KU-575-113

C. W. Reed lives in Whitby. He is married with grown-up children and is also a grandfather. His previous novels include *The Decent Thing*, *All Manner of Things*, *The Foolish Virgin*, *Season of Sins*, *Ties of Blood* and *To Reason Why*.

SILK STOCKING SPY

Travelling alone from India to England in 1940, newly married Cissie Humphreys is captured after her ship is torpedoed. Given the choice of prison or collaboration with the enemy, she works for their propaganda service led by Lord Haw-Haw and falls in love with Sean Munroe, an IRA rebel. Now a secret agent, Cissie accompanies Sean on a spying mission to a fishing village on the North Yorkshire coast. But before long Cissie alone must face the consequences. Now her only chance of survival is to act as a double agent for the British. Where will it all lead?

Books by C. W. Reed
Published by The House of Ulverscroft:

THE FOOLISH VIRGIN
SEASON OF SINS
THE DECENT THING

WRIGHT FAMILY SERIES:
TO REASON WHY
TIES OF BLOOD
ALL MANNER OF THINGS

C. W. REED

SILK STOCKING SPY

Complete and Unabridged

ULVERSCROFT
Leicester

First published in Great Britain in 2006 by
Robert Hale Limited
London

First Large Print Edition
published 2006
by arrangement with
Robert Hale Limited
London

British Library CIP Data

Reed, C. W. (Colin W.)
  Silk stocking spy.—Large print ed.—
  Ulverscroft large print series: adventure & suspense
  1. World War, *1939 – 1945* —Secret service
  —Fiction 2. Women spies—Fiction
  3. Suspense fiction 4. Large type books
  I. Title
  823.9'14 [F]

  ISBN 1–84617–556–9

Published by
F. A. Thorpe (Publishing)
Anstey, Leicestershire

Set by Words & Graphics Ltd.
Anstey, Leicestershire
Printed and bound in Great Britain by
T. J. International Ltd., Padstow, Cornwall

This book is printed on acid-free paper

PART I

DAUGHTER OF THE EMPIRE

1

'Oh, Rani! Am I doing the right thing, do you think? I just don't know! I'm fond of Charlie, you know that. But getting engaged? Marriage? It's so — well — serious. Isn't it?' The light blue eyes, cloudy with the easy threat of tears, gazed appealingly into the compelling, deep brown orbs of the slim Indian girl sitting on the edge of the bed.

The brown hand fell with possessive familiarity on the pale smoothness of the bare arm, stroked in a light but loving caress. 'Come, little mem. You are getting into one of your states. Lie down. Rani will make you better, yes?'

Cissie Humphreys shook out her short, ash blonde hair, and lay back on the brightly coloured quilt. She sighed, her beautiful face already melting into that responsive relaxation which her maid's skilful hands drew forth, as they began again to caress the form so willingly surrendered to their ministrations. It was a clear acknowledgement of the bond that had been forged between them for so long now.

Cissie had been twelve, Rani only a little

more than a year older, when the two had first met. 'This is Rani, your new armah,' Mummy had said. Often, in the seven years which had followed that introduction, Cissie had wondered whether her mother was aware of the exclusive intimacy with which the relationship would develop; if, indeed, Mummy had grown up in such a special relationship herself, for her family were second-generation India. Certainly, Cissie was sure that many of her contemporaries shared the same all-embracing attachment to their armahs that she did. In the enclosed, privileged world of the memsahibs and their sahibs, the bonding of the 'little mems' with their personal servants was taken for granted.

From her prepubescent years until young adulthood, a white girl was attended constantly by her armah, who was generally no more than two or three years older than her mistress, if that. She bathed her, dressed her, played with her, slept with her. It was natural that she should become the confidante, the closest companion, of her charge, closer than parents, or even siblings. There could be no secrets that were not shared.

Cissie had been in great distress just before Rani's arrival, for her father had decided that she should follow Nigel, her older brother, to school in England. Although the sons of the raj invariably returned 'home' for their schooling, even in 1933 it was quite common for daughters to be kept with their parents, to be taught by a tutor — usually a young English graduate of genteel impoverishment — or to attend one of the private schools in the hills. Martin Humphreys' decision, therefore, to send Cissie to England, raised some controversy, not least from his daughter herself, who begged and burst into noisy tears at the news. Though she was used to referring to England as 'home', she had never been there and had no wish to do so. It was a fabled fantasy land to her, and she was desirous that it should remain so. All her family were here, all her friends. It had always been so. Her brother 'Nig' might go on about school when he was back for the summer — and even he had become an ever more remote figure since her early childhood because of the infrequency of those visits from distant Europe — but she had no desire at all to follow in his footsteps. She had heard enough terrifying tales of those few girls unfortunate enough to have suffered from boarding school in the mother country to know that she was not strong-willed enough to survive without much misery in such a situation.

For a disturbingly long time, it looked as

though Martin would have his way, but Cissie had underestimated her mother's influence and subtle powers of persuasion. Delia Humphreys, as delicately languid as any of the other hothouse blooms that abounded in the community of the British memsahibs, put down her shapely foot, in whatever way she found most effective, and Martin finally found himself capitulating, despite his deep and justified misgivings. 'Young girls should get away,' he insisted, even in defeat. Cissie was affectionately tearful with joy, and only a week later Rani came on the scene. And so began the relationship which, more than any other, coloured her young life.

Every morning, from Monday to Friday, Cissie was driven by one of her father's workmen down to the club, where, with four other little mems, accompanied as always by their faithful armahs, she was taught for three hours by Ewan Horner, a graduate in his mid-twenties, supplied by a teaching agency back in England. The Indian maids sat with their mistresses, some with little interest, but Rani took full advantage of the situation to improve her knowledge where she could.

Oddly enough, Cissie found that Rani's presence and that of the other armahs tended to inhibit her relationship with the other white girls, but, like all teenagers, certain topics held priority in their thoughts, and surfaced in their conversation. Boys, and, more obliquely, sex, were matters of prime importance. 'Do you think Mr Horner is attractive?' Cissie asked Rani. 'Margaret Rowell says she thinks he is a worldly man. You know what I mean.'

The armah shrugged dismissively. 'It doesn't matter. Unless you want to find out for yourself!' she added, with a malicious grin, and rejoiced to see Cissie's eyes widen in shock as her cheeks pinked.

It was at her sixteenth birthday party that Cissie first really got to know Charles Pride, the son of one of the more prominent tea planter families, whose estate was considerably larger than the Humphreys'. He was two years older than she was, a contemporary of her brother, Nig. Both boys had recently returned to India after completing their schooling, but whereas Nig was going back in a few months to commence university studies at Oxford, Charlie was staying, to begin work on the family's estate. Cissie was glad.

She could tell at once that he liked her. Not that they knew each other at all, really. It was at least three years since she had last seen him. She remembered him from that time only as one of Nig's oafish and stuck-up buddies, who had no time at all for a skinny-legged girl in faded shorts and scuffed sandals, and who, as Nig derisively put it, was 'as brown as a wog'. But three years on things were excitingly different. Charlie was pale — interestingly so, Cissie thought privately — from his long sojourn in far-away Europe. His hair was as fair as hers, and quite long, brushing his collar, and flopping in a thick, untidy slick over his brow. 'Romantic', was the adjective Cissie's mind supplied, as she thought of poets from those misty climes of the homeland she had never seen, and which she now regarded as a much more intriguing and less frightening place.

'Tell me about England!' she breathed ingenuously, giving him the full power of her blue-eyed gaze, and seeing his own, of a similar but more greyish lightness, spark with an interest and admiration that set her pulse accelerating. Birthday girl that she was, she couldn't keep him to herself anywhere near long enough to satisfy her, but she extracted a promise from him to come over and take her riding the following day. Nigel enjoyed teasing her about her 'conquest' in private, but, though she blushed and pretended to be petulantly angry, she was secretly flattered at this further evidence of his friend's interest in her.

She couldn't wait to tell Rani, who had in

any case been an astute observer on the sidelines at the party. 'He's quite keen on me,' Cissie confessed, bright-eyed, sitting fidgeting in the tub while Rani poured a cooling stream of water down the long, supple back. 'What do you think?'

'He looks pretty. Like a girl,' Rani answered, and smirked at her mistress's squeal of protest. 'All the young white sahibs do,' she went on, in calm condemnation, against Cissie's shrill, indignant remonstration.

Rani was stirred, and startled, by the strength of her resentment when Cissie woke at an unusually early hour next morning and insisted on rising almost at once, to get ready for her visitor and their ride. To be truthful, Rani had always somewhat resented the almost daily custom of Cissie's riding. She did not approve of the habit being continued throughout Cissie's adolescence, when a number of the little memsahibs had willingly relinquished such childish pursuits. It was a pleasure which Rani had never been able to share, though at first she had tried to hurry angrily through the dusty scrub, in the wake of her fast-disappearing charge. She was spitefully jealous of the young syces who accompanied Cissie on another mount, and she never failed to show her contempt for them. It was easy to do so, for they came from the lowliest peasant caste of untouchables.

On the day after the birthday party, Cissie and her visitor stayed out far too long, until the sun had reached its zenith, and burned far too uncomfortably even in that high upland location. Rani scowled in fierce disapproval, and was so brusque in her manner that the affable, easy-going young man commented on it when she was out of earshot. When she was taking her bath before retiring to rest for an hour before the evening meal, Cissie upbraided her. 'Why were you so rude? I was so embarrassed.'

'Why were you out so long? You sent the syce away. He told me. You were alone out there. It isn't right. You should not do such a thing. The young sahib — he is much older than you. The sahib and memsahib would be most angry if they knew.'

Cissie felt herself blushing, with both embarrassment and anger. 'What are you saying? How dare you?'

'You know damn well what I am meaning!' Rani snapped, her dark eyes flashing. Cissie did not fail to note the unaccustomed swear word. 'It isn't fitting to be alone, not that long. With a boy!' Her hands were lacking in their usual gentleness as she tended to Cissie.

The pride and excitement which flickered within Cissie's breast, as well as an intuitive grasp of the emotion underlying Rani's behaviour, caused her anger to dissipate. She began to conciliate and to woo her back to their normal closeness, with such success that presently they lay together behind the gauzy drapes of Cissie's bed, with her blonde locks nestling close to Rani's sleek black tresses.

Cissie's lips nuzzled behind the small ear, her nostrils filled with the musky scent of her companion's warm flesh. She gestured down at her own sprawled, paler frame, scarcely hidden by the short shift she wore. She giggled, a sound which brought them both close to the childhood they had so recently left, and the intimacy they had always known. 'He'll never see as much of me as *you*, my dear!'

But those words, and their conciliatory tone, came back to her suddenly some days later, during another ride with Charlie, and brought heightened colour and a new powerful stirring to that very flesh chastely if hotly hidden beneath the thick stuff of shirt and jodhpurs. A few miles out from the bungalow and its spacious gardens, she reined in her pony on one of the wide grassy tracks through the brush-cleared hillside, above the rolling, vivid green fields of tea bushes and the clustered buildings of the factory. The bright-coloured dresses of the pickers were tiny dots against the greenery as they advanced in neat waves through the low plants, tossing the leaves into the baskets that hung behind on their shoulders.

They dismounted, and Charlie loosely tethered their mounts, before he came and flung himself down beside her on the grass. He had already kissed her, a hard but clumsy wet stab at her cheek, before she had had time to prepare herself, and she had been overcome with embarrassment — and disappointment. He had turned away, already stammering out apologies, his face crimson, and she had not known what to say, totally at a loss, while inside her mind shrieked, Try again! I'm ready now! Well, this time she was, and in spite of *her* blushes, he could see it.

He was as timorous at first as she had feared, and far less bold than she wanted. Despite her tender years, she found herself taking charge, at least in laying all the groundwork, but finally she was as she wished, fully in his arms, and they were kissing, with mounting passion, and even expertise, with tongue-probing enthusiasm, sawing and scraping their faces together, devouring, clashing, until her head was spinning and she leaned back giddily, found herself stretched out on the sward under him, and he put his sweating palm on the small swell of her breast under the thick shirt, and she felt her nipple thrusting, rubbing with exquisite pain against the thickness of the material, and she lifted herself with her arms locked against his neck and pushed herself as tightly as she could against him, until they lay, their bodies entwined through all the layers of cloth separating their flesh.

★   ★   ★

It was now almost another three years on, as Cissie lay on her bed staring up at the gathered misty folds of the mosquito net above her and voiced her uncertainties about her future to Rani, at her side. The morning rides had made great progress; so much so that Cissie was genuinely afraid that her virtue, or what remained of it, was under critical threat. She wondered ashamedly if it was simply lust which had made Charlie stammer out his urgent plea for her to marry him, prefaced of course by the obligatory period of engagement. 'As brief as possible, please!' Charlie had begged. And was it simply her own lust which made Cissie feel the urge to say yes to his plea?

She felt they had some excuse for moving

things along with some urgency, apart from their passion to have sex together. There was an urgent feel about the whole panoply of world affairs, with Europe now plunged into a war of fearsome scale. Nothing was sure any more. Their homeland might well be conquered by Germany. And where would that leave India and all the other countries around the entire world that made up the empire? Even out here, the armed forces were being strengthened, men urged to join up. Her own brother was already in the fray, training to be a pilot in England. He hadn't even completed his studies, and seemed to have little enthusiasm for anything other than the war, and these new aircraft they called Spitfires. And Charlie was chuntering on, like so many of the young men, about signing up, 'doing his bit', whatever that meant. Cissie thought it was all nonsense, so much huffing and puffing and belligerent male pride. She wanted him to do his huffing and puffing for her, in very private circumstances. The battlefield she had in mind was a very confined one. Between the sheets, and if any blood were to be spilt, let it be hers, and in extreme moderation. She was shocked and helpless at the lewd, explicit nature of her own thoughts.

2

Cissie's family combined the celebration of Cissie's nineteenth birthday with the official recognition of her engagement to Charles Pride. The festivities lasted for two days. In addition to the vast spread which they laid on in the garden, where the party ran through Saturday to the Sabbath dawn, with dancing to gramophone records in candlelight, drunken revelry bordering on the dangerous, and amatory assignments among the roses and dim arbours hidden in the trees and neatly clipped shrubbery, there was a curry lunch at the club on Sunday, also acknowledged as part of the young couple's declaration of their love.

'I *do* love you, Cis,' Charlie declared fervently, when the initial fuss over their conjunction had died down a little. 'And I don't think we should wait too long before we get hitched. This Hitler feller means business, I reckon. I know there doesn't seem to be much happening just now, but he's going to call our bluff. We can't just keep on backing down to him. It'll only make him worse. Have you heard from Nig lately? They're all set for a scrap over there.'

Cissie had been present during a number of her parents' sniping altercations at the dining table recently. Delia Humphreys was deeply anxious about her son. She was eager for her husband to order him to return at once. 'There's plenty for him to do out here,' she argued, 'if he insists on wanting to enlist. And if we don't get him back soon, goodness knows when we'll see him. We could be cut off altogether from Blighty if things really kick off.'

But Martin displayed a spirited patriotism so prevalent among his contemporaries at the time. As ever, it seemed to grow in fervour the further away from the crisis centre it was located. 'As far as I'm concerned, he's in just the right place at the moment. I'm proud of the lad, and so should you be! He's doing the right thing, and I hope there's lots more like him, ready to give that blasted little corporal a good drubbing!'

At least Cissie shared her pater's feeling that a tea plantation in north-east India was not exactly the hub of world events. Now, sighing a little, and pretending not to notice Charlie's sweaty palm as it slid sneakily up the smooth bareness of her leg and paused tremulously under the flimsy cover of her thin frock, she pulled her moist lips away from his eager mouth, and batted her wide blue eyes at him in babyish provocation. 'What on earth has what Adolf Hitler gets up to in Europe got to do with us getting married?'

Charlie looked hurt, though his hand remained damply clamped on her thigh. 'I'll have to do my bit, old girl,' he announced patriotically. 'I could be whisked away God knows where. We can't afford to wait too long. Enjoy ourselves while we can, what?' As though reminded by his stirring words, the hand began to move again, and presently its fingers were tentatively exploring the restricting boundary provided by the elasticated leg of her cotton knickers, while Cissie silently cursed Rani, who had refused to let her wear a pair of her best, fetching, lace-trimmed panties.

'You never used to bother so much!' Rani taunted. 'A short time ago, you were just as happy to go bare bummed.'

'Oh well! If you'd prefer me to go without . . . '

With a significant look, Rani had laid out the baggy cotton garments that had served since adolescence. Cissie had decided not to make too much of a fuss. Rani had been behaving distinctly oddly lately, with mood swings to outdo her mistress, and Cissie, of course, knew the reason. She had tried to reassure the brooding girl. 'Listen! Just cos I'm getting engaged, it doesn't mean anything will change between us. I mean, you'll still be my armah, don't you worry!'

'It won't be up to you,' Rani muttered broodingly. 'It will be the sahib and memsahib who will decide. And your young man, soon. He wants to get you into his bed as soon as possible.'

Cissie had gasped in shock and secret, outraged delight, though sex had never been considered as a taboo subject between the girls, from their earliest days together. Indeed, practically the sum of Cissie's knowledge, which was far from infinitesimal, had come from Rani. But now matters had moved dramatically from the objectiveness of the abstract to an immediate and highly personal concern. Cissie had shared with the Indian girl an intimacy both philosophical and physical far beyond any other relationship she had known. That intimacy would be usurped by the young man who had so recently entered Cissie's life. The effect of that entrance would be almost as great on the armah as on his beloved.

And that same young man, with a clumsy but startling boldness in one who had seemed hitherto so timid, was pressing on with his desperate search, while they kissed and cuddled, and Cissie affected not to notice what and where that hidden hand was up to. The ferreting fingers were endeavouring to negotiate a way through the tightly gripping ring of elastic. When they failed, they moved on, over the warm, slightly rumpled surface of the thin material, until Cissie could feign ignorance no longer. She gave a squeal, which was largely muffled by the close contact of their mouths before she tore her lips away, and emitted a kind of whinny, half of fright and half of hunger to know, and feel, more. She clutched at his slender wrist and dragged the offending hand back into view, away from the storm of sensations it had been raising beneath her rumpled frock.

'You frightened me!' she blushingly confessed, over his moans of abject apology. She had an urge to join him in the litany of sorries. 'I've never — you know — I don't want you . . . to think badly of me.'

'I could never do that!' he declared passionately, and his heart beat with wild hope once more at the gentleness of her reaction.

But it was a hope which was doomed for the present to remain unfulfilled, for Rani began to cling to her like a veritable shadow, except that she signally did not disappear with the sunset. The armah's triumphal vindictiveness was increased by the righteous knowledge that she was acting as the proxy of the 'big mem', Memsahib Delia, who was so anxious that her daughter's virtue should remain intact. The couple did snatch moments alone, many of them, but never in a place or at a time when their hot young passions could be fully consummated. In the shady arbours of the Humphreys' garden, or in the even more lushly disciplined spaciousness of his own familial grounds, Charlie was given glimpses or even further tantalizing touches of the heavenly flesh he longed to possess. Rapturously, through the thin stuff of blouse or frock, and, eventually, lace-encrusted bust bodice, his trembling digits traced the swooningly soft contours, or again, felt the divine cool smoothness of upper leg, and even at last the embroidered intricacies of the silken undergarments Cissie had finally and undeniably insisted she would wear for such occasions.

But, wraith-like, the slender figure of Rani was always ready to put in an appearance, like the last-minute trumpeting charge of the rescuing cavalry in the flickering horse-opera epics they showed on Friday nights at the club, her very silence a rebuke. It happened so often that the couple gave up trying to hide the true nature of their grappling, and merely sighed heavily while clothing, limbs and bodies were rearranged to restore decorousness once more.

Later, Cissie was forced, ruefully, to acknowledge that it was her curiosity and steadily mounting frustration that led her to make up her mind once and for all, and to push away the spectres of doubt which hovered on the edges of consciousness about the suitability of Charlie's character and temperament as a life partner. By the time far-away France had fallen, Cissie's reserves had fallen, too. Rani seemed resigned, if somewhat bitter. 'I think I must instruct you very carefully in your duties. It will be my gift to you. You will have to take the lead, I fear, in here.' She tapped the bed on which Cissie was blushingly resting. 'Sahib Charlie looks like a virgin to me.'

Cissie was too distracted to be angry. 'Tell me what I need to know,' she said humbly.

★　★　★

Though swiftly arranged, the wedding was a grand affair, in the best traditions of the small hill station, in spite of the drama unfolding several thousand miles to the west. The word miracle was yet to be applied generally to Dunkirk, as the expatriate community waited for the dreaded news that the hub of empire had been invaded by the Nazis. So everyone was in the mood to forget, at least temporarily, the gloom of Europe in the sunkissed, fluffy-clouded, vivid richness of the Assam greenery, and to celebrate the nuptials of the lovely bride and her elegant groom. The pair drove up the narrow, rough road, further towards the shimmering un-reality of the distant Nepalese peaks, to reach the modest guesthouse for their three-day honeymoon. The staff there were discreet, and had the knack of appearing when required and vanishing when their service was not needed. Cissie felt a sudden and altogether inappropriate longing to have Rani by her side, especially when she saw in the dim lantern light the wide bed, with the fragrant frangipani and orange blossom scattered liberally over the crisp linen.

The reality of sex with her husband did not match her hopes. It never did, with Charlie. She was shocked, even sickened, to discover just how deep her dismay was at this discovery. So deep, in fact, that she worked hard to improve matters. Rani had been right. Charlie was disastrously ignorant, and Cissie had to call on all her reserves of generosity not to feel a burning resentment at the apparent ease, not to say mercurial swiftness, with which he was able to obtain satisfaction, and his total unawareness of her own spectacular failure to achieve a similar state of affairs. To make a bad matter far worse, she found she could in no way enjoy the frankness of exchanging her views with him as she had done throughout her girlhood with her faithful Rani.

Back 'home', living in a bungalow on the Pride estate, things swiftly degenerated even further. She had hoped that Rani would come with her as her maid, and was devastated to find out that this was not to be. 'It never works out, my dear,' Mrs Pride told her, with the overweening confidence of one who ruled at least as consort in this exclusive kingdom. 'It only causes friction in the servants' quarters. We have a lovely girl for you. Munir. Delightful. You'll love her.'

Cissie was further stunned when, perhaps a trifle over-confident herself, she appealed privately to her new husband. 'You know how close we are, Charlie, darling. I must have Rani with me.'

He reddened, and his grey-blue gaze wandered slightly away from hers. 'It is awkward, my love. I've spoken to her, and, to be honest, she's not all that keen on coming over here.'

'That's not true!' Cissie said hotly, then

23

reined in her impetuosity when she saw Charlie's startled reaction. 'I mean — it can't be. You know how — how close we've always been. She'd go anywhere with me, I know she would. She'd die for me.'

'I say, that's a bit dramatic, isn't it, old girl? She's only a Chut, after all!'

Cissie had been well aware of Charlie's lack of empathy with Rani during the brief spell of courtship; his impatience at the success with which the armah had prevented him having his wicked way with her mistress. Not that he would have achieved that much! was Cissie's now ungenerous thought, considering the fact that the exclusive privacy of a blossom-strewn bridal bed and a bride steaming with a desire to be taken had not helped him to rise to the occasion. He was jealous! That was it. He was jealous of her armah's closeness to her, and well he might be, Cissie thought, as the tears began to prick behind her eyes. His next words had an even more overwhelming effect on her, rendering her completely unable to continue the argument.

'As a matter of fact, she asked me a favour. A pretty big one, actually. And because I know how fond you are of her, I agreed to help her. She doesn't want to go on being a servant all her life. She's quite a bright kid, in fact — I could see that right away. She asked me if I could let her have some money — a sort of farewell gift, I suppose. She wants to go off and do some schooling — some sort of clerking course, I think. Down in Calcutta. You know — English, typing, bit of arithmetic, I expect. Thought you'd be pleased, old girl. Keeping it as a bit of a surprise for you.'

Cissie felt the emotion rising within her, so that her throat felt as if it were closing. The tears were stinging hotly now, and she couldn't hide them, or the tremor in her voice. 'I think you — she — could have mentioned it to me.'

'Maybe she thought you'd say no. You know, wouldn't want her to go, and all that. Times are changing, after all. What with the old Mahatma and his gang. We have to go along with some of it. I don't agree with most of his bally ideas, of course. I mean, this India for the Indians thing! Load of bally nonsense! But as far as education goes — done in the right way, of course, I think it's a good thing.'

She had a sudden and violent urge to screech at him to shut up. She felt her fingers curl with a fierce wish to attack him. And then came a great, swamping feeling of having made a terrible, terrible mistake, the whole of her life blighted and stretching before her, as a planter's wife, but always a subsidiary of the big mem here, her role simply a breeder of Prides to feed this private little empire.

She went back to her parents' home, to seek out Rani before she departed. It shook Cissie as she glanced round the bare little concrete cell that had been Rani's room for eight years how very few times she had set foot in here. Mind you, Rani must have spent precious little time here herself, for she had shared practically every minute of her mistress's life, waking and sleeping. The thought brought back the tears that seemed so ready to sneak up on her these days. 'I don't want you to go!' she said, reaching out to take the brown hands in hers. 'I thought you'd come with me. Stay with me over there.' She jerked her head back in the vague direction of the Pride estate. The topi helmet made her delicate face look even smaller, more winsome.

Rani shook her sleek, braided locks in negation. 'It would not have been good, little mem.' She gave a flashing smile and squeezed Cissie's hands tightly. 'Oh! I mustn't call you that any more, must I? You are a memsahib in your own right now. Mrs Pride. How is it?'

There was a hesitation, then the habit of truthfulness they had shared over the years

won out against propriety. The tears over-
flowed. Cissie pulled off the helmet, and sank
down on to the creaking little iron bed
without releasing the hands she clung to. 'It
isn't good, Rani. I've made a terrible mistake!
Why didn't you warn me?'

Rani sat beside her, an entrancingly
graceful figure in the deep blue sari she was
wearing. She pulled the tousled fair head
down to her bosom, and encircled the
quivering shoulders of her little mem. 'Shush,
my dear. Don't cry now. Not over the spilt
milk, eh? You must make the best of it.'

'Oh, Rani! I can't! I wish I was going away,
too. With you!'

Rani began to rock her gently back and
forth in her arms, as she had done so often
when they were children together. 'There,
there! Come now! It can't be that bad. You'll
be having a baby soon.'

Cissie lifted her head and looked at Rani
through watery eyes. She was blushing a little.
'Not yet. Not if I can help it. You remember
what you taught me? I'm being very careful
— not to get caught. It's not that difficult.'

Rani giggled, in spite of her mistress's
tears, and Cissie managed a weak, ashamed
smile in return. 'You mean with the vinegar
— and the sponge? Oh! You wicked child!'

'And the washing — the douche. I don't

want to fall. Not yet. Especially now. Charlie's going away. He's joining up. The army.' Cissie scowled, and Rani's heart was stirred at the memories the childish expression brought back to her. 'Imagine being stuck over there, and having a child. Without even Charlie to back me up. Not that he ever does,' she added gloomily.

'Well, why don't *you* go, too?' Rani held Cissie's face away from her breast so she could meet her gaze. 'I heard talk that even the mems might be called up for the war. Why don't you join up, too, like Sahib Charlie? You know the Simpson girl? Moira? She went to Britain. With her brother. To join the women's army. Or navy, I don't know. You could go to Bombay or somewhere. Maybe Calcutta. We could meet there!'

'Oh, I dunno,' Cissie answered doubtfully, aware even as she spoke how disgustingly feeble she sounded. And Rani's words had implanted a new, beating hope within her heart, however difficult or impossible it might be.

Just briefly, the future was forgotten as the two girls embraced for the last time. 'Gosh! Will I ever see you again?' Cissie sighed. They stood in the dim light of the tiny room and held each other close. She felt she knew the answer already, felt that this was a significant moment, a closing of a long and happy chapter in her life, as significant as the marriage vows she had stammered from beneath her veil only weeks previously.

'*Inshallah!*' Rani murmured fondly. Like most of the native inhabitants of this corner of India, she was a Muslim. For a few precious seconds, race and rank were forgotten, cultures blurred as the girls embraced, their lips touched slowly, and locked in a kiss which expressed a genuine attachment which had crossed at least in some ways so many unfathomable divides.

3

The outside events, so tragic for such a large proportion of the world, seemed to be conspiring to help Cissie with her own private tragedy, for as such she was increasingly inclined to view it, in spite of all her self-urgings not to over-dramatize her situation. She felt worse because of her recognition of Charlie's essentially good-natured, if weak, character. As, indeed, she felt at this moment, as they lay in naked companionship beneath the netting hung over the bed, with the single sheet thrust down beneath their feet. Cooled and calmed by the tepid water in which she had bathed in the adjacent bathroom, she could view with a more philosophical detachment her husband's blissful unawareness of the fever of sensation he could rouse but failed to quell in the breast and other regions of the pliant frame lying at his side. She could almost see and feel the aura of satiated bliss emanating from his own thin body.

'Now we've got Winny back in charge of things at home, I reckon we're going to pull through, old girl.' Churchill had always been popular in India, as a supporter of the raj and an outspoken opponent of those misguided few who were continually bleating on about self-determination.

Charlie wriggled, and nestled his head on Cissie's shoulder, ignoring its delicate boniness. His field of vision was hampered by the pale swell of Cissie's left breast as he surveyed the further fields of fleshly delight spread before him. 'You don't mind my going, do you, sweetie? I mean, we have to do it, don't we? Look at your Nig. I envy him, right bang in the middle of things over there!' Nigel had joined the university squadron before war was declared last September, and was well on his way to completing his training as a fighter pilot in the much-vaunted Spitfire.

'I'll be joining the regiment on the frontier,' Charlie resumed. The defensive note in his voice indicated how he felt about this unglamorous posting to the Burmese border. The Japs had begun a vigorous and belligerently sustained campaign for the British to close the Burma Road, through which the United States had been supplying the Chinese troops under Chiang Kai-shek's command, who were fighting against the Japanese in Manchuria. The beleaguered British government's mind was fully occupied with the catastrophe almost on its shores, and it was about to cave in to Japanese demands. In any case, they had, like most of the western powers except the United States, been steadfastly ignoring Japan's imperial aggression towards China in Manchuria for the past ten years.

Cissie reached across, took his brown hand and placed it on her warm body. 'You know I'm proud of you, Charlie. Worried — but proud.' Her breath caught a little; she felt her tummy wobble as she went on. 'I've been thinking, darling. I'll miss you so much, and God knows when we might get to see each other again. The thought of me sitting here twiddling my thumbs, worrying over you every day — well, it gives me the collywobbles. And you're so right. We're not going to beat old Hitler if everybody sits back and leaves it to the other chap, are we? So — I was thinking — I think I'd like to join up, too. Do *my* bit to see him off. What do you reckon, darling?'

His head lifted from her shoulder. He squinted down at her, with some difficulty. 'What? You mean? Oh well . . . I dunno . . . ' His eyes, already set at a difficult angle, were glad to escape from hers. 'I was rather hoping . . . er, you know . . . we'd have other things, more personal things, to think about.' Now they were directed with shy but unmistakable meaning in the direction of her flat belly, and the sandy tuft at its base.

'Oh, well, of course, that would be different!' she breathed, thinking of her vigorous ablutions just now in the privacy of the bathroom, a now-instinctive conclusion to their congress. For a few seconds she was deeply ashamed of her deceit, and even a little shocked at her skill. Then she was once more strongly aware of how much her present strategy meant to her all at once. She turned on to her side to face him, flung her right leg blatantly across his loins, and blew gently into his red ear. 'P'raps we'd better keep trying then. While there's still time, eh?' She reached down like any immoral tart and delicately picked up his limp, damp member and gave it a playful shake. 'Or has Charlie had enough of his little Cissiekins, then?' She deepened her voice to a growling, sensuous laugh. 'That's a shame. Because she can't ever get enough of this little feller, however often he comes to see her!'

* * *

When she reflected on it, Cissie was shocked again, several times, at her power of dissembling, and her skill as a courtesan, which was the politest word she could think

33

of for her private behaviour with Charlie. The fact that he was her husband and there was nothing at all illegal about what they got up and down to somehow made it all the more shocking to her mind. However, she could not deny the deep thrill of excitement her success brought her.

'Go to England?' Delia Humphreys exclaimed, in tones of utter disbelief, when her daughter disclosed her intention. 'Absolutely preposterous! What on earth is Charlie thinking of, allowing such a madcap scheme? I think the whole world's going absolutely crazy!' She appealed to her husband, who, on this occasion, was definitely more of a mind with her than when she had protested at her son's actions.

But, in spite of their voluble opposition, and the outrage already amply expressed by her in-laws, Cissie's plans were about to be realized, and on a scale far greater than she had originally hoped for. She had seduced poor Charlie — ravished him, practically, she had to admit. He went off to his war, halfway across the vast sub-continent, towards the dusty parade ground and wildly entertaining social life of the officer-cadet training course, with his bemused head still spinning with the fieriness of his young wife's love and desire for him, and ready to sanction just about anything she cared to name or do, and to back it with the necessary financial means for her to do so.

She had travelled as far as Jaunpur on the train with him, where they spent their last few precious hours together, in the high-ceilinged, rather shabby bedroom of the hotel beside the junction station, and she had shamelessly reached out to touch him as they had finished their meal in the oil lamps of the upper gallery, almost before the servant had glided out of sight. 'You're my husband. I want you!' Her eyes sparkled, her hand nestled with delicate indecency in his crotch.

'I say, old girl!' His face was red, with shock, and with a guilty ecstasy of anticipation.

'Mind you,' Cissie confided only a short while later, when, fragrantly and coolly refreshed from her swift ablutions, she returned to their bed under the mosquito veil, 'if you have — what is it you soldier boys say? Knocked me up? — my plans will all be changed and I'll have to sit back home swelling like a balloon and waiting for my warrior's return.'

'Oh, darling!' He clung with sweating rapture to her perfumed breast. 'I couldn't think of anything more wonderful!'

'Nor could I, my darling!' she affirmed,

safe in the knowledge of her comprehensive efforts to ensure the unlikelihood of any such event.

Weeks of frustration followed, and of loneliness. She realized how deeply she missed Rani. She was hurt that she had received only one short note, and even that had been addressed to 'Mr and Mrs Charles Pride', telling them that she had enrolled at a business school in Calcutta. There was an air of finality about the brief letter, so that Cissie felt an extra measure of satisfaction when she replied, telling her that she hoped soon to be sailing for England.

It was not going to be that easy. The outbreak of hostilities meant that the shipping services had been severely curtailed. They listened to the daily news bulletins with increasing anxiety. Delia was more and more concerned for Nigel's safety, especially when the announcement of a wave of air raids on southern Britain was made public. But then, in August, just when the phrase The Battle of Britain had been coined, came a letter informing them that he had transferred to bomber training, and their immediate fears for him were eased just a little. As for Cissie, though she mentioned Nig in her infrequent prayers when she remembered, her greatest fear was that Hitler would spoil all her plans by crossing the Channel before she had her chance to reach the land she automatically referred to as home, and which now, for the first time in her young life, she was so desperate to see.

In September came news of the first really serious air raid on London, then, two days later, Cissie received confirmation that she had secured a berth on the *Star of Indus*, sailing from Calcutta in two weeks. There followed a furious round of buying and packing, and every minute seemed like an hour to her as she waited.

'What about Munir?' Cissie's mother-in-law demanded. 'Surely you're taking her with you?'

'How can I, Mumsie?' The term of affection habitually used by her husband for his mater did not come easily to her lips. 'There's a war on. I'm lucky to get a berth myself. I don't think they'd have room for servants. Anyway, what on earth would I do with her when I got there? She can't come into the WAAFs or the WRENS with me, can she?'

The senior Mrs Pride shook her head and shrugged her shoulders. What a disappointing flibbertigibbet this girl had turned out to be! She should be staying home, learning how to run the house and servants, how to take care of the workers, and having Charlie's babies, instead of gallivanting halfway around the world and probably getting herself blown to bits in the process!

★ ★ ★

'This is your cabin. Bit small, but it's better than sharing, eh? And it *is* an outer.' Cissie glanced across at the scuttle, whose glass was open, and through which the sounds of the busy dockside drifted, along with the oven-hot air and the unsavoury smells of the port. Derek Hargreaves, the *Star*'s second officer, gave her another dazzling toothpaste grin, his brown eyes sweeping with clear approval over her slim figure in the thin floral dress. Cissie should have been annoyed — no, she *was* annoyed, she amended, at his plainly demonstrated appreciation — but she could not help that spark of flattered pride that stirred her at the look. She guessed his imagination would be running riot, and, with a teasing sense of wickedness, she played the game too, in an understated way, acknowledging in turn the Lothario touch of his handsomeness. What did the song say? All the nice girls love a sailor? She had heard tales of shipboard romances, in the encapsuled intimacy of a situation that would never be repeated. She felt her tummy churn with renewed anticipation at the thought of the long voyage ahead, after such a long time of impatient waiting.

'And this is your steward. Anil.'

A young, slim figure, in a white coat even more dazzling than the second officer's teeth, had appeared in the doorway. He bowed smartly. His brilliant black hair, carefully combed back in luxuriant twin waves, gleamed in the sunlit cabin. His eyes flickered respectfully away from hers. 'Welcome aboard, memsahib.'

'We've got our full complement of thirty passengers, as you know,' the second officer was saying. 'So things will be quite lively, I expect. Maybe a little hectic, too.' He laughed easily. 'We're not like the passenger boats. The liners, I mean. But we're fast, and the service has always been good in the past.' His eyes stayed on her face, and she felt a light blush rising, in spite of all her efforts to look poised and seasoned. 'If you have any complaints, come to me. I'll see what I can do for you. Don't forget. I hope you'll have a very pleasant voyage, Mrs Pride.'

Or may I call you Cissie? she fantasized him adding, and felt a responsive smile tugging at the corners of her mouth. 'I'm sure I shall, Mr Hargreaves.'

The *Star of Indus* was indeed a fast passenger/cargo vessel, and as such her prime consideration was the delivery and collection of the assortment of goods she carried. She was not following the usual route up through the Red Sea and the Suez Canal into the Mediterranean. She would sail round to Bombay, then make the 3,000-mile crossing of the Indian Ocean before her next port of call, at Dar-Es-Salaam, before working her way down the African coast, via Durban, Cape Town and round to Lagos, before the Canaries and the European waters leading to London.

'You'll have lots of time to get to know us, my dear,' Captain Fuller told Cissie, their first night at sea. She had been granted the privilege of being among the first group of passengers to sit at his table in the well-appointed saloon. Although tall, he was rotund with the excessive weight he carried, and his neatly trimmed beard was predominantly grey. His attitude towards her was one of jolly avuncularity, which she didn't mind at all. Unlike the junior officers, whose eyes held the same half-concealed message of lechery she had discerned in Derek Hargreaves' gaze. And she found she didn't mind that, either.

There was a narrow promenade deck just behind the bridge, and the first morning she was first out there, stretched on one of the row of empty deckchairs. She had taken care over choosing her new bathing suit. It was a two-piece, in a dusky pink, satiny material. She was self-conscious at its brevity, unable to prevent herself from surreptitiously easing down the cloth where it cut into the crease of her thigh and belly. The waistband was a good two inches below her recessed navel, and she wondered if she had been perhaps a shade forward in buying such a daring little costume. But the quick, hot glances of the stewards, and the bolder, more direct stares of the sailors, not to mention the disguised but hungry eyes of the officers and male passengers, went a long way towards counteracting her initial discomfort.

She soon sensed a shadow standing over her, and opened her eyes, squinting against the power of the sun, to see Derek Hargreaves lowering himself into the seat beside her. His white shorts had knife-edge creases. His knees showed brown, and she noticed the fine black hairs curling above the white three-quarter stockings and the Blanco-white shoes. 'Be careful,' he said, grinning. 'It's amazing how easily you can burn at sea. This breeze can be deceptive.'

Like all people brought up in the tropics, she was well aware of the danger of exposure to the sun. She had been warned from infancy not to go out bareheaded, and when she travelled any distance she had been made to wear the hotly uncomfortable padded spine protector. 'It's all right,' she answered. 'I shall move my chair into the shade soon. I have some cream to put on when I have my bath.' She had a sudden urge to giggle like a schoolgirl as she thought of the effect of these last words of hers on his riotous imagination.

A few hours later, she recalled the exchange as she sat with knees drawn up in the little steel bathtub. The bathroom was a few yards along the corridor from her cabin, which contained only a washbasin. She didn't linger over her ablutions. There wasn't even room to lie back and enjoy a soak. Besides, bathing herself was a chore, she had learnt. No doubt she would get used to it in time, but she had to admit she missed Rani's ministrations, and, more so, the long chats. Having to dress herself, pick out her own things, deal with her hair and make-up, was another nuisance. But well worth it, she had to admit, when she sat after dinner in the crowded saloon and enjoyed the male gazes, which slid over and across her like so many illicit embraces, she thought fancifully. There was no doubt she was the belle of this admittedly severely limited ball, and bathed in the glow of so much male attention and admiration, and failed to notice the growing fixity of the other women's smiles, and the glittering hardness of the altogether different looks they cast on her.

4

During the first days of the voyage, over the great bight of the Bay of Bengal, through the Balk Strait between the island of Ceylon and the mainland, round the southern tip of India into the fierce heat of the Arabian Sea, Cissie enjoyed being, as well as the belle, the cosseted babe of the *Star's* tiny exclusive world. There were four other females, none of whom could compete for either title. As far as Cissie was concerned, they were all old, though the nearest to her in age, at thirty-one, would have hotly disputed being written off as over the hill. She would have disputed most things with Cissie, as she did, in an oblique and sniping, falsely jovial way to her face, and with a vituperative directness in private to her husband, who himself came in for vicious attack for the way 'you moon about with your tongue hanging out after her'. It got so bad that poor old Reggie Gough hardly dare look at the blonde girl, or speak to her in his memsahib's presence.

Marjorie Gough had hoped to attract some of the glamour and excitement of Cissie's present status to herself during the long weeks of the sea voyage. She had happy, heart-fluttering memories of a trip back out from Britain's cold clime nearly five years before, with numerous flirtatious moments with the young deck officers, and some decidedly improper embraces and exchanges with one in particular. Perhaps it did occasionally occur to her now that her husband's sulky jealousy on that earlier voyage was more justified than her own waspish aggression towards him for glancing in the trollop Pride's direction, but then her own bitter envy swiftly dispersed any such fleeting sentiments of objectivity. Just my bloody luck! Marjorie mourned. She was not a bad looker herself, she considered (though in truth she was still maybe lacking in that elusive objectivity) but they would have to pick this bloody ship of all ships, with that simpering, skinny child, with her fluffy blonde locks and baby blues, hardly out of gymslips and bloomers despite her married title. *Missus* Pride indeed! Her hubby must be like the rest of the men surrounding her on this benighted vessel — a bunch of secret perverts who drooled over dreams of adolescents in ribbons and pigtails and frilly dresses up to their knicker legs! The fact that Cissie Pride had displayed none of these accoutrements did nothing to deter from the implacable dislike in Marjorie's much more ample and ripely alluring (in her own modest opinion) bosom.

Cissie could hardly fail to be aware of Marjorie Gough's antipathy towards her. The latter would have been even more galled to know that it gave Cissie an added sense of pleasure, so that, when opportunity presented itself, she vamped, and batted her eyes at the unfortunate Reggie, whose vivid blush suggested apoplexy, and smiled at his grunted, scarcely comprehended, minimal replies to her pleasantries. His tormented gaze before his eyes flicked hastily from hers told it all; even more eloquently on the few occasions when they met without his wife's shadow at his elbow. The other males were of a much more advanced age. She felt very much as she did with Captain Fuller, her role that of a favourite niece as she responded in kind to their mild flirtations.

The officers were a different matter. Patrick McDougal, the third officer, was the chief contender to the claims of Derek Hargreaves, his immediate superior, for the second officer clearly saw himself as chief pretender for her favours in this insulated, sea-bound fiefdom. And he was right. As they headed up the west coast of India, through the oven-like atmosphere of the Arabian Sea, Cissie lay on her cot, the sheet visibly dampened beneath her, while the whirring fan stirred the hot air mockingly over her unclothed body. Because of the wartime regulations, she was forced to keep the scuttle closed and bolted during the hours of darkness. Sleep eluded her, and at last she could bear no longer to be stretched out like the victim of some sadistic torturer. She swung her feet down to the deck, felt the ship's vibrations passing through her limbs as she padded to the basin. She soaked her cloth — even the water was tepid — and sponged herself down. She didn't bother to dry herself, but pulled her silk wrap around her and stepped out into the corridor. The wetness felt deliciously cool at least momentarily against the clinging, thin material, and the illusion of coolness was maintained briefly as she went up to the steady warm breeze of the tropic night on the open deck.

She paused at the top of the companion ladder, moved by the vast panoply of glittering stars in one unbroken expanse over her head. She felt all at once the utter dwarfishness and insignificance of her own soul, and those about her in this tiny bit of metal cutting through the ocean, a shrinking of her very being and of all human endeavour against this vastness of an eternity. And yet the twinkling objects hanging there in that sweep of paleness seemed paradoxically closer than she had ever known them, some comparatively large, of a deeper golden hue, others paler pinpricks, further away in the vastness. For just a moment she was outside of herself, aware of the pettiness of all her hopes and plans and dreams, and the swiftness of mortality. She shivered; became conscious once more of the warm iron throbbing beneath her bare feet. She picked her way quietly up to the small enclosure of the promenade deck, a fanciful name for such a small space, saw the looming structure of the bridge rising whitely above, with two wings standing out at either side, silhouetted against the spangly canvas of sky.

She found a cushion, settled herself down into a deckchair, felt the enfolding sag of it taking her frame, holding her, and lay back, staring up at the sky. She was still cool, freed from the stuffy little cage of the cabin, and her mind returned to her personal world, and her future. She thought of Charlie, wondered what he would be doing now. Probably sleeping, making that funny little flubbering noise with his upper lip. She thought of his rather long nose, its raw, sunburnt look, that comic white band across his brow where his hat had protected his skin against the sun. She thought of how many times she had lain at his side and watched him sleeping. At the memory, she felt that familiar, taunting pulse deep inside, the stirring of her young body kissed by the flimsy silk, its hunger for fulfilment; a fulfilment Charlie had failed to bring to her. She was disturbed and ashamed of the heat of her sensation. Why should she blame him? Yet, in spite of all her efforts, she felt an inner voice condemning him. She had hoped for so much more from marriage. She had tried to shut out the recurring thought that stalked her: that she had made the biggest mistake of her young life when she accepted his proposal. She had tried to fool herself that she was in love. Was it really just for sex that she had agreed to marry him? Rani had known. The admission made Cissie blush even now, in the darkness. Rani. She thought about the armah more than she did of Charlie. Rani was the only one she had been truly close to, had truly loved. Nonsense! She scolded herself furiously, but she felt the prick of tears behind her eyelids as she drifted into a light sleep.

She woke in panic, struggling to lift up her head, feeling imprisoned in an enfolding embrace, not knowing where she was. A dark shape hung over her, and she gave a gasp that was almost a scream.

'Sorry, Cissie. Didn't mean to startle you. You gave *me* quite a fright, I can tell you!'

Cissie struggled harder, lifted herself up on her elbows, felt the hammock-like canvas chair under her. As she identified the soft voice as Derek Hargreaves', she realized that her wrap was practically open, held only loosely by the sash tied at her waist. 'Please, don't look!' she muttered, wriggling awkwardly, half-raising her body to drag the thin silk over her and retie the sash. She sat up, her feet pressed together, holding the silk over her knees. 'How — how long have you been here?' Watching me, she wanted to say.

He crouched on his haunches in front of her, so close that she felt her knees brushing against his clothing, his own jutting limbs enclosing her. His hands rested on her calves, just above the back of her ankles, and then slid upward, over her skin, to the damp hollows behind her knees, his fingers tracing the tendons that had tightened at his touch. She could hardly breathe. 'Don't!' she whispered. But it was not a command, not even angry. Her eyes shone with tears. His hands moved upward again, constrained by the wooden cross-frame of the chair, pushing aside the silk wrap to caress the insides of her thighs.

It seemed an age before she could force her own hands to move, to come down lightly on his wrists, preventing him from further exploration rather than repulsing him.

'I've just come off watch. Came here for a last smoke. Saw you. God! You're beautiful, Cissie! I can't hold off any longer.' The hands left her, came up to her neck, pulled her forward to meet his searching mouth. She could feel his body pressing her limbs tightly against the chair, then her mouth was open and her head spun with the force of the kiss.

'I'm married!' she gasped, when their lips finally parted.

'So am I!' he answered, almost savagely, as his hands pushed aside the robe and his fingers taloned about her breasts, and she thrust against his grip, her shoulders turning in his arms, welcoming his roughness, the fierce hurt of their passion.

He plucked her up easily and she clutched the wrap about her as his arm encircled her waist, and he led her silently back down the companion ladder to the humming lower deck and the narrow door of her cabin. He didn't let go even as they passed through and closed it behind them, then he lifted her and almost tossed her on to the high berth in his desperate need for her.

★ ★ ★

'Wait!' she croaked, as the tapping at the door brought her awake. It opened and closed

51

again immediately at her exclamation, and she fought the thin cover up over her. 'All right.'

Anil came in with her tray, while she lay back on one elbow, clutching the coverlet to her breast. 'It was so hot. I couldn't — ' She could feel her face burning, knew her hair was a wild tangle. Then she saw her silk wrap lying in the middle of the floor. 'Just put it down,' she managed, unable to look at the steward. 'I'll get it — in a minute.' He smiled, studiously avoiding looking at her, or the discarded wrap, and left hurriedly, after he had placed the breakfast tray on the narrow shelf that served as dressing table and desk.

I'm a slut! she thought, as the door clicked closed behind him. She was frightened, yet had to acknowledge the shocking excitement of the word. She realized she had half-suspected as much, from her teenage days long before her marriage to Charlie, when she had lain in Rani's arms and they had talked of things she could never discuss with anyone else. Anil must have seen it all in that one glimpse — her crazy nest of hair, her debauched face.

With a small whimper of dismay, she felt the soreness as she sprang up, then saw the stains on the crumpled sheet beneath her. She dragged it from the mattress, rolled it into as tight a ball as she could manage and stuffed it into the laundry bag. Fear seized her as she recalled the events of the early morning. Adulteress! The biblical force of the term struck her, and the inner conflict began.

If he hadn't come sneaking up on her. Watching her as she lay, as good as naked, on that chair! A gentleman would have crept quietly away again, left her undisturbed. And a lady wouldn't have been sprawled out on deck with no clothes on! Slut! The fear hit her as she thought of all that had happened. She stared down at herself! My God! She thought of her unfailing routine of the marital bed: her rising at once from Charlie's happily exhausted embrace, the race to the bathroom, the painstaking ritual to ensure she would not be impregnated. With Derek Hargreaves, she had lain back, weeping with joy, their frames larded with their exertions, and fallen asleep still wrapped around him. And had woken to feel his hands and mouth on her, driving her wild, then they had made love, again . . . The Lord thy God is a jealous God! The words ran over and over, thundering in her brain as she grabbed dressing gown and towel and raced for the bathroom, while the phrase, less poetic but just as unnerving, Too late! too late! jostled for supremacy.

'We can't do it again!' Cissie hissed, when Derek held her decorously close to the tune of the gramophone in the saloon after dinner. 'I don't know what I was thinking of. You caught me unawares — I shouldn't have . . . have left my cabin. Come up on deck like that — '

She had tried to talk to him seriously, to confess her shock at her own promiscuity. 'I swear I never thought — I've never — with anyone else — '

'Good heavens! Am I the first? I'm deeply honoured. And you've been married how long? Over six months now?'

'You're a bloody sod, you know that?' She was close to tears. His laughter maddened her.

'Don't worry, it's shipboard life. It brings it out in all women.'

She did not have to ask what 'it' was. His smug tone infuriated her, as well as making her thoroughly disgusted with her own cheapness. 'You said you loved me,' she muttered, her lower lip curling, pouting like a tearful schoolgirl.

'I do, and I will. All the way to Tilbury, I swear!'

In spite of her shame and humiliation, she

kept a rendezvous with him the following night, after midnight, in the same private spot on the upper deck.

'I've never known anyone as wonderful as you, Cissie!' he declared, after their first passionate bout of clinches, and when he groped beneath the short flowered cocktail dress she wore instead of an evening gown, he found nothing but her eager flesh waiting to receive him. 'Think of it as the start of you doing your bit for king and country,' he advised, when they lay even more intimately in the steamy solitude of the cabin once more. 'Keeping us gallant sailor boys happy. Who knows what might happen? We could buy it at any minute. These U-boats! Eat, drink, and be merry, eh?'

She moved her head back from his damp shoulder to see his face. 'You're fibbing, aren't you? There aren't any submarines in the Indian Ocean. It's only when we get to the Atlantic we have to start worrying, isn't it? That's why they have this convoy system there now.'

He tapped the side of his nose. 'Don't believe everything you read, or the company tells you, Cissie. There've been rumours.'

'You just want to have your wicked way with me.' But in private she acknowledged a certain force in his argument. Though these leisurely, sun-drenched days made the war and all its horror seem so far away, the world across the ocean was there, waiting. London was being bombed, and other British cities, every night now. People *were* being killed, and in another month or so, she would be in the thick of it. It eased her conscience to reflect on that underlying truth — and there were worse if scarcely less strenuous ways of aiding the war effort!

After a mere two-day pause in Bombay, where she actually experienced the effect of 'sea legs' as she felt the unsteadiness of her limbs on dry land after so long aboard ship, the *Star* headed south-west, over the mighty Indian Ocean towards the continent of Africa. Cissie raised the hearts if not the minds of crew and passengers during the ceremony of crossing the line, as well as raising an almost murderous spite in Marjorie Gough's heart, who, as a fellow sprite and handmaiden of Father Neptune, as portrayed by the bulky figure of the captain, had to watch the ogling eyes fixed on the blonde girl, whose brief costume was such an outstanding success. She and Anil had spent a long, sniggering time decorating her pink swimsuit with festoons of shells and 'pearls' and strands of artificial seaweed, at the same time leaving most of her body exposed to the

56

elements and the gaze of the enraptured onlookers.

In fact, Cissie was one of the handful who had not crossed the line before, but, as a female and one of Neptune's handmaids, she avoided the indignities the male novices had to endure. She got away with having to perform in public, where she sang, with piping, tuneful bravery 'I wouldn't leave my little wooden hut for you,' followed by a ducking in the canvas pool, which left her with a few bruises through the enthusiastic woman-handling of certain crew members, and the loss of most of her festooned finery, beneath which, much to her assailants' disappointment, the pink swimsuit stayed obstinately in place.

It was a memorable day, and she had her certificate to prove it. The party went on late into the night. It was almost dawn before she retired, and the sky was definitely paling in the east when Derek slipped discreetly through her door, and joined her in the privacy of her cabin. 'God! It's been murder trying to keep my hands off you all day, you minx! Come here!'

'Be careful!' she admonished. 'Look! Look what your nasty rough sailor boys have done.' She was showing him her bruises, and he had knelt in order to kiss them better, when suddenly there was a massive thud, as if the ship had suddenly struck an enormous object and been stopped in her tracks. The world erupted in another roar and whirled crazily about them. The deck beneath her gone, Cissie felt herself falling, to smash into the bulkhead opposite the bunk, which was rearing up crazily above her. The light was gone, the furious roar was constant now and some hard object fell across her and something hard struck her on the forehead. She was screaming, she could feel her throat and lungs working, but she could hear nothing as her mind tried to encompass the enormity of her last moment, and the words 'Divine Retribution' blazed in her reeling brain.

5

Cissie was aware of blackness and chaos all around her. She wondered briefly if she were dead, then realized she was fully conscious, with her feet way above her head, almost upside-down. She called out for Derek. Her voice sounded faint, as though it came from a long way away. She became aware of the tortured noise, a rending grinding of metal, a nerve-shattering scream of steam escaping from some torn depths, the mad, banshee wailing of the ship's siren, and, more distantly, a constant chorus of panic-stricken, human screams. A weight was pressing across her, pinning her, and she joined those panicked shrieks. 'Get off!'

She thrust the weight easily from her, and an overwhelming fear seized her that she would sink to the bottom of the ocean in the wreck in which she was entombed. She glanced round, saw that the unreal nightmare scene was lit eerily by flickering light. There was no sign of Derek Hargreaves. Where he had stood, literally at her side, the deck plates reared up in a brief, jagged wall, torn like paper, and she realized that where the door and the corridor outside it had been, there was a swirl of steam and the rush and slap of water. The narrow bunk still hung crazily above her, and immediately to its right, framed by more jagged lumps of iron and twisted girders, she saw the paling dawn sky.

She sobbed hysterically, heaved and rolled and clawed and reached up, inflicting the first real damage on herself as she wrestled and squirmed up, out of the wreckage, through that wide, torn hole to the open air. She squeezed through the hanging curve of the plating to lie gasping on the crazily angled deck, unconscious of the myriad cuts and livid scrapes to her limbs and body. She heard the steady wash of the sea, felt the shattered mass beneath her heave perilously. She scrambled to her feet, which slipped on the oily deck. 'God help me!' she blubbered, as she saw the vast stretch of ocean only a few feet below.

Someone cried out, from the tangled mess of what had once been the superstructure. She screamed as a black figure cannoned into her, knocking her flat. 'Fuckin' 'ell!' She saw a fearfully blackened face, white eyes rolling, teeth flashing whitely. 'Come on, luv! She's goin'!' Large blackened arms clamped about her, plucked her up, and leapt from the shattered vessel into the oily swell. Her further screams were choked as the water closed over her, then she clung like a limpet to the swimming figure, her arms locked around his neck. 'Gerron me back!' he panted, clawing at her, and she gained enough control of her fear to obey, bringing up her knees, gripping him tightly, like a child riding piggyback.

' 'Ang on. There's a boat. See?' Her saviour began to kick out vigorously, despite her clinging weight, and Cissie sobbed with relief as the shape of one of the ship's small boats appeared, heading towards them. Hands reached down, plucked her from the water, and she sprawled across the gunwale, her pale behind catching the growing light of the dawning day, and the men exclaimed in a variety of startled oaths as they beheld the spectacle of her, whimpering and shivering in a state of helpless shock at their feet.

'Ah'm Alfie 'Enderson, miss. That's Dobber, Mick, Jimmy, and the lad there is Richie.' The four men grinned self-consciously, and nodded an awkward greeting.

'Thank you, Mr Henderson,' Cissie murmured. 'You saved my life.'

'Glad to oblige, ma'am.' The round face was liberally smeared with oil and grease, as were his meaty forearms. A large area of his brow glistened more palely, where the thin hair had receded. A short moustache, salted with grey, was severely trimmed almost in Hitlerian style on his upper lip. The much-stained, sleeveless vest protruded roundly from beneath his breast, emphasizing his pronounced belly, which gaped on view between vest and the baggy drawers, which extended almost to his knees.

The others were in similar states of undress. Cissie, conscious of her nudity, was grateful for the coarse blanket someone had draped over her when she was lying shivering in the bottom of the boat, a timeless interval in which they were all recovering, while they watched, stunned, the rapid demise of the *Star of Indus*. It was not long before the ship rumbled and slid below the surface, leaving a widening area of oil and detritus among which no other human survivors could be seen.

By the time these introductions were made, the sun of a new day was already making its warmth felt, and they were bobbing on a long but gentle swell, in a limitless dazzle of ocean. Cissie noticed that the boat was much smaller than the ship's lifeboats, which she had observed during the several drills which had been held during the voyage. She shivered again as she recalled how different, how chaotically terrifying, the real disaster had been when it struck, compared with the well-ordered, jolly exercises the passengers had taken part in.

'What about the others?' she asked fearfully.

Alfie Henderson shook his head. 'No chance! They didn't even have time to get one lifeboat away. This is the skiff. Just for ferrying us ashore an' that. Dobber and Nick were dead lucky to get it off before she went down. She were gone in five minutes. Nobody had a chance, did they, lads?' There was a murmur of corroboration.

Something about their looks and tone disturbed Cissie. 'Wasn't there — didn't anybody survive? Get into the water?'

Henderson stared at her, a suspicion of truculence flitting over his round face. 'Mighta done. We couldn't pick anybody up. You can see. There's hardly room enough for us, like. We just had to get away from the ship, fast as we could, otherwise we'd a gone down with her. When we did have time to look about, there was nobody left. Nowt.'

Something in the gruff, defensive challenge of his words warned her not to pursue the matter. She felt physically sick at the thought of all those terrible deaths, as she remembered her own panic, and that fight to escape. Names of the other passengers, and the face of each one, sped through her mind at lightning speed. And Derek Hargreaves. Dear Derek. She could apply that epithet to him now. They had been close. She felt the merciless pricking of her conscience as she thought of how close, in what manner. She was the one defending now, as she argued with herself. I *was* fond of him. Otherwise I could never have . . . she shivered once more as she vividly pictured just how close, literally, they had been when the disaster had struck. His lips were actually touching her flesh. It was nothing short of a miracle that she had survived.

Her fellow survivors were introducing themselves anew, giving a little more detail. Alf was a fireman, from Middlesbrough. 'It's a bl — miracle I'm here, miss. I'd just come up top for a stand-easy, like.' He shook his head solemnly. 'All me marrers gone. Never stood a chance.' Again his teeth flashed white against his darkened features as he smiled sympathetically at her. 'One thing, miss. All your mates — fellow passengers, like — they wouldn't a known a thing. Asleep down below. Gone just like that.'

Cissie thought of her own nightmare, her clawing fight to live, to get up on deck. She shuddered yet again.

Dobber, a donkeyman, was also from the

north somewhere. Mick was one of the seamen, from Yarmouth. Jimmy was another deckhand, and, finally, Richie, a thin and spotty-faced youth who looked no more than fifteen, had been working in the galley as a scullion.

The lower classes, thought Cissie, intrigued by the idea. She had not come across them before, except for a few of the soldiery in the Indian army, and even then she had had no real contact with them. She was very much aware of their eyes on her, on her pale, scratched knees and legs poking out from beneath the blanket she held carefully around her. She was almost amused by their deference, the way their gaze darted away from her when she looked directly at them. Then she thought of the strangeness of her situation. Naked, alone with the five of them, lost in the vastness of the Indian Ocean.

Although two of the crew were deckhands, Alfie, because of his age and his personality, was automatically accepted as leader of the group. She was surprised, and greatly relieved, to discover that they had a bulky container, with what appeared to be a large amount of food — biscuits, chocolate and the like, as well as three big jerry cans of drinking water. 'We'll have to watch it,' Alfie cautioned. 'Specially with the water. Ration it. One of them cupfuls each a day.'

'We'll be picked up soon, though,' Cissie offered hopefully. 'They'll be looking for us, won't they? There's bound to be other ships passing.'

'Oh, aye. In a day or two, mebbe.' They all glanced at each other for reassurance. 'Something'll come along.'

Cissie said diffidently, 'What was it — you know? A submarine?'

Most nodded in agreement, though Dobber made a tentative suggestion that they might have hit a mine.

'What? Right out there in the middle of the oggin?' Alfie made a rude noise of dismissal.

'Well, I dunno. I mean, from what I've heard, the Jerries don't just sink you like that. I mean, in the Atlantic they usually come up on surface, give the crews time to abandon ship. Then they sink her with gunfire. Save the torpedoes.'

'Naw.' Alfie was still dismissive. 'Don't reckon a mine woulda done all that damage so quick. Ripped the guts right out of her.' He put an end to further conjecture. He glanced at the bobbing horizon. 'Meanwhile, we'd better not just sit here and let her drift. We'll keep pulling. Tek turns at the oars, two at a time. 'Cept for Mrs Pride, of course.' He nodded at her, and Cissie felt greatly comforted by this formal use of her surname. He squinted up at the now-blazing sun. 'That's south-west, intit, Dobber? We'll try and head that way.' He grinned. 'Then we'll bump into Africa somewhere, even if no bugger comes along. Whoops! Pardon my French!' He winked at Cissie and she smiled in reply.

But the men were soon exhausted. The sun glared down, burning them mercilessly, and their efforts at rowing made them even thirstier. 'Rowers are gonner need extra rations,' Dobber grumbled. Alfie shook his head.

The sun was beginning to sink lower in the sky ahead of them when the youth Richie let out a kind of sob, and slumped over the heavy oar. 'Fuck it! I ain't rowin' no more! It's a waste o' fuckin' time! We're not gittin' nowhere!'

'Oy! Watch your language! Ladies present!'

Cissie blushed. She wanted to say something to ease the tension but kept miserably silent. She was crouching near the stem, her back against the thwart. The planking bit into her tender flesh; her bottom ached from its contact with the wet boards. Dark, vivid bruises had come up on her flesh, and the cuts and grazes stung in the salt air. The roughness of the blanket irritated her skin further. Partly to distract from the sudden flare of tension, she rose unsteadily, struggling to smile. She held the blanket around her. 'I'm sorry, gentlemen, but I'll have to use the ladies' room. Will you look away, please?' She waited until their heads had turned to study the horizon, let the blanket drop and eased herself over the side.

The plunging coldness of the water was a blessing, and she let her head go under. When she spluttered blindly to the surface, Alfie's moon-face hung over the side, gazing down at her. 'Don't hang about, miss. Don't forget there's sharks around these waters.'

'Not this far out from land, surely?' But she trod water for just a few more seconds, before she called up, 'Right then. Will you all turn away again? I'm coming back on board.' She reached up, grasping the edge of the gunwale. She was shocked at how high it seemed, and how puny her arms felt. They were at full stretch, and she had no strength to haul herself upward. She scrabbled, grazed her knees painfully against the curve of the hull, felt the sweep of the water ready to pluck her free once more. She gave a helpless sob. She couldn't see anything except the planks of the boat's side inches from her face. 'Help!' she cried. 'I can't climb in. Please help me.'

Hard hands seized her wrists, and she was

plucked, dripping, from the water. Her arms were round hot, greasy shoulders and she was swung inboard and deposited with a wet thump on to the bottom boards. She scrambled for the blanket, wrapped it clumsily round her glistening flesh, half-laughing, half-crying with embarrassment. 'Sorry! I didn't mean for you to see me in my birthday suit!'

'Oh, don't you worry, miss. We had our eyes shut, didn't we, lads?' Alfie chuckled, and there was a gallant if mendacious chorus of agreement.

The great red sphere of the sun was dipping into the sea on their starboard bow as Alfie issued the ration of biscuit, two pieces of the dark chocolate, and the cups of water. There were three tin cups, one with each of the jerry cans, and one was designated solely for Cissie's use. 'Half a cup extra for the ladies, eh?' Alfie said. It was not really a question, and nobody demurred.

Someone even managed to call out jocularly, 'That doesn't include you, gorgeous!' in Richie's direction, and the boy just managed to smother the obscene answer which sprang to his chapped lips.

'No, really!' Cissie protested. 'I can manage, thank you very much. Though it's extremely kind of you. We're all in the same boat, aren't we?' And they laughed in overly loud appreciation of her sally.

'Aye, but *you* paid to be here, eh? We came along for free!' Alfie insisted. She had drained her cupful, unable to resist that sweet few seconds as its coolness flowed down her throat, cleansed her tongue, and now he took the empty vessel from her and poured another couple of inches into it. He got up and leaned forward until he was hanging over her. She was uncomfortably aware of his nearness, and of her nakedness under the draped blanket. He smiled. 'Go on. You take it. Drink it up, there's a good gal.' She felt all at once a disturbing sense of his dominance. She took the cup from him, felt the fleeting contact with his thick fingers, and drank off the liquid obediently.

'Thank you,' she whispered, handing back the tin cup, unable to meet his gaze.

The long night was a weary eternity for her. She wasn't sure whether she slept, whether she was unconscious when the vivid reworking of the nightmare of the sinking ran like a film reel in her fevered brain. The cataclysmic destruction of that safe and pleasurable world was rerun, over and over, along with the hectic pleasures she had known for the first time with Derek Hargreaves, literally plucked from her, consumed in the fires of destruction. Why had she not shared the same fate? She found herself whimpering aloud, shivering violently.

'There there, luv.' A large, rough hand was holding her bare, fragile shoulder, the stubby fingers pressing hard into her flesh. The tears marked shining runnels on the salt-caked dirt of her raw cheeks as she gazed up at Alfie's broad, filthy face. 'You're cold, poor little babby! Come here. Old Alfie'll keep you warm, me luv.'

He slumped beside her, folded his corpulent frame around her, held her close to his side. She could smell the oil and the sweat, feel his body trembling, too, against hers, but she was too weak to protest, too much in need of his warmth and protection, and too afraid of what her refusal of his comfort might spark.

In the chill of dawn she woke to find the blanket had been moved to cover both their shoulders and her body was nestled into his in abandoned intimacy. She felt the great dome of his belly, its damp stickiness against her skin, the coarseness of his underclothing rubbing against her. She gave a smothered cry, tried to squirm free, and his arms tightened about her, hugging her into him. 'Get back to sleep!' he growled.

'Please!' she whispered, crying softly, and

his eyes opened. That great, glistening, dirty face peered at her. 'Let me go!'

She was half up, scrambling to roll away from him, and his great arms clutched at her, dragged her back into his side, his breath warm and stale as he brought his face close. 'Whoa there! You're not at the skipper's table now, missy! Remember where you *are* at, sweetheart. You'd better show a bit of gratitude to the ones what saved your life, sweetheart, instead of gettin' uppity with those your life still depends on. All right?'

Suddenly she was sobbing and screaming and squirming to free herself from his blubbery flesh, fighting as wildly as she had to save herself from the wreck of the cabin back on the *Star*. The fury of her efforts caused him to release her and she crawled away from him, sobbing hysterically. She saw the others, rising from their huddled proximity further forward in the boat, coming awake. Ragged, half-dressed, filthy scarecrows. Yet she saw the look on their pinched faces, felt all their eyes on her body as she crouched there across the after thwart, helpless, trying to steel herself to fling herself overboard and thus face certain extinction. Why, she wondered fleetingly, had she been saved only to face this further ordeal?

'Jesus Christ!'

Her body was taut as a spring: she struggled with the nightmare of a slow drowning, or the even slower nightmare of what would lie in store for her in the boat. But she suddenly realized that the awestruck blasphemy, and the riveted gaze of the boat's occupants, were no longer directed at her. She turned, and then she, too, choked the wild sobs that were rising within. Her jaw dropped like theirs, and she stared in goggling wonder at the vision which reared damascene-like way above the swaying little craft, only metres away, and shining miraculously in the first of the new sun's rays.

The tall black tower was silhouetted against the pale sky and the uniformed figures who were staring back in equal disbelief. They had battered caps, with dull, gold-wired badges. Only their heads and shoulders were visible, their lower bodies hidden beneath the rim of the tower, around which ran a handrail. Their astonished faces transformed into wide grins. They called out, in a language which Cissie could not understand but which she recognized as German, then a voice spoke in heavily accented English. 'Good day to you, fraulein. Sorry to interrupt your . . . er . . . play!'

6

'Give me my blanket!' Cissie hissed, in quiet fury, and Alfie fumbled it to her, unable to take his eyes from the German U-boat rolling blackly in the swell, only yards away from them.

A voice rapped out a staccato command from on high. It was an order that the forward hatch in the cigar hull should be kept closed and none of the crew be allowed on the upper deck, though none of the *Star*'s survivors could understand a word of it. The same voice switched to English once more. 'I am Kapitan Heinz Schmidt. If you please, bring your boat to our side, gentlemen.'

Mick and Jimmy, the two deckhands, scrabbled for the oars and with swift, ragged strokes drew the tiny skiff alongside the bulging round of the enemy's hull, which, close to, was seen to be heavily stained and clustered with small shells and trailing infestations, indicating its long exposure to the tropic sea. 'Thank God you found us, Captain!' Alfie called up fervently. 'The poor young lady here was just about at the end of her tether.'

Even in her gratitude at the timeliness of this miraculous intervention, Cissie registered her furious disbelief at the fat fireman's aplomb. Just as you were about to rape me! her mind screamed in protest, but she remained dumb. She glanced up, and only then noticed the slender barrel of a machine gun angled steeply downward to train upon them. She was startled by this forceful reminder that their rescuers were in fact their enemy. Two seamen in grubby white uniforms clattered down the vertical iron ladder from the conning tower on to the wet hull. They reached forward, and one held the skiff by the thin rope at its bow while the other reached out his hands towards her. He was grinning. His face was young, covered with a thick, dark stubble of several days' growth. He grunted something, clearly meant to encourage her.

She gave a hopeless little cry, trying to hold the blanket to her with one hand and clasp his arm with the other. She was not very successful in shielding herself, and the woollen material fell open as the sailor swung her up on to the hot, slippery deck. She almost fell, and his arms were firm round her as he guided her to the foot of the ladder. 'I think you are not able to preserve your modesty, fraulein!' the captain's mocking voice called from up above. She fought back her tears and let the blanket slip from her as she began to climb. She winced at the bite of the iron rungs on her tender feet, and struggled to pull herself upward, too concentrated on not falling to be outraged at the sailor's hand on her hip, or his close scrutiny of her battered frame as he mounted behind her. She even muttered, 'Thank you,' when, as she was helped awkwardly over the rail of the small circular top, Kapitan Schmidt produced a thin dressing gown and held it open, with elaborate, mocking courtesy, while she turned and slipped her arms into it, then tied it tightly at her waist.

'Please.' His short, fair beard was slightly uneven. The thought flashed through her distracted mind how much more handsome he would look without it, then she was moving obediently to the even smaller open hatchway he was indicating, and she turned clumsily to descend backwards into the interior of the vessel. The fetid atmosphere, thick with soupy malevolence, closed like a fog about her even before she completed her descent of the short ladder, and in spite of the dazzling shaft of sunlight falling from the open hatch over her head. It caught her at once, the evilly rich amalgam of hot metal, oil, stale food, body odours, and sewage, strong enough to make her believe she could taste it at the back of her throat. Later, she was glad that she had so many utterly new sensations to contend with in this alien world, as she obediently followed her guide from the control room, past the avidly curious, grinning stares of the figures crowding there, through the narrow tunnel lined on each side with a maze of pipes hemming her in, so that she instinctively stooped, even though she could have stood upright.

The boy who accompanied her was a junior officer, she guessed, from the gold cap badge he wore, and the single bar on the epaulettes at his shoulders. He drew aside a flowered, dirty curtain from an open doorway and ushered her into a tiny cabin, with a desk fixed to a bulkhead, and a high bunk, neatly made up. 'Nothing to be afraid.' He flushed as he spoke, trying not to stare at her.

What a mess I must look! was Cissie's chief thought, as she blushed in return. Hair stiff with sweat and seawater, face like a blackamoor, body covered with cuts and bruises. 'Rest,' the junior officer urged, gesturing towards the bunk. 'Afterwards, you take bath. Kapitan will come soon.' He turned to go, then turned back, embarrassed. 'You must stay here. For the moment.'

'What will you do with us?'

'You are safe. No problem.' His eyes moved from hers. 'I must go. Please. Stay. Do not move from here.' He went out quickly, swinging the light curtain to behind him.

She glanced around. There were what looked like nautical books and tables on the shelf above the desk. A framed photograph of a pretty, dark-haired young woman holding a baby swaddled in a white shawl was fixed to the bulkhead beside the head of the bunk and the metal lamp. She pinned her hope on this tender evidence of humanity, against the stream of propaganda she had read and heard of the bestiality of the Nazis.

Up top, the five members of the *Star*'s crew made to scramble up from the bobbing skiff, when a sharp command stopped them in their tracks. '*Nein!*' The German commander stared down at them. He nodded at the seaman who had remained on the narrow deck, and the man tossed the painter back into the bow of the little craft and thrust the stem away from the U-boat.

Alfie cried out in alarm. ' 'Ere! You can't leave us behind! We might never be rescued! For God's sake, sir!' His hoarse cry was desperate in appeal. 'At least put us adrift nearer land.'

Captain Schmidt shook his head. 'We are not going to leave you, my friend.' He nodded at the figure who was stationed behind the machine gun. Before the horrified Britishers fully comprehended their fate, the slender barrel spat pale arcs and the shells raked the boat and its occupants, flinging them into jerking motion, shredding their flesh and ripping the life from them. They fell like bundles of rags in careless abandon, the dark tides of blood staining them, and the timbers around them. Another savage burst raked the skiff at its waterline, blew bites out of the low side. The boat began to settle, the water lapped over the freeboard. Only one of the bodies floated free as the craft settled beneath the surface, hanging anonymous, face down, in the heaving swell.

'Below! Secure all hatches! Dive! Dive! Dive!' barked Kapitan Schmidt, waiting by the hatch as the others hastily made their way through.

★ ★ ★

Heinz Schmidt was responsible for all the deaths on the *Star of Indus*. It was his vessel which had picked up and tracked the ship as the sun was setting, followed her submerged, manoeuvring to place her conveniently against the first paling of dawn to send home the two torpedoes which sealed her fate. They had struck within seconds, one close to the bows, the other amidships — a near-perfect strike. The attack had been copybook, like an exercise at the submariner school back in Kiel. A lone ship, complete surprise, for no one had yet discovered that submarines were operating in the Indian Ocean. His was one of the three that comprised the first flotilla to round the Cape of Good Hope, working from a parent depot ship off the south-west Africa coast. The German radio detection equipment, promoted by the energetic efforts of their navy leader, Admiral Doenitz, was far more sophisticated than the British realized. They had learnt of the *Star*'s movements almost from the time she had left Bombay; had lain in wait. Their task was made easier, for, although she was a fast ship, the company believed that there was virtually no risk of attack until she reached the Atlantic segment of her voyage, and had therefore given orders (not to be divulged publicly) that Captain Fuller should proceed as economically as possible on the leg to Dar-es-Salaam and thus conserve fuel.

After their successful attack, Schmidt had not fled the scene as he might have done in the Atlantic theatre, but remained in the vicinity of the sinking in case some other vessel might appear. It was not likely, for the

Star had failed even to send out an SOS, so quick was her demise. Then Schmidt had noted the skiff, the sole survivor. With the small boat as possible bait, he had waited further long hours before surfacing alongside it. He had rescued the naked girl — it would make a great tale back at the depot ship, or in the mess at Kiel should they make it back to Europe eventually. But his gallantry ended there. He realized that the enemy were still for the moment totally unaware of the flotilla's presence. But five extra prisoners to feed, accommodate and guard, maybe for several more weeks before he could offload them, was out of the question. Yet he could not risk the possibility of this handful of men being rescued, however remote it was. They had to die. The two days' grace they had been granted should be looked on as a bonus denied to their shipmates. And they had spent it in the company of a naked woman! Those whom the gods favoured . . .

The great blue eyes stared wildly at him, at one with the general unkemptness of the slim figure wearing his robe. 'What happened?' She was stammering in her anxiety. 'The shooting! Where are my — my friends?'

His eyebrows arched. 'Your friends, fraulein?' He saw her wedding ring. 'Oh, I am sorry.' He smiled. 'You look so young. Frau . . . ?'

There was a pause until she realized what he was asking. 'Pride. Tell me what happened. Where are they?'

'Do not distress yourself. I am afraid they refused to surrender. They attacked one of my men. I had no alternative.'

Her horrified expression reflected her feeling. 'Are they . . . ?' She could not complete her sentence.

'I fear so, Frau Pride.' He gave a rueful shrug. 'They gave no choice. Brave men, perhaps — but very foolish.'

Suddenly all the terrors and calamity of the past two days seemed to avalanche down on her overstretched nerves. The room lurched, the strength drained from her limbs and she folded, collapsed in a heap on the floor, her body shaking violently as she was racked by sobs. She was gathered up, her filthy head cradled, strong arms held her close, and she felt the brush of lips against an ear as the voice whispered tenderly incomprehensible phrases. She clung in grateful exhaustion to him, the weakness of her grief almost comforting as she let herself be swept away on it, aware of her weakness, yielding gladly to it, beyond all shame, not caring that the breast she clung to was a German breast, the strong arms holding her were German arms. She needed them, their shelter, the tenderness that came with them.

An hour later she was nestled in the bunk, freshly bathed, the cuts and bruises tended, wearing a man's clean white shirt and covered by a clean white sheet, drifting off to deep slumber whose approach had been enhanced by the medicinal draught the medical orderly had given her, after he had tended to her cuts and abrasions.

★　★　★

Captain Schmidt cleared his throat, and called out as always. 'Frau Pride?' He waited for her answer before he put his head through the curtained doorway of the tiny cabin he had surrendered to her. 'We are surfacing in five minutes. Come. You may go up on deck.'

'Thank you, Captain.' She studied the polite correctness of the fine features, half-covered yet not at all marred by the more substantial but neatly trimmed fair beard. Again, she noted the lines of fatigue deep about his grey eyes. For a long while now, the label of cold-blooded murderer had not immediately sprung to mind when she saw or thought of him. In the four weeks that had followed, the incident, like the trauma of the sinking itself, had lost much of its sharp and vivid terror, taking on the unreality of disturbing childhood nightmares. Nor were the converging stares of the men she passed as she followed him along the central tube which was the main alleyway fore to aft, and in the crowded control room at the foot of the conning tower, so unnerving.

Things had turned out very differently from the heart-thumping fears which had assailed her the first time she had descended into this claustrophobic, isolated world. For one thing she was no longer naked. The costume she wore was far from eye-catching: a voluminous white, short-sleeved shirt and baggy white shorts whose legs reached down well below her knees, held up by a belt in which several new notches had to be cut. One of the handymen in the crew had adapted a pair of sandals, re-carving the leather soles to fit her feet, and restitching the straps to hold them more securely.

The first night on board she had woken from her drugged sleep in griping agony, to find to her horror that she was bleeding heavily, a darkly viscous mess staining her inner thighs, with spasms in her lower belly which made her groan and whimper for help. Terrified, she was sure she had sustained some terrible internal injury and was about to die. With dedicated professionalism, the young medical orderly had soothed her, cleaned her up, administered to her and dramatically eased the pain with an injection. Embarrassment did not set in until later, when the pain had greatly lessened, and the bleeding had stopped. He asked her questions about her period, and she realized she could scarcely reckon when her last had occurred.

'When you have last sex with husband?' the orderly asked.

'No, no!' Cissie answered, the tide of colour sweeping up into her neck and face. 'He was away. Before I left.'

'I look in books.' He grinned. 'I not meet this before. Not with sailor.'

She giggled nervously. 'No, I expect not.'

'I think miscarriage you have. Usually ten week. Maybe less, after . . . you know.'

'Oh no! It's much longer — ' She stopped abruptly, appalled at herself for not realizing. Derek! When had they first . . . ? Several weeks ago, surely? Could he . . . ? She began to weep, quietly, and the German touched her gently on the shoulder.

'Is all right. Other times, is all right.'

Since then, the only terror she had known had been shared by most of the crew, she suspected, when the klaxon blared and they took up action stations and she was ordered to stay in the cabin. They shadowed their unsuspecting victims, fired their torpedoes and waited to see their effect before making their underwater escape. Cissie was thankful that Captain Schmidt did not pursue the strategy he had followed with the *Star*, of waiting to see if others would come in aid of the destroyed ship.

'Secrecy is no longer our friend,' he told her bluntly. 'They know by now we are here. Soon we must make for home.'

'What will happen to me?' she plucked up courage to ask him, when this confined world was no longer so unfamiliar to her, nor its inhabitants.

'You have nothing to fear. You are prisoner of the Reich.'

His words did little to reassure her, but she began to push the future away from her and concentrate on her present world. She began to see its total isolation almost as a comfort.

The junior officer who had first led her down to her subterranean world was Hans Kuper. She was most relaxed with him, perhaps because, of the half-dozen officers, he was nearest to her in age, as well as the fact that he spoke very good English. Captain Schmidt had instituted lessons in English, for which his officers sacrificed their precious moments of leisure, most of them willingly enough. In turn, they were happy to teach her the rudiments of German. 'You will find it useful,' Schmidt advised her, reawakening temporarily her unquiet about what lay in store.

'He's a bit forbidding,' Cissie confided to Hans Kuper one evening, when they were secluded in her cabin.

Kuper spoke with the glowing enthusiasm of a schoolboy for his favourite master or prefect. 'He is a good man. We are safe with him. You also are safe.'

'I know.' She hesitated. 'But he is so correct. I feel — I don't know. Intimidated. I can't really talk.'

'A captain must . . . er . . . how you say? Keep his distance, *ja*? It is difficult.'

'His wife looks nice.'

Kuper nodded enthusiastically. 'She is, very nice. Beautiful! She is like, you know, sister to us. When we train, she sees us very often. We go to their home, she comes to us. He is a very lucky man, yes?'

'Yes,' Cissie agreed. She was dismayed by the emotion she felt at his ardent words. Could it be that she was jealous of this picture on the wall? The picture that had been removed from near her head and taken to the captain's new abode. Why should it bother her so? She thought of how he had held her, the feel of his body supporting her, his arms so strong about her, the caress of his whispered voice, the feel of his lips so close to her ear.

Now, standing on the island of the conning tower, high over the moonlit waves, the breeze from Africa warm on her face, she knew how much she appreciated these blessed moments in the open, while the boat cruised along, recharging the batteries. She could see him, his silhouette, that misshapen cap, with its grubby white cover, which gave him such a piratical, romantic air. He's your enemy! The shocked inner voice clanged discordantly. The killer of all those souls, passengers and crew, she had shared those weeks with on the *Star of Indus*, murderer of the unfortunate five who had escaped from the doomed ship with her.

She remembered the damply repulsive, smothering flesh of Alfie Henderson, the fierce clamp of his embrace, the animal ugliness of his face as she had fought her way free of his clutch. Heinz Schmidt had saved her life that day, as surely as he had ordered the slaying of those who had been with her in the skiff.

7

The normal pallor of the submariner, shut away as he was for the majority of his time on patrol in the fetid atmosphere of his undersea 'tin fish', was counteracted in the case of U213 by the spell in the tropical waters of the Indian Ocean. Less frequented than its sister ocean to the west, it meant that Captain Schmidt could allow his men the luxury of a spell up top during the early hours of sunlight, as well as the night time, when they cruised on the surface in order to recharge the batteries they depended on. The men would swarm up eagerly on to the narrow central grating of the sloping hull, and even take a quick plunge over the side, in sections of six at a time. The gun crew quickly checked the weapon raised on its forward mounting, then joined their fellows sprawled naked or, in the case of one or two more modest souls, wearing underpants, in the sunshine.

The first time Cissie had inadvertently caught sight of them from her privileged position on the conning tower, she had been a little shocked at the white behinds. 'Don't let the men see you!' Captain Schmidt had called out, somewhat tardily. 'I don't want you to embarrass my poor boys.'

'Don't be such a spoilsport!' she returned boldly. 'They've all seen *my* behind!'

'Not so, Frau Pride. I did not allow them to come on deck, in order to spare you — how you say it — blush.'

Or in order to spare them witnessing your cold-hearted murder of Alf and the others. The thought came like a cold touch, and a reprimand to her lightheartedness. But such sombre reflections came less and less as the long voyage continued. In fact it surprised her to discover by calculation one day that she had spent more time as a prisoner on U213 than she had on the *Star*.

Of course, their morning exposure to the sunlight was brief, and was always tinged with that edge of tension. Lookouts were urged to extra keenness, scanning sea and sky for danger. Cissie was ashamed to find it gave her an excitement that was almost a stimulus to her. There was never any further need for the admonition from the captain to keep herself hidden from the crew below. But it gave her a guilty thrill, too, as she listened to them shouting and laughing and splashing about, to think of them naked. She sat within the confines of the small circular rim of the tower, her back against the curved metal side, the shorts rolled up to her thighs, shirt buttons opened and the shirt lapels turned back as far as decency permitted, her face with closed eyes turned worshipfully towards the precious sun.

And then these welcome interludes ceased; the weather grew suddenly colder. It added greatly to the discomfort of the submarine. Bulkheads grew clammy, and dripped with icy water. The air, cold as it was, became fouler. The young medical orderly, who had looked after her so well, discreetly left a small parcel for her on her bunk. It contained two sets of men's underwear, vests and pants, and a pair of navy serge slacks, as well as two thick pairs of socks. She was glad of them, and the white sweater the captain gave her, though it came nearly to her knees and she had to turn the sleeves up at least six times.

She became much more aware of the motion of the submarine, even underwater: an often unpleasant rolling, which gave her a throbbing headache and an unpleasant nauseous stomach. 'There is much worse to follow,' the captain said, grinning. 'We are near the famous Cape. And we are now into November.' His words added to her queasiness, the shadow of her future looming to the forefront of her mind. 'God willing, you may spend your first Christmas in the Fatherland.'

The nightly run on the surface became a thumping, buffeting, infernally long spell of unpleasantness. 'Can I come up?' she begged, after she had been forced to remain below for several nights. The captain seemed reluctant, but at last he consented. He brought her a sou'wester and a yellow oilskin, with a white silk scarf to fold inside the high collar.

'Do not mind your feet. You can dry when you come below. You will not stay for long.'

She had to be dragged through the narrow hatch, and even though the small circle was protected in some measure by its sides, the wind tore at her, catching her breath. Spray struck her face with the force of small stones, and any sound she tried to make was torn from her mouth and lost in the scream of the elements. For just a moment, the sight through the driving spray was so spectacular she forgot to be afraid. There was no sign of the hull below. The tower seemed to stand alone in a raging, white, boiling sea. Then the bow reared up, and the white cascade parted briefly to show the blackness of the hull, the water streaming from it, until it plunged with a smack she felt through the soles of her soaking feet under the raging sea again. A wall of water reared up, struck and filled the enclosed circle of the bridge with an icy swirl, drained away through the scuppers, and descended with a showering cascade down through the hatch, which was still fastened open.

She was gasping, blinded with the stinging salt, soaked through to the skin beneath the enveloping oilskin. Her hair was plastered to her brow under the rim of her headgear. She stumbled and slid, cannoning into the dark shapes around her, clung white-knuckled to the rail. The captain's lips moved against her ear. 'Enough now. You go.' He manhandled her to the coaming of the hatch, yelling to those below, and swung her through, to where other hands caught and held her, then brought her down until she stood, gasping, dripping and shivering, in the for once welcome fug of the interior.

Her limbs were numb, her fingers clumsy. She stood under the blessed warmth of the shower in the minute cubicle which served as the officers' bathroom, then rubbed herself as hard as she could with the damp towel, all the while banging against the metal bulkheads as the boat seesawed about. In the cabin she dragged on her spare set of underwear, and over that pulled the makeshift nightshirt. She climbed with difficulty into the bunk, huddled under the sheet and the extra blanket, and waited for warmth and feeling to return to her feet.

Slowly warmth began to infiltrate, and feeling too, emotional as well as physical. She thought of the captain, up above in that screaming, wild element. Thought of all the days and weeks and months he must have spent in this metal coffin — she knew that was the term the submariners themselves jokingly used for their craft. Guessed, too, how easily that joke might become a reality. Already she felt as though she had spent half a life-time here. The captain had told her how lucky she was — how easy their present war was compared with the other theatres of the Atlantic or the Mediterranean. 'You will be safe. We will return you safely,' he kept assuring her.

'What will happen to me?' She kept on asking, she could not help it. He was extremely patient with her. All the men were.

'You will be quite safe, Frau Pride.' Why did he insist on addressing her so formally? Time and time she had chided him. He joked about it. 'Your name. Cissie. It is so difficult. I cannot say it well.' He sometimes called her by her proper name. Cicely. Not that he could pronounce it any more easily.

'Don't call me that!' she would wail. 'I hate it. Cissie's bad enough!'

She had pushed the memory of her capture

deep into the background, refused to dwell on it. The fortunes of war. She had watched the hardness clamp down on his features as he explained the reason for the deaths of her companions in the skiff. The hardness distressed her. She had seen it come down like a mask, so many times. When action came, the pursuit of the enemy, the sinking of a ship. They left her alone in the cabin, during the wild excitement after the kill, the drinking and the celebrations. Her fellow countrymen had died up there, and in terrifying violence.

Cissie was shocked to find she could not summon genuine tears for them. Not even, as the immediacy of the events faded, for those she had known on board the *Star*. She decided uncomfortably that it showed some serious flaw in her character, a callowness of emotion. Or was it — an even more discomfiting conjecture — that she could feel only for those who were in close proximity to her? Out of sight, out of mind. Charlie came to her mind now. How easily days went by without her thoughts turning for one instant to him. Her husband. A mistake, a silly, childish mistake! And that led on to Derek Hargreaves. The man she had known for only days before she had betrayed her marriage vows with him. The discomfort became a sharp stab of shame at the thought of how she had enjoyed giving herself. She was right to condemn herself as a slut, for she was nothing less. And now, most shocking of all, she was harbouring such secret, dangerous feelings about Heinz Schmidt. Her enemy, who had killed probably hundreds of her countrymen, including dear, randy Derek, her only real lover, and would probably kill hundreds more. And about whom she was harbouring such private, disgusting fantasies, and envying a picture on his wall. Why should she feel that way? He had been good and kind to her, behaved impeccably. It was a sign of her degeneracy that she should sometimes wish he hadn't.

When she caught glimpses of herself in the small mirror above the washbasin, she was hardly surprised that he should find her physically unappealing. Her face was pinched, her complexion sallow without makeup to enhance it. Her feminine shape, slight enough in truth, was lost entirely in the unbecoming bagginess of the male clothing. Her hair was a dull flaxen mop, like a yokel's about her skull. She looked more like a boy than a girl.

Not everyone was impervious to her virtually non-existent charm. Hans Kuper's naïve, puppyish friendliness quickly gave evidence of developing into something altogether warmer. In response, she was kind;

perhaps kinder than she should be, and perhaps in response to the captain's unassailable correctitude. But Hans reminded her too strongly of Charlie to gain a special place in her heart. Only once did his feelings translate into innocuous action. Across the small folding table, during one of their language lessons, he took hold of her hand and raised it to his lips. 'Don't be naughty!' she giggled, and snatched it away, and he turned a vivid crimson and stammered an apology. She conquered her urge to be cruel, and put on a patiently maternal expression. 'Don't do things like that,' she said kindly. 'Don't forget I'm married. You're my friend.'

The tensions grew, visibly, as the submarine nosed its way north, off the coast of West Africa. She felt a kind of dismay when Heinz Schmidt told her he had hoped to pass her over to their mother ship, a surface vessel, for the transfer back to home waters. But plans had changed, he went on, and they would not be rendezvousing with the ship. 'You will have to stay with us.' Her heart beat a little faster, with relief.

They took risks, travelling for long periods of daylight on the surface, through the buffeting seas. Several times, they were forced to crash dive, when ships strayed into their vicinity, or when planes were detected. As far as they knew they were not spotted. Then came the last and most difficult part of the voyage, up past the Iberian Peninsula and across the Bay of Biscay. They were heading for Lorient, on the northern coast of the Bay, where a new submarine base was being established in the newly conquered territory.

The crew were torn between their relief that the trip would thus be greatly shortened, avoiding the dangers of negotiating the narrow English Channel and the North Sea, and the fact that they would not be sailing into their home port. Heinz Schmidt strove to reassure them. 'I will personally see that you are given leave to travel back home. This has been a long patrol.' They had been away for more than three months. 'And a successful one. We are even bringing back a beautiful prisoner!' Cissie wondered at the great cheer and the shout of laughter that went up.

Later, in the privacy of her cabin, he said, 'Only two more days and we lose you. You are like one of my crew now. We shall miss you — Cissie.' He even struggled to pronounce her name, and she felt a choking lump rise in her throat. Her eyes moistened with the threat of tears. 'But I have told you, do not fear. I shall speak to those ashore about you. I will see that you are cared for.'

'Do you think they might let me go?'

He shrugged. 'It would be good. But I will insist — yes? — that you are taken care of. In comfort. You could perhaps do some useful work, for the Reich.'

She felt herself colouring. Be a traitor, he was suggesting. Work for the enemy. But if it would keep her safe . . . she was no heroine, she was the first to admit it. She wanted only to stay alive. Anybody would do the same. Wouldn't they?

'They will pass word to your family. They will be so happy to find you are alive, yes? Your husband.'

It had come as a shock to her to realize that everyone she knew thought her dead, would be mourning her loss. Her parents, poor Charlie. She wondered if Rani would hear. His words brought it all back to her, and another shocking self-discovery came to light. It struck her that her capture had meant a clean break from her past. Her supposed death was like being born again. A completely new start. Did she really want the old Cissie to be resurrected?

⋆ ⋆ ⋆

The sky was iron grey, the sleet falling, as on a bitter mid-December day, U213 nosed her way through the harbour still being reconstructed to the new pens lining the muddy estuary, and the high hulls of the depot ships moored beside them. A great effort had been made to make the welcome as stirring as possible. A small crowd of top brass stood under a billowing awning, a military band thumped away enthusiastically, and sailors lined both ships and dock to give rousing cheers. There were even a handful of women with the VIPs, among whom was the elegant Frau Schmidt, in fur coat and hat, and soft high boots. At her side the nanny stood holding the swaddled bundle of Heinz Schmidt Junior.

Cissie, waiting below, saw nothing of this. Her teeth were rattling at the cold, her insides churning like the muddy seabed stirred by the craft's propellers. Tears were very close to the surface. Her first visit to Europe! Not quite the way she had intended. She had set off to 'do her bit', as she had proudly told her new husband. Now she was a prisoner in the enemy's hands, without so much as catching a glimpse of the country to which she owed allegiance. But did she? she argued in her whirling mind. Her first duty was to herself. She had to remain alive. And it was the man at this moment receiving the due triumphs of the warrior returned successful from the battle to whom she owed that life.

She had to wait a long time after the U-boat had tied up alongside the depot ship before Heinz Schmidt reappeared, with a small delegation, led by a distinguished older man with gold-encrusted decoration on the cap of his immaculate uniform. 'Welcome to German territory, Frau Pride. You are prisoner of the *Kriegsmarine*. You will be taken care of.' His words went some way towards reassuring her, though the kindly proprietary smile of the captain at his side went a lot further — until she caught the curious and only half-concealed amused look of the elegant and fragrant figure at his heel. Cissie recognized the face from the photo at once. The ruff of the smart fur coat, the saucy angle of the fur hat with its dark, looped veil, the silk-stockinged legs and fashionable Russian boots complemented the aristocratic beauty of the features.

Cissie's face blazed. She hung her head, like a fool, feeling all the weight of the unattractive contrast she must present: the shapeless mass of the thick, grubby seaman's sweater, the shapeless blue serge trousers, boots at least three sizes too big, the straw thatch of her hair and unmade-up features, even sallower after the long recent days of interment in the stale entrapment of the submarine.

'Goodbye, Cissie.'

She knew he was using her Christian name to show how close they had become, and to help her not to be afraid. The tears welled, she could not hold them back. She closed her eyes, felt them squeeze through, to course shamingly down her rough cheeks. She hung her head in complete misery, and her shoulders heaved in a huge and audible sigh. A complete and utter fool! She felt him reach for her icy hand, hold it between both his own, and press it hard. It was the most intimate thing they had shared, and she could not speak, nor even lift her head to look at him. Someone else took her arm, and she moved for the last time from those smelly, cramped confines which had been her home for so long now, and climbed up the steel rungs to the driving wetness and grey light, aware of the clomping and flapping of the ridiculous boots, the stress of the countless new, curious or hostile eyes on her slight form, lost in the shapeless clothing.

She crossed the cluttered deck of the depot ship and down the gangplank to the dockside, accompanied by her strange little retinue of uniformed figures. She saw nothing of the scene through her tears. She kept her head down, stared at the ugly, gaping boots, and climbed into the black car, which sped away.

'She looked a pretty little thing, even in those ridiculous clothes! I'm quite jealous of her!' Frau Schmidt said, leaning into her husband, whose arm slid round her waist. He glanced down at her. She saw the desire in his grey eyes, thought how debonairly handsome he looked in that blond Viking way with that beard of his. She felt the keen thrill of her own excitement, and leaned more intimately into him. The responsive shiver that passed through her owed nothing to the driving winter rain.

8

Cissie could find little to fault in her treatment at the hands of her captors during the earliest days, which she spent in the French port. She was not ill-treated in any way, but the impersonal coldness they displayed, from the military doctor who examined her with clinical efficiency, in the company of his blank-faced nursing assistant, to the civilian wardresses who guarded her in her cell at the back of the police station, made her look back almost with nostalgic longing to the confined, dangerous world of U213, and the comradeship she had shared.

The building was old. The brick walls of her cell were high and cold, and the ugly green paint on the lower half of the brickwork was defaced with numerous scratched initials, and dates, and inscriptions which her smattering of French under Mr Horner's tutelage was inadequate to translate. The bed was a wooden shelf securely fastened to the wall, on which lay a thin mattress, suspiciously stained and with an odour to confirm her suspicions. There was a striped pillow, just a little cleaner, and two thick grey blankets, thankfully cleaner still, and carrying the faint aroma of disinfectant. One of the guards even brought her a third, extra blanket, when she made motions of shivering to demonstrate how cold she felt.

She was greatly relieved to find that, when she was taken to a bleak, high-ceilinged washroom, the water was hot enough to produce rolling clouds of steam, and she stood as long as she dared under the plentiful flow of the shower, using the strong carbolic soap block to wash not only her body but her hair. It had been clipped with rough expertise by one of the U-boat crew — the ship's 'barber', they told her proudly — so that it was still quite short. Like the rest of her person, it had been checked thoroughly by the doctor to make sure it was free from infestation.

And at last, the sailors' clothing she had worn for so long was taken from her, and replaced with scarcely more becoming female attire: the coarse, stiff material of the prison dress hung like a tent on her slim frame, the hem only inches above her ankles. Underneath, the flannel vest and baggy drawers and half-petticoat itched annoyingly, while the thick black woollen stockings, only loosely held by the broad garters, sagged in folds around her ankles, over the heavy wooden clogs.

For two days she was left alone, except for the guard, who led her out to use the lavatory and to wash. Cissie was extremely relieved to be thus roused, in the gloom of a winter dawn. The chipped enamel bucket with a lid on it in the corner of her cell noisomely advertised its purpose. She vowed resolutely not to use it except in the direst emergency. The wardress insisted she bring it out with her each dawn and swill it in the vast stone sink beside the washroom.

On her third day, she was distracted by the faint sound of a band playing, and recognized the melody of a Christmas carol. The familiar tune swept aside her feeble defences and she felt the tears streaming down her face. The weeping fit grew more abandoned, until soon she was lying on the bunk, huddled under her blanket and enveloped in a cloud of misery and self-pity that left her drained, her face blotched, her nose red as a cherry, and her eyes sore and swollen.

'Noel!' she murmured piteously, when the rugged features of the night guard appeared to take her to the toilet after supper.

Finally, Cissie got some sign of human emotion from her gaoler. She had expected at least some covert sympathy from these women, whom she knew were French. Allies, she had thought. Comrades in distress. At last came a reaction, but it was not the one Cissie had expected. The wide mouth, lips even thinner, turned down in bitter repudiation. '*Merde! Les Anglais!* She growled, a deep, throaty sound. Cissie flinched, thought for a second the woman was going to spit at her. '*Sales cochons!*' Cissie stared in wide-eyed alarm. The wardress realized that the English girl could not understand her. She groped for sufficient vocabulary to explain her anger. She made a rapid forward motion with the first two fingers of her right hand, as of someone fleeing. 'Run! They quit us! *A Dunkerque!*'

Belatedly, a startled Cissie understood that what at home was regarded as a gallant last stand and then a miraculous saving of our army from the jaws of the enemy was looked on here as a cowardly retreat and the desertion of an ally.

The following day was the 25th. Never had the festive good wish rung more falsely. Happy Christmas! How many times had Cissie repeated it, heard it directed at her? For the first time in the twenty years of her life, there was no one to say it to, or to hear it from. The tears came again on waking in the cold dawn. She was too afraid to utter a word when the overhead light came on, and the wardress rattled the bars of the door as she unlocked and swung it open. She did not even bark an order, but stood in glowering silence while Cissie grabbed the night pail and timidly eased past her into the corridor.

Did they intend to leave her here for ever? she wondered despairingly, when she was settled back in her cell with her unappetizing breakfast tray in front of her. Gruel and a thick slice of coarse grey bread with a smear of something she hoped was margarine on it. And a tin mug of weak tea whose leaves floated like miniature logs on its surface. Tears brimmed as she watched them swirl. Perhaps they came from daddy's crop, or Charlie's father's. There would be no celebrations at home today, she surmised. Would there be decorations, a tree, the presents heaped beneath, the log fire laid in the hearth despite the sunshine, in honour of the festive season? Mummy would make the effort, she supposed. And Nigel — where would he be celebrating this day? Was he even still alive? Oh God! Please spare him! She had survived after all, against all odds. She knew how dangerous his life was now. Up there in the sky. Even though he and his comrades had fought magnificently, against all the might of this terrible foe. She prayed feverishly for his life to be spared. It was agonizing to think of Mummy losing both her children to this awful war.

But just hang on a minute, you chump! You're *not* dead, are you? You're very much alive, and snivelling in this French prison cell, so stop feeling so damned sorry for yourself and start saying thank you. She must ask, insist, that they inform her parents right away of her continued existence. But who to ask? Certainly not this hatchet-faced French-woman, who had shown a glaring antipathy towards her that had been singularly lacking in any of the real enemy she had encountered, and lived in the closest proximity with for weeks on end. Her thoughts turned disturbingly to Heinz Schmidt, and to his elegant wife. How happy this day would be for them, reunited after such a long, dangerous time; how precious and appreciated as such every minute would be.

It was a cruel torture, the way they left her alone like this, hour after cold hour, with not even a book or a magazine to distract her. She would rather break rocks, sew mailbags or pick oakum till her fingers bled than sit or lie here under the blankets, with only her tormenting thoughts for company.

She must have drifted off, for new voices brought her back to consciousness. But no, she was still dreaming, for one voice was not new, she could recognize its incisive tones anywhere. And it was calling out her name, shouting it as it came closer. She threw the blankets aside, scrambled from her bunk, desperately tugging her hands through her hair to try and make it less witchy in its wildness.

'Cissie! Frau Pride! Where are you? Come! You know this day? We have come for you, your old comrades!'

There he was, clean-shaven — she was amazed at how youthful he looked, his face so relaxed, shining with radiant happiness. They were opening the cell door, he was waving a piece of paper, reaching for her hand to shake it vigorously and to draw her out from her cell. 'Again you are my prisoner for this day! I am your — how you say gaoler, *ja*?'

She was in a daze as he led her out into the open, to a day of gusty wind and high cloud, then they were together in the back of a car, and she sobbed, clung to him, and his arm was around her, her head resting against his wonderful uniform, with its brass buttons and the gold braid on his sleeve. She remembered the comforting feel of his embrace on board his boat, her collapse into that towering strength, the tenderness of his enfolding, lifting her. She could feel those arms again, tight about her, and, with a decadent sense of luxury, she let herself give way to her weeping just for the pleasure of his hold, his lips against her untidy hair.

She had gained some control, had borrowed his handkerchief to wipe her face, smoothed her hair into some semblance of order, by the time the car turned into a pleasant suburban villa, freshly commandeered by the occupying forces. The rest of the officers and the petty officers were gathered there, and Cissie tried to dispel her ignoble thoughts at the sight of Frau Schmidt, in a dark dress which hugged her attractive figure, over which she wore a pale cream woollen cardigan. A twin row of exquisite small pearls curved round her throat.

The men gave a great cheer, and scrummed around Cissie as she blushingly mounted the steps and entered the house. She felt them patting her shoulders, then they were vying with one another to plant quick, brotherly kisses on her cheeks. The Christmas greetings rang out, in German and French, and in English. Someone thrust a glass of dark wine in her hand before she even left the narrow entrance hall, then Frau Schmidt put her arms protectively around Cissie's shoulders. 'Now, gentlemen! You must allow me. I must take my guest away. For a short time only. Please! Come, my dear.'

She followed the elegant figure up the short staircase, and into a bathroom, gleaming with pristine white porcelain fitments and tiles. Frau Schmidt turned on the taps in the tub, and the water gurgled forth, fitfully at first, then in a gush of plenty. A splendid array of jars and bottles stood on the shelf beside the bath. The German woman shook a mixture of fragrant essences into the water, and with her hands whipped it into a foaming richness of perfumed bubbles. 'Come. Let me help you. I shall be your maid. Off with those hideous things. I have picked out clothes for you. We are very close. I am just taller a little. Not so slim.'

Her hands were already undoing the buttons at Cissie's neck. Cissie felt herself blushing. 'Frau Schmidt — ' she said softly.

'My name is Helga, please. I am your friend. Come. You must not be shy with me.' She gave a low laugh. 'You cannot, after all that time you stay with my husband and his men. He tells me. How when they find you.' She put one hand to her mouth, and giggled like a schoolgirl.

Cissie's blush deepened. For an instant she felt a flash of fierce resentment, and remembered the jealousy she had harboured for the figure in the photograph she had never met. And did he tell you, your sailor hero, what he did to my five companions in the boat? She was glad when Helga Schmidt left her, though the German woman returned while she was still sitting in the foam, to help wash and rinse the short fair hair, until it shone and smelt sweetly of the shampoo put to such liberal and energetic use.

In the bedroom, a set of silk underwear and silk stockings were laid out, together with a winter skirt and a jumper of fine soft wool. Cissie sat in a dressing gown at the dressing table while Helga competently brushed and styled the short hair. Cissie no longer minded the appraising looks of the older woman as she dressed in the borrowed finery. 'You look beautiful, my dear,' her hostess declared, with a warmth whose genuine quality could not be doubted. Before they made their way back downstairs, Helga caught her hand, detaining her. 'Later you will meet an important man. Herr Gurtler is from the Ministry of Propaganda. Heinz has spoken to him. He will help you. He can find work for you. To make life easy for you. Please. Talk to him.'

She reached out, took hold of Cissie's hand, held it between her own. They felt cool and wonderfully soft. Cissie recalled Heinz doing the same thing, on the dockside. Was it really only four days ago? Her conscience stirred uncomfortably at her secret thoughts concerning the woman who was holding her. The delicate face showed nothing but compassionate concern. 'I will,' she promised.

It was wonderful to feel herself the centre of their attention, to feel the warmth of real friendship the men showed her. She even thrilled to the hint of devotion still shining in Hans Kuper's ardent look, the anxiety with which he sought her favour, strove to be near, to wait on her and show his feelings. 'Where is your girlfriend, Hans?' she teased.

'He couldn't get them all in here!' someone called out, and his youthful face reddened.

'They're all busy working today!' another voice laughed.

'*Ja*! Most they work at night and in the holiday times!'

'Don't tease him!' Cissie admonished, and reached out for his arm. 'Don't take any notice. Come and dance.'

'Oh-ho! Fraternize with the enemy!' Everyone laughed easily; there was no awkwardness at the reference to her status.

'Your English is far too good these days!' she reprimanded them. 'I did too good a job, I think!'

★ ★ ★

The joking words came back to her later, in the evening, when Herr Gurtler arrived for drinks — and to meet with the English prisoner. Heinz had also spoken to her, urging her at even greater length than his wife to fall in with any suggestions the distinguished visitor might have. 'You will not do any harm to your country. And it will make your life good. Please do it, Cissie. For my sake. For all of us. We have much concern for you.' Perhaps it was just the sentiment of the occasion, and the liquor they had all generously partaken of, that made him take her face within his hands, lean forward and kiss her gently on the lips. She hoped not.

Herr Gurtler was a man in late middle age. He was quite short and rotund. The small circles of his spectacles fitted with the roundness of his face, the hint of double chin and pouting cheeks. His mouth was small, the lips very red. Mincing almost, one might say, if one wanted to be unkind.

He interviewed her in the solitude of a small bedroom, where coats, mostly naval great coats, and uniform caps and scarves and gloves were piled on the bed. 'Normally you would be sent to one of the work camps, in Germany. You would not like that,' he said bluntly. 'It is a very hard life. And even after the war is over, you would remain. There will be many such camps, I fear.'

He smiled and his round, flushed face took on a Pickwickian expression of benign jollity. 'But we do not wish that, Mrs Pride. You are from India, I believe? Your father is planter there, yes? Why do you come to England?'

She shrugged, an admission of helplessness, as though she could hardly explain her action. 'I thought — I'd just been married. And my husband had gone into the army. My brother's over in England. In the RAF. I just thought — I wanted to see ... I've never been to England. Never seen Europe,' she ended, as if that might be explanation enough.

'Have you heard from your brother?' She shook her head. 'I hope he is still alive.' The face was serious again, almost melancholic. 'He is a flyer, yes? They have had terrible losses there. Few survive.' Again the switch to the avuncular smile. He leaned forward, patted her wrist. 'So, more reason for us to wish the war over soon. We still hope that your people see reason. Not like the warmonger Churchill. But things may change soon.' Now he made an oddly boyish gesture, tapping one stubby finger against the side of his button nose, to indicate secret machinations. 'A change in leadership, perhaps. It would be good. Your rightful kind again.'

Cissie's head spun. Edward VIII, did he mean? The man who was now the Duke of Windsor, sent off in exile with his American bride. She had a sudden conviction that this was all outside of her, this province of ranting, cigar-puffing politicians and screaming military leaders and secret plotting. And she wanted to keep it so. She just wanted the killing to stop, for young men like Nig and Charlie, yes, and Hans Kuper, and Heinz Schmidt, to be safe. The nightmare of the *Star*'s end came back to her: the sudden apocalyptic chaos, the shattered cabin, Derek Hargreaves' disappearance, the fight to get into the boat. Alfie Henderson's bear-hugging hold as he plucked her into the sea. Saved her life, then his own blasted out of existence. All of them. That spotty-faced youth. Oh God! She couldn't even remember his name, poor kid! Did Heinz dream of him, she wondered, see their faces streaming before him? He had to do it. He had told her why; she remembered the hard outline of his jaw standing out under the fine blond beard as he spoke of it, the dispassion of the voice, which she knew was a lie, to mask the pain he surely suffered having to do such terrible things.

She would do anything to end it sooner, whatever it took — and whoever won. If she refused this man's offer, what would happen?

She might not survive the rigours of these work camps. 'You would not like that', he had said. She only wanted to live, to get through the present madness of all this hot animal masculine posturing and blood-letting. For God's sake, why couldn't they let women rule in the political arena? There were other ways. There had to be. Meanwhile, she had to survive, to come through.

'There is an alternative that might be possible,' Herr Gurtler was continuing. 'If you would agree of your own free will to do work of usefulness to our cause. Valuable work. Work to end this unfortunate war between our countries.' The Pickwick grin again. 'The country you say you have never seen. What do you say, my dear Mrs Pride? The decision must be yours, entirely.'

'Yes, I'm sure!' she answered, dismissing the twinge of distaste she felt at the fervour of her reply. 'What is it you want me to do?'

PART II

GERMANY CALLING

9

Once again, Cissie looked on the gallant submarine captain as her rescuer. But this time, uncomfortable as it might be, she had to acknowledge his wife as his partner in beneficence. Helga Schmidt's warm friendliness made Cissie wretched with guilt as she thought of her former resentment, and petty jealousy, for it was the German woman who informed her, with such obvious pleasure, that she was not to be returned to the dismal cell in the town gaol, but was to be their guest, 'on parole', for the remainder of the holiday period. Cissie wept with relief, and Helga held her gently while she did so. 'You and the captain,' she sniffled. 'You're so good to me.'

'Nonsense! I knew, as soon as Heinz told me about you, that we would be good friends. He's very fond of you, yes? He wants so much to see that you are well cared for.'

She was treated as an honoured guest. A silk nightgown and robe was laid out for her in a small bedroom, almost stuffily hot from the electric heater placed there. The mattress was soft, the sheets crisply clean, so that it took Cissie a long time, in spite of the unaccustomed amount of wine, to get to sleep. Lots of jokes were made about her unique status. 'We need to put a guard on her,' the engineer officer quipped. 'I volunteer to take the first watch!'

'And who will guard you?' Helga asked drily.

The familiar faces were back again on Boxing Day for a lunch that dragged on and gradually turned into yet another celebration that ran into the early hours. The following morning, Helga herself appeared bearing Cissie's breakfast tray. She was still in her housecoat and sat companionably on the edge of the bed while Cissie ate. She grinned. 'You have a good appetite. Not surprising after all that swill on the boat! Listen!' She reached forward, and with a motherly gesture, pushed the wisps of hair back from Cissie's face. Her features reflected the warmth her words conveyed. 'You must write. You will go to home, I think. To Germany,' she added hastily, in case the English girl should misconstrue her words. 'They find work for you there. But please — tell us what happens. We must stay friends. We could never be enemies, yes? You are our dear friend. Heinz, and for me, too. We have our home in Neumünster. In the north. It is only

122

one hour to travel to Hamburg. We shall meet.'

Cissie nodded, her throat closing. 'Your husband. He saved my life.' It was painful to think back to those strange events surrounding her capture, but equally painful was the thought of saying goodbye to him — to both of them.

There were more tears when she did so the next day. She felt a real sorrow at parting from them, accepted with good grace the chaste kiss on her cheek from him after the tighter, more demonstrative hug from Helga Schmidt. But there was the undeniable hollow queasiness inside at the thought of the unknown future facing her, in the distant homeland of the country she was supposed to be at war with.

The journey to Hamburg took two days of train rides, with hours waiting in the heated first-class carriages filled with German uniforms, whose wearers displayed polite curiosity at the young traveller, accompanied by the Gestapo officials who paid such close attention to her. She was treated with unfailing courtesy, which did a great deal to ease her anxiety, until, finally, her head light with tiredness, she found herself in an official car, speeding through the streets of the vibrant city and port at the head of the long arm of the Elbe estuary, in northern Germany.

The greatly varied countryside during the long trip had looked bleak in the grey bitterness of mid-winter, but was full of interest still for someone who had never seen Europe before. Cissie was glad of the warm clothing newly provided for her — a whole suitcase full of things, as well as a smart leather travelling case stocked with cosmetics, a parting gift from Helga. Even her legs and feet were warm, in the woollen stockings and ankle boots. The imposing buildings and wide, incredibly clean avenues and the disciplined bustle of the traffic in the city fascinated her, so different from the hot and noisy throng of Calcutta's busy streets, and the brief glimpse she had had of Bombay, the only other conurbations she had any experience of. She wished that the two male companions either side of her were a little more talkative. She had an urge to chatter, to share the novelty of these impressions, but they were not forthcoming, and she was too shy to attempt to breach their reserve. A little casual talk might also have helped to counteract the increasing nervousness she felt as their long journey approached its end.

The car pulled up outside an unimposing grey building whose outer walls were thickly padded with sandbags. Cissie had time to glance up and notice that the roof was sprouting with a miscellany of aerial masts and antennae. She was taken to a small room, which led off from a much larger office housing a considerable crowd, of both sexes. She was once again sick now with anxiety. Her hands were clenched, and wet with a nervousness she hoped she could disguise sufficiently.

I must make a good impression! she urged herself. Yes, let them see how eager you are to become a traitor, a conflicting inner voice fired. Her mind was jolted into this reminder that she was still a prisoner, in the heart of the country that her people were at war with. She felt ashamed that all the visible evidence, of smart uniforms, of language, of the flags bearing that sinister spider-like symbol of Nazidom, had failed to register its significance with her. Was she forgetting her allegiance already?

One of those dark uniforms appeared before her now, and automatically she made to rise. Although the man was slight of figure, the black uniform was tailored effectively, and of a smoothly superior quality of cloth. The eagle badges, the buttons, and the buckles and the leather of the belt and what was known in the British army as the Sam

Browne, all gleamed to perfection. 'Please!' His carefully manicured hand waved her back into the chair. He gave an exaggeratedly wide smile as he took his place behind the desk. '*Wilcommen* — welcome — to Hamburg, Frau Pride.'

He had brought a slim file with him, which he opened. He read the information aloud. 'Cicely Pride. Born 6 April 1921, in the Assam province of India. Married 15 July 1940, to Charles Pride, serving with British forces in India. Taken prisoner, 3 October, after sinking of SS *Star of Indus*. Landed at Lorient, 20 December.' He looked up, and again came that bright smile, which held little warmth, Cissie felt. 'An adventure story, yes? And now.' He spread his arms in a theatrical gesture, entirely appropriate, Cissie thought, for that was how he seemed to her; an actor rather than a military man. 'You are here. I believe you wish to help us with our work?' His English was heavily accented, and far from fluent.

Cissie cursed the hot blush she could feel rising from her neck. She nodded. What should she do? Show her eagerness, appear brimming with enthusiasm? Wouldn't such an overzealous exhibition make them suspect her motives? And wouldn't they be right to do so?

'You have never visited England. You have

126

not family there?' She shook her head, cleared her throat to confirm, when he snapped, 'You have your brother there, yes? He is with the British Air Force. A pilot.'

Now she was blushing, vividly, and she stammered like a child caught in a lie. 'Oh — yes. I see what — he went there — he was studying — he stayed. Joined up. I'm sorry.'

Again, the transformation of the rapid smile, the waving of the elegant hand acknowledging an oversight. Cissie's brain was racing. How had they known about Nig? Of course! She had told Herr Gurtler, at the party at the Schmidts' house on Christmas night. Why did she have this feeling of a confidence betrayed? She was behaving like a ninny. She must be on her guard. This smiling manikin had power over her. Real power, and she was far from Heinz's protection now. She was sitting forward, on the edge of the hard chair. She was sweating profusely; she could feel the dampness inside her clothes. She breathed deeply, struggling to relax, to ease the tension which had clenched all her muscles.

'You feel loyalty to your mother country?' he asked her. 'I mean to England, of course.' He smiled again. The question had not been framed in an aggressive way. It was almost as though he was expecting her to affirm this, as though that would be the right answer for her to give.

She felt a second of panic. She had to make a blind choice, choose the right path of two turnings, with no idea which was the way to go. She cleared her throat, felt her heart bumping. 'I don't — I don't want the war.' Her voice was low and hesitant, she knew. He was leaning forward slightly, and she lowered her gaze from the eyes watching her closely. Herr Gurtler's words came to mind. 'If a way could be found to end it . . . I don't want people to die. Anyone . . . '

'You do not want to avenge our conquest of Europe? Our march into Poland?'

She felt rather than saw his mocking smile now, heard it in his teasing, affable voice, and felt miserably that she had blundered herself into a corner. 'I don't know about the politics. Treaties and that kind of thing.' She was muttering now, back to the guilty schoolgirl once more, and she felt a swift but fierce disgust at her own feebleness.

'Of course, Frau Pride. For what sweet young lady should concern herself with such things? Good!' He closed the file decisively. 'Wait, please. I am sure we can find work for you. Excuse, Frau Pride.' He stood and clicked his heels before he swept out. Weak with relief, Cissie sagged in the hard chair, stifling the hysterical urge to giggle.

She was left for an uncomfortably long time to her racing thoughts. She could hear the buzz of muted voices, the click of typewriters, from the outer office. Clearly, this was some kind of headquarters, she guessed. But it did not have that military feeling to it, in spite of all the uniforms. And it certainly didn't look like a prison. She had had no watch since the night of the torpedo attack, and there were no clocks in this stuffy little room. She began to be afraid she might have to leave to find a toilet. She was startled but relieved when the door opened to reveal a smartly dressed and neatly groomed young woman, with short black hair, who advanced on her with a smile not as wide as the uniformed male who had interviewed her but with infinitely more genuine friendliness in it.

'Hello. Cicely Pride? My name is Inge Langer. So glad to meet you.' Her English, too, was much better than his. Precise, the accent very slight. Cissie reached for the hand held towards her, feeling gauche and somewhat unkempt despite her new wardrobe before this striking figure.

'Please. Everyone calls me Cissie. Pleased to meet you, er . . . Miss Langer.'

'Let's not be formal. Please, call me Inge, yes?' Cissie nodded, still bemused at this overwhelming friendliness. The German girl was not wearing uniform, but a heavy, knitted cardigan over a white blouse, whose gathered frills showed at the neck, where a small brooch was pinned. The skirt, of excellent tweed, was narrow and hugged the slim hips and limbs. Beneath its hem, which ended at mid-calf, shapely legs and ankles clad in fine silk stockings showed. 'Now. If I know our beloved *Geheime Staats Polizei* — Gestapo,' she translated, 'you're probably wondering where on earth you are and what is going to happen to you, yes?'

Cissie thought of her two virtually silent travelling companions, and felt a surge of gratitude towards Inge Langer. She nodded.

'Well, to begin with,' Inge continued with quick efficiency, 'you're in the Radio Hamburg building. That's our headquarters. We're attached to the Ministry of Propaganda. Civil Service. We disseminate information, over the air, leaflets, articles, et cetera. The English section deals with overseas material, of course. Our head is a fellow countryman of yours. You may have heard of him? William Joyce?' Cissie shook her head. 'Well, you'll meet him in due course. An interesting man. Came over to us just before the outbreak of hostilities, a fervent supporter of the Führer.' She smiled disarmingly. 'Confidentially, sometimes he can be a little too much of a fanatic. None worse than the converted, you know.' She laughed again. She had a deep, infectious gurgle, and Cissie smiled involuntarily in return. Then she blushed as it suddenly occurred to her that such remarks, indeed, this whole appearance of feminine chumminess, might be a trap. Once again she told herself she must be on guard, always.

'You will start work with our section. I have been assigned to look after you and see that you are settled down nicely. You will stay at a government hostel. I will take you there. First we'll make sure you have all you need. In the way of clothing.' She pulled an attractive face of complicit mischief. 'I know you've been given some things, but I know what the military mind is like. 'Panties, pairs two, females for the use of',' she intoned, in mockery of officialdom. In spite of her caution, Cissie found it impossible not to be charmed by Inge's warmth. 'After you, my dear.' The light hand on her back steered her towards the door, and the arm was linked with firm comradeship in Cissie's as they passed through the veiled, curious stares of the outer office.

★ ★ ★

The work she was put to was far from strenuous. It consisted mainly of reading through articles and leaflets written in English. All Cissie had to do was check through them, editing for mistakes of grammar, punctuation or spelling, or any structures or expressions she felt might be clumsy or 'un-English'. Inge supervized her closely, and Cissie's greatest embarrassment came from the fact that it quickly became apparent that Inge's command of written English at least was clearly superior to her own. 'I never went to school,' Cissie confessed, to the German girl's astonishment. 'Not properly. We had a tutor. A fellow out from England. He taught four of us. But I'm afraid I never showed much interest in lessons. I never saw the point.'

'The idle rich, yes? Good marriage, children.'

Cissie was startled at Inge's summary of the mapped-out route of Cissie's existence, but she nodded slowly. 'I suppose so,' she admitted apologetically.

'Never mind. It is not too late. We shall teach you how rich your language is. Like our own. Which you must start learning at once. You will start lessons tomorrow.'

She was as good as her word. To her surprise, Cissie found there was a large number of foreigners gathered in the city, and the language lessons, for two hours every afternoon, were well attended. She was afraid at first that she was too academically dim to make much progress, but, surrounded as she was by examples, both spoken and written, of the language, and forced to speak it increasingly just to get by in her new surroundings, she made quick progress. Another early task, which Inge set her, and which took up a great deal of her time for a while, was to write, in English, a detailed account of her life so far, to portray her class, her culture, the colonial background she had been brought up in. 'I want to know what it is like to be one of the memsahibs. The daughters of the empire the English are so proud of. You shall work on it in the evening — your homework, yes?' Cissie found, to her surprise, once she had managed to get started, she enjoyed her task.

It was not work which she found distressing. Far from it. The stuff she was reading through meant little to her, to be truthful, going on about the philosophy behind the Nazi doctrines, the benefits that the Führer had brought to the country and to the common people, the Aryan culture which had been so threatened by the ignoble strains of other races, in particular the Jews, the Bohemians, and others. And the dogma of the communists as a means by which these inferior peoples were trying to infiltrate. And writing up her own life quickly became not a chore but a pleasure. It was what happened in the long hours after work in the radio building that began more and more to distress her.

Her fellow inmates at the government hostel were from a variety of European backgrounds. There was quite a large French contingent, several Poles, Czechoslovakians, Belgians, even a few hard-faced German girls — ex-prisoners, prostitutes, even — who, unofficially, ran the place with sometimes cruel and often wanton authority. Cissie was dismayed at the level of antipathy shown towards her. The attitude of the warders during her brief stay in the cells at Lorient had helped to disabuse her of any false hopes, but the relentless malignancy of the group of French girls hit her hard — in more ways than one. 'Feelthy English! Cowards, who run from us! Run into the sea!'

Cissie found herself trying to apologize, even to deny her own heritage. 'I've never even been to England!' she pleaded. But they refused even to acknowledge her language, except to use the relentless phrases of abuse to hurl at her. The verbal attacks and their unceasing vitriol were unpleasant enough to endure, but it began more and more to exceed these demonstrations of their feelings. Once she came from the recreation room, as late as she could, to find mattress, blankets and the iron bed head itself pitched down the stairwell. And another time she climbed between the sheets on an icy February night to find them soaked in a liquid whose ammoniac pungency discounted any faint hope that it might be water.

Cissie endured her mistreatment for a long while. The matron and her few assistant cleaners showed little interest, and the hard-faced German mafia seemed amused by if not openly approving of the situation. But then, one night, after one of the first bombing raids on the city, confined to the dock area around the river estuary, matters became far worse. She was 'scragged'.

She had heard the term used by her brother and by Charlie, referring to their schooldays in England. She remembered in particular one incident they had talked of, when she was fourteen, during one of their long summer vacations. They did not get out home every year, so it was comparatively rare for her to see them as she grew through her adolescence. They were rather grand, and remote, invested with a glamour more than their two-year seniority over her might have warranted. Nig talked, with a great deal of salacious sniggering, of this unfortunate pupil who had been set on by his fellows on the train, during the end-of-term ride up to the capital. Their sixteen-year-old contemporary had been stripped naked and held outside the carriage, pinned against the side of the coach, while the train roared through the summer countryside, and past the astounded gaze of all who observed it. 'When we pulled him in, he was as black as a coon and blubbing like a baby!'

The image had haunted Cissie. In fact, it became the emblem of one of the earliest truly erotic dreams she could remember, then the object of many similar waking fantasies, as she tried to visualize the poor, sprawled, weeping figure, the pale beauty of his slender body, becoming stained and sullied by the engine's smoke and soot.

There was nothing erotic in the assault to which she was subjected one chilly night in Hamburg. At least not for her. Stripped of her thick pyjamas, she was paraded, held high above the shoulders of the French harpies, and one or two of the German whores, in a fine example of entente, through the dormitories then out on to the landing. For one terrifying moment, she was afraid they were going to fling her over the rail to the ground floor below, but they proceeded in howling triumph to the bathroom, where they contented themselves with dumping her into a tub full of icy water, and standing in a jeering ring around her while she sat and shivered violently and blubbed in a misery to equal that of the sooty schoolboy, symbol of her adolescent fantasies.

10

Cissie had struggled valiantly not to let Inge know of the difficulties she was facing from her fellow inmates. The German girl had been so friendly, genuinely caring, and understanding of all Cissie's worries, not least that concerning her ability to do the work assigned to her, that she did not want to burden her with any additional personal problems. And she was still extremely unsure of just how safe she was from a much harsher fate, of work camps and downright brutality. She even wondered if her superiors might in fact be well aware of the situation at the hostel, that it might be some sort of test of her stamina. But the painful humiliation of the scragging broke the back of her resistance.

Next morning, she could not hold back the tears. Inge had already noted the red eyes, and nose, the general air of woebegone-ness about the drooping figure. 'You're not coming down with anything, are you?' she asked sympathetically. The bouts of cold and influenza dogging everyone as the severity of the winter lingered on into the advent of March had made the offices a hotbed of virulent germs as people snuffled, coughed and sneezed, and blew delicately or trumpeted blatantly into their soggy hankies.

The gentle question was enough to open the floodgates. Soon, Cissie's sloping shoulders were heaving, and she derived much comfort from Inge's arm about her as she stammered out her sorry confession. 'I duh-didn't wuh-want to tuh-tell you!' she spluttered.

Inge's reaction was more than Cissie dared hope for. 'Wait here,' she ordered her firmly. 'You cannot possibly go back to that place. I won't be long.'

Cissie tried to direct her thoughts towards the autobiography she was writing. Inge had given her the guidelines. 'We want to read about the privileged lifestyle of the white society. Try to see the perspective of the native peoples, how oppressed they are. That sort of thing. It would be good to show how immoral the practice of British imperialism is.'

But surely Germany had colonies, too, until after the Great War? Cissie thought, but kept the query to herself. Inge had talked at length of the racial inequalities, the yoke under which the native populations groaned, the coming of a new world order to improve their lot. Were Norway and France and Belgium and Poland — and Britain itself, if German plans were realized — to benefit, too? Wisely, she kept her doubts and scepticism to herself. She thought of her beloved Rani. Inge would be shocked if she knew just how close the relationship between the little mem and her armah had been. Cissie had already written about it — she had thought she had conveyed some of the intimacy they had shared, had altered her script, toning it down when she understood what it was they wanted from her. But Inge's comments had surprised her. '*Mein Gott!* It is like the Roman Empire, yes? You had your own personal slave in this poor creature!'

The remark hurt her, though she made no reply. She even tried to convince herself that maybe Inge had a point. Anyway, it seemed to be what she wanted to hear, or read. But the word 'traitor' rose spectre-like in Cissie's thoughts once more, no matter how hard she tried to push it away from the forefront of her mind. It's just a job you're doing, she reassured herself. A way of saving yourself from who knew what horrors. No one would condemn you for wanting to stay alive. Besides, no one would be influenced by this stuff. Nobody would see it, probably, except for Inge and her bosses.

This morning, her mind was far too troubled to concentrate on it. It was hard enough to take it seriously. She sometimes felt that Inge was like a far prettier version of Mr Horner, with his tasks: 'I want an essay, of at least four hundred words, ladies, by next week. I mean it!'

She was glad when Inge came back, even gladder at the wide grin which adorned her face. 'How would you like to stay at my place? You might have to share a room with me for a few nights, but Frau Muller will find you a room soon enough, I am sure.'

'Oh, Inge!' There were tears again, briefly, but for a very different reason. Impulsively, she flung her arms around Inge and they hugged tightly. 'I can't believe it! You're so good to me! I don't deserve it!'

Cissie slept on a camp bed in Inge's room, on the third floor of an old tenement building in the district of St Georg, not far from the main station. It had a faded, genteel shabbiness, but the apartments were well maintained, and the big rooms, with their ornate ceilings, in good repair. It was a little less than two miles east of the notorious St Pauli area and a great deal more respectable. 'We will have to arrange a trip out there for you,' Inge said, with that deep laugh, and

Cissie was half eagerly curious, half apprehensive.

In a few days, the landlady, Frau Muller, had cleared out a small, partitioned space in the attic, with room for a single bed, a locker, and an elegant armchair, which, like the building, had seen better days. But Cissie was delighted. 'It's pretty grim,' Inge observed, 'but if you wear your flannel pyjamas and woollen socks you will survive. Besides, it is only for sleeping. You can spend all your time with me. Except when Dieter comes to call.'

Dieter, thought Cissie privately, after she had met and got to know the tall, thin man, with a slight stoop and the look of an ill-nourished academic, was a bit of a thorn in the side, as far as she was concerned. He was a frequent visitor to the flat, and clearly on intimate terms with Inge, though the German girl never gave any blatant displays of affection, beyond the hug and brief kiss of greeting. No doubt there were more extreme physical contacts, Cissie guessed, for he stayed very late sometimes. Cissie was a little ashamed of her spying, on the occasions she tiptoed out on to her cold, tiny landing, and heard the discreet click of Inge's door, the whispered parting late into the night. She was just a teensy bit jealous of him, she conceded, and the claim he had on Inge, for she and the

German girl were even closer now that they were living together. Several times, Cissie almost summoned up courage to ask her outright if he was her lover, but was never quite brave enough to do so.

One day Inge came to her desk at work and put a hand on her shoulder. She was grinning impishly. 'Duty calls tonight, Britisher! Now you'll have the chance to see a bit of the decadence Hamburg has to offer. You can wear that green dress of yours. And silk stockings you have? No? I can lend you some.' She giggled. 'You will have to turn them down a few times.' She was a good four inches taller than Cissie. 'You have to accompany Dieter and I. We are entertaining a guest from our ministry. Newly arrived. A pal of our beloved leader, Joyce. Make no mistake, this is vital work for the war. You must please this man. Make him fall for you, my English spy!'

Privately Cissie thought that Dieter was hardly the man one would choose for a wild night on the town. He wasn't bad looking, in a haggard, ascetic way — if you liked that type, which she didn't. But though he was unfailingly polite, he had that stiff Germanic manner. She had once overheard a remark she was not meant to hear at a club do back home. The man was describing one of the most sought-after young princesses of the eligible circle of their small world: 'She looks as though she's got a poker stuck up her arse!' How apt to sum up Dieter, Cissie smirked. But she was excited as Inge went on to give more details, switching to German to do so, despite Cissie's groan of protest.

'You know we should speak only in German,' Inge insisted. 'Anyway, the lessons are going well. Already you speak almost like a native.'

It was true that Cissie's proficiency had increased tremendously. She still attended daily classes and was proud of her achievement in such a short period. Especially because, she reasoned, her superiors other than Inge would be pleased with her progress.

'The visitor, Sean Mullins, is from Ireland,' Inge told her. 'He has been working against the British there, but he was almost caught. He was lucky to escape. Now he has been assigned here, in Hamburg, so I guess we'll see quite a lot of him. You must make a good impression, as I'm sure you will. You can borrow my crystal necklace. He won't be able to resist you.' Cissie poked out her tongue.

However, she was extremely glad that she had followed Inge's advice and made the effort to make herself presentable. It would have been difficult to find a greater contrast between the reserved and serious Dieter and the Irishman. About the only thing they had in common was their height, for Sean Mullins was also around six feet tall. But his build, like his personality, was much more robust. Broad shouldered, he had the frame of an athlete, and the ruddy, rugged, open-faced appearance of a farmer. Unruly, tight red curls crowned his head, his features stamped with an almost perpetual appealing smile, with a hearty, booming laugh to match. Cissie could feel herself falling under his spell within the first minutes of their meeting.

The whole evening gave promise of being a special one. She was excited by Inge's promise that they would see something of the throbbing nightlife of the notorious St Pauli quarter, with its risqué cabarets and clubs. They dined first, in a small but fashionable, expensive restaurant, where both Dieter and Sean stood out as among the very small minority of men not wearing immaculately tailored uniforms. 'Bleddy staff officers, I'll bet my life on it!' Mullins declared airily. 'Never heard a shot fired in anger!' Cissie was privately delighted at the way he kept insisting on speaking English to her, blithely ignoring the curious and, in one or two cases, disapproving glances it drew. Inge soon gave up attempting to steer them back to her native tongue. 'I'm not all that hot in German,' Sean confessed cheerfully.

'Oh, you must let Cissie teach you,' Inge answered quickly. 'She's rapidly becoming an expert.'

'I'd like that, by God!' Sean declared, so enthusiastically that Cissie blushed and giggled.

He was quick to lead her out on to the crowded intimacy of the tiny dance floor, once they had reached the coffee and liqueur stage of the meal. She felt a quiver of pleasure pass through her at the way he folded her into his arms, and the bold directness of the large hand he rested on her flank, the more discreet but equally telling rubbing of his knee and thigh along her own. Her face was nestling close to his shoulder, but when their eyes met she saw, unmistakably in the clear, twinkling gaze, the attraction that mirrored her own.

'Well now, Cissie,' he murmured, in his softly lilting accent, which seemed to add to the bubbling humour of his words, 'I hear you've had quite an adventure getting here. Torpedoes and submarines and all manner of dangers. Is it true you spent days and days in an open boat with a bunch of hairy-arsed sailors as your only company?'

She gaped a little at the coarseness of his language, and sniggered. 'Yes — well, a couple of days, actually. I'm not sure about their hairy — what you said — though.' She remembered what their fate had been, and was ashamed of her laughter. But then he said something which made her gape even more.

'And are you happy enough to be playing the traitor here, or are you just after saving your pretty little skin?'

For an instant, she was too amazed to be angry or to answer, but then, though she crimsoned, she rallied. 'I'm not doing anything that can really hurt my people. I don't know all that much about the rights and wrongs of this war. I keep telling everybody — I've never even been to England. It would have been my first time if — Anyway, what the heck has it got to do with you? Yes, I bloody well *am* saving my skin! Is that so wrong? What are *you* doing here? Aren't you doing the same thing?'

'Whoa there, my little spitfire! Did I say it was wrong? And as for me, I'm fighting the good fight against you oppressing colonial bastards, beg pardon, ma'am. I've been fighting Albion a damn sight longer than these Nazis, thank you very much. Still, whatever our reasons, let's remember we're both on the same side here, that's what counts. I'm certainly looking forward to being your friend, Cissie, and that's a fact. You're the prettiest sight for sore eyes I've seen in many a long time.'

She soon forgot her brief irritation, and readily forgave for it, too. Nor did she mind when, only a minute later, he asked, gently this time but with his usual directness, about her husband. She found herself being a lot more honest with this stranger than she expected. Or maybe it was the plentiful amount of wine she had drunk. 'Charlie's all right,' she said ambiguously, with a slight shrug. 'I've known him since we were kids. And yet ... ' She paused, and sighed, overcome by a sudden longing to open up. 'In some ways I feel as though I hardly know him at all. Specially now.'

'Does he know you're safe?'

She felt herself blushing again, and snuggled closer, hiding her face against his shoulder. He had unwittingly touched a nerve. During the first days of her captivity, she had asked several times if her captors had let her family know of her captivity, or internment, or whatever it was. 'The International Red Cross will inform them,' she was told. But when she heard nothing from them, she had repeated her request, saying that she would like to write to her husband and her parents to confirm she was indeed alive.

Now she gave a little shrug. 'I'm not really sure. I've heard nothing from him, from anybody at home.' She lowered her voice to a whisper. 'Do you think they really have let them know? I'd like to write.'

'Might be a bit awkward, like. You know.' Her head lifted; he saw her look of enquiry. 'You doing what you're doing. Working for the Germans. They could shoot us for it if we ever go back.'

Ever go back? His words rang like the U-boat's klaxon in her brain, and he saw her wide-eyed expression, which showed the effect of his words. 'But what's the use of worryin', eh? The song's right, me lovely. We might as well pack up our troubles, for there's damn all we can do about it!'

His attitude was infectious. As the night wore on, and she drank more wine, she felt a recklessness that responded to his devil-may-care mood. Reluctantly, Dieter was persuaded to go on, deeper into the unsavoury district, into the narrow streets of the clubs and bars, outside which the clusters of garishly made-up women proclaimed their profession. The cobbled streets were closely packed with noisy, wandering groups of servicemen, and the entrances to the many establishments paid no more than fleeting lip service to the blackout regulations, despite the air raids which had taken place several times, always under cover of darkness. 'They only bomb the docks,' the jovial revellers proclaimed. 'Stay out of the sailors' brothels and you'll be fine. Besides, it's only the RAF. They've only killed a cow on one of the farms so far, and *it* only died of heart failure!'

They chose one of the clubs, and pushed their way through the crowd of servicemen, pimps and prostitutes. In spite of his reluctance, it was Dieter who produced a card which had an immediate effect. The doorman ushered them through the heavy curtain at once. They trooped down a short flight of narrow stairs. The tiny space was packed, and they had to stand at the miniature bar at the back for quite a while after they had bought their drinks. 'No wonder it's officers only,' Inge commented, over the noise of a trio of violin, piano and drums struggling valiantly against the buzz of conversation. 'It would take a month's pay for a private to buy a round in here.'

The drums crashed out deafeningly, the dim lights dimmed further, except for the brilliant white spotlight on the little platform of the stage. A heavily made-up but attractive-looking girl with flaxen hair twisted into two thick plaits like a milkmaid began to sing an outrageous song. Just as she began, a waitress tapped Inge's shoulder, and they squirmed through the darkness in her wake, and through the murmurs of protest, to a table which had just become vacant right at the front, on the very rim of the brilliantly lit circle.

The girl was singing some outrageous ditty, winning uproarious applause, and even more for the way she shed her clothing as she sang. The white cap and apron went with the first verse, the black dress with the second, and the shoes and white stockings with the third. She was left with what appeared to be a brassière whose straps and two conical cups were made of leather. The garment around her loins, of matching material, was briefer than any Cissie had seen, or imagined. At the front it was no more than a cache-sexe, a triangle of shining blackness, which did no more than cover her sexual parts. Shocking, Cissie thought, until the girl turned around. She advanced, turned and thrust her rear literally under their noses, and waggled it as if to catch their attention — a totally superfluous manoeuvre. The garment's back consisted of no more than a strap a couple of inches wide, running up the divide of her generously proportioned and exquisitely symmetrical buttocks. 'Will ye look at that?' Sean breathed reverentially — also an entirely unnecessary injunction, for all eyes, including Cissie's, were riveted on the spectacle.

It was well after midnight when the car drew up outside the hotel, for government personnel only, where Sean was staying. He caught Cissie's wrist and hauled her out after him. 'Won't be a minute,' he said, and led her a few yards away, into the shadows by the wall. 'Listen. I have to see you. Properly. Alone. Tomorrow. All right?' His head bent and she felt his warm breath, as she lifted her mouth eagerly to meet his kiss. 'I'll pick you up after your German class. Unless you'll come up with me right now and keep me warm in me lonely bed? We'll make love all night long!'

'I don't — we can't — I don't know you!' she gasped, outraged, astonished, and fiercely excited by his disgraceful proposal.

'You soon will, my beauty, I can promise you that.' Another fierce kiss and, with a low laugh, he spun her round and pushed her gently in the direction of the waiting car.

11

'Jesus! no wonder you're frozen, my little darlin'. Come here and let me put some life into you.'

Suddenly the tears started from behind her lowered eyelids, and she blushed furiously, standing there in the pink cami-knickers, staring down at her bare feet. Her toes curled with embarrassment, digging into the thinness of the worn carpet. His little room was almost as bare as a cell. Her skirt and jumper lay on the one chair the room boasted, together with the petticoat and the thick black stockings she had just discarded. She was ashamed of the ugly red rings around her upper thighs made by the tight garters. He scooped her up easily and carried her to the metal bed, which squeaked loudly as he deposited her on its lumpy mattress.

He pulled back the blankets. 'Get in before you freeze to death.'

She obeyed, wishing she could stop the tears, scarcely knowing what they were for. He must think I'm a complete slut, she thought. What else could he think, me jumping into bed like this, with someone who, only a few nights ago, had been a total stranger? I'm no better than a whore. I should ask him to pay for it! But, despite her self-admonitions, she could feel the eager beat of her body, her desire for him.

She tried to push away the apparition of Derek Hargreaves, as she watched Sean undress hurriedly, with no false modesty. The sight of his nakedness thrilled her even more. Apart from a small patch of light gold curls between his nipples, his torso was smooth and pale, faintly dusted with freckles in places, strongly curved with muscle. Their cold flesh came together, his legs and arms closed about her, and she clung, hiding her face against his chest, and inhaled the smell of him, of both their eager bodies, changing from the cold of the dull grey March afternoon, already heading towards dusk, to the sealed-in warmth they generated.

His fingers were nimbly busy, fumbling without pretext at her crotch, even as they kissed passionately. The gurgle of laughter was there again in his voice. 'Now then, let's see what you're made of, my little Indian maiden. These things are the divil to unfasten. No! Don't help me!' he commanded gruffly, dipping his head beneath the sheet. 'I have to learn. It's a knack.'

He finally succeeded in releasing the three

tiny hooks from their eyes, and the silk parted. Now the tears were gone, and the shame and the vestige of modesty, swept aside as easily as the thin silk, to expose her needy, ready flesh. 'Oh God! I want this!' she groaned, honest at last in her craving for him, and she cried out ecstatically, when they came together. He held himself back. He was a considerate as well as an experienced and unselfish lover, and she wept with happiness now, and knew nothing except the total joy of physical consummation.

Afterwards, their damp bodies still locked, she rested on his chest. Her tears had dried on her cheeks, and she drifted slowly back to awareness, and found she could no longer feel the sense of shame which had at times so overwhelmed her during the few days which had led inevitably to this moment. 'You must think — I don't know what you must think of me,' she murmured, after a long while. But now she sought only confirmation of her own feeling, which she received from him like a benediction.

'You're beautiful. I love you.'

'We don't know each other,' she attempted, with tired blissfulness, and felt the tremor of his flesh against hers as he chuckled.

'Well, now, ye could have fooled me, darlin'.'

Much later, after they had slept and woken in each other's arms, and made slow, gentle, then equally passionate love once more, with the room now in darkness, she sighed. 'I don't want to get up. I don't want to leave this bed, ever.'

'We've got to keep our strength up,' he chuckled. 'I'll be needing me grub if I'm to keep you satisfied, my little spitfire.'

'Don't!' she cried, pouting, striking at his arm around her waist. 'You think I'm . . . one of *those* girls, don't you? A — a — floozy!'

'Now how would I know what one o' them craytures looks like? A simple laddie like me, straight from the bog?' At her small groan, he dropped his teasing and his stage brogue, and took her gently into his embrace. His soft tone was completely serious. 'We're just so lucky to have found each other, Cissie, my love. In this time when all hell's breaking loose around the world. So we've known each other a few days. In other times and places, we'd have talked politely, I'd have raised my hat to you. After a couple of months I might have plucked up courage to speak to you. Another month and we might even have got around to going out for tea, or the pictures.' He paused. 'Or more likely, darling, someone like me would never have got within spitting distance of someone like you. Isn't that the truth, now?' She stirred against him, made to frame some sort of denial, and he stopped her with a soft kiss. 'But times are not what they were. Anything could happen, to either of us. And the world we knew is changing. The old world's gone for ever, Cissie. Make no mistake about that, whoever wins or loses. Let's just be thankful we've found each other and have got some time to share. That's our luck, and I thank God for it!'

And so did she, she had to acknowledge, in the days that followed. She was alive inside for the first time, ablaze with love for Sean Mullins, jealous of every hour, minute and second spent away from him.

She was more than a little hurt at Inge's failure to appreciate her enthusiasm, and at the German girl's sounding of the notes of caution. 'Please be careful!' Her face showed her concern, and because of that Cissie smothered her resentment at Inge's attitude. 'You don't know much about him. He's led such a dangerous life. And he will not be staying. When — '

'Why? What do you mean? Tell me! What do you know?'

Inge coloured and looked at her uncomfortably, and Cissie felt that little shiver of apprehension, afraid that Inge knew more than she was telling her. As though to confirm her fears, Inge went on, 'I can't say too much. You know that.' She sounded as though she were appealing to Cissie not to pursue the matter. 'But he has a special job. When he has spent time here, when he is more familiar with our language et cetera, he might move on.'

Inge refused to say more, denied that she knew anything definite, and when Cissie met Sean she told him of the conversation she had had, pressed him to be honest with her.

'I'm not a desk man, Cissie, you know that much. I'm not like Dieter, or Joyce, or any of these professor types they've got working here. Writing reams about the rights and wrongs of this and that. I'm a field man. I need to be up and doing.'

'You're going to leave me then.' Her face wore a stricken look. 'We've only just met. Found each other. I knew — '

'Hey! Come on! Stop it, me girl! Right now I'm here, and I'm not going anywhere, except that bleddy language school and a desk in that blasted radio hutch! What am I always telling you? Make the most of what we've got. Don't spoil it with worriting over what's going to happen, or what might happen, or what might never happen! Come here, darlin'. Let me show you what I mean, you gorgeous Indian maid!'

But the fear came, bleak and undeniable, and far too soon, not long after they had celebrated her twentieth birthday, in an April bright at last with some hope of a springtime, though small patches of a late snowfall still loitered in the countryside and under the shrubbery of the city's parks. It was, Cissie was ashamed to admit to herself, the happiest birthday she had known. She couldn't tell anyone except Sean and she felt privately disgusted with herself when she recalled her last birthday celebrations: the marquee and the champagne in the garden at home, when she and Charlie had celebrated their engage-ment and she had looked forward so much to being in the state of wedded bliss. Now, poor Charlie was probably broken-hearted, believ-ing himself the grieving young widower, while she was in the heart of the enemy and never happier, with her only, her eternal lover, and the third man she had made love with in her mere twenty years.

'What's wrong, darling?' She had waited until they were alone, and he was lying back on his bed watching her undress.

They had never tried to hide their relationship. It had become increasingly blatant. Inge's timely warning had sobered her somewhat. 'You *are* taking care? You know what I mean.' Inge's glance towards Cissie's stomach was plain enough. Cissie had nodded, unable to hide her blush, and Inge went on urgently. 'If you became pregnant it would be disaster. They would not let you stay here. You would be sent away to a camp. Your baby would be taken from you. Sean could do nothing for you.'

Cissie thought of her bleeding, her terror that night on the U-boat. Maybe she no longer needed to take precautions. Perhaps that miscarriage had meant that she would never be able to have children. But she had begun to take more care, to go back to the rituals she had first learnt about during those now far-off giggling bedroom confidences she shared with Rani.

Now, at her question, he sat up, unfastening his cuff links, and for once not looking at her as she reached behind to unclip her brassière. 'I've got to go away, me darlin'.'

Her hands fell away from their task. She stared at him, suddenly hating that bog-Irish imitation he did so often. Her face reflected her shock and hurt at his announcement, even though she had tried to convince herself she would be prepared for it. 'Why? Where are you going?' The tension was palpable, in her voice and in the air.

He rose and came over to her, standing behind her and continued the undressing of her she had begun. 'For some special training. About six weeks or so. Then I should get some leave, and straight back to you, like an arrow!' He unhooked the undergarment, then slipped the cups from her breasts and the straps from her shoulders. She just stood there, rigid and quivering. The brassière fell from her arms across her feet. He folded her in his arms, bent his face to her golden hair, which had grown and curled softly around the nape of her neck and her ear. 'You know I'm not happy with this pen-pushing.' His tone was apologetic. 'I want to do something more. Get into the war. Properly, I mean.'

She spun round, faced him, her eyes gleaming with tears, staring at him. 'Aren't you happy with me?'

'You know I am, my love!' he protested strongly. 'But we can't just ignore the war. It's going on all round us. I love you. You know that. But I have to do what I can. I believe in what we're doing.'

'And what exactly is that?' Her dismay and fear made her voice sound harsh, and also the implied rebuke in his words, none the less stinging because she recognized its truth. 'Tell me all about this special training of yours. What does it involve?'

He suddenly looked almost hang-dog, like a guilty child. 'I can't talk about it, Cissie. You know that. We knew it had to come — '

'And you can't tell me. Can't tell me where you're going, what you're doing! Why? Because I'm not to be trusted? Is that it?' She suddenly pushed down her last garment, thrust it furiously down her legs and kicked it free, then folded her hands on her hips. 'Right, then! Seems we both know what I *am* good for, so let's get on with it.'

She yelped, with shock and pain, as he suddenly swiped her hard across her flank, a resounding slap with his open palm, and she burst into a torrent of sobbing. 'Bastard! You filthy sod of a bastard!'

He grabbed her and bundled her over to the bed, fell on her, and began to make love, with a rage and a desperation to match her own, until everything went from her except her love and need of him and she clung and wept and returned his kisses, and murmured like a prayer, 'Oh God! I love you, I don't want to lose you, I love you.'

★ ★ ★

He had told her, reluctantly she felt, that he was not leaving Germany, that he would be away in the east somewhere, and that he would be back after six weeks. It seemed like a long prison sentence to her. She could not help herself, could not pretend to be brave, wept herself to exhaustion on their last night before he left. She wanted him, wanted the wonder of their loving, the ferocity of its passion, its exclusiveness. What did it matter what went on around them? The world had gone mad. Bombing, killing. She hated both sides for the madness. It was nothing to do with her, with the two of them. Except that, for Sean, that wasn't true. She wasn't enough, and the knowledge of that was a constant pain inside her. For all her rage and tears, and begging, she could do nothing about that.

After he had gone, she felt heavy and listless; life was drained of any pleasure. Over the past months, and especially after Sean's arrival, she had gone on working quite happily, none of it mattering: office work, dogsbody to Inge, reading through documents in English, checking for errors, still scribbling bits of trivia about her life in India. Now, the tedium of it all weighed her down, until even Inge began to show her irritation. 'It's all right for you!' Cissie flared one evening, when yet again she had refused to accompany Inge and Dieter out for a meal and the cinema. 'You've still got your chap with you!'

Inge was scornful. 'Good God! You think I

wouldn't be proud if Dieter was on active service somewhere? How can you be so selfish, Cissie? I really thought you believed in what we're doing here.'

A few days later, Cissie received a summons to present herself at Joyce's office. The alarm bells began to clang in her brain. Had Inge reported her for her moody outbursts? Fear gripped her insides. Sean's promised letter had not materialized. What if they were about to banish her far from here, dismiss her to one of those distant work camps they had threatened her with when she first became a prisoner? She might never see Sean again! It must be something serious. She had scarcely spoken to the legendary figure who headed their organization, though she had seen him often enough, and listened to his propaganda broadcasts aimed at Britain. The nasal whine of his opening, 'This is Germany calling, Germany calling,' might sound vindictive, but Cissie could not understand why her fellow countrymen had now dubbed him 'Lord Haw-Haw'. It was Inge who explained that, in fact, it had been a previous broadcaster who had earned that sobriquet with his exaggeratedly aristocratic drawl.

Some said there was still a discernible soft lilt to his voice, which indicated his Irish parentage, despite the fact that he had been born in America and held a British passport. His open features were dominated by the scar that ran like a deep fold horizontally along the right side of his face. His voice on its own had a gently hypnotic effect, Cissie thought, but, in his presence, she felt the sinister force of his personality. The eyes were cold and impersonal, yet with a power greater than his voice, which told her she was right to be afraid. But somehow she could understand how he could command obedience, and even loyalty, especially in this land which was so in thrall to the magnetism of its own charismatic leader. After all, Joyce had led a following in Britain, forming his own British National Socialist party four years before, on his expulsion from Mosley's Fascists.

The thin features were split by a sudden wide, disconcerting grin. 'I'm sorry I've left it so long before having a proper chat, Mrs Pride. But you seem to have settled in very well. I read your article on the British raj. I might well use some of it in my broadcasts, if you don't mind. You would have no objection, would you?'

'No, sir, not at all.' Suddenly she reddened. 'My name . . . it wouldn't be mentioned?'

He chuckled, an oddly warm sound, as though they were sharing an intimate joke.

'Modesty forbids, eh? You don't want claim to any fame?'

'I was wondering — my family — I still haven't heard anything from them. I haven't been able to communicate — ' she stammered.

'Ah, well now. That brings me to the point. We won't waste too much of your valuable time. You're not ashamed of the work you're doing here?'

She could feel the red tide sweeping up once more, knew how crucial her next words were. 'No. It's just — I wouldn't like to make things difficult, for my family. My husband,' she added. It sounded like the afterthought it was.

'You wouldn't want them to know you were working for the Reich?' He waited, but she said nothing, could not meet that piercing, cold stare. 'Your husband is in the army, I believe? And your brother a pilot? How do you feel about that?'

She glanced up at him helplessly, in mute appeal. She shook her head. 'I don't — they had to go. All the young men . . . I'd like to stop the fighting.'

'Of course you would! You've become close friends with Mr Mullins, I understand?' Cissie's body was afire with hot shame now. She was staring dumbly, like a small animal trapped by its pursuer. 'I'm glad you've found such a good companion. You're a very lucky young woman, I'd say. Very fortunate indeed. Surviving the shipwreck, plucked from the sea by Kapitan Schmidt. Almost like being born again, given a second chance.'

In the midst of her shame and her fear, Cissie was startled at this phrase, which had so often suggested itself to her.

'You have done very well, Mrs Pride, have no fear of that. I should be very sorry to lose you.' He glanced down at an open folder. 'However, we might just have to let you go. It depends on you. I have a request from General Schoenburg. From our Military Intelligence. He wishes to interview you. Only if you are willing, of course.' She gazed at him, hardly able to breathe. The knowing smile transformed his face again. 'How would you like to work more closely with your friend, Mr Mullins? On work of a very vital, and confidential, nature?'

12

General Klaus Schoenburg was an impressively handsome figure in his resplendent uniform. He was tall enough to carry the excess weight around his middle, which was in any case discreetly and invisibly disciplined by the short, tightly laced corselet into which his batman, equally discreet, laced him during his morning levee. His grey hair added to his distinction, and was, like everything else about him, carefully groomed. 'He's a ladies' man,' Inge had warned Cissie. 'Definitely the green dress for your interview. And maybe we should take it up a few inches, yes? And nothing but silk stockings will do. Make sure he sees plenty of them, and your best slip, too.'

Cissie squealed in delighted outrage. She had done little but grin like an idiot and giggle like a schoolgirl since William Joyce had told her of the general's interest in her. Inge had blown hot and cold. First, she had looked downright dismayed, but had quickly thawed at the English girl's delight at the prospect of working in conjunction with Sean Mullins. 'It's not definite, though, is it?' Inge had cautioned. Then, seeing Cissie's disappointment, she had changed to a more cautious optimism. 'It will probably work out for the best, I'm sure.'

Cissie was convinced Inge must know more about the proposal than she was prepared to admit, and begged her to tell her more. The German denied any more detailed knowledge, but then added, 'He is a senior officer in Military Intelligence. That means a lot of hush-hush work. Secret operations, that kind of thing. He must want you for some post in his organization.'

Cissie didn't care what it was, as long as it meant she could go on being with Sean. And Inge had given her some very useful information on making the best of herself at the interview. 'He's got a very keen eye for a pretty girl. Your looks are your biggest asset, sweetheart. Bat those big blue eyes at him. You must look the part.' Inge gave a cheerful sigh of mock envy. 'I must admit you've got it in the looks department. The Aryan ideal. Blonde like a Rhine maiden. Even if there is nothing in that pretty little head of yours!'

As soon as she saw the look the general gave her as he rose courteously and waved her to a seat, Cissie was glad she had heeded her friend's advice with her appearance. She could still hear Inge's voice urgently whispering in her brain as she nervously sat and smoothed down the skirts of her dress. 'You have to sell yourself, darling. Convince him you're devoted to the cause. None of your wishy-washy 'I just want to end the war' stuff!' Cissie had smarted at the dismissive contempt her friend had shown for her views, but she appreciated the motive behind Inge's sharp criticism and resolved to follow her guidance. She remembered her other tips, and, with studied nonchalance, she crossed her legs, making something of a business of it, swinging one elegantly high-heeled foot aloft before she once more smoothed down the slightly displaced hem of the dress. She saw his eyes flicker over her. Full marks for that manoeuvre, she guessed.

He beamed his lit-up smile at her, then glanced down at the file on his desk. 'It is now almost eight months since you became a prisoner here, yes?' He spoke in German, and she was glad of the efforts she had made to become fluent in his language as she answered his questions easily.

'Yes. That's right. And I've been most happy here,' she added, without his prompting. 'I'm not ashamed of the work I do for the department. The sooner we can bring this war to a close the better, for everyone, I believe.' Careful, Cissie. Don't overdo it, you goose. You sound like one of the characters in those idiotic sketches they churn out at the office.

'That's good. I've read your superiors' accounts of your efforts. You have done well. But perhaps it's time for you to play a different role. A more important role.' He paused. 'How would you like to go to England?'

For all her preparations, the sudden question caught her totally by surprise. Her mouth hung open; she goggled speechlessly. He laughed, clearly pleased at his effect. 'You've never been, have you? A delightful place in many ways. I thought you'd jump at the chance.'

'I'm sorry — sir — I don't understand,' she floundered. 'You're sending me . . . ?'

He held up his hands, smiling charmingly. 'Oh, let's not jump the gun, Frau Pride. It's early days. But I've been told you're a friend of Sean Mullins. He is working for us. A devoted member of our small group, in fact. He speaks very highly of you. He had recommended you. It will mean you having to pass through a great deal of training, pass some very stringent tests. If you come out successful, you could find yourself working with Mullins, somewhere on the British mainland.'

Her mind was spinning. 'You'd trust me?' she said ingenuously. 'Let me go? How would you know I wouldn't . . . betray you?' Betray? Was that the right word, she wondered, when she would be returning to her own people, her own heritage?

General Schoenburg chuckled. He shrugged. 'We wouldn't. But I know you English are sticklers for honour. For doing the right thing. Fair play, you call it, don't you? You would join our forces, take the oath of loyalty to the Fatherland. We would trust you.' There was another short pause, and he laughed again. 'Then there is the matter of Sean Mullins. I am aware of just how *friendly* you and he are. You wouldn't betray him, would you? And he would keep a very close eye on you, I'm sure. You'd be partners together.'

Cissie drew a deep breath, like a swimmer about to launch into space from the top board. 'He knows how I feel.' Her voice was soft but very clear. 'You're right, sir. I would never betray him. Never.'

'Good.' He sat back casually. 'You're ideal in so many ways. Converted to the cause, a native speaker. And with only your brother who could possibly recognize you. And, more especially, my dear, even he is convinced you are dead.' Her eyes widened again, as he pushed a newspaper clipping towards her. 'Look at that.'

The extract had been taken from the *Assam Provincial Times*, dated back in February. An item had been circled by pen:

A memorial service was held on Tuesday for Mrs Cicely Pride, wife of 2nd Lt Charles Pride, and daughter of Mr & Mrs Martin Humphreys, planters, of Kandla Station. The church where nineteen-year-old Cicely (Cissie) was married less than a year ago was packed . . .

Cissie scanned swiftly through the remainder of the brief article, which stated that it must now be assumed that no one had survived the torpedo attack on the *Star of Indus*, after approaches to the German High Command through the Red Cross.

'You see, my dear. Unknown in England, yet indisputably British — dead to everyone you knew. A new identity, a new beginning. New glory.' He stood, came round the desk. He leaned over her, his hand almost touching as it rested on the back of her chair. 'A whole new life awaits you, you lucky girl!'

★　★　★

And that was what happened, with bewildering speed. Within days she had bidden Inge a tearful, clasping farewell and left in one of the military staff cars, on a long journey, to an old castle, draughty and ancient, somewhere near Cottbus, deep in the forest close to the Polish border, to begin her arduous training to be a secret agent. A spy! Among her own people! She tried not to think about it, but with little success. To be with Sean, she told herself desperately, to be at his side, to share his danger. That was all that mattered. But there were many formidable obstacles to overcome before that could happen. She had to qualify.

There were three other women on the course. One was French, the other two German. There were six men in their class also, with whom they combined for most of their lessons. Remembering her experiences in the hostel, Cissie was apprehensive, but the atmosphere here was very different. Nationality seemed immaterial. They were all in the same boat. The castle was occupied by thirty other trainees, at various, more advanced stages of progress, but everyone was friendly, all imbued with a common purpose: to achieve qualification and pass out as an accredited special operative.

For a large part of the day, they did not

even use names, only numbers. Cissie was Number Four. 'Four! Shift your arse or you'll go round again!' the instructor screamed, as they struggled through the slippery woodland paths, or round the muscle-testing obstacles of the assault course. A great deal of time was spent in the first days on reaching a high standard of physical fitness. Cissie had always considered herself to be in good shape, with the traditional outdoor pursuits of her upbringing, the riding and the tennis and the swimming in the small outdoor pool of the club. But that had been a while ago, and she had lived quite a sedentary life since her capture, except . . . But she could not list the most strenuous activity she had indulged in most in recent times, however comprehensively exhausting it might have been. The climbing of ropes, the complicated team manoeuvres she took part in, swinging over streams, moving heavy objects from one difficult place to another, rigging up precarious bridges and hauling themselves over them, were all foreign to her. 'Come on, Number Four! You're bloody hopeless!' She began to loathe the impervious male drill instructors and their constant barked abuse.

She was better in the classroom, learning the various methods of coding and decoding messages, the assembling and use of the radios, the ingenious methods of hiding them. And the instructors were far less abusive.

The head of the spy school was Colonel Voss. He was grey-haired, with the appearance of an aristocrat, and the manners and speech of a diplomat. He was the one who first told Cissie of her new identity. 'Your name is Jane Freeman. Unmarried. Civil servant, ex-India. Invalided out, after recurrent enteric fever.' He smiled, passed across one of the English newspapers, which lay plentifully at hand. 'That's where we got the idea for your name.' He pointed at a strip cartoon, entitled, simply, 'JANE'. You remind us of this delightful young lady. Though I hope you'll manage to keep your clothes on a little more successfully.' She glanced at the drawings and blushed as she saw what he meant.

She plucked up courage to ask Colonel Voss about Sean. She had built up her hopes that the Irishman would be here at the castle, in one of the courses senior to them, and was bitterly disappointed to find this was not so. She had heard nothing of him or from him, not a single written word. He had promised to write. Surely he could have found time to scribble a few lines to her, just to let her know he was still alive, still loved her?

'Ah! Mr Mullins has moved on. He wasn't

with us long. He was no novice at our kind of games, as I'm sure you're well aware. He's gone down south, I believe.'

'Did he . . . ? Did he know I would be coming here?'

The colonel shrugged. 'I shouldn't think so. He wouldn't be in on a decision like that, though I understand he put your name up for it.'

'But now, he must — is it possible to get in touch? For me to write to him?'

'You have to concentrate on getting through the first part of your training here, Jane.' The use of her new name was still entirely foreign to her. The colonel's manner was as urbane as ever, but she coloured, aware of a hint of rebuke behind his polite words. 'That's all that matters for now. We require the highest level of dedication from all our operatives. We don't allow any outside communication while you're here, I'm afraid.'

'Yes, of course. Sorry, sir.'

His voice was even kinder as he continued. 'You know, my dear, one of the most important lessons of all for any operative in the field is not to let personal attachments interfere with dedication to the task, or cloud our judgement in any way. To do so might be fatal.' He held up his hand as she mumbled an indistinct acknowledgement of his warning. 'I'm not saying such attachments are wrong. In fact, they may play an important part in our work. Just as long as they don't get in the way. You understand?'

She nodded. But his words, timely as they were, did nothing to ease the burden of her thoughts. She could tell no one the truth, but she had to admit it to herself — the only reason she was mixed up in all this was because of her love for Sean, and her desire to stay with him, whatever danger that might lead her into. She didn't want to think about what that danger might be, or where. But already, at the very outset, things seemed to be going terribly wrong for them. She needed at least to hear from him — anything, just a line — and her gloom deepened as the days went by. The days were full enough to end in virtually total exhaustion, but they couldn't alter the growing sadness whenever she had the time to dwell on her situation.

The German woman, Leni, who was almost thirty and therefore a much older figure to Cissie, commented on her withdrawn mood, so that Cissie felt obliged to tell her at least a little of her problem. 'God! Surely you can forget boyfriends out here, my girl? I'm too shagged out to think of anything.

I'm out like a light when my head hits the pillow!'

Cissie had never felt so alone and abandoned. She wept into her weary pillow as she thought of Inge, and the way they had shared so much of their time and their thinking. And as the first three weeks ticked away, there came a further, increasing worry — that she might fail the course and be returned to the department at Hamburg, or, maybe, now that she had seen what went on in the forest around Cottbus, some far bleaker fate might befall her. You must pull yourself together! she commanded herself. Of course Sean loves you! He's probably just as worried about you. They won't let him get in touch. Maybe it's all part of the test, for both of you.

She did better in the weaponry training, coming ahead of the other girls in the small arms marksmanship, and beating two of the men in the class. The unarmed combat was a different matter. She had to keep telling herself it was not all some perverse game, as their NCO instructor, drafted from one of the commando units, showed them how to disable, how to kill, with knife or wire or bare hands. It all seemed so fantastic and unreal, but there was nothing of fantasy about the livid bruises she suffered over her limbs and body as, time after time, the sergeant threw or slammed her down in the sand or the mud, knocking the breath from her, or immobilizing her in some vice-like grip, in his efforts to transform her into an efficient killer.

Finally, though, she made the grade, or, in the sergeant's words, 'scraped through', with enough marks to register as a pass. 'Mind you,' he said, with a leer so plain in its meaning that Cissie could not but feel insulted, 'if it comes down to it, Number Four, and you're really up against it, my advice is drop everything, lie flat on your back and leave everything up to nature. Know what I mean?'

'You've made it through the first stage,' Colonel Voss told them after their six weeks had passed. 'Congratulations. You have a seventy-two hour leave, then you return to begin Part Two. Time for you to go into uniform. For the moment, you are part of the Auxiliary Reserve. You have already taken the oath of secrecy, and you are on trust not to break it, not even to your nearest and dearest. Understood? Good. Now, make the most of your leave, and don't be late when you return.'

The uniform was dark green, and had been tailored to fit their individual measurements. There was a neat forage cap to go with the skirt and jacket, shirt and tie, and Cissie was pleased with the sight that met her, when, ready to depart, she gazed at her reflection in the long mirror of the women's barrack room. She had a travel warrant to Hamburg. She had still heard nothing of Sean, and she could think of nowhere else she could go. Helga Schmidt had written a couple of times, but she had remained with the infant in the quarters in France, which was now the established base for the U-boats operating in the South Atlantic. Cissie tried to console herself. It would be good to see Inge again, and the people at the radio building. She was too embarrassed to ask Colonel Voss again about Sean. All she could do was wait, and hope. The sickening thought came to her that he might already have gone into the field. Perhaps he was even glad to be free of the encumbrance she represented?

It took most of a long day to reach Hamburg. She felt glad to be in uniform, and even a little proud when she climbed the stairs of the Radio Hamburg building to find Inge and the others. They crowded round with congratulations, and Inge hugged her tightly. 'Listen,' the German told her. 'I've got to work late tonight. As you can see, there's plenty happening. We've been getting regular raids from the RAF lately. Frau Muller is jam-packed. You can get in at the Hoffnung, at least for tonight. Come in here about ten tomorrow. I'll be able to get some time off.'

The Hotel Hoffnung was familiar to Cissie, achingly so, for it was where Sean had stayed throughout his time in Hamburg. They had shared a good many nights there in that cell of a room, which had become such a haven for her. And for him, she had believed blissfully. Now she was far from sure that that had been true, and the knowledge sickened her. And now even Inge was too busy to welcome her properly. She told herself she was being petty and childish. What had she expected? Flags and bunting and a brass band? With Sean standing on the platform waiting to enfold her in his arms?

Surely, though, she thought some moments later, fate was being particularly cruel to her, when she was given her key and recognized it at once as the very room Sean had occupied. Darkness had fallen. 'Make sure you draw the blackout before you put the light on,' the elderly concierge admonished her. 'The curtains won't have been drawn, and those bloody English bombers come nearly every night now.'

Was everything conspiring to make her feel deserted and alienated? The staff here had never been so uncooperative. Surely a maid could have closed the heavy curtains, shown her to her room? All right, she only had her light service valise to carry, but such normal courtesies cost little. She felt her eyelids prick with incipient tears as she opened the door and dropped her case in the narrow little vestibule. She fumbled her way across the dimness, making for the narrow square of window showing the night sky. At least there was nothing for her to trip over except the bed and that rickety old chair, she thought, with nostalgic longing. She felt her heart catch at the thought of switching on the light and seeing the place again. How lonely it would be without him.

Then her heart was racing with fright. A hand clamped over her mouth, cutting off her scream, and a hard body pressed intimately against her from behind. She felt the point of a knife at the side of her neck. 'Don't make a move,' a thick voice hissed in German, 'or it'll be your last! Understand?'

She nodded, against the smothering grip of the hand, which left its clamping hold. He remained pressing against her, but now his hands were moving with obscene intimacy over her body, plucking open the buttons of her tunic, the buckle of the belt, digging into her waist, unzipping the skirt, giving it a tug to assist it in its soft fall around her ankles. She gave a whimpering sigh, as he stepped back a little and roughly dragged the jacket off her shoulders.

'Jaysus! Where's all this unarmed combat they're supposed to have been teaching you, me darlin'?'

She spun round, gasping with amazement and sobbing joy. 'Sean? Oh — my God! Oh, my darling! Oh, you bastard!'

He gathered her, bore her expertly to the bed in the dimness and fell happily on top of her. Their clothing fluttered down on all sides as they shed it in desperate eagerness.

Some time later, they heard the rising wail of the sirens, and watched through the still uncurtained window the fingers of search-lights scanning the summer sky. 'Should we go down to the cellars?' Cissie murmured sleepily against his ear, as the first anti-aircraft batteries opened up.

'No. You know what they say about the RAF. Besides, I vowed to myself I'd never let you wear a stitch of clothing for the next forty-eight hours at least!'

13

'Steady! steady! hold her there, Skipper. Wait for it.'

Nigel Humphreys stared ahead through the front screen of the cockpit. They had broken through the heavy blanket of cloud, and he could see the paler shape of the Elbe estuary, the prickling little orange dots of the explosive that had been dropped by those in front of them. His mind screamed the usual obscenities at the droning bomb aimer, lying on his belly just behind him. For Christ's sake! This will do, won't it? There's the river. The docks must be down there somewhere. Besides, we must be over the city now. Hamburg is a big place. Let them go, for God's sake! Wherever they fall, they'll still kill Germans. Come on, damn you!

Each one would count towards his avenging Cissie's death. It was funny. He hadn't expected to be so upset by it. She'd always just been a skinny little kid to him. He'd never really got to know her; she was an irrelevance, a whining background to his home life, an even more remote figure once he'd been packed off on the long voyage to

185

school in Blighty when he was ten. He probably hadn't spent even a single year in total back home, since that day twelve years ago now. His family could only afford to pay for his passage home for the vacs every other year. His mother had been over to England twice, but she had come on her own, his father once. Poor Cissie had never made it. That made him feel even worse, that and the fact that she had at last been on her way when she had died. And there was the awful manner of her death.

He hoped she wasn't frightened, though he guessed that might be a forlorn hope. He knew what fear was. He couldn't shy away from it, no matter how hard he tried. Fear made him physically sick; he could almost taste vomit in his mouth right now, feel its thickness in his throat. He hadn't really known it until his first combat. He had actually got through the training to be a fighter pilot without any bother, was thrilled at flying such a wonderful craft as the Spitfire. But on those first sorties, during the earliest German raids across the Channel, aimed at the aerodromes along the south coast, those opening preliminaries of what was to be the Battle of Britain, though no one had realized it then, he had suddenly found himself literally in a cold sweat, his brain scarcely functioning in his terror. He had hung back, used the excuse of wingman to avoid the chaotic whirling, diving dog fights that were the approved tactics — 'getting stuck in', as they put it. His section leader had spotted it at once. But they were too gentlemanly to accuse, much kinder to him than he was to himself. He went along with it, the transfer to bomber training, the move up to East Yorkshire. After all, the biggest fear of a coward was being found out.

It had happened just about the time he had got the letter from his mother telling him of Cissie's engagement to Charlie. By the time he learned of it, and of their plans, the wedding was practically taking place. He was delighted, of course. He had known how badly Charlie had fallen — he had to admit he was shocked himself when they had both returned home, school over, in '37, to find this quite striking young woman, with all the right attributes in all the right places, instead of the brown skinned waif as dark as her armah, who was always at her side.

He had missed old Charlie when he returned to Britain, up at Oxford. He didn't find it all that easy to make new chums, and they had grown up together. School was just another adventure, their biggest so far. He could face most things, he reckoned, with a real chum alongside. That had been the trouble with this fighter business. No one with whom he could really let his hair down, so to speak. No bosom pal. He hadn't found it easy, either at college or when he had joined the service full-time, to make real friends with anyone. He was quite lonely, really. Perhaps that was why hearing of Cissie's death had hit him so hard, especially after that awful gap of waiting, clinging on to some hope that she might somehow have survived. The announcement and the service back home had brought things to a conclusion.

He jerked all his thoughts back to the terrifying present, as he saw the puffs of the ack-ack clouds spreading in a mottled carpet below them, and away to starboard the white fingers of criss-crossing searchlights. 'Steady! Steady!' The mechanical voice buzzed in his earphones, and he heard the stream of profanities running like a prayer through his brain.

'Bombs away!' At last. He released his breath in a noisy rush. 'Let's get to hell out of it, skip!' Nigel could hear the cheers in his headset as he banked the heavy Stirling bomber round in a wide turn. There was no other turn to make in these unwieldy crates, and he was yet again bitterly regretful and envious of the sweet way the Spitfire had been able to twist and turn and stand up and beg, practically, and hurtle through the sky at a speed this old lumbering heap could never dream of. The fighter boys had it cushy nowadays. The Luftwaffe had virtually given up daylight raids, and the Spitfire and Hurricane jockeys lorded it all over the place, heroes of the hour, shagging all the prettiest girls, while Bomber Command went out, night after terrifying night, flying hundreds of miles over enemy territory to get to their targets.

HQ Ops must have been loonier than ever, ordering the raid for tonight. Half the force had been lost before they even got over Germany. He didn't even know where most of his own squadron was. He had been amazed when they had dipped below the cloud to find how close they were to the target. One up for Matty Dean, he had to admit, though their intrepid navigator had looked more than a bit surprised himself to find how accurate his calculations had proved.

At his side, Matty was grinning now like a school kid. 'Should get a gong for this one, old boy!' he shouted, easing his mike away from his mouth, and bellowing over the roar of the motors.

189

Their tenth mission, well on the way to completion now. God, how much longer could their luck hold out? Training had been dicey enough. At least in a fighter if you cocked up you only wrote yourself off. It was just one more sickener to know that in this thing you had six other lives in your hands, too.

He had very nearly pranged the kite during one of their early training runs, landing at an unfamiliar airfield in North Yorkshire. Ginger Evans had sworn at him. 'You nearly killed us, you stupid fucker!' Nigel had been going to put him on a charge. That was another cock-eyed thing about this crazy set-up. Matty and he were the only officers in the seven-man crew. Matty was senior in rank to him, a flight lieutenant, whereas Nigel was a flying officer. The others were all non-coms, sergeants and flight sergeants. A flight sergeant calling you a stupid fucker! What an outfit! And when they weren't bawling you out, it was all 'skip' this and 'skip' that. Not a 'sir' in sight. It wasn't really on. But these aircrew types were a law unto themselves.

'Christ, skip! Fighters! Three o'clock! Turn, turn for Christ's sake!'

Evans' shrill voice pierced his brain. He heard the clatter of the upper turret as he banked desperately, wrestling the controls, the right wing dipping as the cumbersome craft began its move. There was a ripping sound, and the plane lurched sideways. He felt a blast of icy air, heard the scream of the wind, the flapping of canvas and grinding metal. Half the cockpit seemed to have caved in to his left, and the bomber slammed downward, like a lift out of control.

'Jesus!' he wept, fighting with the controls, his body soaked in sweat despite the icy blast. After a couple of terrifying corkscrew turns, to his disbelief he felt the plane begin to respond, and straighten out. He could see the dark mass of the countryside levelling off. They were well below the cloud cover, but they had lost the fighters. We'll stay down, he thought. We can't be far from the Dutch coast. We'll risk the flak. A hysterical relief grabbed him. 'We're all right!' he shouted into his headset. 'Keep your eyes peeled! We're staying down below cloud level.'

'Skipper! Skip!' Sergeant Williams, the Engineer, was shaking him furiously, and he turned in irritation. Christ! What did they want now? Couldn't they see he was flying a crippled kite here? Let me get on with it, for Christ's sake! Then he saw Matty, flung back like a broken doll in the ruins of his seat, the left side of his body a dark mass of tattered cloth and blood. The glaring eyes were wide, the mouth gaping open in the rictus of his final scream. He was very clearly dead.

Oh God, no! Nigel began to shake violently. He forced himself to concentrate on flying the damaged machine, while the tears poured unchecked down his frozen cheeks.

★ ★ ★

'I thought I'd wait, until after the funeral,' Nigel said awkwardly. 'Give you a chance . . .' He was going to add 'to get over it', and realized how stupid that would sound, coming only days after the ceremony.

'Yes,' Midge Dean answered quietly. 'What can I get you to drink? A G and T all right? I'm afraid I might well turn into an old soak.' She brought the drinks, sat opposite him in the low armchair, and he tried to keep his eyes off the limbs, in the dark silk stockings. Her face was extremely youthful, in spite of the lines of grief, the washed-out look of the eyes. She had the fine-boned, aristocratic lines he so admired in a girl. Her skin, unmarked by any make-up except a hint of lipstick, was flawless.

Nigel had met her quite a number of times. Certainly he felt much closer to her than the other surviving members of the crew, for Matty had invited him back to the cottage in

Barmby Moor, the small village practically at the end of the runway. Midge's family had taken the cottage in order for her to be near her new husband during training. It had been an added bonus that their squadron had begun operations from the same 'drome. As a brother officer, Nigel had been granted the privilege of being admitted to this private area of Matty Dean's life, an honour he had not been so eager to share with the rest of B-for-Baker's crew. In fact, most of them had met Mrs Dean for the first time at the funeral, which had been held down at Matty's home, in a Derbyshire village near Buxton.

The ceremony was a military one, with bugles and guard of honour and a volley over the grave, but it was clear the social divide between the two families was great. Midge Dean's maiden name was Goresby-Harrington, her familial home an eighteenth-century manor house in its own rolling parkland, her father Sir Roland Goresby-Harrington, Bt., which made her mother 'Lady'. Matty's father was a partner in an undistinguished solicitor's firm in Buxton, and his wife's title was 'Mrs'.

Nigel had always visualized Midge's tall, willowy frame in jodhpurs and hacking jacket, rather than the severely neat black dress she was now wearing. Her voice, already deep, had an extra huskiness about it, which Nigel found even more attractive, then thought penitently that it was probably because of the amount of crying she had done over the past days. There was also a brittle abruptness in her tone, which indicated the stress she was suffering. 'Please — don't think me horrid, but I don't want to hear — any details you know — of what — of how it happened. Last minutes and all that.' She stared down at the glass in her lap. 'As Daddy said — thank you for — for getting him back to us. And jolly well done, making it back to England and all that. Saving the lives of your men. The others, I mean.'

Nigel felt that great cold canker of misery swelling within him. There was some talk of his getting the 'gong' Matty had spoken of — his last words, Nigel thought. They had had a week's leave, but now there was a replacement kite ready for them. And a replacement navigator, too, but a flight sergeant this time, which meant Nigel would be the only officer on board. Well, he wasn't going to take any more shit, especially from that bolshy carrot-head Evans! But there was far worse than that to think of. There was the growing conviction that he simply could not face going out on another op, ever again. Just when they were all hailing him as a hero, too!

Cometh the hour, cometh the man. He had somehow, by the grace of God, probably, got crippled B-for-Baker back home and on to terra firma, sat there weeping in the soggy evidence of his terror while they cheered and thumped him on the back. His hour had come and gone. Never again! blazed in the forefront of his mind.

He gulped suddenly at his drink, and rose abruptly. He shook his head. 'There's nothing I can say.' His despair was a weight, pinning him to the spot, when all he wanted was to get out, to run, anywhere. 'That's the last thing I'd want — to talk — about any of it!' He tossed off the rest of the drink and put the glass down, trying to stop the violent tremble of his hand. 'I'd better be off.'

She stood quickly, too, and he heard the soft rasp of silk, which jarred his strung-out nerves like a jolt of electricity. She put her hand on his sleeve, kept it there. 'Were you and Mat close? Did he talk to you? About us?'

He shrugged, diverted from his own angst by her question. He struggled for something to say, for a convincing lie. 'Well, when you're in the same crew — you get to know each other. You know how it is.' Of course she doesn't, fool! he lashed himself. And neither do you. He hadn't got close to Matty at all. Not really. Schoolboy reminiscences, a kind of recognition of their different status from the rest of the crew. That was all.

'Do you have to go?' she asked. Her voice seemed to carry an intensity, reflected in her swift look. 'Come for a walk with me.'

In the tiny hallway, he helped her into a light mackintosh, watched while she bound the silk scarf round her dark head, tied it under her chin in a loose flowing knot. As soon as they were outside the low wooden gate, she seized his arm, thrusting her own through it, pressing it against her side tightly, with a shocking familiarity. They set off past the grey stone wall of the churchyard, and the long, leafy lane. Through the hedge he could see the long hangars, and the squat building of the control tower. A line of Stirlings stood in seeming haphazard parking on the grass.

'Are you flying tonight?'

He shook his head. 'They've just got a kite ready for us. A replacement. And — ' He stopped himself in time from mentioning the replacement navigator. *The king is dead. Long live the king.* 'We'll take her up in the morning. Then we'll be on at night.'

'I'll be listening for you. It's like thunder. I keep thinking you're going to knock the chimney off.' She squeezed his arm, a startlingly intimate little gesture, and he felt the softness of a breast against him. 'You don't have to go back yet, do you? You could stay and have some lunch with me.'

He was suddenly terribly nervous, and apprehensive, yet excited, too. 'I suppose you'll be packing up. I mean, going back home. To your folks.'

She gave a bitter little laugh. 'I dunno. I suppose so.' She turned, glanced at him sharply. 'I was bloody glad to get away, to be honest. It was getting me down, nobody knowing what to say, Mummy wanting to tell me to buck up, pull myself together.' There was a pause, then she went on with quiet intensity again, 'They were dead set against it — Mat and me, getting married. They were just starting to come round to it . . . I know why!'

This last remark was made with such vehemence that Nigel stole an anxious glance at her. 'Don't upset yourself,' he said inadequately.

'It's because Daddy wants to make sure we have an heir, somewhere. A male, I mean. There's only my sister and me.' Again, a low, bitter laugh. 'I don't think he's ever forgiven Mummy for delivering two girls. Not up to scratch at all!' She strode ahead again, practically pulling him along with her. She turned again to him, and he felt helplessly trapped, as he saw the gleam of tears in the brown eyes, and a fury, too, that both frightened and aroused him. 'Mat promised me a baby! He swore he'd give me a child! He broke his promise to me, the bastard!'

They finished the walk in brooding silence, and once more Nigel felt the urge to make his escape, and began a rumbling attempt to do so, which she cut off summarily. 'You promised you'd have lunch with me. Or do you break your promises, as well?'

'I just . . . don't seem to be helping you very much,' he muttered miserably. 'I'm sorry.'

'No, no! My fault entirely! Take no notice. I'm the one to apologize. I'll lighten up. What we need is another drinkie. A good stiff one, eh? Fix them, will you, darling?'

He felt his nerve twitch at the carelessly flung term of endearment. His pulse raced.

She made some sandwiches, huge doorstop slices, with almost equally thick slices of cheese, and dark homemade pickle. 'Made by our cook back home. Takes the silver plating off a teaspoon!' They washed it down with more generous helpings of gin and tonic, and her mood was transformed to one of equally intense merriment, while Nigel sat there, his head swimming and his emotions in a bigger whirl. He felt helpless yet willing to be the victim of this divine enchantress.

'Come with me!' She gave the command

imperiously, and rose with that typical, abruptly decisive movement. He followed her from the room, and up the steep and narrow stairs of the old cottage. His eyes fixed on the delicate tendons at the back of her ankles, the little black oblongs rising from the heels of her shoes, the lines of the stocking seams which ran from them, up the slenderness of her legs.

The high bed, with its bright eiderdown, seemed to fill the small room. The low ceiling was beamed, the small cottage window latticed, through which he could see the brightly sunlit garden. She was reaching behind her impatiently. 'Unzip me.'

'What?' He stared, goggle-eyed, and she repeated her demand in an urgent, hissing undertone. With a start he moved to obey, drew the zipper down to the small of her back, revealing the slip beneath. 'I say!' His face was hot. 'We can't — I mean — '

She shrugged the dress forward, off her arms, pushed it down from her hips. 'You were close. The nearest to him. Don't you want me?'

He gazed helplessly at her, saw the outline of her undergarments beneath the silk of the slip. 'Yes, yes. Of course I do.' And part of him did, too. Definitely. And besides, it seemed the right, the gentlemanly, thing to say.

14

'Go on!' the instructor's voice came from close behind, in her ear, over the roar and the rush of the icy air, and Cissie whimpered like a puppy in her paralysing fear. He pushed hard at her haunches, but she clung on to the heavy metal handles above, her knuckles whitened. She saw the miniature fields, the slope of the woods, the dark, dividing lines of hedgerows, clear in the harvest moon — 'bombers' moon' they called it nowadays. They were far below, framed in the vast open doorway of the plane, and terror gripped her by the throat.

She strove with all her might to overcome it. Now, at this last of all minutes, to fail at the jumps, after she had negotiated every other obstacle in the long path. Since Sean's miraculous, dramatic re-entry into her life, and the glory of their two days together, she had been transformed, her zeal and determination reinforced to make the grade, to pass out, to be worthy of his partnership. He had promised her she would go with him, and she had never doubted him, nor questioned her own motives or beliefs. She loved him, completely, and that was faith enough for her. She had made it so. Sheer hard work and resolution had got her through, not impressively, perhaps, but enough to pass out, despite the rigours of the long completion of the course. Except for this last insurmountable hurdle. She had feared it more than any, and now the tears streamed down her face at her inability to overcome her fear and thrust herself out.

The sergeant instructor knew he had to act, and quickly. They would be out of the dropping zone in a few more seconds. He liked the slim little English girl. She was a bit of all right. He knew how hard she had had to drive herself, knew about her liaison with the big Irish fellow. He couldn't let her fall at this last fence.

But her hands were clinging like limpets to the handles overhead. It would be a hell of a struggle to prise them off. He knew what blind panic could do to a person's strength. He checked that her chute was clipped on to the wire above, and his own, for he would be following her out. Pulling out his short service knife, he hacked through the belt of her trousers, dragging the garment down from her waist. The pants fell down to her thighs and, as he anticipated, she tried to grab them. He struck her forcibly in the back with his shoulder, knocking her easily out into the rushing air. He heard her dying, terrified wail as she spun away, a small, black, hunched shape against the paleness of the sky, and he fell out after her.

Cissie's world spun crazily, the wind whipped the breath from her, and, for some time, she felt she was not falling at all. A vague impression of the aircraft's bulk shot by, slightly below her, and she actually experienced the sensation of rising for a few seconds, then she was tumbling, over and over, her mind numbed to all except her fear. This was it. Death! Only it wasn't. She found she was still alive, screamingly so, earth and sky dancing crazily all about her. Something had tethered her legs. What was it? She saw her bare legs up above her, trousers flapping around her calves. Conscious thought flooded back; she clawed at the harness at her chest, tugged viciously, and there was the blessed whoosh, the tremendous jerk at her armpits, and the chute crackled and flapped, blossoming out, the webbing all around her, and she was right side up, hanging swaying under the comfortingly vast canopy.

She looked down. There were her white legs, the pants round her ankles now, the green fields below her feet. Green fields rushing to meet her, with a speed that set the alarm bells jangling again. Brace yourself. Desperately, she plucked the scraps of training to mind. Knees bent, feet spread. Except she couldn't spread her feet. The damned trousers were caught, wrapped around her boots, and she sobbed again, kicking out furiously, scissoring her legs, and she whimpered in hysterical relief as the pants detached themselves and spun away from her.

Just in time. She was down, she could see individual tufts of grass, there were low bushes all about, then she hit the ground, with a jar that shot up to her helmeted head, and she tried to double up and roll, as they had been taught on the mat at the gym.

She was on her front, being dragged with amazing speed, bouncing along, through and over the tufts of spiky meadow grass, and she remembered she should have hauled on the rope to spill the wind out of the chute. Too late. She screamed at the agonizing whiplash of hundreds of thorny branches as she was hauled through a thicket of brushwood. Her body was flayed, she felt torn to pieces, until, at last, the forward rush ended, and she lay there, half-conscious, sobbing hysterically, in fright, and relief, and pain, the chute flapping around the bole of a sturdy tree.

There was a shout, and a crashing of feet in the tangled undergrowth, and she lay limply, shaking and sobbing. The sergeant crouched, turned her over, inspecting her swiftly to make sure she was all right. His sweat-smeared face was grinning down at her. 'My God! You made it! Covered in cuts and bruises, but you made it!'

She clung to him, half-laughing, half-weeping, as he helped her to her feet. She stared down at herself in shock. Most of her clothing ended in a bunch at her midriff, caught in her webbing. From below this point, she wore only the baggy khaki knickers and the thick grey socks and her combat boots. Her thighs and knees were a mass of raw grazes and a-glint with the blood from a myriad of small abrasions.

'Reckon you're living up to your name, eh?' He grinned, nodding down at her battered limbs. Everyone at the school knew the circumstances of her assumed name, and regularly followed the misadventures of the original in the old copies of the English paper which abounded. 'Sorry about the debagging, but it was the only thing I could think of to get you out.'

Her face was filthy, too, liberally smeared with sweat and muck, diluted and spread by her tears. But she beamed a smile at him and, lifting her head, kissed him soundly on his cheek. 'Thank you, Sergeant. I'd never have jumped, would I?' She giggled bravely. 'The things you have to do in the line of duty, eh?'

★　★　★

'Congratulations, Mrs Pride. I know you won't let us down.' Colonel Voss held on to her hand. The pressure was maintained for long seconds, while his eyes seemed to pierce through to her innermost thoughts. The message in the lean, distinguished features was crystal clear, and Cissie's heart beat fiercely once more, just as it had earlier, when, in a voice that quavered shrilly with nerves, and the breath that seemed trapped within her chest, she had sworn the oath of allegiance to the Führer and to the Fatherland, in front of the room full of spectators.

The use of her proper name startled her. It was a long time since she had heard it. Number Four. Jane Freeman. And a whole host of far less polite epithets through the months of the training which had led to this crowning moment. She had been very conscious of her lover's presence in the audience as she took the oath, wondering what he was thinking as he listened to her promise of loyalty and life to Germany and its leader. Did he doubt her? As she was sure everyone else doubted her. Why not, when she doubted herself? Was she really swearing to betray her upbringing, her background, the Empire? All the things she had taken for granted since she was a little girl?

All she had thought of, all that had kept her going through the formidable routine of the latter part of her training — the radio course, the Morse code, the cryptography; the fierce grillings when she had been worn down to weeping, almost hysterical exhaustion, until the torture had seemed all too real; the exercises, the use of explosives, the mock killings again — all that she clung to was the hope of being with Sean, and of being free. Who knew what might happen once they were in England? Maybe she could make him forget the war, forget causes to die for. Maybe she could make him, instead, cling to something to live for, as she had. A very personal and private world of love. Was it hope? Was it some rosy, vague dream? She dare not look again, or even examine too deeply the inspiration that had brought her to this seminal moment.

When the colonel finally released her, she looked round anxiously for Sean. Their eyes met, she saw his gaze fastening on her, and she thrilled to its unspoken but clear message. She knew she looked good, in her new, dark green, expensively cut uniform. The fine material was of the highest quality, and it made the most of her slender frame. It was a pity she would scarcely wear it. This was only the second time she had done so, and presently it would be returned to the locker, to remain there — for ever? Cissie refused to look beyond the mission, whatever it might be, and their departure.

'Well, Frau Lieutenant,' Sean murmured, bending so that his lips brushed her ear. 'When the hell can we get away from this shindig? That uniform is far too alluring. I can't wait to get you out of it!'

She giggled, pulling a face of disapproval. 'You're an insatiable beast! I'm starting to worry about what you'll be like when we're stuck with each other day after day, in the field.'

That night, in the warm, wide hotel bed in Dresden, they lay naked, still dreamily entwined, and gloriously lethargic after making love. Sean rubbed his crooked finger along the side of her jaw. 'Final briefing starts tomorrow. This is it, my love. Schoenburg will want to speak with you alone. Make sure you say the right things to him. He's the boss man. Absolutely. What he says goes.'

'I'm scared, Sean,' she whispered. Her head was resting under his chin, and she could feel the rise and fall of his damp chest, the soft tickle of his body hair against her face. 'Why does he want me on my own? We're going together, aren't we? Can't you talk to him? Tell him? Tell him he can trust me,' she added tensely.

Her head bounced as he laughed quietly. 'You don't tell a full-blown general what you want, me darlin'. Especially not one like Schoenburg. He's one of the Führer's favourites. Next in line for a marshal's baton, they say. So you be nice to him. Don't be scared — but be nice.' He reached down; she felt his hands intimately searching for her. 'Not as nice as this, though, my little Mata Hari!'

★　★　★

Her interview with General Schoenburg was, as she expected, a last pep talk. And something more. 'Of course, you have sworn the oath of loyalty, and believe me, the Führer is personally aware of your courage and your efforts for the Reich. It will not be easy, once you are back among your people. Although you might find the reality of England rather different from the ideas you have held of it from India. Nevertheless, you might begin to have doubts, about your allegiance to us, to the ideals we are fighting for. But you must always remember where your duty lies. Never forget that Herr Mullins' life depends on that duty. It would be him you were betraying, as well as our cause. A cause he is prepared to die for. He is completely dedicated to his task. Close as you are, he would not hesitate to take the severest action should he suspect you of any treachery.'

She was staring at him in dismay, her lips parted. He smiled coldly. 'Oh yes. Make no mistake, he has given his word he will be watchful — and ready to act to prevent any danger to the mission.' He sat back, studying her with such dispassionate attention she felt as though he were reading her confused mind. 'Then of course there is the matter of your family and your friends. Should you elude the punishment Mullins might deem suitable, we would be forced to make known your activities here. Your folks would be shocked to discover you were after all this time alive, and that you have been living in utmost comfort here, serving the Reich very ably. While they might be thankful that you are not dead, they would not take kindly to what they would see as your betrayal of them. Even the British authorities would find it hard to trust, or forgive, you. As for proof, perhaps you were not aware, but the glorious moment of the oath of allegiance has been captured on film.' His smile broadened as he saw her start of surprise. 'Oh yes. We will be forced to release it, should you fail in any way to complete the operation.'

She was drained, her clothes damp with sweat, when she finally emerged from the interview. Hiding in the toilets, she wept bitterly, and spent a long time repairing the damage to her features before seeking out Sean, who, at one look, could see the experience had been harrowing. 'They've invested a great deal in you,' Sean told her, holding her comfortingly in his arms, 'of time and effort, and of trust, too.' He paused significantly. 'And so have I, my love. I've gone out on a limb over you, sweetheart. Don't let me down.'

She gave a wounded cry, rearing back to stare tragically up at him. 'Do *you* doubt me, too? Oh, Sean! If you knew! I love you, so much!'

'I know, I know!' he soothed. 'Of course I don't doubt you. I'm crazy about you. I'd go into the flames of hell itself with you by my side, and don't you ever forget it!'

★ ★ ★

The details, and arrangements, of their operation, in the briefings which followed, seemed unimpressively vague. They had what appeared to be fairly sound cover stories, as long as no one went digging too deep. Their papers were good. Sean had authentic identity card, ration book, and even driving permit, in his own name. Cissie had queried this early on. 'But don't they know you already? Weren't you in trouble back home? I mean in Ireland?'

He grinned. 'I've had all sorts of names but never me own, me darlin'. Sean Mullins is as pure as the driven snow, as far as the English are concerned.'

They were given the name of only one possible contact, in north London, though they were being sent in over 200 miles further north, for this was their immediate task: to ascertain as many exact details as possible about the north-eastern coastal defences, from the River Tyne down to the Tees, and, if possible, beyond. It was over this area that most of the bombers raiding Britain flew on approaching the island, and the losses incurred were becoming worryingly high. 'Hellfire corner', the aircrews had started dubbing it.

Even Cissie, woefully inexperienced in espionage as she was, concluded that the agency was seriously inadequate. The very small number of agents they had tried to infiltrate into Britain had virtually all been rounded up either immediately or shortly after their arrival on enemy soil. Still, she was delighted to discover, at this late stage, that they would not after all be required to make that terrifying leap from a plane in the darkness over unknown, hostile territory, but were to be transported by U-boat across the North Sea, and landed on a hopefully quiet, preferably deserted, coast, by rubber dinghy in the dead of night.

Cissie's huge relief at not having to parachute in was somewhat tempered when she thought of the imprecision of the whole operation. No one waiting to receive them — at least no friendly face — it seemed naïvely optimistic to her mind to expect to land undetected, especially when she herself had read in English papers brought to Hamburg of the thousands of ordinary citizens, ancient and youthful, who were flocking to join the Local Defence Volunteers — the 'Home Guard', as it had been unofficially christened. Lord Haw-Haw might mock at their training with broom shanks because they had no weapons, but they had eyes, didn't they? And even if, by great good luck, they should succeed in making it ashore on some wild northern beach, how should they suddenly emerge and pass themselves off as ex-India types, slotting without suspicion into the British life around them, while they slipped up and down the coast making careful notes of all the anti-aircraft batteries and other means of defence?

Then, for Cissie, came the most disturbing thought of all. She was a Briton, a Daughter of the Empire. If she was caught clambering ashore, she could, she deduced, claim her birthright, convince them that all that had happened to her had been through no fault or design of her own. And just where did that leave Sean?

They spent their last night in Kiel, sharing a cabin on a submarine depot ship, very like the one Cissie had seen when she had left U213. The low cigar shape they boarded at dawn the next day was identical to the vessel she had spent almost two long months in, or so it seemed to Cissie's informed gaze. 'God! How did you stand it?' Sean asked, as they waited in enforced idleness in one of the narrow messes, when the boat had submerged to make the dangerous crossing. Yet again, he insisted they ran through their cover story.

She was Miss Jane Freeman, ex-government official, embassy material from the secretarial upper echelons, clearly true-blue middle-class type, home from India, and recovering from a debilitating and serious tropical illness. That was how their romance had started, at the School of Tropical Medicine, in London, where Captain Sean Mullins, late of the Fifth Gurkhas and also laid low by exotic disease, had been sent home to recover. They would admit readily enough to the curious that they were lovers. Captain Mullins had married young. He and his wife were separated; neither family approved. 'Even the most hard-bitten ould biddy of a landlady won't be dry-eyed when she hears our tale of star-crossed love!' Sean declared, with a confidence Cissie was far from feeling.

Two nights later, the U-boat waited for the tide, far enough out from the small fishing village of Kingstaith to avoid any of the inshore fishing cobles. There were not likely to be any underwater defences on this stretch of the north Yorkshire coast, and the captain took his boat as close to the high cliffs as he dared, and thanked God for the moon-obscuring clouds, as they hastily launched the dinghy, and two of the crew propelled the two spies into the narrow, steep shelf of beach under the sandstone cliffs. 'Good luck!'

The noise of their stumbling feet sounded terrifyingly loud as they scrambled up to the shelter of the high rocks at the foot of the cliff. They squirmed between them and lay there, breathing hard and recovering. Cissie could feel the icy wetness seeping through the heavy boots and thick socks under the waterproof leggings. Her teeth were chattering, more from tension than cold, and her whole body shook uncontrollably.

Sean moved closer, put his lips to her ear. 'Looks like we've made it, darlin'. Welcome to England, madam. Is this your first visit?' His grinning impersonation of a tourist guide or customs officer infuriated her, then she leaned gratefully into his embrace, and wept with relief.

PART III

MOTHER OF THE FREE

15

Sean found a small cave a little way along the beach. There were several such, some quite large, but this was a narrow aperture, more of a fissure, running at a sharp angle from the line of the cliff, thus making it harder to spot from any distance, with a jumble of rocks about its entrance, which acted as a further screen. 'Come on, we'll get a fire going,' he said encouragingly, for Cissie's face looked pinched, and she couldn't stop shivering. He knew it was partly reaction to all the tensions that had been building up over the past days and hours.

Her eyes widened in alarm. 'Someone might see it.'

'No. I'll build it back there, no one'll see it, from sea or land. We'll be as snug as a pair of bugs in a rug! We can get our wet socks off and dry them out.'

He was right. The small fire, which he started with quick expertise from the dry sticks hidden in the caves, was well concealed, and just the sight of its cheery glow heartened her, as she lay wrapped in his arms and pillowed on their rucksacks, watching their socks and boots steaming gently in the heat. They had stripped off their heavy walkers' outer coats, which he had draped over them as blankets, and he had taken her frozen red feet between his legs and massaged them into renewed life and warmth. A heavy fog came up with the dawn, hanging like camouflaging smoke just yards from the sea's edge, out of which the white waves rolled from the eerie calmness. 'Not bad for October,' he said, enveloping her in his embrace. 'It could be blowing a gale on this coast, at this time of the year.'

'You know more about England than I do. Tell me about your boyhood. I want to know all about you. I've told you everything there is to know about me.'

'Yeah, I know. Privileged little memsahib, with poor little native girls to do everything but wipe your backside for you! Or did they have to do that, too, the poor haythens that they were?'

She gave a squeal of outrage, and struck him hard on his encircling arm. 'Beast! My Rani lived just about as well as *I* did! Same food, everything!' His teasing had diverted her, and she felt a sudden, throat-tightening nostalgia at her thoughts of home. Renewed awareness of their danger brought back the sombreness of mood. She nestled down against him, not looking at him as she continued softly. 'Sean. If things went wrong . . . if say, you thought I'd somehow let you down . . . betrayed you . . . what would you do?' She waited, and when he didn't answer, she said, 'Would you kill me?'

'I might,' he answered starkly. The shock of it was like a blow to her, before he went on, with a shake of his tousled head, 'But I doubt it, darlin'. I doubt I could do it. Not even to save my own life.'

'Oh, darling!' She turned into him, clung fervently to him, seeking out his mouth, murmuring against it. 'I love you so much! I'd die rather than ever hurt you, I swear!'

Her heart was thumping like a drum when they moved from their refuge into the grey murk of a new day. Hoisting their packs like the hikers they were meant to portray, they slipped and scrunched along the narrow slope of the beach, until it levelled out to a wider sandy stretch, where the wall of the cliff on their left ended dramatically, to mark the mouth of the narrow creek along whose sides the village had come into being. Only the nearest cottages loomed into sight, and the distinctive wooden cobles hauled up on the hard: open boats nearly thirty foot long, and seemingly modelled on the old Viking ships. The foot of the stems were lined with

221

coppery metal, the grandiose names painted in white on the bow. *Star of the Sea, Hope, Resolve*. Lobster pots were stacked in high, neat squares, and the nets with their lines of floats draped over wooden frames.

The fishermen, in cloth caps and high-bibbed oilskins over their identical dark 'Ganseys', the heavy knitted woollen jerseys, were already about, working on the boats or mending nets and pots. Most of them had pipes clenched between their teeth. One or two of the younger ones drew on cigarettes. All eyes turned towards the two strangers who appeared startlingly out of the fog, but no one even nodded a greeting.

'Good morning,' Sean called out, with ringing confidence. 'No fishing today?'

One of them, his mahogany face wrinkled and sporting a fine white stubble, waved his hand towards the sea, invisible except for the few yards of lapping waves rolling to the shore. 'Can't see 'and in front o't face.' Clearly, he thought the question superfluous, but then strangers said daft things anyway. 'Winnat lift today.' Cissie could feel all eyes on them and wished only to hurry away, but Sean had stopped, ready to chat. The old man squinted at them, pointing with his pipe in the direction from which they had emerged. 'Come along t'beach, 'ave yer?'

'That's right. Thought we'd get an early start. Could do with something warm inside us, though. Is there anywhere we can get breakfast?'

'Aye. T'Ship's the place. Keep straight on.' He gave a grunt that might have been a laugh. 'Ye can't git lost 'ere. It's at Bank Top.'

Cissie nodded. 'Thank you,' she said curtly. 'Good day.' She began to move, and Sean bade them farewell. Why didn't he hide his Irish accent? she wondered fearfully. He was quite capable of doing so, as she well knew. She told him so, when they were safely out of hearing, and trudging up the wet cobbles of the High Street — the *only* real street, as far as she could tell, for only narrow alleys and courtyards ran off on either side, the cottages piled higgledy-piggledy under the cliffs on either side of the beck, sometimes with hardly room for a single person to squeeze between them.

'You're not forgetting what you were taught already, are you?' He grinned back at her. 'Stick as close to truth as you can. Never dissemble more than you have to. Makes the lies a damned sight easier.'

That was why he had decided, at the last minute, when they were waiting to board the submarine, that she should keep her real name of Cissie, in spite of the papers which identified her as Jane. They had tried using the pseudonym, but the way she reacted to it was wrong. Caught unawares, and because of the deep intimacy of their relationship, one of them might slip up at some critical moment, which could destroy them. So Cissie she would remain, much to her relief. 'We'll say it was a pet family name from infancy.'

They were both panting by the time they had climbed the steep bank and the cliffs had fallen away on either side. They saw the hanging sign, in need of a coat of paint, though the lettering and the drawing of the sailing vessel could still be seen, 'SHIP INN', and, over the door at the top of three worn stone steps, 'Prop. Robert Price'. Sean knocked loudly on the door. It was opened by a young woman whose black hair, wound in tight metal rollers at the front, showed over the flowered scarf that was knotted like a turban about her brow. She wore a similarly patterned apron, which could not disguise her attractively full figure. 'We were wondering if we might get some breakfast,' he said exerting the full power of his charm. 'And a bit of a warm. My friend and I are on a walking holiday. We set off early this morning. We thought the fog would lift.' He pulled a boyishly rueful face. 'We surely got that wrong, I reckon.'

Cissie was sure she had seen the woman's eyebrows flicker at Sean's use of the word 'friend'. But she stepped back and ushered them in, with a surprisingly shy smile. 'Oh, yes. Come in. I've only got one gentleman staying at the moment. I was just fixing him some breakfast. I can soon have something ready for you. Take your things off. Hang them in the passage. Sit in the bar there. I'll soon have a fire going. We don't open the pub till eleven, of course.' She introduced herself. 'I'm the landlady. Mary Price. My husband's away, I'm afraid. In the army. North Africa.'

'I'm sorry,' Cissie answered automatically, and Mary shrugged. She gave her a warm smile, which seemed to transform and light up the thin face.

'Oh, well. You know what they always say nowadays. There's war on, eh?' She laughed, and they nodded in sympathy. 'If you'll excuse me. I'll see about some grub. Porridge all right to start? And I can do you some scrambled egg on toast. Bacon's a bit short, I'm sorry. Usually I can keep a slice or two by, but it's a bit low at the moment. This blooming rationing, eh? And not much AUC round here, as you can imagine! Different in the big towns, I expect? Where are you from?'

'We've come from London,' Sean told her. 'Both on a spot of leave. Convalescent, as it happens. We're both home from India, as a matter of fact.'

'India!' Her brown eyes were wide, with interest and excitement. 'My word! You poor things! You must be frozen, with our weather. Hark at me, stood gossiping away, when you're both starving!' She coloured, and said, with shy hesitancy, 'If you wouldn't mind — you could come through to the kitchen, if you like. While I cook you something. There's a nice fire on there, for the stove. It's warm.' She gave another nervous laugh. 'We're not posh or anything — but you're very welcome.'

'Love to, wouldn't we, Cissie? Very good of you, Mrs Price.'

They followed her along the dark passageway towards the rear, past a staircase with a high, polished newel post, and into a large room where half of one wall was taken up with a gleaming, black-leaded stove, whose high grate held a banked, glowing red fire throwing out an encompassing heat. 'Draw up your chairs.' She indicated two wooden captain's chairs, with thin cushions tied to the time-polished seats. 'Take your boots off if you want. Warm your toes. You can eat your porridge in front of the fire. I'll soon have the eggs done.'

'What's AUC, Mrs Price?' Cissie was

trying to relax, to make conversation as the landlady busied herself preparing the meal. 'You said just now you can't get it round here.'

'Eh?' Mary Price stopped beating the eggs in the basin and stared at her in surprise. 'You've not — ' Then her face cleared, and she gave a quick chuckle, nodding in comprehension. 'Of course. You've come from India, haven't you? Don't suppose you're bothered with rationing and all that over there. AUC — it means, 'Anything under the counter?' You know. Extras, like. Bits your grocer keeps for his favoured customers. We've only got the one shop here. We used to get into Whitby or up to Redcar before. But now, with Bob away . . . ' Her voice tailed off.

Cissie felt herself reddening, her ears hot, and she was glad to have the excuse of the fire glow to explain it. She didn't dare look at Sean; wondered if he would be angry at her indiscretion. But he was full of good-natured ease as he filled in details of their history for Mary, who was quick with her interest. This was clearly well out of the ordinary for this little community. 'So you just met at the hospital?' she said, her face alive with eagerness to learn more.

'Yes. We were hundreds of miles apart in India. Never knew each other existed.' He cast Cissie a look of such telegraphed affection that she felt herself colouring, and once more could not in all honesty blame the fire's heat. Mary was evidently no hard-hearted publican, for she was entranced at this whirlwind, wartime romance. So much so, that Sean decided to play this unexpected good fortune for all it was worth.

After they had eaten, he pushed back his cleared plate and sighed with noisy bliss. 'That was good, Mrs Price, and no mistake.' He beamed that special smile at her, then moved to include Cissie in its aura. 'Listen. I don't suppose you could put us up for a few nights? Say a week or so? We've got this leave, and — well, we were planning on walking about here — the dales and the coast, you know. Cissie doesn't know this part of England at all, so I've promised I'll show her how special it is. We were just planning to put up where we could. But really, this would be an ideal spot to make our base.' He rolled his eyes and rubbed his stomach appreciatively. 'And my God! With cooking like this, well! We'd be fools to pass it by! Could you do that?'

'Of course!' Mary answered at once, her face lit up by her enthusiasm. Then he saw just that shade of hesitation that put a tiny touch of heightened colour in her cheeks.

'You've got your ration books — and identity cards and all that?' Her voice was apologetic. 'It's the law now. They can be quite strict, if the inspectors call in.' And her hesitancy and embarrassment was even more obvious as she continued, 'That's . . . er . . . rooms — what would you be wanting — I mean — '

'Oh, yes, I see what you mean!' Sean laughed easily. 'Two rooms, of course, if you can manage it. Wouldn't want to cause any scandal, would we, Cissie, my love?'

'No,' she managed faintly, her own face crimson yet again. She avoided his amused glance. She knew the 'my love' had been a deliberate addition, its intention clear for their hostess. At least he was keeping to the precept he had urged on her during their toil up the hill after their encounter with the fishermen. 'Stick as close to the truth as you can.'

⋆   ⋆   ⋆

'I think we should move on. It's too dangerous sticking in one place like this. Someone will get suspicious.' They were under the eiderdown in Cissie's bed, which was a high, old-fashioned double. Solid enough but inclined to rattle slightly, and creak, when put to over-strenuous use, which

229

Cissie found inhibiting, and so alarming in the late-night silence after the last customers had filed out into the blackness and Mary Price had drawn the heavy bolts of the front door into place, that she had swiftly banned any physical intimacies beyond some restrained embracing and sweet-nothing whispers.

'She knows fine well what's going on!' Sean objected, causing Cissie to blush for shame, even though she asserted fiercely she was not ashamed. 'She's not stupid. Besides, don't tell me she isn't all for it. She's as excited as hell, the poor wee thing.' His voice took on that teasing quality Cissie knew so well now, and which she both loved and was infuriated by. 'She's in her prime herself, is she not? A fine-looking woman. And her hubby away out in the North African desert, amusing himself with those hot little Arab girls! She must be missing it, poor soul. She's all for us. We couldn't have found a better berth to land up in. I reckon we're here for the duration. And once we're established, I can quietly go about the business we're here for, and nobody any the wiser.'

Cissie was still unconvinced. 'Make her your friend, Cissie,' Sean urged, and she knew he was serious now. 'That's your job, darlin'. Keep her sweet and on our side.

Star-crossed lovers. Don't forget.'

Before the week was up, Sean and Cissie were regulars in the small, crowded public bar. Cissie was tolerated as a guest in this traditionally male preserve, but Sean soon put her wise to the form, and she took to retiring early, with her plea of tiredness, and the fishermen nodded and grunted and called out their 'good-nights'. 'Lassy's still not fit, the' knaas,' they agreed sagely. Sean stayed until 'chucking-out' time, and was quickly the life and soul, with his tall tales and earthy humour. And Mary Price was soon firmly under his spell.

He took to helping her clear up the glasses, and moved through to the glowing fire in the kitchen to sit with her for a while. 'I miss Bob,' she confessed, in her reserved way, one night, staring at the dying sea-coal. 'We hadn't been married that long. Five years, nearly. Courted for three before that, of course.' She sat forward, her arms resting on her knees. 'No bairns yet. And I'm not getting any younger.' She gave an embarrassed little flutter of a laugh. 'Thirty-four next. My mum had four of us by then.' She gave a loud sigh. 'I hope to God he comes back all right.'

'He will, my dear. And you've time for a houseful of kids yet.'

She looked very young as she glanced with

shy gratitude at him, and he saw the sparkle of tears at the ends of her thick, dark lashes. 'What about you — and Cissie?' she added hesitantly.

He grunted, shrugged his shoulders. 'She's a sweet kid. I didn't mean for it to get . . . so involved. You know how it is.' He could feel her sympathy, knew how great a weapon it could be for them. 'I married young. Far *too* young. Hardly out of my teens. Before I went abroad. My wife's family are well off. They live up in these parts. Or at least they have a big place hereabouts. Inland. That's how I know the area. We're separated. She's down south. Her folks have property all over the place. We don't have children. But divorce — well, it's tricky.' He made an impatient sound in his throat. 'I've made a bit of a mess all round, I'd say.'

'She's a lovely girl,' Mary said warmly. 'And she loves you very much. I hope things can work out for you.'

He sighed. 'So do I, Mary, love. So do I.' He rose and touched her briefly on the shoulder before he left her.

★ ★ ★

Cissie had to admit that Sean had been right. Slowly the tension and fear eased. 'I've a

232

feeling about this,' he told her. 'We've landed on our feet. Give it a little while. These folk will be all right. They're just like the peasants back home. They believe in us just because we are so different.'

After a couple of weeks, the locals were nodding and smiling. Mary Price was their champion and friend, thanks to Sean's winning, blarney-kissed ways. Instead of the low profile Cissie had thought was essential for their task, he was the life and soul of the bar each evening, doing badly-needed maintenance about the pub for his grateful hostess, and even serving as well as entertaining her customers.

One morning, when Cissie was still in her dressing gown after a late breakfast, and Sean was out working on one of the dilapidated outhouses at the back of the property, Mary tapped lightly and entered her room. 'Brought your washing,' she said, and laid the neatly folded articles on the bed. She was no longer piqued by Cissie's casual thanks, as she had been at first, when the blonde girl didn't even seem to notice that she had ironed them. Sean had told her how Cissie had been brought up in India, how everything was done by servants out there. 'Very nice, too!' Mary had commented drily.

'Listen, love,' she said now. Her tone

indicated the awkwardness she was feeling. 'There's no need to pretend — with me, I mean.' She put her hand involuntarily on the black metal rail of the bed foot. 'I know you have to have the two rooms. For the look of things, and that. But it's all right. I know how you two feel. Captain Sean's told me about it. Not that I needed to be told.' She gave that shy smile and Cissie, who had tightened with embarrassment, suddenly relaxed. 'I could see how things were between you right away. And I hope it all works out for you, my dear.'

'Thank you, Mary!' Impulsively, Cissie moved to her, and they hugged each other. 'Bless you!'

16

Eight weeks before his sister would step for the first time on an English shore, just over sixty miles to the north-east, Flying Officer Nigel Humphreys was lying, torn between racking guilt and a wild and dizzy elation, in the Deans' bed, still hot and damp from the exertions he had shared with the week-old widow. It was also just a week since he had, unknown to both of them, been no more than a mile above and five miles north of Cissie when he had dropped his bomb load and Matty had met his violent death.

Nigel was almost equally stunned by the enormity of what had happened here, in this little room, since. It was still unreal in his head, despite the painful, exhausting reality of his sore and sated flesh, the throb and burn of the red weals and scratches which angrily flamed on his back and shoulders, and his upper arms, where Midge Dean's long, desperate nails had clawed at him, urged him on in frenzy.

Had he satisfied her? Part of his brain told him that he hadn't. He had come far too quickly, he was sure. Mentally, he squirmed away from the vision of her mad flinging, the way she had fought round from under him, battering herself against his thighs, riding with those savage thrusts, and those strange, barking cries, before she flung herself violently from him and lay sobbing, deep, guttural, wrenching sobs from deep within her, her whole body lifting, juddering, so that at first he had been frightened that she was having some sort of convulsive fit. Yet within minutes, as he lay beside her, frozen, powerless to move or speak, she had suddenly recovered, her face red, smeared with her tears, and smiled, and plastered her wet flesh against his again, only tenderly this time, and whispered hotly against his face, 'That was good, wasn't it? Lovely, wasn't it?' And he had agreed, and she had wrapped herself round him and they had lain still, drifting through the late summer afternoon.

The persistent knocking had roused them, and the frenzied barking of Peter, her black and white spaniel. She had sworn, and pulled a long pink dressing gown over her nakedness before padding downstairs. 'Stay there!' she commanded. 'And don't make a sound. I'll get rid of them.'

He could hear the buzz of voices below. Whoever it was had gained entry to the cottage. He was trapped up here. Even if he dressed, he could hardly wander downstairs into the middle of their conversation. He had a sudden, ignoble urge to make his escape, and was deeply ashamed. He had already told Midge that he had only to telephone the guardhouse to report that he would not be 'sleeping in', and he could spend the night here, need not go back to the station until 10 a.m., in time for their test flight. Of course he wanted to stay! He admonished himself for his cowardice. He had done all right, she had said so. And maybe he would have the chance to perform more competently for her, though he had no idea how.

Shame again, as he admitted to himself the paucity of his sexual experience. Not quite a virgin, but scarcely better than. All the bragging and lying at school, the wild tales and claims of fictitious conquest, and still 'unblooded', even through his time up at Oxford. His innocence had been lost, at last, between the capable and meaty thighs of one Vivien Brown, a WAAF from the training camp outside Hove. And even that had been a disaster initially, for, after she had hiked up her tight skirt about her middle and slipped off the service 'passion-killers', he had spent himself, shamefully, at the first touch of her nimble fingers, and she had sworn with startled, vivid contempt. However, his anguish, and unmanly tears, had softened her compassionate if too easily won heart, and she had generously offered to 'try again', at a later date, and with a little more planning. The second attempt had taken place in the luxury of a bed in an establishment in Brighton, which hired out rooms to people without luggage and did not insist that guests should stay overnight. Success was sweatily achieved, and she even declared a degree of pleasure and satisfaction in the congress, though later, in painful self-examination, he conceded this might have had, again, more to do with her acknowledged generosity of heart.

But now, on this, his second awfully big adventure, he was bemused by this merging of his familiar world of solitary, indecent fantasy with apparent reality. Except that the reality was even more unbelievable, tilted with madness. The lovely girl who was Matty's wife, a week after her husband's death, and still wearing her widow's weeds, had dragged him up here to make love, literally in her partner's place. Those weeds were still scattered across the floor. The brassière hung in a tangle of straps over the back of the chair, the black dress, the silk knickers and dark stockings, the trailing suspender belt, formed a little nest on the faded cushions.

How unbelievably decadent the whole episode was. Surely he would be damned for this? Of course, people would say, and Mrs Dean could well plead, that grief had rendered her temporarily insane. Unsound of mind, though clearly nothing that wasn't working in her body. Which made him the arch demon, the perverted devil of all this. He wasn't a religious sort of chap, in spite of years of attending chapel every morning, and Sunday worship, both at school and in the small wooden church, far less frequently, back home. But he believed in God all right, and God must be feeling jolly pigged off with him right now, and who could blame Him?

So why did he feel so much like the helpless victim, with the stigmata of his suffering so redly evident on his pale skin? 'Come with me.' He had felt she was dragging him along, even though she had mounted the stairs ahead of him. He thought of the fury of her passionate assault, and once more acknowledged his powerlessness against it. And the thought of that long, supple body, the working limbs, that fine horsewoman's behind, clenching and rippling, stirred him with renewed desire, and he sprang up, hot with shame, before he remembered the visitor and he froze with apprehension. He tried to move noiselessly, as he drew on underpants and trousers, slipping the white canvas braces over his tender shoulders, before creeping like a cat burglar barefoot on to the tiny landing. He could hear the stranger's voice now — the clear, decisive tones of a female, organizer of many good works, chairwoman of many church committees, the vicar's right-hand 'man'. She would have been swiftly at home in Kandla Club, ordering the native servants about.

'I can see how awful it must be for you just now,' Mrs Edith Westcott said, with no trace of sympathy in her tone. 'But the only thing to do is to pull yourself together, rally round. Times like this when we must show what we're made of. Backbone! That's what's called for, my gel! Not loafing round undressed, diving into the gin bottle. WVS are crying out for volunteers. Come round to the village hall tomorrow afternoon. We'll see — '

'Mrs Westcott. I've no interest whatsoever in contributing to anything to do with this bloody war. I've given them a husband. Surely that's enough, wouldn't you say?' Midge Dean's voice sounded perfectly controlled, almost a parody of her visitor's authoritative vigour. 'So now if you'll excuse me I'll get back to that gin bottle. And please don't bother me again, or send any more of your do-gooding friends round to save me. I have all that I need right here to get me through. Let me put it to you plainly, Mrs Westcott — bugger off and leave me alone!'

'I'll assume you're not yourself,' Mrs Westcott muttered stiffly. 'Perhaps later, when you've — '

'*Goodbye, Mrs Westcott!*'

The front door clashed shut. Nigel stood at the top of the stairs, letting out an awed bleat of laughter. Midge turned back and stood there, grinning up at him. 'There! How was that? Think she got the message?'

'I'll say!' he answered, in hushed reverence. 'You'll be the talk of the district!'

'Suits me!' She tugged open the cord of the gown, and let it fall open to display herself. She stood legs astride, in a flauntingly obscene pose. 'What are you doing with your pants on, you 'orrible little man? I'm coming up there to deal with you on the double!'

'Oh God!' He groaned to aching conscious-ness, to find reality once again far more grotesquely wonderful than the kaleidoscope of dream and fantasy he had been inhabiting hitherto. She was kneeling astride him, her long thighs, leanly muscled, splayed out either side, her warm weight crushing him

— until she lifted, and her hands ferreted and captured him, and recaptured him in that splendid union of their flesh where the weary pain was part of the pleasure, prolonged until she began to grind and pound and crush him into the creaking bed. She yelped echoingly as she folded herself upon him and he was drowned, a willing sacrifice, in her and beneath her.

'I have to go,' he said, a timeless age later. 'I'll be on a charge. I'm absent without leave. I should have taken the kite up. They'll have the police out for me.'

'I don't want you to leave me. I want you to stay, right here with me, in this room, for ever and ever, amen. I want to keep on doing it, over and over.'

In spite of his sickness and his fear, he felt the spark of wicked excitement still burning brightly. 'I have to go.'

He was up, crouched over the stained bathtub, running in tepid water. She fitted herself gently round his curving back. He felt the brush of her breasts and thighs, the scrub of her belly, and felt his sickness and fear, and his weakness.

'I don't want you flying again,' she said flatly. 'You have to tell them you're sick. Tell them it's your stomach. They can't declare you fit. I won't have it. I'm going to call someone I know. A doctor. He doesn't live too far away. He's a friend of ours. He'll arrange to give you a chitty. You have your bath. I'm going to ring the station now.'

He looked at her in alarm, and she smiled with cool reassurance. 'Don't look so scared, you big baby. You're just like Mat, you know.' She giggled, reached down and shook his flaccid member. 'Except in that department. You're an absolute beast. A perfectly greedy little piggy down there.' She released him and turned away with another rich laugh.

Oh God! What was happening to him? Maybe she *was* crazy, unhinged by Matty's death. He suddenly saw Matty's shattered body again, that singed mass of cloth and blood, that terrible, wide jaw of glaring finality. The rush of wind and the crazy lurching and juddering as he fought the aircraft through the long hours of their return, with Matty's yawning corpse sitting beside him. He didn't want any of that again. He could not face climbing into another cockpit, heaving that lumbering beast off the ground, knowing the odds were running relentlessly out. A court martial, gaol. Anything would be better than flying, going on ops again. Maybe that strange girl downstairs could make it happen for him, save him from the nightmare. He'd give her a baby gladly. A whole nursery full of kids, if that's what she wanted. He climbed shivering into the cold tub and splashed away the tears he could feel on his face.

★　★　★

The next days were an ordeal of a different kind, almost as draining on his nerves. He had to keep telling himself he was not flying. Whatever was happening, he was not going up in that kite, and however much people thought he was lying, however much he despised himself for acknowledging the sickening truth of his cowardice, he was no longer on ops. He had to go briefly back to the station, endure the embarrassment of seeing the faces he knew, the men who had acknowledged his status as a flyer. No one accused him of lack of guts, but it lingered like a bad smell, that air of embarrassment, in the flickering sideways movement of glances, including his own, the gruff falseness of tone in every conversation, however casual.

He almost began to wish for more honesty, until he met with Ginge Evans, who declared with jovial mock-camaraderie, 'You jammy bastard! How the devil did you work that then?'

He seethed with vitriolic hatred as he tried

to fix on a smile. 'I'm cheesed off about it, believe me, Ginge! It means you lot will have completed your tour long before me. I'll be stuck on ten till I get back again.'

'Still,' Evans said, grinning, with a twist of the knife, 'at least it means you won't have the chance to wipe us all out any more!'

I saved your blasted lives, the bloody lot of you, except for poor Matty! Nigel thought, though he said nothing, merely smiled sourly.

There was no more official mention of a gong, however. He was glad to be transferred from Pocklington, to a hospital near Weybridge, which was a commandeered mansion in its own grounds. 'Nervous exhaustion' was the accepted phrase for his condition. 'Those stomach pains and the headaches — all down to nerves,' the service MO told him. 'I'm afraid you'll have to come off flying duties for a while.' Nigel struggled to look suitably crestfallen. Besides, he had practically succeeded in convincing himself of the genuineness of his disability. His nerves were shot to pieces all right. He would only be a danger to anyone who went up in a kite with him. The odious Evans was probably right after all, sod him! Though it didn't make Nigel's view of the flight sergeant any less hostile.

But at least he had an increasingly powerful

distraction in the alluring form of Midge Dean. As soon as he could obtain permission to spend nights away from the hospital, she came down to stay in an unpretentious studio flat in Kingston — a haven of torrid fleshly delights which left Nigel breathless, and, for the first time in his life, less than abysmally ignorant of sexual matters and a woman's bodily needs. He was shocked by what he learnt — and still secretly persuaded that Midge's appetite and voracious demands were far in excess of what could be considered 'normal'.

He was at first horrified when she announced that he was to go with her to spend the weekend at her ancestral mansion, and meet Daddy, Sir Roland the baronet, along with his good wife, Lady Julia. 'It's a bit, er, soon, isn't it?' he queried feebly. It was, after all, less than two months since Matty had been ceremonially laid to rest.

She raised a well-defined dark eyebrow. '*Soon?*' she echoed scornfully. 'You've been bedding me for the past two months, old chum!' She waited, and added with studied nonchalance, 'And I rather think you may have got me up the spout. Not absolutely certain yet, but mum's the word, I'm pretty sure myself.'

'Oh God!' he murmured faintly.

'I'll take that as an expression of your unqualified rapture, shall I, darling? Trouble is, I fear folks may well have to count on fingers *and* toes to measure the time twixt conception and parturition if I try to pass it off as Mat's.' She dropped her pose of cool detachment and came closer, to wind her arms around his neck. 'Don't you think I'm growing a little rounder, ripening a little? Won't you make an honest woman of me, do the decent thing? You've no need to worry. The parents won't have you flogged or anything. I've already told them how special you are to me — without going into graphic detail, of course. I've just painted a glowing picture of you as knight in shining armour, consoler and champion of this dame in distress. Which is true, darling. As a matter of fact, they're quite taken with you. They're tremendous supporters of the Empire. I'm afraid they think your background far more respectable than poor old Mat's and his dreary little clerking lineage.'

She backed him into a chair and twined herself on his knee. 'And Daddy can fix things for you to be posted to the Air Ministry. There's a little *pied-à-terre* going for us in Knightsbridge. It would be perfect, darling.'

'But — I mean — it's still a bit soon, isn't

it? You know — after . . . ?'

He could feel her coil like a spring as she sat up, leaned away from him to stare at his face. 'You think Mat wouldn't be overjoyed with us getting together? You don't think he gives us his blessing now that he's not here?'

He blushed, pulled her down to meet his kiss. 'Of course he does, darling,' he answered obediently.

'I have to go up to Barmby again for a couple of days. Just to finalize everything. Close the house down and so on. I promised I'd have a farewell drink with some of your crew. I'll pass on your good wishes.'

'Yes, do. And hurry back, won't you? I can't imagine how on earth I managed before you came along.'

'Nor I. I'm completely besotted, you wicked creature! But you know that damned well, don't you, you brute?'

★   ★   ★

'You're a byootiful lady and you've got the arse of an angel.' Ginge Evans lightly kissed the curve of her left buttock, then gave it a resounding slap, and she yelped and knelt up, rubbing the red mark vigorously and pouting at him over her shoulder.

248

'You're an uncouth bastard, but I shall miss you.'

He grinned. So would he, he acknowledged, though he didn't tell her so. She liked it rough and ready, this high-born lady, and no frills attached. No wonder poor old Dean and that supercilious prick, Humphreys, couldn't satisfy her. What a shame! All those wasted months, when he could have been giving her a good seeing to — discreetly, of course. She wouldn't mind where she got it, from haystack to hedgerow, as long as she got it. But the skipper! Dear God! Out of the frying pan into a damp squib, if ever there was one.

He studied the soles of her narrow feet, wrinkling as they were folded uppermost on the crumpled sheet. The big toes were long and broad. Be a brilliant high jumper, he thought. The soles were a light dusty brown on balls and heels, where she had padded downstairs to get another bottle of wine. 'The last of Mat's cellar,' she had said unaffectedly, and he grinned.

'Always save the best till last, do yer?' She was lovely all right, and a real high-class lady. But she needed a real man to satisfy her needs, and he'd never met a bird who needed it more. 'Listen. You're not really gonna shack up with the skip? Not that bloody pillock?'

She rolled over on to her back and patted her belly. 'I've told you. The little sprog needs a daddy. Don't be too hard on him. He and Matt — they're very similar. They can't help themselves. Public school and all that. They never learn anything about this sort of stuff.' She waved a hand at their naked frames in illustration. 'Anyway, he adores me.'

'Modest little mare, ain't you?'

She giggled like a schoolgirl. 'This little chap is really B-for-Baker's offspring, after all.' Her hand still rested on her belly. 'I had thought of working my way through the whole crew, but if they're all like you I'd be worn out in next to no time!'

'What do you mean, *chap*? Don't tell me you can organize that and all?'

She reached over and caught hold of his penis, shaking it in friendly fashion. 'Whatever its sex, let's hope the little bugger doesn't emerge with bright red hair, what?' She began to wrestle, trying to pin him down, and he swung her round, trapping her and spreading her arms out above her head, holding her by the wrists, 'Say goodbye to me again,' she murmured throatily, and he moved to oblige.

17

Mary Price tapped at the door and called out as she entered. Cissie was sitting up in bed, propped on the pillows. 'Here's your cocoa.' Mary smiled. 'Just listen to that wind. You really feel it up here on Bank Top. Sometimes I think the roof's coming off. Wouldn't be the first time, either. Poor old Bob used to get sick of going up and down the ladders putting slates on.'

The wind was indeed roaring about the old building, rattling every windowpane. To Cissie, still enjoying the advent of the winter season of western Europe, only the second she had experienced, the storm emphasized the cosiness of the room, its lamp-lit snugness, the warmth of the cocooning blankets and heavy eiderdown.

Mary handed over the steaming mug, and sat beside her, on the edge of the bed. The landlady was wearing her checked, woollen dressing gown, beneath whose long hem the bottom of her winceyette nightgown showed, above her felt slippers with their worn edging of fur, and thick woollen men's socks. Her black hair, with the row of metal crimping curlers, was covered by a white net. 'I must look a right sight,' she said apologetically. 'You look so pretty,' she added wistfully, and Cissie pinked with pleasure. And a twinge of guilt, too, for her first thought, when Mary had appeared in such unflattering night garb, had been, Huh! It's easy to see Sean's not around.

At first, she had been amused, even flattered, at the older woman's growing attraction to Sean, which showed itself in so many little ways to Cissie's discerning eyes. 'She fancies you!' she had told Sean, sniggering at the idea, aware of how mortified their very proper landlady would be if either of them suspected it. But it was true. Though she doubtless believed she kept it decently hidden, and though it was innocent in the extreme, Mary's attention to his every comfort, the favourite dishes she prepared especially for him, the care she began to take with her looks (such as the swift disappearance of curlers in his presence), the rosy flush which so easily appeared at his constant appreciative compliments, and, above all, the look in her artless brown eyes, were eloquent testament to the accuracy of Cissie's giggling deductions.

Sean denied it, but rather preeningly, to Cissie's way of thinking. 'That's just the way the womenfolk are round here,' he explained patronizingly. 'Just like back home. They're homemakers, they look after their men folk. That's their job in life. What would you know about it, brought up out there, with a poor little subservient race to run around at your beck and call?' As usual, his attitude towards her privileged background infuriated her, especially as she could never come up with any convincing argument to counter his accusations.

Anyway, he was a fine one to talk about subservience. Wasn't that just what he demanded of her in everything they did? That was why they were separated now, against all her wishes, for he had suddenly declared that he was going to go off and leave her, to take his own first proper steps to carry out their assignment. Not that she had given in too readily. They had quarrelled last night, in furious, hissing whispers. She was devastated when he announced his plan to take off alone for a few days, to make his survey of coastal gun defences, around the River Tyne. 'I thought we were working together!' she said, tearfully.

'I can do this better on my own,' he replied, with harsh frankness. 'It's a dangerous game. I don't want to be responsible for you as well as myself. I know what I'm doing.' When she continued to argue vehemently against his idea, he hurt her even more. 'You know, I wonder if you're not trying to con me altogether with this game. Did you mean any of it when you took the oath of allegiance back there? Or is your blue English blood winning the day after all? Would you rather we just sat out the war in this cosy little pub, humping away merrily till the victory bells ring out? And whose bells would you like them to be, eh?'

She had burst into floods of tears, and hastily he had gathered her to him, smothering her face against his chest in order to muffle the noise of her weeping. His cruel attack had left her too wounded to make an answer. He knew he had hurt her deeply, and his hands and lips were tender in their soothing, and his whispered words when he had calmed her grief. 'Listen, my love, I need you. I couldn't do anything, couldn't even *be* here, if it wasn't for you. It's like I said, we're accepted here now, we're a team. Keeping our base here is vital. Keeping Mary sweet is vital. As long as you're around, that's just how she'll be. That's why I've told her about me having to go off to see my wife's folks. To try to come to some sort of arrangement, for our future together. As long as we're around, or one of us is, she'll believe in us. She won't have time to sit down on her own and start thinking, maybe wondering.'

By now, Cissie's anger was dissipated, and feelings of a very different nature were stirring at his caresses. 'Besides, I mean what I said. It *is* tricky, creeping around about these coastal batteries. It'll be easier if I'm solo. In and out, a quick look-see then away. I don't want to risk you, darling. I'll ring here every night, as near six as I can. I shouldn't be more than four days away. I'm only doing around the Tyne, north and south. We'll leave the Wear and Tees till later.' His hands were gently tracing the contours of her yielding body. 'If you don't hear from me by phone, or don't receive a message for more than thirty-six hours, pack your bag and clear out. Make sure you're well away from the area before you send the signal. They'll issue instructions. You have the London contact.'

She clung fiercely to him. 'Oh God! Make sure you come back, please!' Later, she had held him again, more calmly, and said anxiously, 'You do believe in me, Sean? I'd never let you down. I love you.'

He nodded, smiling down at her solemn regard. 'You look after Mary. Keep her sweet, me darlin'.' His grin broadened, and she saw that humorous gleam in his eye once more. 'Fine-looking woman, isn't she, for her age?

And missing her man terribly, I reckon. Like I said, that sort need a man to look after. And to be looked after by. Know what I mean?' She had sworn and punched his arm hard enough to bring up a bruise as a souvenir.

Now she eyed Mary Price speculatively as she sipped at the mug of steaming cocoa. 'Just the two of us tonight,' she said. 'I hope there isn't a raid or anything.'

'Nay. Jerry's not bothered about Kingstaith. We're in far more peril with this gale. Bloomin' December! Reckon we'll have snow before Christmas.'

The brown eyes regarded Cissie solemnly, and Cissie sensed that the older woman was a little embarrassed. Clearly she wanted to broach a matter of some delicacy, and Cissie waited, catching something of her tension.

'Listen,' Mary began awkwardly, 'I hope you don't think I'm sticking my nose in, or speaking out of turn, like. But I hope you're not put out — about Captain Sean going off on his own, to see those relations of his. They aren't worth bothering about. Don't you let them get you down.'

Cissie managed to disguise her first great feeling of relief, then mastered her instinctive reaction of annoyance, at the woman's infernal cheek. What right had she to be so impertinent? Then she saw the concern, and indeed diffidence, in those great brown eyes, and she felt immediately guilty at her unkind thoughts. Sean was right. She didn't know the ways or manners of these country people. She grunted, looking suitably ingenuous and confessional. 'Yes,' she answered, as though girlishly reticent. 'I was a bit miffed, actually. We had a few words about it, as a matter of fact. I wasn't keen on him going.'

'He's doing it for you, you know. Trying to get things sorted, for you and him. Families can be a nuisance, sometimes.'

In spite of herself, Cissie once more felt that spark of irritation at this woman's presumption. Sean must have taken her far more into his confidence than he had let on during those late-night cosy chats of theirs in the kitchen.

Mary stood, reaching out to take her mug. 'Finished? There's a good girl. Come on, snuggle down. I'll put your lamp out, shall I?' She tucked in the covers about Cissie's shoulders, let her hand brush lightly across the fair locks at her brow, then bent and swiftly touched her lips to the golden curls about the temple. 'Night-night. God bless.'

Yet again, Cissie experienced another pang of guilt as she murmured an identical reply.

In her own room, Mary Price grimaced at the sight of her reflection in the narrow, smoky mirror of the dressing table, as she slipped off the dressing gown and turned back the sheets. Her gaze moved, as it did habitually every night before she climbed into bed, to the photograph standing there, darkly framed, of Bob's grinning, self-conscious face under the foreign-looking forage cap, the ugly buttoned-up collar of the battledress. She felt herself blushing hotly. Poor Bob. Automatically she prayed for his safety, wondered if he was in danger right now.

Unable to turn her thoughts from it, she recalled Sean's kiss, in the fire glow of the kitchen, two nights ago, the way his lips had pressed insistently on hers, the surrender of her open mouth, his arms squeezing her tightly, moulding her body to him, her yielded softness against his throbbing manliness. She could not disguise the nature of their embrace, the raw, sexual hunger of it. Sorry, Bob. She wanted to say it aloud. Her eyes stung with tears as she turned away and turned down the lamp by her cold bed.

She tried to empty her mind, and failed completely to tear her thoughts from the memory of the kiss, the feel of his hands and his body. Overlaid with images of Cissie's sweet young face, the fragrance of her, and the brush of that soft yellow hair against her mouth. Night after night she had tried not to lie there straining to listen for sounds from their room. Last night Sean had not lingered after closing time, quite rightly, but gone straight up to his bed and the waiting Cissie. When Mary had settled into bed, she was sure she had heard the sound of weeping. Don't let them quarrel! she had prayed, still overcome with guilt at that stolen kiss.

Even now, she could not escape it, nor the excitement mercilessly ensnaring her in its power. She was trembling. Despite the cold and the roaring gale outside, she could feel her body hot and damp under the bedclothes and the thick nightdress. She had a sudden urge to fling back the blankets, to free her body to the cold caress of the air. Tormentedly, her mind conjured the memories of the nights she had spent here with her husband, how her passion had rarely been met or satisfied by him, how she wept secretly with shame after she had shut herself away behind the locked door of the bathroom to ease that merciless hunger of her blood. She had all but conquered such secret vices as her marriage settled down to the habits and routines of all steady relationships. Now, all that painful sense of unfulfilment had returned to haunt her, with the added affliction that, this time, it was not Bob's kindly, unremarkable face that was the object of her fantasy.

* * *

Next morning Cissie was woken by Mary, bearing her breakfast on a tray. She could see at once that the landlady was agitated about something. 'I've just heard on the news. The Japanese attacked the American fleet. We're at war with them and all now! And the Americans are in on our side! Surely to God this'll end it now!' Her face was red with excitement, but all at once she was startled by the look on Cissie's sleep-marked features. The girl looked stunned, but not with joy. 'Surely that's good news, isn't it?' Mary floundered.

'Eh? Oh yes! Of course! The best!' Cissie sat up, quickly recovering herself. 'Sorry. I wasn't properly awake. I thought you'd heard something — about your husband.' She knew that Mary had been acutely worried at the recent news of the launching of another British offensive by the Eighth Army in the Western Desert. She scrambled up, out of the blankets, furious with herself at her moment of carelessness, struggling to match Mary's mood. 'What happened? Where was this attack on the Americans?'

'Yes.' Mary was immediately stricken with remorse. 'You're quite right, love. Here's me going on about what good news, when more folks have been killed. I should be ashamed of meself, shouldn't I? That's what war does for you, eh? Place called Pearl Harbour, I think,' she continued in answer to Cissie's enquiry. 'Not sure where that is. Might be in the paper. It hasn't come yet. It's always late these days, like everything else. You hop back into bed. Here. Let me wrap your dressing gown round your shoulders. Get this while it's still warm.'

Cissie discovered that the 'Yanks' had been dragged in willy-nilly on 'our' side, for Hitler had not waited but had declared war on the United States within hours of Japan's own declaration and its simultaneous treacherous attack. A mistake on the German leader's part possibly as costly as that which was only just turning into glimmers of doubt in some military minds: his opening of the Eastern Front against Russia, back in June. The American President, Roosevelt, had long been antagonistic towards Nazi aggression, but there was a considerable body of opinion in the USA that, in the wake of Pearl Harbour, felt that the war which had been going on for the last two years in Europe was still Europe's affair. However, in his

261

megalomaniac zeal to be centre of world stage, the Führer had flung down the iron gauntlet.

The *Daily Mail* was delivered every morning to the inn, but Cissie was determined to read the reports in some of the other newspapers. Mary was already working in the bar when Cissie came down, dressed and ready for outdoors. 'I'll walk down to the shop, get a *Telegraph*, I think. Anything you want?'

Mary shook her head. 'No, you're all right, love. The lad'll be bringing the order up later. I can order the *Daily Telegraph*, regular, if you want. There's not much call for them posh papers round here,' she answered, smiling. '*Daily Mirror*'s more to folks' taste in these parts. You know. The one with that cartoon in. That lass with your name. Jane. I bet that's why you don't like it, isn't it?'

'No, of course not. I told you. I've been Cissie to everyone ever since I can remember.' When they had first arrived in Kingstaith, she had explained to anyone who would listen how the pet name had come about. 'I think it started with my brother. He used to call me Sis, or Sissy, when we were little. It just stuck. And anyway, I like it much better than plain Jane.'

But the news of most significance to Cissie,

when she was settled in the small 'best room', at the rear, along the corridor, and next to the kitchen, was not that of the perfidy of the Japanese, which covered the front page and a great deal of those inside, but the smallest and most discreet of announcements, among the Personal columns of the inside back page. The bar was deserted this early weekday afternoon, and Mary was keeping her company. She heard the half-stifled exclamation, and looked up from her woman's magazine. 'Good God! Cissie, love! What on earth's wrong?'

Cissie felt the wave of giddiness; the colour drained from her face. Mary had risen, seeing the ashen complexion and glazed look. 'What's the matter?' she repeated.

Cissie drew a great gulping breath and made a furious effort to gain control of her emotions. 'No, I'm all right,' she murmured faintly, waving a hand as though to keep Mary from touching her. 'Just a bit of a shock, that's all. Someone I knew, out in India.'

'Oh, dear! Bad news, is it?'

The blonde head shook. 'No, no! Not really. Silly of me. It's just that — we were quite close, sort of. Long time ago.' She strove to rally herself, but it was too late to divert the older woman's keen attention. 'A boy I knew. We were just kids, really.'

'What's happened? You said it's not bad news. What . . . ?'

Helplessly, unable to think of a further lie in the face of Mary's concern, Cissie pointed to the brief paragraph.

The wedding took place yesterday at 11 a.m. of Mrs Margaret Dean (née Goresby-Harrington, widow of Ft Lt Matthew Dean) and Ft Lt Nigel Humphreys, at the parish church of St John, Highcombe Down.

18

'Here. Try a drop of this. Damned good stuff. Hope my supply lasts out. Can't get hold of it for love or money these blasted days!' Sir Roland Goresby-Harrington poured a generous measure into Nigel's proffered glass, and the rich fume of the spirit seemed to penetrate his head. He reached over at his father-in-law's invitation, and selected a Havana from the wooden box on the desk. 'So! How do you think married life will suit you?' Sir Roland asked, in an ostensibly jocular tone.

Nigel, however, had a sense of unease. Like the vintage brandy, life was having a heady effect on him. He thought of responding in similar jolly vein that two days was rather a brief interlude on which to make a judgement, but decided that would not be an appropriate answer. 'Very well, sir.' He hoped he was putting the right amount of enthusiasm into his reply. 'I never thought — I realize how extremely fortunate I am. I hope you know how much — I want you to know I think the world of Midge. I can't believe I've been so lucky. I haven't come down to earth yet. I don't think I ever will.'

Oh God! That sounded wrong as well. What did he mean by 'lucky'? Lucky that he had bumped into those night fighters, got poor old Mat wiped out while not suffering a scratch himself? Lucky that he had got Midge up the spout, practically first shot, whereas again poor old Mat had been trying for two years?

'You'd better, and damned quick, young feller!' There was no hint of humour in Sir Roland's voice now. 'She takes a lot of careful handling, as I'm sure you've already learnt.' He paused and blew a cloud of blue fragrance towards the ceiling, where it hung in the lamp light of the study. 'Tell me something. I want you to be perfectly honest with me. Were you and Midge . . . Were you seeing each other — you know what I mean — before Dean's death?'

'Oh, no! I can assure you . . . ' Nigel hesitated, suddenly assailed by the alarming thought that that might not be the right answer, either. 'Well, I mean we . . . I was greatly attracted to her — who wouldn't be? We got on well. But I would never have . . . never tried to come between them.'

'Well, I'll be brutally frank with you, Nigel. We never approved of the marriage, as I'm sure you're aware. It was as much a case of kicking over the traces as anything. The main motivation was to spite us, I'm damned sure of it! She was barely out of school, didn't know what the hell she wanted. Then the war was brewing up. She just went off the rails, if you ask me. And Dean was the first young feller that took her fancy. He was just joining up, going into the Air Force. Flyer. He wanted to be a fighter pilot, but didn't make the grade. He probably thought he was going to land himself in clover when Midge came along. Sorry to sound so unfeeling but I believe in being honest. A spade's a spade, eh?

'What I'm saying, old boy, is that we're prepared to give you a go. Make the best of the way things have turned out. Hope it all works out for the best. Good background, solid colonial stuff. Look forward to meeting your folks when this nonsense is all over, what? At least *you* can sit a horse, eh? Ride to hounds! Poor young Dean was entirely out of his depth. And couldn't handle a spirited filly like our Midge! Not a chance! We told her it would never last! Of course, didn't mean it to end the way it did, mind you.

'Never mind. All in the past. Now it's up to you. I'll give you fair warning. You'll have to keep her on a tight rein. She's always been a headstrong gel, needs a firm hand. We'll try to make sure you don't get bent or blasted by Jerry. I've had a word with Tubby Bleaseby. You're to join Air Staff. Air Commodore Harris. Know him? He's just come back from America. About to be made up to Air Vice-Marshal. He headed the RAF delegation out there. Chances are he's going to be head of Bomber Command any day now. Chap of your experience. Just the kind of feller he's looking for.'

'Thank you, sir.' My experience? Nigel thought. Ten missions, two near prangs, and three cock-ups. And for a grand finale bringing home the body of my shot-up navigator and leaping into bed with his wife the week after we buried him. Could any tale be more surreal?

He found it hard to think so, when, a couple of hours later, he lay in a chilly four-poster bed in an even chillier bedroom known as the 'Blue Room', in an eighteenth-century mansion, and watched the daughter of the house approaching him wearing nothing but a big smile, and with nipples standing out like light switches with the cold. 'For God's sake, you effete colonial wimp!' She knelt over him, dragging back the sheets, ignoring the chill atmosphere as she plucked at the buttons of his pyjama jacket, then yanked the cord of his pants, before stripping the garments from him. She straddled him, and he gasped at the touch of her icy fingers as they delved, and captured him. 'I'll show you how to keep warm, you foolish boy. And when you've had *your* fun, we'll see about lighting *my* fire, my little chimney sweep!'

★　★　★

'Bet this is a bit different from your usual set-up, eh, milady?' Ginge was sitting up in bed, watching Midge as she drew on the artificial silk stockings, and clipped them to the ribbons of the suspenders. She was well aware of his scrutiny, and made quite a performance of dressing, just as she had when discarding her fashionable clothes two hours earlier. The room was shabby. The cheap old furniture had been repainted several times and was chipped. The bed squeaked, the bed linen was of dubious quality and cleanliness, the taped-up windows were encrusted with the London dirt. They were in a first-floor bedroom of a dingy old house close to King's Cross, where most of the neighbouring properties were put to similar casual use, though perhaps more commercially motivated. 'Every other gaff's a bleedin' knockin' shop,' Ginge Evans told her cheerfully.

'Good heavens! And here's me giving it

away for free. Or would you like me to chip in for the hire of the room?'

He chuckled. 'No, I reckon I can stand the tab for this dump! Bit different from your pad in Knightsbridge, though, ain't it? Not that I'm ever gonna get the chance to compare, of course.'

'Quite right. You certainly aren't. I absolutely daren't take you there. We have a commissionaire who misses nothing, believe me! Talk about the eyes and ears of the world!' She grinned. 'I'd hate to give you ideas above your station. Anyway, you know how I get all worked up when I'm slumming!'

'I certainly do. I should think they heard you across at the station. Probably thought it was the Flying Scotsman leaving from platform nine!'

'Are my seams straight?' She turned, and presented him with a splendid view of her long limbs.

'Do you have to go? I've still got the room for three more hours. I reckon we could manage another gallop, what do you say, sweetheart?'

'I say thanks but no thanks. Honestly, Ginge, I'd love to, but I'm definitely running late as it is. Nigel seems to be doing bugger all up at that Ministry HQ of yours, so he's never late. He'll be home already. Let's hope he's not wondering what I'm up to.'

'Oh yes? And just what *are* you up to, as far as he's concerned? What is it this time? Dressmaker? Massage? Visit to the doc again?'

Her voice was muffled as she drew the slip over her head, then stepped into the dark, narrow skirt and fastened it at the waist. 'Running out of excuses, you 'orrible little man. Which is why we'll have to forego our little assignations for a while, my randy little Red. You can count this afternoon as your Christmas box. We've got to go down to the country again for the holidays. Needless to say, Nigel's not on duty until next week. Wouldn't think there was a bloody war on, would you?'

He laughed sourly, and clambered out of bed, dragging the eiderdown clear and draping it round him. 'There isn't for your sort, my lovely. How's he getting on with your old man? Doing better than poor old Matty, is he?' He watched her keenly as he spoke, waiting to see if there was any reaction to her late husband's name. There was none that his keen eye could notice.

'Oh yes. He can sit a horse. That makes him halfway home at least with Daddy. And a few-hundred-acre tea estate in India's a sight more respectable than a piddling quarter-acre garden in the wilds of Derbyshire.'

'Well, good job he can ride *something*, I suppose!' Evans chuckled lewdly. 'I know one little mare the poor sod can't handle at all, eh, milady?'

She finished tidying up her hair and make-up, then pulled on the tight-fitting costume jacket and buttoned it up. She turned from the divided mirrors of the small dressing table, after arranging the small hat at a chic angle on the back of her skull. 'So I guess I should say thank you for the gallop, what? I'll let you know when we can next exercise, all right? Through the usual channels?'

She picked up the dark fur coat and held it out to him. 'Come on, you peasant!' she said, when he made no move to take it.

'Oh, yes! Sorry, your ladyship! Do forgive me.' His grin widened as he let the eiderdown slip from his shoulders and stood naked to take her coat. She turned her back and he held it so that she could slip it on. He felt its sleek, cold silkiness against the front of his body, and he pulled her close, his chin resting on her shoulder, his lips nuzzling at her fragrant neck. She shivered responsively. She turned, then pursed her lips for a fleeting kiss. 'Sorry, but I can't mess up my lipstick. Have a splendid holiday. Will you be on duty?'

'I expect so.' He was still grinning, his brightness a challenge to her.

'How's your skipper? Settled in now? One of the boys?'

'Too true! A *real* flyer! Flight sergeant, common as muck. Just like me! Not a ruddy officer on board now. We might even make it through the tour now we've got rid of your Nigel!'

'How many is it now?' Her tone was as casual as if she were enquiring about a cricket score, and he appreciated her deliberate coolness. That's right! he thought. No big deal. It's all a fucking game, and that's just the way to play it. She was just like he was, however vast the divide in their social ranking. What a dame!

'Five to go. But we're not counting.' He nodded down to her loins. 'Just like you and the sprog. Does your old man know? I mean your dad. Sorry! *Daddy!*'

'He's got a pretty good idea, I think. He's not totally a fool. I don't think he believes it was entirely young love that got me rushing up to the altar with Nigel. Even we toffs can count, you know.'

'Isn't there just a chance he might think it's Matty's?'

'What? When I foal almost a year to the day after Mat's death? As I said, he can count, certainly up to nine — and a bit beyond!'

'Do you know whose it is?' Ginge asked, with bold directness.

She didn't bat an eyelid and answered at once. 'Of course, you silly man. It's Nigel's. My beloved husband's. Who else's could it be?'

'Let's hope you've got a ginger nob somewhere in your blue blood then, eh?'

She bent forward and gave him a last light peck on the cheek. 'I'm sure we have. We put it about rather a lot in the past, I believe. Now be good, and don't prang that bomber of yours, you hear?' She returned the look he had directed at her, and nodded down at his penis. 'It mightn't look very impressive at the moment, but that's some secret weapon you've got there, Sergeant. Merry Christmas.'

★   ★   ★

Approximately three and a half thousand miles to the south-east, and sitting almost on the Tropic of Cancer, some thirty degrees south of where Midge Dean and her adulterous lover had wished each other a merry Christmas, Lt Charles Pride muttered the same time-honoured festive greeting to himself, with far less enthusiasm and meaning. He was sitting in his khaki drill shorts and nothing else, and the sweat was glistening on just about every exposed inch of his skin, in spite of the languid efforts of the punka wallah, a diminutive boy of ten or eleven years, who was sitting by the open doorway of the small room. The cord which led up to the fan made of woven reeds was looped round the boy's big toe. The skinny leg bent and straightened, bent and straightened, the calloused bare heel scraping softly along the dusty stone floor, thus agitating the mat-like structure suspended from the ceiling in the middle of the room. The subsequent feeble currents of hot air felt like someone opening the door of an oven.

Charlie was feeling sorry for himself He had stayed in the mess for a few drinks after he came off duty, but there was no mood of celebration; rather the gloom of impending, unavoidable disaster. Everyone was awaiting news of the fall of Hong Kong to the Japanese. It could come tomorrow, on Christmas Day itself. The garrison had held out far longer than anyone had expected. Cut off as they were, it was impossible to get help through to them, and Charlie was well aware that the feeling for some time had been that the station was expendable. But even more alarming was the way the Nips were advancing through the Malayan jungle, threatening the Burmese capital, and the fortress of Singapore itself.

Charlie had spent a considerable time up at the frontier, before all the fun had started, and had considered himself lucky to land a plum staff job back here at HQ. The very day he was packing, the envy of all his brothers-in-arms, the news had come that Cissie's ship was overdue, posted missing. He was even more grateful that he was in the city, and spent every hour he could pressing the shipping line and the government offices for information. Bound to be all right, he kept telling himself, the dread growing coldly inside him with each passing day.

He had been startled one day when a slim, sari-clad figure appeared in the doorway of the tiny cupboard they called his office, and there stood Rani Mishala, Cissie's former armah. Charlie recognized her right away, even though he found himself shocked at how well groomed and presentable she was. His corporal was treating her like a lady, and she was acting as such, he thought. But then, suddenly, she gave a great wail of grief, and was beating her shapely breast and crying with a force that brought several people running with avid curiosity to see what all the noise was about. 'Please! Please! My dear Rani! Don't distress yourself. Come on now.'

She was in his arms, they were clinging together, and, to his horror, he felt his own eyes moistening with tears. 'Please — leave us,' he managed to say thickly. 'This is an old friend — a friend of my wife's — of the family.'

'Oh my God! How could this happen? Oh, my little mem!'

Her black hair was fixed in a neat bun. He could feel it under his nose, and he breathed in the rich, aromatic scent of her. Exotic, and shamefully arousing, he found. He had taken time off, walked from the HQ building to the Alexandra, a hotel and restaurant where whites and the better class of Indians met with perfect ease, took tea together. Some even played tennis at the hotel sports club, and the very liberated even shared the swimming pool — males only, of course, as far as the indigenous were concerned.

That was how their relationship had started, in those shared tears of mourning for someone they had both dearly loved. Rani was now working for some company, in their office, something to do with transporting goods, both nationally and internationally. 'I'm doing very well,' she admitted, with shy pride. 'They think very highly of me. And I owe it all to you, Mr Charlie. Oh yes! I know that. You encouraged me, at the first. I would never have obtained my diploma. You put me on the way. I will never forget you.'

They met for meals and for trips to the cinema. Times were changing, at least in the big cities like Calcutta. Things were much more free and easy. The races were mixing, and the sexes, too, and not just the Tommies and the whores who plied their painted trade in the red light district. Good girls, educated girls, of good background — like Rani, Charlie was pleased to acknowledge. His eyes misted when he thought how Cissie would have been so happy at his advanced liberalism. He had always advocated it, he could reassure himself. He grew more and more fond of the Indian girl, and reliant on her to lift his mood and his ego. He liked her kind of naïve deference, the way she looked up to him, hung on his every word, when they discussed the grave world situation, and the ever-growing threat on India's doorstep. He was able to do her a favour. Her 'cousin-brother' had joined up, was part of the Fifth Indian Brigade. The family were concerned as to where he would be posted. Charlie bent the rules a little, disclosed classified information, to let them at least know the worst if not to put their minds at rest. The Fifth was to be part of a desperate stop-gap measure to try and save Rangoon, and stem the rapid

Japanese advance. 'I shouldn't be telling you this,' he said, with a winning smile. 'You could get me shot.'

She was extremely grateful. Those wonderful dark eyes of hers glowed with warmth and tenderness. She reached up and let her lips touch gently against his, and he felt the powerful stirring of his desire at the nearness of her supple body, so beautifully enhanced by the colourful silk of her native costume. She's beautiful! he thought, and it struck him like a revelation.

He had no intention of their becoming lovers. It happened in spite of those intentions, good as they were. And it was wonderful, and shameful, too, for Charlie was saddened to have to admit to himself that he had never known such sexual excitement and satisfaction in his brief interlude of wedded bliss with his beloved wife. He had loved Cissie — loved her still, though now, like a good many of his colleagues, he had an Indian mistress. Whom he loved, too, he was also forced to admit, and not just for that hot and churning brown body so trustfully abandoned to him, so capable of stirring him to hitherto unimagined heights of passion and fulfilment.

He loved the way she was so interested in every aspect of him, of his work, his views on what was happening, and what would happen, in the world. His solutions — and those of his peers — to all those dire problems. He had access to a great deal of privileged information, and he revelled in his role of pundit and keeper of secrets when he shared it with her. After all, she was entirely trustworthy, otherwise he would never dream of being so careless with military confidences. And he always warned her not to pass on anything he disclosed.

His gloom was already lifting at the sight of her slim silhouette, which appeared against the fierce light of the doorway. She dismissed the young servant at once, and threw herself into Charlie's waiting arms, her mouth seeking his with a hot eagerness that more than matched his own. Such urgent business demanded immediate attention. It was much later, when he was sitting with knees drawn up in the small tin bathtub, and she was kneeling devotedly beside him, squeezing the sponge to allow the cool droplets to trickle over his pale shoulders and curving back, that she was able to turn her mind to other pressing matters. 'What on earth is going to happen to us, Charlie? How are we going to stop those damned Nippons from invading us? Haven't we got any more forces we can call on to help us? What about East Africa?

Can't they send reinforcements to us? Or the navy! What the hell are they doing to help us?'

He began to talk, and she listened avidly, unmindful of the way his hands were playing with her breasts, and the tingling arousal caused by his caresses. After all, they were *her* weapons of war, and she was using them to full advantage. Her new masters would be well pleased with the information she was extracting.

19

In spite of the exigencies of war, Christmas at the Ship Inn was truly festive. Mary had got hold of an extra barrel 'or two' of ale, from dubious sources, delivered before dawn two days before Christmas Eve. 'Santa's early this year!' Sean chuckled as he helped her stack them in the cellar in the freezing lamplight. Afterwards, he sat at ease around the kitchen fire, which had been banked with sea-coal and was soon revived to a cheery red glow, flinging out the heat over their companionably stretched-out limbs. Mary's slender ankles showed palely above a fetching pair of embroidered slippers and below the thin lace of her nightdress peeping from beneath her soft pink housecoat. Though a light silk scarf, knotted turban-like at the front, bound her black hair, no trace remained of the metal curlers which had confined her locks during the hours of rest.

She tried not to blush at the thoughts racing through her outrageous mind, as she peeped with surreptitious pleasure at him over the rim of her steaming tea mug. He was such a fine figure of a man, lounging there in those old corduroys of his, his toes curling in the thick grey stockings. Army issue, she guessed. The striped shirt was unbuttoned in a deep V at his chest, the collarless rim carelessly unfastened also at the base of his thick column of a neck, the sleeves rolled up above the elbows, to display the muscled manliness of his forearms, the fire glow highlighting the light russet, fine hairs covering them. The glorious tightness of the curls that crowned his head seemed to spark with the gold-red unruliness she found so attractive.

The sudden memory of Bob's thin brown hair, receding already at the temples, the feel of it through her fingers when he lay with his sweating head on her bosom, was a cruel stab of conscience, as was the fever of excitement beating through her at the proximity of her lightly clad body to Sean's powerful, relaxed frame. Instinctively, she drew her legs away a little from his. 'I hope we haven't woke Cissie with our goings-on. I wonder if I should just pop up and see if she's awake. She might fancy a cuppa, if she is.'

'No, Mary. You stay where you are. You spoilt her far too much while I was away. She told me. Breakfast in bed, bringing her cocoa at night, tucking her in. She's a big girl now, you know.'

He gave his easy laugh, and let his large hand fall carelessly across Mary's knee. She felt its weight, and warmth, like a brand across her flesh, felt every inch of her pulsate in response to it. She had to swallow hard to find a voice to reply. 'Oh, I feel so sorry for the poor lass. All on her own here. She never seems to hear from her family. And there's no one here . . . ' Mary's voice died away uncertainly. She felt again the great struggle going on within her. Would she be betraying a confidence? Had Cissie already mentioned it to Captain Sean, or didn't she want him to know?

'What is it, Mary, love? Something's bothering you, isn't it? I can tell. Anything I can help you with?'

The brown eyes were large with worry, yet she could not turn away from his steady gaze. She felt helpless, the colour flooding up from her neck. 'It's just . . . while you were away . . . I don't know if I should . . . didn't Cissie tell you?'

The feeling of helplessness increased as she continued to gaze at him. She felt him take her by the wrist, felt his firm hand caressing hers. 'What is it, Mary? Tell me.'

The brown eyes were beseeching now. 'Please — don't say anything — I mean, if she hasn't . . . maybe she doesn't want you to know. She said it was nothing, just someone she knew ... p'raps it's someone she was fond of when she was, you know, just a kid.'

Sean was all gentle patience. 'I swear I won't say a word. Just between you and me till you say otherwise.'

She rose and he was still holding her hand, and his smile seemed to pass right through her like a gentle caress. He released her and she went across to the old-fashioned bureau, which stood in the dark passageway between the kitchen and parlour and the bar. She came back with a small clipping from a newspaper and passed it over to him. Her face showed the doubt and anxiety she was experiencing. 'I don't mean to be nosy or anything. Promise me you won't tell her — say anything, please? It's just — she looked so upset. White as a sheet, she was. When she saw it. She just said it was someone she'd known — quite close, she said. An old sweetheart, I expect.'

He read it quickly, handed it back. 'Stow it away again, will you? We'll say nothing. Like you say, an old flame, eh?' She gave a grateful smile, turned to replace the clipping, when he caught hold of her arm and pulled her round to him. 'Hey! Thanks, Mary, dear. You're a good friend. I appreciate it.' He drew her close, kissed her lightly on the forehead. She was trembling. Suddenly his arms were round her, enfolding her as they had before, and their mouths were joined, their bodies pressed together, the kiss one of mutual passion.

She was still in his arms, leaning in to him, gasping. 'Don't! You mustn't! I shouldn't — let you — '

'You're a woman, Mary! A *real* woman! I'm sorry, but I can't help myself.'

Somehow, she managed to push against him, to release herself from his embrace. 'No, no! We can't. That poor girl! Things will work out for you. There now. You go up to her. I've got . . . to get on.' She turned and almost ran from him.

★ ★ ★

The small bar was crowded on Christmas Eve, the air thick with pungent pipe smoke. Sean and Mary were busy behind the bar. Cissie hovered awkwardly, but she was very conscious of being out of place in that masculine sanctuary, and was glad enough to retreat through to the warmth of the kitchen, where the long table was covered in the cold foods Mary had managed to prepare for her customers. Cissie couldn't help feeling piqued at her alienation from the boozy jollity; an alienation she realized, to her chagrin, that was not shared by Mary, the only female in that noisy throng. As for Sean, he was, of course, loving every minute of it, fitting in as though he had been born into it. In fact, his own native community was probably very similar to this small fishing village, she surmised, which did nothing to ease her own sense of isolation.

'Don't you mind? All those men?' Cissie asked, when Mary, red-faced and still laughing at some ribald remark, came along the passage to begin carrying through the plates of sandwiches and pies. Mary stared at her in puzzlement. 'You know! You the only woman, among all those men. Why don't their wives ever come in? Or complain about them spending their time in here?'

Mary laughed. Her rosiness owed something to the several port wines she had taken, as well as her efforts as landlady. '*I'd* be in a bad way if they did now, wouldn't I? It's our livelihood. Nay, the wives have better things to do, love. Specially tonight. They've got plenty to occupy them — giving the place a good clean, getting all the stuff ready for tomorrow. They'll all have managed something special for the Christmas dinner. Goose or duck or chicken — there's still plenty of fowls about round here. Even if they do cost the earth! There's some folks are far too greedy these days.'

And I wonder if *you've* been giving any beer away, or dropped your prices in honour of the season! Cissie thought bitchily. She had the grace to feel a little ashamed of her meanness, but, really! Since Sean had come back from his trip up the coast, he and their hostess had become thicker than ever, so that, at times, particularly on this special evening, Cissie could not resist the pangs of jealousy which assailed her. We have to keep her sweet! Sean kept telling her. Well, he was positively dripping honey over her. And Mary was responding in a manner far from becoming for a married lady whose husband was away fighting for his country.

The enormity of her own hypocrisy made Cissie's ear tips burn. How dare she accuse poor Mary? She who had betrayed poor Charlie from the very beginning, by marrying him when she had known in her heart she did not really love him. And cuckolded him practically from the moment she had stepped aboard the *Star of Indus*, and long before she had met the love of her life, Sean Mullins. Contritely, she made a great effort to be extra sweet to Mary. She even stifled her involuntary flash of annoyance when Mary said casually, 'Bring those plates along to the bar, will you, love?' and obediently turned herself into a skivvy to cater to the roaring, crude clientele, who hooted and cheered and practically stripped her with their glances when she followed Mary into their midst.

Christmas Day was, by contrast, pleasantly private, for the pub was, of course, closed. In spite of not retiring until the early hours of Christmas morning, Sean was, as always, up and about before Cissie had woken, rousing her by his appearance with a laden tray, on which, along with the breakfast things, lay two wrapped gifts. One was a necklace, strung with small local seashells and coral. 'It's lovely!' She sat up in bed, bent her head and moved the hair from her neck so that he could fasten it for her. It scratched her skin a little. She would have to wear it over a blouse, perhaps. The other packet was a small book, *Poems of Sentiment*, by Ella Wheeler Wilcox, bound in soft calf leather, and beautifully illustrated. The date of publication was 1910.

'It's lovely!' she repeated. He had written *With all my love, Sean* across the flyleaf. 'I'll treasure it always. I love you.'

'Hey, careful!' He clutched at the tray as she launched herself at him to kiss him. 'Wait!' she squealed, scrambling out of bed and diving underneath. She pulled out a large and lumpy parcel. 'I was going to wait. We always used to open our gifts after lunch. But here.' She pulled a mock-rueful face. 'It's not much, but honestly, what is there to buy round here?'

It was a knitted sweater, a blue Guernsey, or 'Ganzey', as the locals called it. 'See? It's got the special stitching that shows it was made here. All the villages have different ways of stitching. Do you like it?' He was pulling it over his head. The red-gold curls came thrusting through, and his face beamed.

'Perfect! Talk about fitting in, eh? I'm really one of the boys now.' He strode over to the door, calling as he went. 'Mary! Come and have a look at this. I'm one of your bonny fisher lads now, aren't I?' He went out and Cissie heard Mary's little shriek of laughing protest, then he came back, shepherding her through the doorway, she still protesting, and taking care not to upset the contents of the tray she was holding.

'It's the first time I've been woken up by a strange man in my bedroom bringing me breakfast in bed!' The two women stood gazing at each other. Mary's cotton night-dress, a little more substantial than Cissie's satin garment, was still prettily embroidered about the short sleeves and bosom and ankle-length hem with a thin band of lace.

'Hop into bed, the pair of you, come on!'

He snatched the tray from Mary's hands and put it on the dresser, before steering her firmly by the shoulders. 'Go on! In you get, this instant! My own private harem, eh, girls? I've never known a Christmas like it, have you? Have I died and gone to heaven, me darlin's?'

Looking just slightly embarrassed, Mary and Cissie found themselves obeying, sitting side by side under the covers, which Sean tucked around them. 'Do you not think there could be room for just one more little 'un in the middle there?' They squealed in giggling, scandalized protest when he made to follow up his request with action.

★　★　★

'I want you to take the transmitter. Go along the cliff top, the path along to Brackengrave Harbour. The ruins of the old cottage. Send this signal.'

Cissie was staring at him. 'On my own?' She had never used the radio. Sean had always been the one to make contact. 'Wouldn't it be better if we both went? One of us could keep watch.'

'No. I have to go into Whitby. I'm meeting someone. I'll be away all night. This message is vital. It has to go tomorrow. The seaward side of the ruin is a great spot. You're off the path. No one can spot you from the land. And if there's any fishing boats out they'll be too far away to see anything. Just set up and send these figures. Dismantle and pack up. Easy as falling off a log.'

She was still staring at him in dismay. 'Why can't I come with you? Who is it you're meeting? We're in this together. What if something should happen? We ought to stick together, Sean.'

'Why do you always have to argue?' She could see he was struggling to keep his temper with her. He had been showing increasing bouts of irritation with her since the Christmas period. 'Let me remind you, *lieutenant*' — his German pronunciation of her rank was starkly emphatic — 'that I am the senior officer in this operation. We are not love's young dream, sheltering from the harsh realities of the war. That's our cover, Frau Pride, just in case you've forgotten that fact!'

She recoiled from his controlled fury, staring wide-eyed, her face pale, before she flung herself on the bed and burst into anguished sobbing.

'That's right! Let Mary hear you wailing, you spoilt little brat! So much for your oath of loyalty and your dedication to the cause.'

She thrust her face deep into the pillows, to

stifle the gut-wrenching groans and sobs of her despair. Her frame shook with the violence of her smothered grief. She felt physically sick at the lash of his cruelty. All she had done was to beg to be allowed to share the danger, but he had repulsed her, declaring his intention to go off yet again, on another solo mission, this time south to the area of Middlesbrough and the River Tees. He had stayed away for a whole week last time. 'Mary's going to start getting suspicious of these trips of yours,' Cissie muttered, like a sullen child. 'Leaving me alone with her. There's nothing for me to do here except go for walks. And it's usually too bloody freezing or wet, or blowing a gale! Unless you'd like me to turn myself into a barmaid, like her! Watching all those oafs swilling beer and ogling me the whole time!'

'Heaven forbid you should ever dirty your precious hands with a drop of real work, me darlin'! That would be a real turn-up for the books, would it not?'

Mary! Mary! His precious Mary! She was growing heartily sick of the way he was constantly singing the landlady's praises. And as for those great cow eyes of hers! She was about as skilful as a six-year-old at hiding her feelings for 'Captain Sean'. Cissie was frequently ashamed of the bitterness of her thoughts towards the older woman, but it was sickening the way they simpered and flirted with each other — sickening, too, the invidious jealousy that was eating away inside Cissie, despite the countless times she urged herself not to be so stupidly juvenile.

Now, she had a chance to prove herself to him. Was that what he needed? By asking her to carry out this assignment, of sending this information through to Germany, he would have proof of her active commitment to his cause. But hadn't she proved that already, over and over, in the weeks they had been here, under cover? The very fact that she was with him still, had not betrayed him to her fellow countrymen, was evidence enough of her loyalty, to him, if not to the Fatherland.

Her feelings about that were cloudier than ever. Sometimes she had thought, when she saw these fishermen, and their hardy, hard-faced women, that she had far more in common with Heinz and Helga Schmidt, and Inge Langer, and William Joyce. Or was that merely class-consciousness operating? No doubt the fisherfolk of Germany, the miners and the labourers, were no different from those she was living among at present. But the daily accounts she was reading in the papers, carefully censored though they surely were, of the fortunes, or misfortunes, of the war, particularly the nightly bombing raids, disturbed her conscience more and more. Mary had told her of the children who had been evacuated to the rural villages of the surrounding area from towns like Middlesbrough or Newcastle, where homes had been destroyed, in some cases parents killed. 'I'm only glad our boys are doing the same to them Germans!' Mary declared righteously, while Cissie suffered more and more from her conflicting emotions.

Sean had already encoded the message she was to send into its surface meaninglessness of letter and number groups. Cissie thought it must be important information about the coast defences he had just been investigating around the mouth of the River Tees. She was surprised that he was trusting her with this task, the first time he had done so. They had transmitted very few messages from their new home territory. 'It's too good a cover to rouse any suspicions,' he had argued. 'Not that I'd guess there was much monitoring going on around these parts. But you never know.' When she reminded him of the risk now, he said, 'You can transmit this in a matter of minutes. Unless you've forgotten all you've learnt! Then you get packed up and away. Be back here fast as you can. You can leave when I do, in the morning. Tell Mary you want a good long hike, clear your head. It'll do you good. You can walk down as far as Runswick, then make your way back. Wait until dusk. It's dark so damned early these days. Don't leave it too late. Back to the inn for tea, and you can sit and warm your tootsies in front of the fire, and have a cosy little chat with Mary. A real heart-to-heart, eh? And I bet my ears will be burning all night long, if I know anything about you women!'

'Yes! You'd love that, wouldn't you? To think we'd spend all night chatting away about you. You should be so lucky!'

He winked at her, and grinned infuriatingly. 'I bet Mary wouldn't mind, the darlin' wee girl!'

20

The January gloom was so thick it was almost dark, even though it was only four in the afternoon. The ruined pier of Brackengrave Harbour 200 feet below her was hardly visible through the slanting drive of sleet cutting across from the north-east. It was a sleet which was thickening by the minute, and would soon be falling as snow. Cissie could see the white tumble of the breakers marking the weather side of the crumbled breakwater. A detachment of Royal Engineers had come and blown it up back in 1940, when a German invasion was expected any and every day. They had also put down wooden and wire tank traps on the short slope of beach, and several solid concrete blocks. There was a 'pillbox' concrete gun emplacement not many yards from where she stood, sunk danger-ously into the lip of the sandstone cliff, which, according to the locals, would end up splattered on the beach below within a few more months. 'Cliff's fallin' away like rotten teeth,' the fishermen had assured the newcomers. They still talked with morbid pleasure of the time nearly eighty years ago, when a whole street of the old village cottages had slid into the sea one night.

The pillbox was not occupied. It had been empty almost from the first. The Home Guard had used it for a while, but it was too damp and prone to sudden leaks, and they had swiftly given it up. Now it served as a temporary refuge for the more adventurous courting couples. They would need to be pretty desperate, thought Cissie, to be about and amorous on this raw January afternoon, though she had checked it, just in case, squeezing through the barbed-wire fence and glancing in from the three steps that led down to it. Black water gleamed in the dimness, and it smelt of damp earth, underlaid with a faint lavatorial odour, which had made her retreat in haste.

Such thoughts reminded her of her present discomfort with her bladder, but she sternly rejected this sign of nervous tension. She was afraid, she didn't mind admitting it. After all, unlikely as it was that she should be caught, it was a hanging or a shooting offence if she was. Even as she crouched against the old stone wall of the cottage, and quickly rigged up the transmitter, sheltering it as best she could from the elements, she was still considering whether to alter the message the paper safe in the pocket of her waterproofs contained. Just a few numbers jumbled, the odd letter or two changed, and the information would be useless: gobbledygook, which nobody could decipher. Sean hadn't bothered to tell her what the message was, only that it was 'vital'. 'The less you know the better,' he had told her dramatically. She hadn't been scared when they were whispering in bed last night. It was different alone here, in this freezing gloom of isolation.

She had a sudden urge, not to urinate, but to weep. What the hell had brought her to this, crouched on a cliff top, in a country that was as alien to her as Germany, the besotted slave of a lover who believed he could make her do anything for him? A lover who might well be right! she reflected miserably. Angry at the tears which did, indeed, blur her vision, she knelt, feeling the cold seep through the knees of her overalls, and savagely pulled the paper from the folds of her over jacket. Maybe she would make a mistake anyway! she thought defiantly as her frozen fingers clicked out the groups of digits and letters. But she was careful, painstakingly slow, to ensure that no errors were made, and her tears spilled over at her own merciless condemnation of her treason.

She switched to the receiver and waited for the acknowledgement, which seemed to take an age to come. When it did, she hastily packed away the gear in the rucksack. She rose, feeling the stiffness and cold in her joints, and stumbled off through the soaking dead grass, passing the fence with its Ministry of Defence skull and crossbones warning, sealing off the precipitous descent down to the deserted remains of Brackengrave — a thriving harbour in the last century, thanks to the then flourishing iron mining.

She was weary, looking forward to a long soak in a hot bath, a good meal, and Mary's tender ministrations. Cissie had parted from Sean outside the Ship soon after dawn that morning. He had made his way to the station at the top of the bank; she had turned down the steep cobbled road to the clustered cottages of 't'au'd town', as the villagers called it, by the miniature harbour with its twin tiny piers and the hard on which the fleet of cobles were drawn up.

She had been simmering inside, still, at his refusal to take her into his confidence as to whom he had to meet in Whitby, and why. 'What if something goes wrong?' she had asked. 'What if you get picked up?'

'Then like I said, the less you know the better. If I'm not back by lunch tomorrow, you leg it out of here, get the emergency code sign off and head south.'

She had toyed with the idea of following him, of making her own way to Whitby. But unless she could keep him in sight, it would be nothing but a waste of effort. And boarding the early train at the village station, with less than a dozen passengers and a few fish boxes, without his seeing her was a feat beyond her capability, in spite of his jocular references to her as Mata Hari. Instead, she had, as always, done exactly what he had advised. She had walked along the beach, past the spot where they had landed three months ago, then climbed again, an easier ascent to the top of the cliff, where the next sheltered bay protected the neighbouring village of Runswick.

There had been a few curious glances. After all, she was a stranger here, as anyone would be coming from a full five miles further up the coast. 'Funny them Kingstaith folk!' was the general, fast-held opinion. But Cissie was willing enough to explain her even more exotic fictitious background to anyone willing to listen in the quiet back room of the village pub. From the reaction of the landlady and her three customers, Cissie might well have dropped in from the moon. One elderly man looked up sagely from his seat at a high-backed bench near the fire. 'Our Bessy's lad was out there, like, wi' t'army. Tom

Sanders, 'is name is. Mebbes ye come across 'im?' When Cissie denied all knowledge of him, the old man nodded philosophically. 'Aye, well. Reckon it's a fair size, India, eh?' Cissie nodded her bemused agreement.

Once again, the Ship Inn was quiet during the weekday evening, and Mary was able to spend much of it keeping Cissie company in front of the kitchen fire. Cissie had already put on her night things after the much appreciated bath. They ate their supper together, and sat with their mugs of tea before the flames.

Mary had received a letter from Bob. Cissie thought privately she had seemed oddly reluctant to talk about him. She pressed the landlady for details. 'They've got this new general in charge now. Taken over from that Wavell feller. He's doing all right, Bob says. He can't say much.' She indicated the heavy censor stamp on the back of the thin envelope. 'But now Tobruk's been relieved they should keep them on the run.'

'You must be worried.' Impulsively, Cissie reached over and put her hand on Mary's wrist. The older woman blushed a little, and glanced at her with shy gratitude. She's very pretty, Cissie acknowledged, with something of a shock. No wonder Sean finds her attractive. The sudden thought disturbed her.

302

'He's always telling me he's miles behind any real action,' Mary was explaining. 'Him being in the artillery. Them big guns are miles behind the lines. They've got guns that big they can fire from here to past Whitby, he says.'

'Well, then. He's probably right. You've nothing to worry about.'

Mary smiled and nodded. 'Aye. Look, love. You go up. Take the hot-water bottle with you.' She nodded at the cylindrical pot object, with the legend *Stone's Ginger Wine* in black lettering on its side. 'I'll lock up and clear away, then I'll be up. I'll bring your cocoa up. Off you go. An early night'll do us good. You must be worn out after that hike.'

No Sean for you to sit up and chat with! Cissie thought, then suffered the usual pang of remorse at her uncharitableness.

Cissie spent a restless, miserable night, drifting in and out of dream-tossed sleep, with long, wakeful periods and even more disturbing thoughts. Surely Sean must be ready to move on soon, even though they had as far as she was aware amassed little useful information for their masters? They had been here three months. Even the inhabitants of this little backwater must be starting to wonder at the young couple who had dropped in from nowhere and had settled in so nicely. More importantly, Mary Price was no fool. Army captains and young female civil servants were not allowed the luxury of months of leave, convalescent or otherwise, with precious little evidence of illness or doctors' attentions.

Cissie could no longer claim to be a passive observer on the sidelines of this war. She had taken an active part, Sean had seen to that. She had sent out valuable secret information, information which might well contribute to Britain's ultimate defeat, certainly to more deaths of its citizens. She was a traitor, there was no way she could deny it now, and it grieved her deeply. She was aware more than ever that that ceremony she had gone through, the oath she had sworn, the fine uniform she had briefly donned, had meant nothing to her. She did not believe in the Third Reich, or its strangely charismatic Führer. And however much she might feel distanced from this hostile, cold climate, and the natives of this out-of-the-way little village, her cultural heritage lay within the shores of this beleaguered island; the values of her people, everything she had been taught to believe in as a Daughter of the Empire, was rooted here.

But she loved Sean. She stretched out from the warmth to the cold emptiness of the bed beside her, and felt her body stir with its hunger for him. Was *that* what love really was, the instinct to mate, to share one's body the way she did, that wild joy of abandonment? Whatever it was, it was something she had only known with Sean. She was deeply, penitently ashamed of her deception with Charlie. She hoped the poor boy would find someone to love him, for that was one thing she had not done. So where did her true loyalty lie? To England, that misty abstraction she had sung and prayed to in her unthinking childhood, or to that real, consuming ferocity of longing and passion of heart and body fused with the man she loved? How could she ever doubt that singularity of purpose so central to her when she thought of him?

Next day, as the morning hours ticked by towards noon and he did not appear, Cissie felt the cold beginnings of foreboding, its sickening rise towards a choking panic, which she tried, with little success, to hide from Mary. 'What's wrong? Where the hell is he? Why hasn't he come?'

Disturbed by the younger girl's growing distress, Mary felt her own insides churning unpleasantly. 'He must have been held up by something. Nothing to worry about, eh? He'll be along later.'

Unable to sit still, Cissie pulled on her

outdoor things, and crunched through a thin layer of new snow, under a truly leaden, laden sky which threatened further heavy falls, to the low, dark buildings of the small station. She sat in the chill of the fireless ladies' room, listening to the jarringly relentless tick of the wall clock, until the midday train from Whitby came chuffing in, to add more clouds of hanging, pale smoke and steam to the atmosphere. Her throat closed, she waited anxiously, praying to see him descend from one of the three carriages. He was not among the alighting passengers.

She hurried back to the inn, slipping perilously in her haste. Pack and leave, he had commanded her. Get as far away as you can before you send the emergency call sign which would alert the department back home. *Home?* This is your home, you fool! her racing mind screamed. These are your people. No, no! She must not let him down. He had her allegiance, otherwise how could she love him? She must do as he said. Pack her bags, get away. She could head north. The next train to Middlesbrough, then south. Make for London. The contact they had been given.

When she got in, entering round the back to avoid the drinkers in the bar, Mary called out and came along the passage. 'Oh, there you are, love! Are you all right? You look white as a sheet. What's the matter? Come and sit down, get warmed up. He's rung. Just after you left. He's been delayed. Says he'll be back later tonight, he hopes.'

'Oh God! Mary! Thank God!' She was shivering violently, and she broke down, the tears streaming down her face, and Mary clasped her to her, her expression almost mirroring Cissie's distress. 'There there, love. Don't take on so. What's wrong? You didn't think he'd run off and left you, did you?'

Cissie made a great effort to control herself, to try to discount the violence of her reaction. 'Sorry! I've been feeling — nerves, you know. Bit worn out, what with one thing and another. You're right, I don't feel too good. Be all right in a minute. I'll just go and have a lie down, I think.'

'Should I send for a doctor? I can ring Doctor Martin. Have you got your medicine?'

'Yes, yes. I'm all right now, thanks. Don't fuss. I'm sorry for being such a baby.'

'You go up and get into bed. I'll bring you up a cup of tea. What about a Beecham's Powder? You could be coming down with a chill. You're not used to our blooming weather, don't forget.'

When Mary tapped on the door and entered the bedroom a little while later,

Cissie was in bed, the covers pulled up to her chin. Her eyes were red from weeping, and she sniffed and gave a pathetic little watery smile. 'Perhaps you're right. Maybe I have got a touch of cold or something. I've got my socks on, and my vest, and I'm still shivering.'

'Now don't argue!' Mary said firmly. 'Drink this tea. Then I'll bring you a Beecham's, and a tot of whisky in some hot milk. You'll be a lot better by the morning.' She sat on the edge of the bed, watching while Cissie, propped on her elbows, sipped obediently at the tea. 'Listen. There's nothing worrying you, is there? I mean special, like. No problems?' Her eyes moved away from Cissie's gaze, and she gestured towards Cissie's form, hidden beneath the blankets. 'Nothing to do with you — and Captain Sean?'

'Eh? What — ' Cissie's face crimsoned as she realized Mary's implication. 'No! Certainly not!' She toned down her instinctive sense of outrage. 'No, honestly. Nothing like that, I — we — we're very careful.'

Mary was equally embarrassed. 'Of course. Sorry I asked. Only — if there was — it wouldn't — I mean there's folk can help. I know someone — '

'I've told you, it's nothing like that. Really.' Cissie could not help the sharpness of her tone, or its abrupt note of dismissal.

Sean came back down to the kitchen's warmth, and smiled crookedly. Mary, her housecoat tied tightly about her waist, looked up from her chair in front of the fire. 'She's sleeping like a baby,' he said. 'I gave her something a bit stronger than your powders.'

Mary was watching him gravely. He lowered himself with a sigh into the chair at her side. 'What is it?' she asked worriedly. 'Something's wrong — between you two. I'm not daft. I'm your friend. You can tell me. I wouldn't — '

'I know what you are, Mary,' he said quietly, leaning towards her, taking her hand in his and holding on to it. His grey eyes were full of trouble. 'Oh God!' He groaned quietly. 'I need to talk to someone, that's for sure. I feel so bad.'

He moved, so that he was kneeling, his arms lying heavily across her thighs, both his hands holding hers now, imprisoning them in the tightness of his grip. He bent, and leaned his head with utter weariness against the cloth of her robe at her lap. She kept still against the storm of emotion he was stirring inside her. It was hard for her to speak. 'Tell me,' she whispered.

'It's Cissie.' The red-gold curls moved, and

he raised his head, staring appealingly up at her. He shook his head. 'I'm going mad with it. I had to go . . . to meet with someone from the War Office. Intelligence. I still can't believe — they want me to find out more — ' There was a pause, while Mary held her breath. 'She's not who I thought. Not the person I fell in love with. They . . . think she's a spy!'

Mary's eyes were huge with incredulity. She stayed silent, never taking her gaze from him. 'That thing in the paper. That wedding announcement. The way you said she reacted. She never told me about it. I thought it was like you said — maybe an old flame, something she didn't want me to know about. But . . . they showed me a photograph of this chap. Humphreys. I saw it, straight away. The likeness. They say he's her brother. Turns out her name's not Jane Freeman at all. Cicely Humphreys, they say. They had some old picture of her, when she was a kid. Got it from this RAF feller. Only *Cissie* Humphreys — that's what she always called herself, he says — was killed, at sea. Torpedoed on her way to England from India. No survivors. That was way back in October '40.'

Mary stared at him. She had forgotten the fact that he was crouching at her feet, pressing on her legs, his arms resting in her lap. Their hands were still intertwined. 'You mean . . . she's pretending to be this girl?'

He shook his head again. 'No! That's the weird thing! The pictures of Cissie — the real Cissie, this fellow's sister!' His head jerked up, nodding towards the ceiling. 'The photos are when she was just a kid but there's no mistaking — it's Cissie all right. *My Cissie!* No doubt of it.'

'But . . . but you said you'd met her in the hospital. You — '

'Ah!' Sean cut in quickly. 'I was convalescing, in an officers' nursing home. I was still attending clinics at the Tropical Medicine School. So was she, I thought. We used to meet there, every day. We got chatting, went for walks. Met for meals. She had all her papers, knew all the docs and everything. So I thought! And she certainly knew all about India. About Assam and the frontier, where I'd been stationed. No bloody wonder! Turns out she was telling the truth about all of that, because she really is Cissie Humphreys. It's just how the hell she got to be here and working for the Jerries that's got everyone stumped.'

Mary moved, and Sean drew back as she stood and slipped past him. 'I can't believe it!' she said decisively.

'Neither could I!' he answered, and gave

another deep groan. He pressed his hands to his temples, as though to restrain his head from bursting with the knowledge. 'I still can't! Oh God, Mary! What am I to do? They want me — they've ordered me — to carry on, to keep close to her, find out what she's doing, who her contacts are. They want me not to let her suspect anything. To trap her.' He threw her an agonized look. 'They said I shouldn't tell anyone. And I've already broken my word. I've told you. But, Mary — I think I'll go mad. I had to tell you. You're the only one in the whole world — I need you, my love . . . '

The tears glistened in his eyes. She stepped in to him, and he came to meet her, and they were both weeping, whispering, their lips moving over wet faces, lapping salt tears, until their mouths came together with an undeniable hunger and need for each other. His hands were inside her robe, feeling the soft, full roundness of her breasts, their nipples hard through the cotton of her nightdress, and she moved again, thrusting herself against him, careless of the opening gown, lost to everything except that pounding need for fulfilment she had known since she was a young girl.

21

Sean slipped from Mary's bed while it was still dark, and entered his own room. In the pitch-blackness, he could hear the reassuring, soft snoring, and smiled as he thought how angry his proud, golden-haired beauty would be to be told she had been sounding off like a sawmill all night long. He had slipped enough of the sleeping powder into her evening drink to guarantee her unconsciousness well into the morning. Carefully, he groped his way around the foot of the bed, and pulled back the heavy blackout curtain and the ordinary drapes behind them. No stars or moon were visible, only the silent flakes of snow incessantly lighting on the glass. A thick fluff of fresh snow several inches deep had gathered on the stone sill.

Still without making a sound, he gathered his clothing from the chair and held it in front of him as he crept out and made his way naked down the creaking stairs and into the lesser chill of the kitchen. The high-banked fire looked dead, but he quickly broke the crust of dark sea-coal with the poker, exposing the red glow beneath, and riddled the high grate until the glow spread, and cast its rosy light and heat over his grateful flesh. He pulled on his clothes quickly, smelling the scent of Mary's perfume and musk on his skin and acknowledging that spontaneous spark of excitement even now at its powerful reminder. He was glad he had had her; he hoped their night of love would remain a sweet memory for her, whatever happened. He doubted it could be repeated, for he had too much to do in the hours that lay ahead. And by tonight he hoped to be far away.

He was counting on his luck holding. He had had some near squeaks, and his last trip around Teesmouth had convinced him he should move before it ran out altogether. He had actually been discovered, by a couple of the Home Guard — a self-important, plump little sergeant, who had not looked old enough to be past the age of conscription, and a bespectacled youth who must surely be awaiting call-up. He was nestled in the dunes above the seashore, south of Hartlepool, not far from a steelworks, just after first light. He had made rapid sketches of the position of the ack-ack batteries below the works and others closer to the town along the closed-off section of the long beach. He had even jotted down brief notes of the beach defences themselves, the anti-tank obstacles, and the extent of the barbed wire enclosures. They were there, in the top of his rucksack, along with the bits and pieces of the transmitter and the folded antenna. One quick search and he was done for. These two LDV stalwarts even had a service rifle each.

His quick-talking silver tongue saved him, though he was glad he had worn the khaki military gear for this expedition, to give credence to his tale. 'Captain Mullins,' he said confidently, in pukka officer accents. 'Haven't seen a couple of youngsters wandering about, have you? Cadets. White tab jobs! Officer training. We've lost a pair of the blighters. Night exercise. Couldn't find their way to their mothers' tit, bloody idiots! Oh! You'll be wanting to see my papers, eh? Could be a Jerry spy for all you know, what?'

He flourished his identity documents, which they barely glanced at before flashing him a clumsy salute, which, not wearing his cap, he remembered not to return. 'Well, better get back to the road, otherwise they'll be sending out a search party for *me*, too. If you come across them tell them to get back to Seaton, chop-chop. Keep up the good work, men.' He strode off, trying not to run, and trying not to look too ridiculous as his feet sank deep into the soft, sloping dune.

He would be glad to get away from this

bleak corner of England. He had been transmitting a lot of messages recently, so many that it was odds-on that the British would be aware by now that an agent was operating somewhere on this stretch of coastline. They might even know the content of his signals. There were rumours of a hush-hush listening post in the south somewhere, with highly sophisticated equipment, as well as some ace code crackers. Which was why it was necessary for him to disappear — and why, sad though it was, it was necessary to ditch poor young Cissie, and to leave her to take the rap. He guessed, in spite of her professed undying love for him, she would soon be blabbing like a deathbed sinner to a priest in an effort to save her pretty neck — and who could blame her? That's why he had to implicate her some more, if he could. All he really needed was to buy some time, and the tangled web of deceit would take some time to sort out. Poor Cissie might even have to spend some time in pokey. She was a traitor, after all. But he doubted she'd end up with a rope round that same pretty little neck. She might even learn a little humility from such experiences. And if they got caught together, he knew that, despite all her bedroom vows, she'd shop him when the shite hit the fan.

But, most important of all, he had made his own arrangements for a new phase in his career — if that's what his dedication to fighting for Ireland's cause against perfidious Albion was. He had made contact with his first and only real love, the freedom fighters of the Republican cause, and was ready to take up the sword on their behalf again. That's what this last meeting with your man in Whitby had been about, and which, finally, had borne fruit. He had never been really convinced of the Nazis' support for United Irish independence. They were interested only in causing dissent and rebellion to weaken the British war effort. And fair enough. They were using the cause, and him, just as he was using them. They could continue to work together, if they chose. But on his terms now. He'd done what he could up here in this north-east wilderness and he was moving back into his own fight — with their help or not.

It was ironic. When he had first got to Berlin and met up with that other so-called Irishman, Joyce, they had recognized each other right away as implacable enemies. In the old country they would have been literally at one another's throats, for Joyce was an out-and-out Unionist. Home Rule and United Ireland were red rags to a bull for him. In fact, Joyce had fled from Galway while still in his teens, following death threats from the IRA. Oswald Mosley's Black Shirt mob had been like meat and drink to him. It was during one of their bouts of thuggery on the London streets that he had had his face almost sliced in half by a razor, giving him the scar he thought made him look so hardened. But he was, literally, all mouth. As Lord Haw-Haw, he was listened to by most British households in his regular propaganda broadcasts. Mary never missed him if she could help it, and Sean was convinced the English population were as ready to believe his wild claims and dire predictions as they were to accept the heavily censored news put out by their own information services.

So, beautiful young Cissie, hot little lustful, loving, golden-haired daughter of the raj, would have to be sacrificed. Regrettable. But totally necessary. And Mary, his new, and equally lovely if more mature lover, of one night only, would have to be another victim of his machinations.

★   ★   ★

Cissie struggled to fight her way to alertness through the heavy fog of drowsiness, whose enveloping weight was dragging her down, beckoning her back to that sweet warmth of oblivion. She whimpered at the iron grip of Sean's hands on her bare arms, the violent shaking that buffeted her whole frame, and made the bed in which she was lying rattle and squeak. He let go and she fell back with weak relief on to the softness of the pillows, but he was back and she cried out at the ice-cold wetness on her face that trickled down her neck and on to her breast, and was soon soaking the thin satin of her nightgown. 'Please!' she blubbered, trying to turn her head away.

'For God's sake!' He thrust the wet flannel hard over her features, and the blonde head twisted in a vain attempt to escape. 'Wake up, will you, Cissie? What the hell's wrong with you?'

'I don't know,' she wept helplessly. 'I don't know — I feel doped. Oh, Sean, something's wrong. Am I ill?'

'You've got to listen! Come on, get up!' He dragged her up, hauled her out of bed. She would have fallen if he hadn't held her tightly. She felt the enveloping coldness of the air as he roughly dragged the thin nightdress up and over her head, but the shock of standing naked brought her closer to awareness. She swayed, but stayed on her feet, holding on to his gentler touch now.

'I'm sorry,' she was blubbering. 'I can't help it.'

'I have to go!' he said urgently, shaking her once more in his desperation to make her understand. Her blue eyes were still foggy, but they focused on him, her face screwed up with the effort to concentrate. 'We're in trouble, Cissie. But I'll lead them away from here. What you have to do is be brave. You'll be all right. Just do as I say. Will you? For me, sweetheart? You know I love you? I won't let anything happen to you. You've got to be brave.'

She was nodding, still whimpering like a frightened child, striving to understand. 'What is it?'

'They might be on to us. But they'll come after me. They don't know about you. You'll be all right, as long as you stay put. I'll try to get back if it's safe. Or I'll get a message to you. But listen. You *must* get this message away. Send it today. Four o'clock. Same place. It has to go. I'm counting on you entirely.'

'Yes, Sean,' she murmured. She leaned against him, lifted her face, and he kissed her gently. He put the message pad on the bed.

'That's my brave girl. God! I love you, my darling!' He crushed her to him now, and his hands were holding her, moving possessively, caressing her back and the swell of her haunches, and she moaned with renewed need of him, and of his love.

'I swear I'll try to get back to you. Or send word if it's safe for you to come to me. We'll be all right, my love.'

She blinked again, felt her jaw aching in its desire to release a massive yawn, then he was sealing her mouth with another kiss and she clung desperately to him. 'Can't I come with you?' she whispered, meekly.

'You must stay here. Stay free. For my sake, not for anything else!' She wept again, but there was a sweetness this time in her tears. 'If you haven't heard by tomorrow night, send the emergency code sign. They may have a message for you. Keep trying. Every two hours. You'll have to risk transmitting from in here. Make sure Mary's down in the bar. I have to go. Here. Keep this safe.' He put the paper on the bedside table. 'Whatever happens, it must go off this afternoon.'

'Sean. I'm frightened. I don't know — '

'It's going to be all right, my love. All will be well. I love you.' He was shepherding her back under the still-warm covers, kissing her one last time. 'It's early. Go back to sleep. I'll see you soon. You have my promise.' He bent and brushed the hair from her wet face, kissed her a last time, softly on the lips.

Half an hour later, fully dressed and his pack ready to be swung on to his shoulders, he clasped Mary to him, and kissed her, with equally convincing passion. 'God, Mary! What would I do without you? I'd have gone mad, I think. I certainly couldn't have gone through with all this. Just keep an eye on her, watch out for anything out of the ordinary. She shouldn't stir outside on a day like this. If she does, try to see where she goes. Without letting her know — '

Mary's brown eyes were wide with alarm. 'Oh, Sean! Can't we tell someone? The police? Army? *Somebody*! I can't — I mean, what can I do? On my own? We need — '

He grabbed her arms, shook her lightly. 'You can do it, Mary, my love. I know you can. I'm relying on you to help me through this. I'll get back as soon as I can. If there was any other way, believe me . . . we have to find out, once and for all, what she's mixed up in. Who she's working with. There could be a whole network of them. We must know. Think of all the damage she might do. The lives that might be lost. I know it's hard, Mary, but I know how brave you are. You can do it — for me, eh?'

The tears rolled down her cheeks. She thought of the night, the love they had made together. Beautiful. And wicked. She had betrayed her marriage, betrayed Bob. This was one way she could atone. Superstitiously, she believed it was a way she could keep Bob safe, by finding the nerve to do as Sean had asked, otherwise God would surely punish her by taking her husband's life. But then Sean would be back, and the nightmare would be over ... and she knew for a certainty, as she trembled and clung to him in their parting embrace, that she would sin again, that her body cried out for him again, even now.

★　★　★

'You can't go out in this!' Mary prayed that she could inject the right note of reasoned and innocent incredulity into her voice. 'It's nearly pitch-black already and blowing up for a blizzard. There's a foot of snow and drifts all over the place. You've been in bed all day. You'll catch your death of pneumonia. Have some sense, lass!'

Cissie's face was white, her youthful features racked with her anxiety. 'Just a short walk. I won't go far. Just to the end of the lane. I have to get out. Get some fresh air. My head's splitting.' She was already muffled in her outdoor clothing and heavy boots, her rucksack hanging from one shoulder.

'What do you need your bag for?' The question came out more accusingly than Mary had intended. Her heart was hammering, and her face as pale as Cissie's. For a second they glared at each other in silence.

'What is this? An interrogation? Am I a prisoner or something?'

Now Mary felt herself colouring up. 'Don't be so daft, lass! But you're not yourself. Mebbe you're a bit delirious with the fever. Captain Sean would never forgive me. Come on. Get them things off and come and sit by the fire. I'll make us a cup of tea, eh?' She saw the panic in the girl's eyes and felt a similar emotion. What could she do if she simply refused to take notice? If she just walked out into that snowy gloom? Should she try to stop her? Did she know that Mary suspected her? Was she about to make her escape?

Mary almost gasped with relief as she saw that wild look of desperation fade from the blue eyes, to be replaced by an expression of defeat, and of surrender.

Cissie sagged visibly, slipped the sack from her shoulder and held it by the strap. 'You're right,' she said, almost inaudibly. 'I'll go and change.' She tried a smile of reconciliation, which failed dismally. 'Sorry, Mary. You're right. I'm not thinking straight. I'll be down in a while.'

She turned back, went up the stairs and into the bedroom from which she had just emerged.

Mary heard the door close. What on earth was she intending to do, going out into this awful afternoon? Whatever it was, Mary had prevented her from doing it. She went along to the kitchen and set about making a pot of tea. Her hands were shaking so badly. She was glad Cissie wasn't on hand to watch her, or she would know at once there was something seriously wrong. Another great wave of fear and loneliness overwhelmed her. Oh, Sean! How could you make me do this? I'm no good. Not brave at all, my love. I'm just ordinary. A coward. That's the trouble. You. Your love. That girl upstairs. It's all just too much for me, I can't take it. Get a grip, girl! Come on! Frame yourself, as Bob would say. And he's out there, in that North African desert, risking his life for you — while you're being unfaithful to him in his bed! The thought slammed into her mind like a knife. Do *something* that might make him proud, for God's sake.

She went to the cupboard, reached in to the back, and pulled out the twist of paper Sean had given her. 'If things get desperate, you can use this. Slip it in her drink. It'll knock her out for at least eight hours or so, like it did last night.' She clutched it in her hand, felt her heart thumping, then slipped it into the pocket of her pinafore.

She made the tea, fitted the cosy over the pot and sat listening to the ticking, the soughing of the wind round the old house. Nothing from above. She padded along the dark passage to the foot of the stairs, stood listening again. Nothing. Then she thought she could hear something, but could not decide what it was. Something rattling? It stopped and started up again, a soft clicking noise. Knitting needles? Surely not? It was not a pastime she would associate with a girl like Cissie, and in all the time she had been here she had given no evidence of it. Mary edged up the stairs, wincing at the soft creaks. She stopped on the dim landing. The clicking was louder now, rapid bursts of sound, then a pause, then more clicks. She felt as though her heart must leap up into her throat, but somehow she found the resolution to put her hand on the door handle and turn it, calling out shrilly. 'Tea's made, love. Do you — '

The door was locked. Mary called out Cissie's name and tapped on the door. The clicking had stopped. Mary cleared her throat. 'You coming down for tea? Or would you like it up here?'

The key turned and the door swung open

violently. Mary stepped back involuntarily. Cissie's face was wild, and paper-white. Her eyes were huge, awash with tears, and her vivid mouth was twisted. 'Can't you just leave me alone, for Christ's sake? What's wrong with you? I'll be down when I'm ready! All right?' The door slammed in Mary's face and the key turned again in the lock.

Mary retreated down the stairs, shaking from head to foot. She was breathing quickly, short, shallow breaths through her mouth, the tears ready to spill from her eyes. She thought of that startled, startling face. The fear, and the hate she had seen. There could be no further doubt. The girl was as guilty as hell, she was sure of it. And therefore a danger to everyone Mary knew and cared for. Once more, she felt the sickening helplessness wash over her, as she sat staring into the red heat of the fire, the courage draining from her. If she was so certain of Cissie's guilt, then the girl would surely know, too, that Mary knew her secret. Get up right now and telephone for the police. Tell the operator to send Constable Gibbs up here at once. But Sean had said they must not alert Cissie; that there were others in this spy ring that must be caught. She bit her lip, to suppress the cry that almost escaped. Come back, Sean! she prayed fearfully. I'm not up to this. That sweet girl up there was a complete sham. She was the enemy. And she could well be deadly. Mary gripped the sides of her chair, ready to lift herself up, to head for the telephone in the passage.

She heard the door upstairs click open, heard the tread of feet above, then the steps coming downstairs, towards her.

22

Cissie's nerves were stretched to the limit. Her racing mind was racked with indecision. To make matters worse, she was still suffering from this sensation of having lost a good number of hours from the last twenty-four. She wondered if this fogginess of memory was in itself an indication of the extreme fear, not to say panic, she was undergoing. It was like surfacing from a great depth when Sean had jolted her awake this morning. She could scarcely take in his urgency, the way their exclusive and cherished world seemed to be crumbling all around her. Strange as it was in this dangerous adventure they had embarked on, that was just how she had felt these past three months, cushioned and safe, in spite of all the hazards. But now that cocoon had burst, and she was lost and terrified. If only he had confided in her, instead of letting it fall on her with the suddenness of a thunderclap, when she was least prepared for it.

Of course, she knew that he had tried desperately to prevent her from being threatened and afraid. That was why he had told her nothing, why, even now, she had no idea of how exactly this present danger had come upon them. But she wished with all her heart he had not been so lovingly determined to shield her. It just left her all the more alone and lost now. It was so hard to think, to try to plan what she must do. Nothing, for the moment, according to Sean. Except for getting his message off — and even that she had made a mess of. But Sean couldn't blame her for that. She could not help this terrible weather. Mary was right, she couldn't have gone blundering into the darkness of a blizzard, not without appearing totally deranged. As it was, that was her most important task now, to try to reassure Mary that she had not taken leave of her senses, to find some explanation, and to try to atone for her appalling rudeness when Mary had come knocking on her door. Had the landlady heard the Morse keys? Would she know what the distinctive sound was? Surely not? These people were village folk, ignorant of most momentous things that were going on beyond their own doorstep. She could convince her somehow, make her believe her story. She must!

But all Cissie's resolution teetered perilously at the first glance when she went along the passage and opened the kitchen door.

Mary's great brown eyes gave her away at once. 'Mirrors of the soul, your eyes,' Sean used to tell her teasingly, back in Germany. 'That's what you've got to learn, my darling. Lying with your eyes. That's the secret of this spying game.'

'Like *you* can, you mean?' she had riposted, and he had chuckled in acquiescence.

'When I need to, my love. That's what's so nice about being with you. I've no need to, have I?'

Well, she had to now. Sean's life, and maybe hers, depended on it. Mary's brown eyes looked terrified. She almost backed away at Cissie's appearance. Cissie strode forward swiftly, with a penitent cry. 'Oh, Mary! I'm so sorry! I don't know what's the matter with me — I'm so on edge. Please! Let me talk to you. You're the only friend I have here!' Her voice caught in a sob. She could feel the tension in Mary's body as she clung to her, registered it as she released her and sat down on the worn cushion of one of the two chairs facing the black range and the hotly glowing fire. She made a great business of collecting herself — it was not all acting — and blew her nose on the hankie she dug from the pocket of her dressing gown. 'I don't know what came over me just now.' She jerked her head upward towards the bedrooms. 'I'm just so worried about Sean . . . and what's going to happen to us.' She cleared her throat and carried on in a husky murmur of contrition. 'Will you forgive me, Mary?' She waited an instant, and when there was no reply, she said humbly, 'Is there still some tea in the pot?'

Mary could hardly trust herself to speak, or even to look at the seated figure. Cissie's gold hair had been brushed out. When she had first come it had been cut short. Sean had trimmed it lightly once, but it had grown again. Now it hung in simple twin long strands on either side of the pale face, just curling slightly at the ends, where it rested on the lapels of her sensible, thick dressing gown. She looked so young, so pretty and helpless and woebegone, sitting there before the hearth.

All this was like a dream, some hideous nightmare, Mary thought. Then she heard Sean's urgent voice, the catch in it that betokened his own shock, and misery. What must it have been like for him, to learn that the girl he had been ready to give up everything for — his wife, family, all his friends — was a world away from this lovely innocent slip of a girl she had seemed? And then Mary remembered that other desperation — a mutual desperation, which had brought him to her own arms, and to her bed, in that wonderful fury of passion. Her body still ached with it, and at its powerful reminder, she steeled herself to act. 'I'll put a drop of water to it. It'll be a mite strong by now.'

In spite of her determination, another violent fit of trembling seized her when she fumbled with the pot again, and she turned her back, praying that Cissie would not notice her agitation, or that she would simply put it down to her distress over the scene that had taken place between them upstairs. She reached for a clean mug, shielded it with her back. She could feel the sweat clinging to her; her fingers shook so badly she feared she would not be able to perform the simple task of extracting the twist of paper from her pocket. She fumbled it open, shook the white contents into the mug of steaming liquid, and followed them with two heaped teaspoonfuls of sugar, the grains spilling on to the oilcloth at her unsteady hand.

She stirred vigorously. 'To hell with the ration! Here! There's two spoons of sugar in that. Reckon you could do with it. Drink it all up, there's a good lass. Now, are you going to tell me what's up between you and Sean? What is it that's got you so worked up?'

Cissie smiled gratefully, cupped her hands

round the comforting warmth of the mug, and sipped. She just prevented herself from grimacing at the overpowering sweetness, and the too-generous measure of milk. She thought of the bright green of the rows of bushes back home in the bright beat of sun, the sense of space in the blue above, with those drifting high white clouds, and the distant mountains. The other side of the world. Another world! What was she to do, all alone here? Sean wasn't coming back. She knew that, in spite of her befogged mind, from the way he had spoken, and held her, this morning. She had to make contact again, send that dreaded code word to alert the listeners back in Germany. Just sit tight, Sean had told her. Please don't let him be caught! she prayed. And the first thing she had to do was to allay the fears and doubts this woman beside her must be having at the drama enfolding around her.

Cissie began to talk, eloquently she hoped, of their love, the feeling of despair, of doom, she was beginning to suffer. It was not hard to be convincing. So much of it was true. It brought genuine tears to her eyes; the pathos of the love story caught her. And it was working. Mary was listening, silently, but she could feel the woman's sympathy, her compassion. 'Come on, drink up, it'll do you good,' she encouraged, and Cissie obeyed. She reached out, took Mary's cold hand, and held on to it. She was winning her over once more.

'If we could just be free . . . of all this . . . this . . . be on our own . . . ' Her head jerked back; she was startled at the echoing quality of her voice inside her brain. What had she been saying? She couldn't remember. She stared down at the mug tilted in her lap. Mary just caught it before the dregs spilt out; took it from her fingers. They felt clumsy and it took a great effort to move them, to extricate them from the handle of the cup, which Mary had taken from her, was placing on the table. Cissie's neck felt weak, her head too heavy as she lifted it to follow Mary's movement away from her.

All at once, a great, heaving sigh turned into a yawn, a vast, loud groan of utter weariness that seemed to transmit itself through her entire body. She blinked. God! What was happening to her? It was like . . . like what had happened to her last night, this utter draining of her senses. Something wrong . . . seriously wrong. It was hard to speak, through that cotton-wool mist closing down her mind. 'I have to go — upstairs,' she murmured. She began the struggle to lift herself from the chair, pushing down with her arms, but her body seemed a tremendous weight, and her limbs were dead. 'Have to — have to send . . . Sean's message.'

She blinked owlishly up at Mary, who suddenly loomed over her, dark, menacing. Beyond her dark shape, the room looked fuzzy, unfocused. 'Must get up . . . upstairs. The message . . . '

'It can wait. You're not going anywhere.'

Mary's voice sounded strange. Harsh, unfriendly. 'You don't know . . . don't . . . '

'Oh yes, I do. I understand fine well. Sit down. You have a good sleep.'

Mary was holding her, the thin, strong hands like clamps on her arms, hurting, thrusting her back against the hardness of the wooden chair, pinning her there. Cissie began to cry. 'Please, Mary. I have to go.' But the older woman was holding her firmly, by the shoulders now, sitting on her, preventing her from moving, and, weeping softly, Cissie slid into the waiting oblivion.

★　★　★

There was the pain, biting, searing, as Cissie surfaced from her fog of doped unconsciousness. Her arms: something was digging in to the softness of her upper arms, excruciating. And her ankles, she realized, were burning her. Dim light filtered through her gummed eyelids and she made to rub them, but found she couldn't move. Panic assailed her; she tried to move again and threshed against the burning restraints, powerless. She began to whimper, believing she was still wrapped in that last moment of fearful dream, fighting to wake up and end it.

The pain helped to dissipate the clinging clouds of unreality. Awareness came, slowly, and with it utter incomprehension. She was not in bed. Her whole body was a mass of pain. The fearful noise she could hear crashing in her head was Mary's vigorous riddling of the fire. She saw the bent form, kneeling a few feet away. To her amazement, Cissie found that she was sitting strapped to her chair. Or, rather, not strapped, but bound, with strong rope, to the wooden back. The bonds, of washing-line thickness, ran tightly just below her breasts and trapped her upper arms, hence the sharp pain, even through the thickness of her dressing gown. The searing pain at her ankles was caused from their being similarly tied together, and the rope tethered in a complicated ravel of knots to the chair's front legs and the rung that ran between them.

Cissie blinked, felt the seal of the unregistered hours like a mask on her dishevelled features, her skin stained with tears and saliva and her eyes hot and stinging. Her voice was a hoarse croak. 'Mary! For God's sake! What are you doing?'

Mary rose. She still held a brush and dustpan in her hand. 'So! You're awake then? I've made sure you'll stay right where you are. I know all about you. I know what you are, what you've been doing.'

Cissie tried to turn her head sufficiently to see the clock. Its face on the wall to her left swam into focus. Oh God! It was almost nine o'clock. Full daylight. She must have been unconscious for fifteen hours or so. But why? How? Mary must have heard her using the transmitter. But how? 'You doped me!' she said incredulously.

Mary nodded grimly. 'It was the only way I could make sure you didn't get up to any more of your filthy tricks. All this time! When I think!' She made a choked noise of disgust.

'You fool!' Cissie's voice cracked. 'You don't realize. You've put Sean's life in danger — '

'Shut up!' Cissie flinched at the force of Mary's cry. 'I know your filthy game! I know what you are! Sean told me. As soon as he gets back they'll come for you. I hope they shoot you!'

'You fool! You don't know anything! Sean's

the one who'll be shot! What on earth has he told you? We were working together. Something secret. You've got to let me explain. Let me go. I have to get a message off. Upstairs, there's — '

'Is this what you mean, eh?' Mary pointed towards the table. Cissie turned her throbbing head. There was her bag, her clothes, all in a jumbled heap. And there were the valves, the earphones, the antenna, the keypad of their portable wireless set. 'That's what you want, is it? To get a message off to your Nazi friends? Germany calling! is it?' Her voice was choked with her revulsion.

'It isn't what you think!' Cissie gabbled, thinking frantically, still struggling to clear her cloudy mind. 'Sean and I — we're working under cover. For our side — *your* side! Nobody must know. That's why I have to get this message off. It should have gone last night. Sean's life could be in danger. Trust me, I beg you. I know how much Sean means — '

She cried out as Mary stepped forward, swung her right arm back and gave her a ringing slap across her face. The force of it sent Cissie's head swinging, the blonde hair flying. Her vision was lost in a blaze of redness as the fire of the blow seared her tender cheek, its crack ringing in her head.

Tears streamed down her face; she tasted blood inside her mouth. She hung her head, gasping, blinded, her sobs deep and gut-wrenching. Mary's voice was unsteady; she was fighting tears too as she spoke. 'Wicked bitch! I'd like to kill you right now, like you deserve! That poor man! To think you could deceive him so! Trick him, use him. But he knows now, he'll see you get what you deserve. He told me — '

Cissie's effort to lie her way out of the crisis burst in the crimson rage of her own despair, as she contemplated the overwhelming fact of his betrayal. He had left her, sacrificed her, so that he could escape. He had made sure that she had stayed behind, given Mary the means to incapacitate her, even made sure that Cissie would incriminate herself finally in that desperate attempt to get off the message he had coded. Told her to stay here, to go on transmitting their emergency call sign, no doubt ensuring that the British authorities would have traced her very quickly. He had even warned Mary not to inform anyone of the truth — not until he had made sure he was well away from danger. It was now well over twenty-four hours since he had made his escape. He could be anywhere in the country. Or out of it. She felt hollow with despair as she thought of him back in Germany — the accolades he would receive, the laughter he would share with Schoenburg and the others at her role as sacrificial lamb.

Her head was hurting and her branded cheek ached abominably. She could feel her lips and gum swollen. The desperation and rage ebbed from her, and her body relaxed. She sat limply, accepting all the pain and discomfort. 'He won't come back,' she murmured dully, not looking at Mary. 'You can sit here till doomsday. You won't see him again.'

Physical discomfort turned to torture, as the endless hours ticked by. Cissie wept like a child, begged for release. 'My arms and ankles!' she croaked pitiably. 'They hurt so much.' Her feet were purpled and swollen, the ropes making deep, chafed indentations in the tender skin. There were other humiliations to endure. Mary fed her sips of tea, and water, holding the cup to her sore lips, the liquid trickling down to stain her robe. 'I need the lavatory,' Cissie wept, her tears increasing when Mary returned bearing an enamel chamber pot. 'I can't!' Cissie gasped, and Mary gave a callous shrug.

'You'll have to sit there and wet yourself then!'

Sobbing bitterly, Cissie finally endured the shame of squirming, still tightly bound, to lift her bottom while Mary rearranged the night things and slipped the pot under her so that she could relieve herself. 'I'll scream!' Cissie threatened, when opening time approached.

'Go ahead! I'll let the lads come and see the Nazi spy for themselves. Then I'll leave them to it. They might have some fun. They're not gentlemen, you know. Just fisherfolk.'

Cissie was almost tempted to carry out her threat when, finally, a couple of customers entered the bar. But, while no one else was aware of the truth, Cissie felt there might still be a measure of hope, however faint, that she could extract herself from this crisis.

By early evening she was ready to face anything, even death, in order to end the agony she was suffering. She was afraid the circulation in her limbs had ceased altogether, while the unyielding hardness of the chair she was imprisoned in seemed to have penetrated through her flesh to the bones beneath. She was drifting in a nightmare half-world of real pain and frightening conjecture when the end came, first in the disbelieving regard of the village constable, then a quartet of self-conscious Home Guard members. When they released her, they had to lift her from the chair, and her body remained folded in its shape for some agonizing minutes while the blood flowed freely once more. Her skin was marked like shackles where the rope had bitten into it, and she moved eventually like a crone.

She crawled upstairs, where Mary, torn between bitter hate and genuine compassion, sat with her while she took a much-needed bath. She even helped her to dress in warm underclothes, sweater and slacks, before the black car, bearing two plain-clothed policemen, came to take her and her few possessions away. Mary hardly knew what it was that made her reach out and catch hold of Cissie's bruised arm and squeeze it hard. She leaned in close to the flinching, pale figure. 'He slept with me, you know,' she whispered. 'Tuesday night. After he gave you that dope. We spent the night together.'

'I hope it was worth it,' Cissie managed bravely, but Mary could see how much she had hurt the beaten girl. She felt bad about it forever afterwards. As she did, some weeks later, when she found her period had not come, and, after a great struggle with conscience and with her fierce desire to have a child, she went to see Emmy Harkness down in the village, for the necessary means to terminate the new beginnings of life within her.

One night of love. She would never hear the Puccini aria again without weeping.

23

'Come on then, Freeman. Time for walkies!'
Sarah Barker was a statuesque woman, with a
plain, open, no-nonsense face. Her brown
hair, trimmed to rest above the collar of
her khaki shirt, was usually neatly confined
beneath a net, except when she accompanied
her captive out to the small yard that served
as exercise area, for which she jammed on the
unbecoming soft hat with its dull ATS badge
centred above the crumpled peak. She was
already wearing her long greatcoat over the
uniform skirt and blouse. It was not unlike
the military clothing Cissie was wearing,
apart from the black diamond patch sewn on
the sleeves of all Cissie's garments, which was
their only insignia, to delineate her status as
a prisoner. Prisoner without trial, Cissie
reflected apathetically. She had begun to
wonder if she was simply to be left to rot here
in this most famous of gaols, for days had
dragged into weeks of dreary and uncomfortable incarceration, once the initial terrifying
brutality of the interrogations had ceased.

She pulled on her greatcoat against the
grey blustering of late February. They would

345

not allow her a hat or a head square, not that it mattered, she supposed. They had cut her hair in an ugly fashion, straight by the lobes of her ears, with a fringe at her brow that made her look like a schoolgirl. She was full of cold anyway, in this terrible, chilly fortress. Unless the weather warmed up soon, she would probably solve all their problems — and hers — by contracting double pneumonia.

'Come on, Freeman. Step out. It's stopped raining. Look lively.' Down the narrow, worn staircase, the stone steps saucered in the middle by generations of unfortunates who had trodden them. The interior of the great thick walls was whitewashed, though the unevenness of the stones was evidence of their antiquity. They smelt of centuries of damp, as did her cell, with its totally inadequate wall heater, which in any case was switched off most of the time.

'Why do you keep calling me Freeman?' Cissie asked, for the hundredth time at least. 'You know that's not my name.'

'It's the name that's on all the papers,' Barker answered patiently. 'Till they tell me otherwise, that's your name.'

They passed the khaki-clad figure, armed with rifle, standing as sentry by the arched narrow doorway through which they emerged into the open air. Open mostly above, where the low, grey clouds passed rapidly overhead. The whitish-grey, high stone walls, castellated on the side away from the solid mass of the building, marked the boundaries of their restricted movement. The sentry and Sarah exchanged greetings. The man's eyes seemed to pass over Cissie as though she were invisible. There was no acknowledgement of her presence at all. All the guards behaved in identical fashion. She hardly seemed to exist for them, and she had a strong urge to challenge him in some outrageous way. But she took no action. Her life, such as it was, was precarious enough, without making further trouble for herself. Besides, she was too dispirited to show any tokens of resistance. If they told her to jump, she would ask, 'How high?'

She just wanted to be left alone. Broken-hearted. She had heard the trite phrase so often; it was the province of crooners and those trashy True Confessions magazines. But she feared the words might mean something truthful after all. Sean's betrayal was as terrible to her as her capture. Her anger had not lasted. The blow had been too severe for that. Even Mary's last words, hissed into her ear as she clutched at Cissie's painfully bruised arm, had taken her beyond rage, stunned her with the thought that he could be so callous, so unrelentingly cruel. Nothing matters any more, she had told herself, as they led her out to the waiting car, and the curious, dead-white world.

Of course, fear had soon reasserted itself, once they had brought her to this forbidding legend of a place. The Tower of London! She had scarcely been able to comprehend it. Traitors' Gate. The Bloody Tower. Beheadings. This was a fabled place, unreal to her. She had imagined all kinds of things that being captured would mean, but not this. It was like being walled up, even with electric light and hot meals, and the rare luxury of the heater. Windows were barred, and were slits cut in stone three feet and more thick. This was still the world of dungeons and dragons and medieval tortures.

And they had threatened her with torture, these refined men with voices like professors, who looked odd and out of place in their uniforms. She hadn't known if they were joking. 'We still have the thumbscrews and the rack,' a bespectacled figure with a smile like a parson told her. 'Not that we've used them for ages. But we can still be crude if we have to. We can pull out your nails, hands and feet. Slowly. One by one. Count to twenty, eh? I've known tough guys who have sung like canaries before we got to five. Or other nasties, more scientific. Electric wires, inserted in certain delicate parts of the anatomy.' She was staring at him, wide-eyed, open-mouthed, too shocked to weep. 'Makes the eyes water. In the end you'll be begging us to let you talk. Tell all you know.' His pleasant smile was macabre.

The threat was enough. In fact, he needn't have bothered, for, sobbing in the dank darkness of her new prison, she had determined to give them as much information as she could. Nothing mattered any more. She remembered the ceremony in Berlin, the oath she had taken. She had betrayed already. And been cruelly betrayed. She talked at length, and told the unvarnished truth about all that had happened to her. They listened, took it all down painstakingly, occasionally joked about it. 'So! You were one of Lord Haw-Haw's playmates, were you?' the bespectacled one snickered.

She was shaken from her apathy in those early days, when they began to cross-examine her, going over every aspect of the time from her rescue by U213 to her sojourn in the Ship Inn. The questioning was aggressive. She was afraid they didn't believe her. They woke her in the middle of the night; she had to drag on her trousers and battledress blouse over the ugly nightshirt, while her two male escorts watched her unblinkingly. They sat her on a hard chair with a harsh lamp trained on her like a theatrical spotlight. There were two figures who were mere dim silhouettes behind a table. They shouted their questions at her, hardly listening to her answers. She was left sitting there trembling for hours, it seemed, then it started all over again, the same questions until she was sobbing and pleading with them to believe her. 'Everything! I've told you everything!' she blubbered, staring blindly, her face streaming with tears.

She was deeply relieved when the interrogations stopped. But now the days had settled to a dreary routine of nothingness. Meals were brought to her cell. There was a small recess without a door, where there was a lavatory and a washbasin. She was allowed to shower twice a week, in a bleak bathroom somewhere on the ground floor, in the implacable presence of Sarah Barker. At first her wardress steadfastly refused to engage in conversation, but gradually humanity if not humaneness won the day. Now they could at least talk — not heart-to-heart confessionals, but it was an acknowledgement of her existence as a person.

An army padre visited weekly. The poor man had looked startled when Cissie declared herself to be 'Church of England' and willing to receive Communion. It was through his visits that Cissie picked up snippets of war news — Sarah Barker resolutely refused to pass on any information from the outside world, as per her orders. It was he who told Cissie of the fall of Singapore, and looked suitably abashed at his indiscretion at bringing what might be termed as 'comfort to the enemy', until he was reassured by Cissie's obvious dismay. 'Oh gosh!' she pondered. 'My family — they must be getting worried out there. And my husband — ' She felt the flood of colour mounting. She guessed that the priest must know, as everyone else seemed to, the story of how she had been living in England with her Irish spy lover.

Home had been on her mind a great deal. Would her parents and Charlie know by now that she was still alive — and a traitor shut up in the Tower? She rather hoped not. She would rather remain decently dead and buried to her dear ones than be resurrected as spy and traitor. Maddeningly, the officer whom she still saw once a week refused to answer her question. 'Not at liberty to say,' he said, poker-faced, as she strove to swallow back her impatience.

'What is going to happen to me?' she

asked, as she did at every opportunity. 'Will I be put on trial? Or will I be left to rot here for ever?' She sounded a mite melodramatic even to her own ears. His answer did not reassure.

'An act of treason merits capital punishment in wartime. A civil trial is not necessary. Military tribunal, king's signature. That's all it takes.'

'But I've told you everything! Surely I've helped? I only did it — all that stuff in Germany — to save my life!'

The poker face remained as the Intelligence officer answered her. 'And stayed under cover with your lover up in Kingstaith, while passing vital information to the enemy. It might interest you to know that there was a raid on Sheffield in early January, when the Luftwaffe passed over the coast undetected. They came south of Redcar. Missed all the heavy anti-aircraft defences. First time they'd crossed there. Why was that, I wonder? Forty-odd people lost their lives that night. Civilians. If we'd a mind to, I dare say we could charge you and your boyfriend with murder.'

Cissie could only stare in mute horror. It preyed on her mind a lot during the long days that followed. More days of total isolation. She spent long periods of the daylight hours lying in bed, dozing and reading. They brought her books — all novels, British classics, of which she was woefully ignorant. Dickens, Hardy. She loved *Tess*, until she came to the final pages, with which she felt she could identify far too closely. She even woke from a sweating nightmare, in which she felt the rough rasp of the noose, and the smothering blindness of the hood. Would they post a notice somewhere at an outer gate, proclaiming her execution? Would they tie her to a post, offer a last cigarette before the firing squad? Could she die bravely? 'No, thank you. I don't smoke.' Somehow she thought not.

'Come on, get off your pit, Freeman! You've got a visitor. Tidy yourself up a bit. Brush your hair.'

Barker's voice startled her. Who was it now? More Intelligence types? The wardress's tone had indicated something rather more unusual. The word 'visitor' had never been used before. Her stomach began to churn, her pulse quickened. Barker's voice hadn't sounded ominous. Quite the opposite. But Cissie's hands were clammy as she stood nervously a few minutes later at the clink of the door being opened.

Barker was ushering in a man, who stooped automatically as he passed through the low doorway and down the two steps to the stone-flagged floor. A uniformed figure, in air force blue, slipping off his cap as he came forward from the dimness. His hair was fair, like her own, his face scarcely less pale or tense than hers. She gaped, her mouth hung open, her eyes bugged. 'Nig!'

Nigel Humphreys managed a twisted smile. 'Hullo, Cissie. What a damned mess you've got yourself into.'

He stayed in the middle of the room, but she hurtled across the space between them, flung herself at him with a force that rocked him on his heels, her arms locked about his neck as she raised her face avidly for a kiss. He held her awkwardly while she collapsed against him, weeping unrestrainedly. At last he spoke. She could feel his hands gently easing her away from him. 'I say, old girl! Steady, eh? Bit of a turn-up for the books, eh?'

She fought hard to control herself, turned to find a handkerchief to wipe her streaming face, conscious of so many things all at once: her scruffy, unkempt appearance in the ill-fitting prison clothes, in such contrast to his well-groomed, masculine fragrance; the immaculate uniform, with its proud wings above the left breast pocket, the two thick rings and one thin on his sleeve, denoting the rank of squadron leader, she remembered,

354

from her weeks of training at Cottbus in the forest; but, most significant and hurtful of all, his clearly all-too-confined joy at seeing her alive after all this time. Bitter shame swept up, from her curling toes to the roots of her stiff, ill-nourished hair, at the terrible knowledge of her treachery, and at the inescapable fact that he must be fully aware of every aspect of her crimes — and all who had known her would be filled with the same disgust.

'You've let the side down, Cissie!'

The inadequate, juvenile phraseology carried all the weight of their shared despair. 'I'm glad you're unhurt. Alive,' she mumbled huskily, and there was a measure of unconscious reproach, as the awful thought assailed her that her family might not feel the same about her. 'Does everyone know? Back home? I haven't heard a thing.'

He shook his head, and she stared at him bewilderedly. 'Then how . . . did you . . . ?'

'I'm the only one. Nobody else. Charlie. Pater and mater.' He shook his head fiercely. 'Listen!' he said urgently, all at once. He glanced round towards the door. 'We have to talk! They let me see you — because there's a way you can get out of here. Save yourself. And maybe make up for the way you've behaved. Make amends. It's your only chance!'

The 'chance', Cissie learned, a day later, from much more senior and devious sources than her brother, in a carefully screened cluster of offices occupying the two top floors of a large London building housing a large department store beneath, was for her to resume her role of traitorous spy. A small, grey-haired man, with neatly clipped moustache and dark-rimmed glasses, whom Cissie would have designated without doubt as a bank manager or senior civil servant, and not only because of his black morning coat and pinstripe trousers, explained in detail.

'We want to run you as a double agent. The only people who know about you are your brother, and that woman up north. Mrs Price, your landlady at the Ship Inn. We felt we had to let your brother in on it, in case we needed him to talk sense into you. Make you see what a black you've dropped and so on. I'm glad to see you're co-operating fully. We've spun the Price woman a yarn. Mistake all round, you were really on our side after all. Sworn to secrecy — I think she'll keep mum.' He smiled, but the gesture did not warm Cissie towards him. 'We're able to do her a bit of a favour. Got her husband a posting back here. Thirty miles from home. Coastal defences. Home to pipe and slippers every other night, I should think.' Another, wider, cold smile. 'That's the secret, eh, Mrs Pride? What's in it for me? Works every time, as I'm sure you agree. Work for us and you avoid a lifetime's lodging in the Tower, or some other of His Majesty's establishments. Or even a noose round your, if I may make so bold, pretty neck!

'The only nigger in the woodpile is that Irish inamorato of yours. Captain Mullins, or whatever his name is. Gone to ground in his native peat, we suspect, but we'll just have to take our chances. It might be your being brought back to life as it were will smoke him out. So! You'll start resuming your glamorous spy role. That contact you gave us. We've kept an eye on him. He's pretty well dormant. But then, in all modesty we may claim that the espionage network here is virtually non-existent. You'll reappear miraculously like Banquo's ghost, turning up at Fossbeck Road, with the tale of how you lied, cheated, squirmed and charmed your way out of trouble and then laid low for a while. You'll make contact with your masters in Deutschland, and feed them gems we'll supply you with from time to time — from your new lover, a chap who works in the Air Ministry, as a matter of fact. Chum of your brother. Squadron Leader Humphreys is of course privy to our devious deeds. He will become your cousin, for the foreseeable future. That will be part of your cover. He's looking forward to entertaining cousin Jane, introducing you to his new family.

'You'll love it. Sir Roland has a beautiful estate. Highcombe Hall — rural Essex. He's even managed to prevent it from being commandeered by the government. Takes in the odd wounded soldier, I believe. Officers only, of course, and just for convalescence. You'll be able to soothe their fevered brows and get them back into the war machine that bit quicker.' Again came that hard little laugh, clear in its condemnation. 'You'll probably come out of this with a gong, my dear, for your patriotic efforts. And if by any mischance we should end up losing the game, you still might be able to claim you were on the winning side!'

24

'I can see it's been a while since you sat a horse. How does it feel?'

It felt damned uncomfortable, Cissie thought, aware of how bedraggled she must appear in comparison with the svelte and as always immaculate figure of her 'cousin-in-law', Midge Humphreys, née Goresby-Harrington. Less than three months ago, on the last day of July, Midge had given birth to a girl, Angela Verity Louise, yet here she was, more blooming than ever, cutting a full-bosomed dash in her hacking jacket, her riding breeches elegantly moulding those firm thighs and — it galled Cissie to have to admit — that exquisitely curving backside. Her own skinny rump was decidedly sore. She was squirming uncomfortably in the saddle, and letting her mind dwell longingly on a hot bath, a stiff drink, and a warm fire against the autumnal chill.

Try as she might, though she found it hard to try hard, she conceded, Cissie had found it impossible to like Midge in the half year she had known her. She remembered the saying from childhood about 'silver spoons', and that other less decorous expression about pokers inserted up rectums. If ever they applied to anyone they applied to the insufferable creature at whom she was smiling right now. The chief reason for her antipathy towards her was doubtless her attitude towards Nigel. His wife treated him with scarcely veiled or, more often, entirely uncovered, contempt. Cissie had been shocked when, while Midge was still ladying it from her grand bed after the confinement, bosoms practically spilling from peach satin and lace, she had declared roundly, 'You've let the side down badly, Nigel! Daddy's furious with you. And I must say I'm deeply disappointed, too. Next time you get me up the duff you'd better make sure it's with male issue, otherwise we'll be out on our ears!'

Cissie had soon gathered that these barbed witticisms were not jokes. Sir Roland was more circumspect in showing his displeasure, but displeased he undoubtedly was. It made Cissie feel bad. She had never felt close at all to her brother as they grew up, and she was surprised now at the depth of affection she carried for him. Perhaps it was something to do with the way she had come back from the dead, as it were. And, though Nig had found it hard, once he had got over the shock of her treachery, he had returned that affection in full measure. It gave her a warm glow to see his response to her. She knew that it was due in large measure to the way he felt alienated from Midge's family — and in so many subtle ways from his wife, too. There were many, many times when Cissie had itched to slap that cool aristocratic face at the way she treated Nig like some dim retainer, or, worse, like one of the yapping family pets. 'Go here. Fetch this. Stand there. Sit!'

There was something else — Cissie couldn't put her finger on it — that disturbed her about Midge. Something that didn't ring true, something hidden — and Cissie had become an expert in deceit over the past two years. She wished she could tell what it was, for it disturbed her more than she cared to accept. And it was not something she could ever discuss with Nig, not even indirectly. He was loyal to a fault. He was extremely upset now by the fact of hiding their true relationship from Midge and her family. Several times he had insisted he was going to tell Midge, 'in confidence'.

'I trust her implicitly!' he asserted fiercely, at Cissie's voluble alarm.

'It could be dangerous,' Cissie pleaded. 'Anyway, you're bound not to disclose it to anyone. Official secrets, remember!'

Privately, Cissie had serious doubts about

the value of what she was doing. She had been quaking literally with nerves when, in April, she had knocked on the door of 45, Fossbeck Road, to Mr Alex Harben, and his wife, Greta. The Harbens had lived in Finsbury Park for four years — 'handy for Holloway!' he had joked. He liked 'a laugh', as he never tired of telling her. His wife bleated dutifully at everything he said. Greta seemed to be fully aware of his clandestine activities, but always vanished whenever he and Cissie got 'down to business', as he put it. Their cover was that they had left Austria when the writing was being scribbled on many walls. 'I'm a lapsed Jew, but that makes no difference over there!' he told anyone who would listen, and most did, sympathetically. He was known and liked in the neighbour-hood.

To Cissie it was amazing that the Germans accepted her story of escape and evasion so readily, but, apparently, they did, and so she became an infrequent visitor to Finsbury Park, where she handed over information supplied by her new masters from the offices above the department store, for Alex Harben to pass on to the old firm in Berlin, or Hamburg, or wherever they operated from. The less she knew the better, Cissie felt, and exhibited a distinct lack of curiosity for detail from either of her employers.

She hoped some good would come out of it in helping the Allies to win the war. She knew she had to atone for her weakness — more and more she could attribute it as time passed by to the blindness of her love for Sean Mullins, or 'whatever his name is', as her controller, Mr Penn, above the store, said. The Irishman had disappeared without trace. The sudden resurrection of Cissie as an agent for the Fatherland had not brought him out of hiding. She was uncertain whether to be glad or sorry. She was still waiting for her heart to mend.

In the meantime, she had acquired another lover, one Squadron Leader Derek Humsby, the source of most of the 'plants' she brought to the Harbens' door. She was disconcerted when one day Mr Penn introduced her to a tall individual in air force uniform and sporting the now fashionable flowering bristle of whiskers from his upper lip known as a 'handlebar'. 'This is your lover,' Mr Penn said, eyes twinkling behind his glasses. 'We think it's about time you two met. He can drop you off or pick you up at Fossbeck Road next time you meet your friends. Touch of realism, what? You can start by being seen about town. Two tickets for the Adelphi for tonight. Spot of dinner and dancing afterwards. Nothing too outrageous, mind.'

The squadron leader took his cover far too seriously. In the taxi, he put his hand on her stockinged knee even before they had dined and wined. On the late return trip, he was much more determined — and specific. She wrestled with him quite energetically, and turned her cheek when, finally chastened, he lunged for one desperate goodnight kiss on the steps of her billet close to the Ladies' Automobile Club in South Audley Street. 'Look, Derek.' She was polite, almost kind, but firm. 'I'm already spoken for. In fact, I have a husband, who's out East.' Not perhaps very convincing as an argument. Half the female diners and winers were married and were accompanied by someone other than their husband. Perhaps, she thought later, with a scandalous giggle at her shamefully macabre humour, she should tell him what happened to the last poor Derek she had kissed. Alas, poor Hargreaves! She had certainly known *him* well!

Nigel was highly indignant when she told him about her latest acquisition. She was touched, and pleased. 'The blighter! Derek Humsby? Never heard of him! Nothing to do with our lot.' 'Our lot' was Bomber Command. It was just as well, Cissie thought fondly, that she had been turned, and was no longer a faithful employee of the Reich. Nig had told her far too much about the mountainous workload he was swamped with these days — and many nights — with the regular thousand bomber raids over occupied territory, and the German mainland itself. He also travelled about the country as a liaison officer with the American Army Air Force, establishing itself in bases all over England. 'Poor beggars are taking some stick. They insist on daylight bombing. They're getting cut to ribbons.'

He had also nearly dropped them in it much nearer home — *at* home, in fact — when, not long after her renaissance, he called her 'Cissie'. Midge had pounced at once, and 'Jane' had launched into her voluble and fortunately ready explanation of the nickname. 'My brother's fault,' Cissie had laughed. 'It just stuck with members of the family.'

'Brother? Where is he?'

'He's out in India,' Cissie answered quickly. 'Or, rather Burma, now, I think. Haven't heard for ages.'

'Strange types, you Indian wallahs, eh?' Midge chuckled. 'I wonder what I've let myself in for sometimes.'

The senior Freemans were out in the sub-continent, though hundreds of miles from Kandla and her parents. My ruddy family's growing by leaps and bounds, Cissie reflected. Her life here was scarcely any less of a lie than when she had been secreted up north with Sean. Poor old Charlie. First she had made him a widower, now she had relegated him to the role of brother. Still, why should she imagine her life any different, when the whole world was in a mess? Charlie came far too infrequently into her thoughts, or even her prayers these days. She tried to offer some restitution as she prayed for his well-being now.

★   ★   ★

Poor old Charlie! Rani thought, a smile playing about her vivid lips. She studied his slim, pale form as he stood there. His penis was brown and squat in its shroud of foreskin, above it the small scrub of dark curls, the only evidence of hair on the pale smoothness of his body. She liked to keep him naked after their lovemaking, after they had bathed — and after she had dressed. She was wearing her lemon sari, and she felt the stirrings of excitement again beneath the clinging folds of the light material. It was an excitement which she had taught him at least and at last to assuage. A shame, she thought, with a genuine and tender regret, that she had not been able to instruct him thus for the brief period when the little mem had been his bride. She still thought often of her charge, the long, happy days, and nights, they had spent together. The memory of Cissie was kept separate, locked away like a shrine in her heart, totally apart from what her life had become now, its dedicated aim.

She felt another smile tugging at the corners of her mouth as she beckoned him to come to her, and he moved at once, obediently. She placed him on the bed, his body as slim and graceful as a girl's, as her little mem's. But then there was that stirring difference, as she began to stroke and fondle, slowly rousing him again, rejoicing in his soft, sighing, helpless submission. Mistress. His mistress. That was her title now. And never had it been more true.

She was acknowledged as such. She met his fellow officers, and the girls like herself they proudly gave the arm to, smug in their new-found liberalism. 'Going native.' There was no stigma to it now — as long as you didn't go too far, of course. Bed but don't wed. That would be unthinkable. But maybe not in the new world and new society she and those she was working with were striving for.

Charlie had been useful to her. Helped her

to get to the city, to find a job, get an education, then better jobs, so that she could break through barriers, work her way up through the ranks of clerkdom. But most of all he had helped her quite unknowingly, giving her illegal access to military matters, enabling her to meet others from whom she could learn confidential information, for her secret and more vital occupation, as agent for the destruction of British sovereignty over her country and her people.

There were some who still argued that independence would come soon after British victory in the war. Before war had broken out, Labour politicians like Macdonald had talked of self-government. But the current British leader was a diehard opponent of self-rule. Others were pinning their hopes, foolishly, on the Japanese advances through Malaya and Burma. But Nippon was just another colonial power, or was hoping to be. They would be just as oppressive as the British, if not worse. As for the Mahatma, he might support the Quit India brigade, but strikes and non-violent methods would not bring success. Too many people, men and women, bore the scars of the long batons on their backs, or were buried in mass graves, testament to how the British dealt with non-violence.

The small cell of which Rani had become a vital part looked elsewhere for help — and it would be forthcoming. The foes of Britain in Europe — the Germans — offered a more positive and decisive hope. They were aiming at the destruction of the British rule in India and everywhere else in their empire, and offering freedom in its place. Contacts had been made, in Delhi, in Bombay, and now here in Calcutta. Rani was to be accorded the great honour of playing a major part — she would be sent to London itself to further these clandestine ties, to discover how Indians could participate in the struggle against tyranny, and bring about the fall of British rule.

As she worked on the slender form twisting and whimpering beneath her caresses, the nostalgic sympathy and regret she had been experiencing at the thought of this relationship which was so soon to end faded, and was replaced by fierce resolve, and contempt for the effete, degenerate society Charlie Pride represented, whose fate she controlled and held literally in her busy hands.

★ ★ ★

The advent of 1943 was celebrated with renewed enthusiasm throughout Britain, as people were convinced for the first time that the war would be won. Sir Roland and Lady Julia had thrown a party the like of which Highcombe Hall had not seen since the days of peace, and in London the celebrations had lasted for many nights. So optimistic was the general mood that Cissie, tiddly on champagne and the notion that life might be worth living after all, and after Sean Mullins, had almost given in and allowed her 'lover' to spend the night with her. Almost but not quite, much to 'Dreary' Derek's disappointment. The tide had turned on the Eastern Front, it appeared. The Reds had held up the Germans at Stalingrad, and were actually breaking out after months of siege. In the North African desert, the Eighth Army had halted the Desert Fox's seemingly unstoppable advance on Egypt, at El Alamein at the end of October, and had proceeded to move west, over the territory they had previously yielded.

Cissie had hardly recovered from many late, wet January nights, when, on the very day that the Allies entered Tripoli, Mr Penn summoned her to his den. 'How are things in the typing pool?' he asked as he waved her to a seat before his desk. He was referring to the cover Cissie had assumed, which fooled very few of her colleagues in the department, in view of the time she spent at her desk and her two-fingered stabs at her machine.

'Far too exciting for me to regale you with, sir.' Their relationship had mellowed considerably from the days when he had resorted to threatening her with incarceration or the gallows to persuade her to do her duty.

'There's something come to our notice,' he said. 'Something just up your street, I should think, given your background.' He saw the beginning of a blush steal over Cissie's attentive features, and went on hastily. 'I refer of course to your upbringing in India. There's a group of our dusky brethren over here — naughty boys — who've been trying to form an alliance with Jerry. The usual Home Rule bunch of misguided souls, who seem to think they'll get us out of India much quicker if they team up with the Hun. Damn nonsense, of course, but we thought we'd better look into it. We've got wind of one of them who's coming over here from the homeland. Already docked, we understand. A woman! Which makes it even more your cup of tea, wouldn't you say? You'll be her Jerry contact. We've picked up the Hindi chappie delegated to meet her. He's been most co-operative.'

How easily the words tripped off his tongue. Cissie recalled the dank gloom of the

Tower, the interrogations with those cold, bespectacled Intelligence types, their dispassionate regard as they threatened her with all kinds of horrors. She hoped that the unknown Indian had been as sensible and as cowardly as she had been, if not as patriotic.

'We know the rendezvous. Tomorrow, ten o'clock. It should go swimmingly. She won't suspect a thing. Get chummy, find out all you can. Names, places, as much as you can squeeze out of her. There's a bed-sit in Bayswater. Move in today; we've allocated a driver for you, to help with your stuff. Take her back there tomorrow. Get cosy. Pump her for all she's worth. We'll see how to play it from there. But I should think a couple of days should do. You can even let her see you're in contact with Deutschland. Send out a signal or two — it'll impress her no end. Keep her at the flat. We'll wait for you to get in touch. You might be able to keep the thing going, who knows? She certainly won't be very clued up, not if the bunch over here are anything to go by. Should be quite enjoyable for you. You'll be able to have a jolly old chinwag about home, eh?'

Cissie tried hard to emulate Mr Penn's breezy casualness next morning, as she paid off the cab and made her way through the barricaded gateway off the Mall, and into the park. The seat near the bandstand, on the left, heading west. She swallowed, and strove to ignore the sick feeling, which seemed to be stirring her breakfast uncomfortably. She was ashamed of a sudden hope that the seat should be empty, that the unknown spy would fail to make the meeting. She was so confused as to her own emotions about this. Why should she feel a double sense of deceit because the stranger was Indian? She was clearly one of those who would stop at nothing. Someone who was prepared to see Britain suffer defeat at the hands of the Germans in order to bring the raj down. How dare she? Cissie tried to rouse her sense of outrage to help her in the task that lay ahead.

The path through the park was crowded, though most people were striding ahead purposefully, not loitering at their leisure. Cissie glanced ahead. Yes, there she was! Muffled in a dark winter coat, with a blue woollen scarf draped hood-like about her head. Of course she would be feeling the cold, poor soul, especially if this was her first visit to Europe. In fact, it was rather a stupid place to choose for a rendezvous, given the time of year, for she was the only figure sitting hunched on the bench, and every other seat within sight was empty. The thought gave Cissie courage. She would be a match for these people! She hurried forward. She must get this stranger up and away as quickly as possible. She prepared the polite Hindi greeting she had not used for so long, as she saw the brown features, looking small and pinched in the upturned collar, the blue wool. Cissie held out her hand as she gave the greeting with a bright smile.

She reared back in horror at the wild vision of terror which crossed the face. The slim figure rose, gave a piercing shriek, which made the passers-by stare with alarm. 'Oh my God! Little mem! Are you a ghost? Is it you? Please!'

Cissie reeled. 'Rani?' she muttered faintly, and echoed her former armah. 'Is it you?'

Then they were standing, clinging together, sobbing, while around them people stared, then moved on in resumption of their myriad separate lives.

PART IV

LOOSE ENDS

25

The meeting with Rani brought all the devious and disparate roads and byways of Cissie's life into cataclysmic junction. It went way beyond coincidence. It seemed like the drawing together of all the complicated threads she, and the circumstances of her complex life, had woven, by a god much closer to Hardy's President of the Immortals than the one Cissie had acknowledged and prayed to each unthinking night of her childhood, and worshipped in her Sunday frock at the family's side in the white wooden church at Kandla. It was a watershed, and Cissie knew that on the other side of it things had to be different.

Rani seemed equally moved and stunned. In the cab, they sat holding gloved hands. Tears kept rolling down the brown face, and she murmured 'Little mem!' over and over, in a voice of wonder, with those great dark orbs fixed on the figure at her side as though she might disappear at any second.

In the gloom of the bed-sit, almost as unfamiliar to Cissie as it was to her guest, they made tea, and picked at the sandwiches

Cissie struggled to prepare from the grey slabs of the 'British loaf'. 'What animal is this?' Rani asked suspiciously of the slices of jelly-coated, cold meat, which she declined to eat or touch. Her suspicions were well founded for, had she eaten of it, she would have broken one of the fundamental laws of her faith. 'Bread will do fine,' she said, eyeing the doughy slabs with little enthusiasm. 'And a nice cup of tea!' she added bravely, in an effort to dispel the lingering atmosphere of shock, and the chill physical atmosphere which enveloped the dark and shabby room in the grey noontide. Rani had not even discarded her heavy coat, beneath which she wore a thick, ribbed sweater with high, rolled collar, and navy blue slacks.

'I've never seen you in western clothes.' Cissie stared at her, with a wistful, tremulous smile. The doubts and questions gathered like the gloom of the day about them, impinging on the wonder of their miraculous reunion. 'We have to talk,' Cissie said solemnly. She was possessed by a simple stroke of inspiration. 'It's freezing. And I don't have any coal. Let's go to bed!'

They removed coats and shoes and climbed under the sheet and blankets. As they turned to clasp one another again, the years fell away, and Cissie realized that this shivering, tawny figure in her arms was the one person she had known and loved uncomplicatedly in her young life. And she could not deceive her.

Rani's great, solemn gaze remained riveted on her while she told the monstrous events of the past three years. It took a long while, and was punctuated with many incredulous questions from her listener, as well as many pauses for Cissie's choking sobs, and the fervent consolation of the arms and kisses she had grown up with. Cissie scrambled for a handkerchief, dabbed at her swollen eyes and blew her crackling nose. 'So you see,' she sniffed, in confessional conclusion, 'I've made a thorough mess of things. A bad show all round. I've been unfaithful to poor Charlie . . . he'd be better off if I never came back from the dead!'

She had pulled no punches in describing the passion of her relationship with Sean, and was awaiting, almost with a morbidly masochistic pleasure, the castigation from her confessor. Rani's answer was therefore even more of a bombshell. 'And poor Charlie has been unfaithful to you. Though at least he has the excuse that he thought you were dead.'

All these moments beneath the blankets of Bayswater were seminal moments of truth. '*You?*' squeaked Cissie, sitting up from the embracing arms and staring bug-eyed. '*You?* He went to bed with *you?*'

For an instant, all the intervening momentous events of their separate histories were as nothing, and Cissie really was the little mem once more, and Rani the little brown playmate-serf, who was there to do her pleasure and her bidding. 'Yes! *Me!*' Rani fired back. Eloquently, she grabbed Cissie's hand, locked it firmly in entwining fingers and held them up before Cissie's nose. The dark intricately knotted and combined with the paler skin. 'Was that such a terrible thing to do? He needed comfort, and love.' But Rani was not, in the last instance, ready to unburden herself as completely as her former mistress. She did not mention the motive behind her provision of that comfort for the grieving widower. Instead, those dark eyes flashed challengingly. She captured Cissie's other hand, held them both in tight imprisonment, and pressed her face close until they were almost touching. 'Is that such a terrible thing, little mem? Do you feel betrayed? Brown and white! Do you feel disgust?'

Cissie's head was spinning. 'No!' she whispered. She fell back on the pillow. 'No. Of course not.' She began to cry again, and Rani's tears mingled with hers. Their faces pressed in contact as close as their joined hands, and their lips met.

★　★　★

'It's all a dreadful mess, I'm afraid, sir. I've made a terrible hash of the whole bloody thing! Sorry, sir!' Cissie appended at the use of her expletive. She groped in her jacket pocket for her handkerchief. My nose must be like a cherry, she thought disconsolately. She had blown it so many times — she was almost out of face powder. She wondered where Rani was, in this great, alien city, and what would become of her. The significance of their sudden meeting and parting still imposed its awesome spiritual dazzlement on Cissie's spinning mind. It was, it had to be, a turning point.

She had let Rani go. She had extracted nothing from her, had made no effort to do so. Instead, she had warned her of the degree of skilful penetration of MI5, its knowledge of the enemy's inadequate spy networks. She told Rani of her own dual role, of the task she had been assigned, to help track down those plotters of the downfall of the raj. 'They already have one of them. That's how I came to be there in the park.'

'If it had not been me, would you have

381

done it? Betrayed us?'

Cissie blushed, but she nodded. 'This is my country. I've already betrayed it. I've tried to make up for it.' She drew a deep, shuddering breath. 'But no more. I'm finished with all of it. I don't care what they do. They can shoot me if they like!' she asserted, with tremulous bravery.

There was more of the tremolo than the bravery, however, as she faced the impassive countenance of Mr Penn in his office the next day. The sword of truth was slightly nicked, as she lied a little. 'It just threw me when I saw my armah — maid — of all people, sitting there on the park bench. I think she saw through me straight away. We talked over old times, mostly. All day and half the night. I was just — you know — trying to allay her doubts about me. Then, when I woke up this morning, she'd gone. No note, nothing! I must have gone out like a light last night. Didn't hear a thing.'

'Perhaps she doped you,' Mr Penn said, still impassive. 'At least this one didn't leave you tied up and helpless.'

Cissie crimsoned, glancing up at him in surprise. Was he trying to be funny? It was impossible to tell. It scarcely mattered. Now it was time to return to the truth. The big truth. She swallowed, to ease her dry throat.

'The thing is, sir, I think my cover's been blown. I think — I can't really go on with this whole business. I can't take any more, sir. I've had enough!' She tried to rein in the note of rising nerves and panic. 'I want to end it, sir. I — I don't really care what you do to me! You can lock me up again if you like. Or — shoot me!'

They didn't shoot her. The urbane calm of Mr Penn's reply dumb-founded her. 'We were pretty much coming to the same conclusion ourselves. Jerry seems to be taking your sterling efforts on his behalf with liberal pinches of salt. Certainly he's not acting on the titbits you've been passing him. And no one's slipping ashore or dropping in from the skies these days. It's time we pulled in the Harbens. Our friendly neighbourhood Jew has had a good run for his money. As for this latest little viper's nest of empire destroyers, we'll just have to make do with the little bird we've got. See if we can make him sing a little more.

'Shame about your ex-nanny, though. Still, she won't get far, I suspect. Alone in the big city, fresh off the boat. In February, too! Brrr!'

She mightn't be as easy to catch as you think! Cissie reflected. She had given her some useful tips, and all the limited cash she could muster. She thought again of their last passionate embraces, in the glimmer of the cold dawn. And she thought of that lithe brown body cleaving fiercely to Charlie's, night after night. Just as I did to Sean! Cissie's conscience rebuked. Yes, she confirmed resolutely. I hope she makes it back home.

And it was home thoughts that assailed her overwhelmingly at Mr Penn's next, and most startling, words. 'You know, I think it's time you were resurrected, Mrs Pride. Officially, I mean. You've done your duty. A little tardily, perhaps, but we'll say no more about that. You've paid your dues this past year. Account cleared, shall we say? You're due a spot of home leave. And you can trail your clouds of glory with you. Captured in Germany. Fooled them into thinking you'd fallen for their guff — sneaked back into Blighty, to beat them at their own devious game. Hail the conquering heroine, eh? Don't give that poor hubby of yours a heart attack, though, will you?' And now he gave a full-throated chuckle, and allowed the sparkle behind the spectacles to break through. 'I'd better break the news to our friend, Humsby. Poor Derek! He'll be devastated to lose you — as we all are.'

★ ★ ★

'What? You mean to say you're his — ' Midge swivelled her gaze on to her husband, and her astonishment was replaced by a look of fury. 'She's your *sister*?' Her voice rose to a venomous shriek on the last word. Nigel was looking suitably wretched, like young George at the fallen cherry tree. Except that poor Nig *had* been telling a lie, and maintaining it for the past year and more.

'I had to, darling!' he pleaded abjectly. 'Official secret and all that. In view of the job she was doing. Hush-hush — '

'My God! To think you could keep something like that from your own wife!' Her righteous outrage was magnificent. Her anger took in both brother and sister, who looked even more alike as they stared in sheepish discomfort at the carpet before her wrath. 'What a devious pair you are! I wonder what other nasty little secrets you've been keeping from me!'

Nasty secrets? The phrase stung Cissie, and she felt a fierce reply springing to mind. We've been working to save our country, not sitting on our fat backsides, or exercising horses, or spurning the peasants toiling on our land, or living off the illicit fat of that land available only to a privileged few in wartime England. But she kept silence, enduring the verbal assault with what she hoped was offended dignity. A spirited defence would only make matters worse for poor old Nig in the long run. And she would very soon be abandoning him, leaving him alone in this unfriendly feudal fiefdom of Highcombe.

Midge was still in full flow. 'There should be nothing that can't be told between husband and wife. Complete honesty in all things. Is that too much to ask? Surely — '

'Mamma! Dadda! Bad boy? Dadda naughty!'

The door had crashed open, and Angela staggered on sturdy but unsteady legs into their midst, nappy sagging, her green eyes alight with glee at Mummy's angry tones. Followed by a nervously apologetic maid, the infant teetered towards her mother, with arms outstretched, and Midge scooped her up efficiently before she fell. From her enfolding arms, Angela swung round to survey the others. To Cissie, those green eyes, and that long, pale and freckled face, below the vivid halo of light gingery curls, glanced at them with a cocky worldliness impossible in one who had not long celebrated her first birthday. Certainly a chip off the old block on the maternal side, Cissie surmised. But precious little evidence of Nig's gentle, easy-going nature, more's the pity!

Then Cissie observed something quite remarkable. Midge had stopped in mid-flight. A dull tide of redness swept up from the neck to flood the patrician features, and the tirade magically ceased, for which Angela's new aunt was grateful, if somewhat puzzled.

She was not to know the truth. No one ever was. Midge had not seen or had any contact with Flight Sergeant Ginge Evans since several months before Angela's birth. Midge was not aware that Evans had been posted missing after his bomber was shot down over Essen, his so far unidentified remains consumed along with his fellow crew members in flames on German soil. Lack of this knowledge did not worry the precocious little girl bouncing in her mother's arms. She already had a hero for a daddy. Even if Mummy did give him a good ticking off now and then!

★   ★   ★

Martin and Delia Humphreys, along with Charlie and his parents, had had well over a month to absorb the astounding and miraculous news of Cissie's reappearance in the world of the living. The local papers were full of it, despite the efforts at censorship. Details were scarce, but it was beyond doubt that she had played a dramatic and heroic part in the distant European war. And a hero's welcome awaited her, with the red, white and blue bunting dug out to decorate the club, and Union Jacks fluttering everywhere.

She was flown back. The journey took more than a week, with several hops involving nightly stopovers and several exotic (at least on the map) places *en route*. But eventually the final plane touched down on the strip at Jaunpur. Charlie had pleaded to be allowed to go alone to meet her. The welcoming hordes would meet the train at Kandla Halt the following evening.

Cissie was sick with apprehension throughout the last bumpy plane ride, and her legs felt as though they might not carry her down the aircraft's short steps on to the baking dust in front of the simple single-storey little building. Truth! she urged herself. She clung to the word like a lifebelt. She must be honest with him; she would no longer carry her baggage of lies and evasions.

Then she found herself sobbing in his arms, and he was crying, too, the tears running down his thin, tanned face. He looked as boyish as ever in his khaki drill, and more so when later she saw his naked paleness, with the deep contrast of tanned neck and face, and mahogany hands and forearms.

She felt as shy as she had on her honeymoon, and far less certain. I *will* tell him! I will tell him everything! She opened her mouth, and he fell on her, crushing her, bearing her backwards on to the creaking bed, where the mosquito net hung folded on its metal ring, like a cloud above them, and he did not stop to unfurl it, and she gasped, staring down at his body, then she cried out, sobbing now with her joy and her desperate need to be one with him.

'I love you!' he whispered, much, much later, and she recognized that the words were superfluous now, but she murmured them in return, rejoicing in their wet and sweating flesh and her sorely sated body. This was truth, too, and it would do for her for now.

The return to her home was everything she could wish for, and she and Charlie stuck it out manfully until dawn before they fell into bed in her old room and slept in innocent inebriation in each other's arms.

Surfacing at lunchtime, clad only in a cotton wrap, Cissie smiled blearily across the table, set for breakfast still, on the veranda. 'This came for you, darling,' her mother said, passing across a postcard. 'Probably travelled out with the mail on your plane. Dated a month ago. Posted in London, by the look of it, though God knows what the picture is. Some little English fishing village, by the look of it. Some cheeky blighter!' Her words indicated that she had read its brief message.

Cissie glanced at the front, and her heart quivered as she saw an old photograph of Kingstaith, taken long before the war. On the back was a brief, bold scrawl:

Glad you made it. Fight the good fight, me darlin'.
As ever, Sean.

'Who's it from, sweetheart?' Charlie asked curiously. She tossed it on the table in front of him. 'Just some cheeky so-and-so I met in training, ages ago. An Irish chap. Full of blarney. You know what they're like.'

He nodded and smiled tenderly at her, reaching for her hand. She blushed a little at his demonstrativeness in front of her parents, but returned his smile. 'This damned sun!' she said lightly. 'I'm not used to this brightness any more. Makes my eyes water.' And she brushed away the moisture clinging obstinately to her lashes.

Other titles published by
The House of Ulverscroft:

THE DECENT THING

C. W. Reed

David Herbert lives a privileged life in Edwardian society but is dominated by his sisters, Gertrude and Clara. At public school he suffers bullying and at home his only friend is Nelly Tovey, a young maid . . . Living on a pittance in London after being disowned by his family, he becomes seriously ill and is nursed by the devoted Nelly. Although certain of their love, Nelly is aware of the gulf between them. David must find the courage to defy convention and breach the barriers to their happiness.

SEASON OF SINS

C. W. Reed

When Johnny Able, reared among the
pirates of the East African coast, miraculously reappears at Strenshaugh Hall at
the end of Queen Victoria's reign, his
grandfather is delighted. His lordship's
dreams of his heir's marriage to the shy
and virtuous Rose appear to be fulfilled.
But Johnny's upbringing has left him sadly
unfitted for his elevated role. A scandalous
affair with Rose's maid and his profligate
lifestyle in London cause Rose to reject
him. Embittered, he leaves England once
more. Rose turns to a former suitor for
comfort, but after a disastrous marriage,
she risks all to follow Johnny . . .

THE FOOLISH VIRGIN

C. W. Reed

In the beautiful North Yorkshire Dales, a wartime relationship develops between Land Girl Ruth Palmer and captured German flier Holger Fichtmuller. This almost unthinkable affair transcends the prejudices of two nations locked in world combat. Kept apart for more than two years, the couple correspond through a sympathetic chaplain. When, eventually, Holger is transferred to Yorkshire, fortune seems to favour the lovers, despite family opposition. However, as an Allied victory in Europe finally approaches, news of death camp atrocities brings a crisis of conscience to Holger.

STAND AGAINST

POLLUTION

AND

WASTE

Georgia Amson-Bradshaw

W
FRANKLIN WATTS
LONDON • SYDNEY

Franklin Watts
First published in Great Britain in 2020 by The Watts Publishing Group
Copyright © The Watts Publishing Group 2020

Produced for Franklin Watts by
White-Thomson Publishing Ltd
www.wtpub.co.uk

Editor: Georgia Amson-Bradshaw/Izzi Howell
Designer and illustrator: Mimi Butler

Every attempt has been made to clear copyright. Should there be any inadvertent omission
please apply to the publisher for rectification.

ISBN 978 1 4451 6823 4 (HB) and 978 1 4451 6824 1 (PB)

Printed in Dubai

FSC
www.fsc.org

MIX
Paper from
responsible sources
FSC® C104740

Franklin Watts
An imprint of
Hachette Children's Group
Part of The Watts Publishing Group
Carmelite House
50 Victoria Embankment
London EC4Y 0DZ

An Hachette UK Company
www.hachette.co.uk
www.franklinwatts.co.uk

CONTENTS

KNOW YOUR TARGETS: Pollution and waste

Humans produce a lot of waste, and we're not just talking the stuff we throw in the bin. Waste chemicals and gases are constantly being pumped out in huge amounts around the world. When waste gets out into the environment, it becomes pollution, which hurts people and the planet.

WHAT A WASTE

Packaging, used or broken objects, uneaten food and all the things we throw away at home or at school are obvious kinds of waste. But what we don't see is that before the things we buy even get to us, a whole load more waste will have been produced while the objects were being manufactured.

THINK AND ACT

What was the last thing you threw away? Could you have **reused** it or **recycled** it instead?

MAKING THINGS

Take a single cotton T-shirt, for example. Growing cotton plants creates waste because some parts of the plant aren't used. Spinning and dyeing the fabric uses water and chemicals that become liquid waste. Making the fabric into a garment leaves waste fabric in the offcuts that aren't used. The T-shirt is wrapped in packaging to be transported and sold – which also becomes waste.

POLLUTION: THE MAIN CULPRITS

Air pollution is caused by harmful gases being released into the air, while water pollution is caused by chemicals or rubbish being dumped or leaked into waterways and the ocean. The dumping of litter or chemicals from farming and industry on the land and in the soil is land pollution.

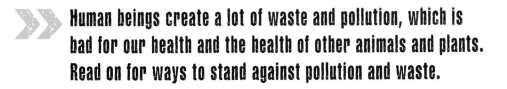 Human beings create a lot of waste and pollution, which is bad for our health and the health of other animals and plants. Read on for ways to stand against pollution and waste.

WHERE DOES POLLUTION COME FROM?

Pollution is everywhere. Even in the Arctic, or in the middle of the ocean, the effects of human pollution can be found. So how does all this pollution get released into the environment?

VEHICLE EMISSIONS

One of the biggest sources of pollution is from vehicle engines. Vehicles burn fuels such as diesel and petrol, which release toxic gases, particulates (tiny bits of soot) and greenhouse gases (which cause climate change) into the air.

THERE ARE OVER A BILLION CARS ON THE ROAD WORLDWIDE.

INDUSTRIAL POLLUTION

The majority of our electricity is produced in power plants that burn fossil fuels such as gas, oil and coal. Like car engines, these create air pollution. Industry (that's factories such as chemical plants, metals and plastic factories, mills and mines) also releases polluting gases. Industry is a key source of water pollution, too, as chemicals from industrial processes leak or are dumped into waterways and the ocean.

AGRICULTURE

In many countries, agriculture is the largest source of water pollution. Pesticides applied to crops spread into the surrounding environment. Fertilisers, animal manure and eroded soil washes off farmland and into waterways, causing 'eutrophication'. This is when extra nutrients in water cause algae to grow too much, blocking out sunlight and using up all the oxygen in the water. This kills off water creatures such as fish and plants.

WASTE MANAGEMENT

Solid waste, or litter, is another type of pollution that ends up on the land and in the sea. Many places around the world don't have good waste management, and litter is often simply dumped on the land or in waterways, where it makes its way eventually to the ocean. Scientists estimate that up to 2.41 million tonnes of plastic waste enter the ocean each year from rivers.

THINK AND ACT

Do you see a lot of **litter** in your area? Could you pick some of it up and **put it in the bin**, instead of just leaving it where it is? Why not solve the problem yourself, rather than leaving it to someone else?

IMPACTS OF AIR POLLUTION

How serious can some gases in the air be? After all, there's so much air in the world! The answer: very serious. 4.6 million people die every year directly because of air pollution, and that's only the start.

HUMAN HEALTH

Have you ever found yourself coughing because of vehicle exhaust, or blown your nose, only to find your snot is all black? Yuck! That's air pollution. It can have very serious effects on our lungs, causing asthma, respiratory diseases such as emphysema, bronchitis and lung cancer.

As well as lung problems, it can increase the risk of heart attacks, strokes and diseases including Parkinson's and Alzheimer's. Air pollution is particularly risky for young children and babies in the womb, affecting brain development. Governments around the world monitor air pollution levels, and have targets to reduce it, because it is so important for improving citizens' health.

THINK ABOUT IT

HOW MANY OF YOUR FRIENDS AND CLASSMATES HAVE ASTHMA? DID YOU KNOW THAT THREE TIMES MORE PEOPLE HAVE ASTHMA TODAY THAN 50 YEARS AGO?

WILDLIFE

Plants and animals are at added risk from air pollution due to the effect of acid rain. When certain pollutants in the atmosphere mix with rain, it becomes acidic. When the rain falls on forests, lakes and streams, it can destroy trees, and make the water toxic to the fish and other creatures that live in it. Birds and animals that rely on the plants and the fish for food are also affected.

DAMAGE TO ATMOSPHERE

Ozone is a type of gas. High up in the Earth's atmosphere, there is a band containing ozone gas called the ozone layer. The way ozone reacts with sunlight protects the Earth below from the harshest UV rays.

However, when certain types of air pollution get into the atmosphere, they react with the ozone, causing the ozone layer to break down. This allows dangerous UV rays to get through, causing skin cancer and harming ecosystems. For example, extra UV rays can stop plankton from reproducing. Plankton make up the bottom rung of many food chains, so this reduces food for other animals all the way up the food chain.

>> Greenhouse gas emissions are one of the most serious types of air pollution, as they cause climate change. Read more about them on pages 38–41.

MEASURE AIR POLLUTION

Compare pollution in places you visit. You won't be able to measure gases but you can measure particulates (tiny pieces of solid pollution) such as dust and soot.

You'll need: white card, scissors, a hole punch, string, a permanent marker and Vaseline.

STEP 1 Cut the white card into twelve 6 cm x 6 cm squares. Punch a hole in the top of each one. Tie a piece of string through the hole, creating a loop so you can hang it off a tree branch or similar.

STEP 2 With an adult's help, think about four locations for your experiment (such as your bedroom, a friend's garden next to a busy road, your school's car park, and so on).

STEP 3

Use the marker to draw a small square on each piece of card. Smear a thin layer of Vaseline inside the square.

STEP 4

Hang three squares in each of your chosen locations, and leave them there for 7–10 days. (You might want to label them with **'science experiment – please do not touch'** on the back.)

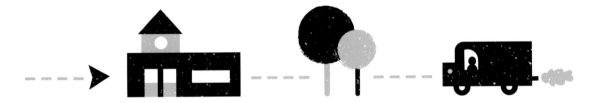

STEP 5

Collect the squares after 10 days. Examine each card with the magnifying glass. You should find small particles stuck in the Vaseline. These are pieces of air pollution. **In which area did your card capture the most air pollution?**

Check **waqi.info** for real time information about air pollution around the world.

Are you driven to school in a car, or do you walk, cycle or take a bus or train? In the past, it was much more common to walk or cycle to school compared to now. But with so many parents driving, there is more air pollution from cars around schools.

TOXIC AIR

The exhaust fumes from cars on the school run create areas of heavy pollution around schools, which exposes pupils to very high air pollution levels. This is especially dangerous for children, as air pollution affects their development. **So what can you do about it?**

 Why not encourage your schoolmates to walk to school by organising a **Walk to School Day?**

On a **Walk to School Day,** everyone walks (or cycles or takes public transport) to school. You can use the day to draw attention to the **health and environmental benefits of walking to school**.

STEP 1

Get your headteacher to approve the **Walk to School Day**. If they need some persuading, explain to them the health benefits for children and the benefits for the environment.

STEP 2

Promote the event to other students and parents. You could put up **posters** and **give out flyers**, or put an article in the school newsletter. It's good to talk about things that will motivate your schoolmates and their parents. Are they interested in health issues, or the environment? Is their local concern about road safety? Try to tap in to the issues that are important to your school community.

STEP 3

If you want, you could plan some 'walking buses' or 'park and strides'. **A walking bus** is where a group of children and a couple of adults meet at an agreed time and place, then walk to school in a group. It's safe and fun to do. **Park and stride** is good for people who live too far away from school to walk all the way. Instead, the parents can park a walkable distance away from school and the child walks the rest. It means that air pollution from the cars isn't all concentrated around the school.

STEP 4

Remind people the day before. **Hang up some banners** to greet everyone when they arrive at school the next day.

IMPACTS OF WATER POLLUTION

Water is essential to all life on Earth. But water pollution is a growing threat to us and other living creatures.

DIRTY WATER

2.3 billion people around the world don't have access to proper toilets. Even in places with toilets and sewage systems, the waste water isn't always treated properly. When sewage and waste water get into the environment, it can spread diseases such as cholera, dysentery, typhoid and polio.

Dirty drinking water is estimated to cause 502,000 deaths each year.

UNDERGROUND POLLUTION

Groundwater (water that is found underground inside porous rocks) can be polluted by chemical and industrial spills, or often by runoff from cities and roads. Roads get covered in bits of tyre, spilled fuel and exhaust emissions. When it rains, this pollution is washed onto the land where it can seep down into groundwater.

DETERGENTS

When we clean our homes, do our laundry and wash our dishes, we don't usually think about what happens to the chemicals and detergents that we wash down the drain. When the detergents aren't treated properly in waste water plants, they can poison aquatic life such as frogs and fish.

FARM WASTE

Over a third of the world's land is used for agriculture, and the runoff of animal manure, fertilisers, pesticides and other chemicals can cause big problems. As well as causing eutrophication (see page 7), pesticides can escape into the environment and kill wildlife.

OIL SPILLS

A very obvious type of water pollution is the oil spills that we see every so often on the news. Very major oil spills are quite rare, but when they do happen, they have very serious effects. Animals that swallow the oil are poisoned. Oil also destroys the insulating ability of birds' feathers and the fur on animals such as sea otters. Without the ability to repel water and insulate from the cold water, birds and mammals die from hypothermia.

>> **Less than one per cent of oil-soaked birds survive, even after BEING CLEANED.**

INVESTIGATE WATER POLLUTION

How polluted is the water in your area? What is the quality of your drinking water? Try these activities to find out.

Whenever collecting samples from rivers and lakes, ALWAYS wear gloves, have an adult present and take care at the water's edge.

In this experiment, compare the quality of your tap water, some bottled water and water from a local stream or beach.

You'll need: Three jars, water from a local river or beach, bottled water, tap water and water testing strips (available online, such as the Watersafe brand).

STEP 1
Collect your water samples in jars to be tested. It is essential to have an adult present when collecting water from a river or beach. Be very careful around the water's edge.

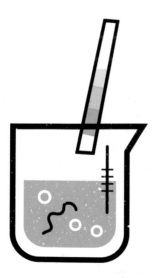

STEP 2
Use a strip to test each water sample as per the strip packet instructions (usually the strip is dipped in the water for 60 seconds).

STEP 3
Compare the colours on the strips to the chart in the testing kit. The colour of the strip will show you the levels of contaminants such as lead, nitrates (which often come from fertilisers used in farming), as well as how acidic the water is.

INDICATOR SPECIES

Scientists use the presence of 'indicator species' to judge how polluted water is. This is because some animals can survive only in clean water, whereas others thrive in polluted water. See if you can find indicator species in a nearby stream or lake with this project.

You'll need: A white plastic tray with deep sides, rubber gloves, a digital camera and internet access.

STEP 1

With gloves on, collect some water in the tray – about 2 cm deep. Take care at the water's edge.

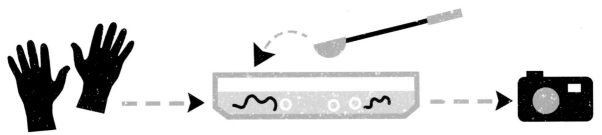

STEP 2

Take pictures of the creatures that you find, then count and release them. On a computer with internet access, see if you can identify the creatures. In particular, look for mayfly larvae and stonefly nymphs. These are indicators of clean water. If you find freshwater shrimp or caddis fly larvae, this indicates some pollution. If you find bloodworms or rat-tailed maggots, this indicates high pollution.

MAYFLY LARVA   FRESHWATER SHRIMP   RAT-TAILED MAGGOT

OCEAN PLASTIC POLLUTION

You may have heard about the problem with plastic pollution in the ocean. But although people are waking up to the problem, we are still using millions of tonnes of plastic every year, with huge amounts of it going into the ocean.

PLASTIC EVERYWHERE

We use plastic to make everything, from clothes, packaging and toys to vehicles such as planes and cars! Its versatility and durability means it's very useful. But even though plastic takes hundreds of years to break down, we treat it like it's disposable, making plastic items and throwing them away after one use.

ESCAPED WASTE

In less economically developed countries (LEDCs), the lack of waste management systems means a lot of waste simply gets dumped on the land or in rivers, then washes into the ocean. Even in countries with better rubbish collection, plastic still escapes into the environment through littering and being washed down the drain.

THINK AND ACT

Do you ever see people at school throwing plastic bottles and other containers in the bin? Ask them to **recycle them instead.**

PROBLEM FOR WILDLIFE

Up to 12.7 million tonnes of plastic end up in the ocean each year. Much of this is litter from the land, but a huge amount is also lost or dumped fishing gear. Plastic fishing nets go on catching fish even when they have been dumped, killing thousands of animals every year.

STARVING SEAGULLS

To many animals, such as turtles and seabirds, plastic looks like food. Other creatures that filter feed, such as whales, can't help but swallow plastic while they are eating. The plastic these animals swallow can't be digested, eventually filling up their stomachs and starving them to death.

TOXIC SNACKS

It isn't just the big bits of plastic that we can see that are a problem. Tiny fragments of plastic called microplastics absorb toxic chemicals, and are then eaten by small creatures such as shellfish and plankton. When the small creatures are eaten by bigger fish and birds, the toxic microplastics are passed up the food chain – eventually to us! The chemicals in these microplastics can have harmful health effects for the animals that accidentally eat them.

>> **If nothing changes, by 2050 there will be more plastic in the ocean by weight than fish.**

Solving the problem of water pollution might seem like a huge problem, but there are lots of things we can all individually do to help. And the more people take action against pollution, the more others will be encouraged to change their behaviour, too.

CHOOSE ECO-FRIENDLY DETERGENTS

There are a wide range of eco-friendly cleaning products available, including dish soaps, laundry liquids and surface cleaners. They still clean effectively, but if they escape into the environment they won't harm wildlife. Ask your family to buy eco-friendly cleaning products when they next go shopping.

AVOID PLASTICS

Explain to your parents the problem of plastic pollution, and try to avoid using so much plastic as a family. Could your family buy loose fruit and veg, instead of stuff wrapped in plastic? Avoid buying single drinks in plastic bottles such as fruit juices and fizzy drinks, and carry a reusable bottle filled with cordial instead. Ask your parents not to buy individually-wrapped snacks for your lunch – why don't you make your own snacks to take instead?

ORGANISE A BEACH CLEAN

Take action against the rubbish that has already escaped into the environment by organising a beach clean. If you don't live near a beach, you could do a river clean instead. Here's how to organise a clean up.

» **FOR ACTIVITIES NEAR THE WATER, ALWAYS have an adult present and take care at the water's edge.**

You'll need: rubbish bags, gloves, litter pickers (optional)

STEP 1

Pick a time and date. Nice weather will make more people want to come. Low tide is the best time for a beach clean, as that is when more rubbish is exposed on the beach.

STEP 2

Spread the word. Get as many people to come as you can by promoting it at school, on social media and on local websites, with the help of an adult. If you anticipate a lot of people coming, it's a good idea to let the local council or landowner know you're doing it.

STEP 3

Get your supplies: make sure there are enough gloves and bags for everyone. It might be nice to provide snacks, too.

STEP 4

Make it fun! Turn it into a game by awarding prizes to whoever collects the most, or whoever finds a list of particular items (such as plastic bottles, straws, etc.) first.

THROWAWAY CULTURE

What do you do with things you have broken, but don't want anymore? At best, you probably give them to a charity shop, but it's just as likely you throw them in the bin. But this habit of always getting new stuff and then throwing it away is a problem.

TAKE, MAKE, DISPOSE

Remember the problem of 'disposable' plastic, that we use then throw away? We have the same basic problem with everything we use. All our stuff follows a 'linear system': the materials to make it are extracted from the land, are made into things, transported and sold, used and then thrown away. But the big problem is that there won't always be more resources to extract, and the 'away' we throw things to just means landfill: big rubbish dumps that take up space, and pollute the local air and water supply.

DAMAGED PLANET

Making items uses a lot of raw materials, such as oil and minerals from underground, or wood from forests. Extracting these materials requires energy and land, and causes pollution. Turning the materials into objects and then transporting them uses even more energy. Worldwide, most energy is generated by burning fossil fuels, which releases greenhouse gases. These stay in the Earth's atmosphere, trapping heat from the Sun and causing climate change. Read more about this on pages 38–41.

TOO MUCH STUFF

Not only do we waste resources by constantly making new stuff then throwing it away, the sheer amount of stuff we consume means we are using natural resources, such as wood from forests, far faster than the Earth can replace them. Globally, we are using 1.7 times more resources each year than the planet can sustain. This is called 'overconsumption'.

THINK AND ACT

Do you have any unwanted clothes and toys? **How could you make sure they don't get wasted?**

WHAT DO WE WASTE?

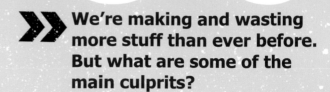 We're making and wasting more stuff than ever before. But what are some of the main culprits?

FAST FASHION

The world now consumes **80 billion items of clothing every year**. That's four times as many as just twenty years ago. A lot of this increase is driven by 'fast fashion', where shops sell very cheap versions of the latest trends, which people wear only a few times and then throw away. Very little textile waste is recycled either – about 12 per cent around the world. Most of it is sent to landfill.

PACKAGING

A huge amount of what we throw away is packaging, particularly food packaging. Plastic wrappers keep our food fresh, but only 10 per cent of plastic is recycled globally. Most gets sent to landfill, where it can take hundreds of years to break down, if it ever breaks down at all.

THINK ABOUT IT

It takes an average of 10,000 litres of water to make 1 kg of cotton. The cotton industry also accounts for 25 per cent of the world's insecticide use: toxic chemicals for killing pests, which damage the environment.

ELECTRONICS

Unwanted electronic goods, or e-waste, is one of the fastest growing types of waste product. Only 20 per cent of this type of waste is recycled, but making electrical devices has a big environmental impact.

Rare metals used in smartphones are often mined using very toxic chemicals, and are taken from natural places such as the Amazon rainforest. Vast amounts of energy are needed to extract the materials, contributing to climate change.

THINK AND ACT

If you are thinking about replacing an electrical device such as a mobile phone, think about whether you could **repair or improve it, rather than get an entirely new one.**

BUILDING WASTE

The construction industry (that's building houses and roads) produces a lot of waste in the form of rubble from the building site, unused materials and chemicals used in the construction process. Concrete particularly is a problem. It is the most used material in the world after water, but old concrete is rarely recycled.

MEASURE YOUR WASTE

How much waste does your family produce each week? You'll probably be surprised. Try this project to find out how much waste you are generating, and look for ways you could reduce it.

 You'll need: Separate boxes or bags to separate different types of waste and a set of weighing scales.

 STEP 1 Explain to your family the problem of waste, and how you'd like to measure your combined output over a week. As an option, you could ask them to bring rubbish they produce at work or school home too, so it can be included in the weigh-in.

 STEP 2 Set out some bags or boxes for everyone to put the waste in. It's a good idea to separate the waste into categories, such as recyclables (glass, cardboard, tins, and so on), non-recyclables/things that are rarely recycled (plastic films, Styrofoam, coffee cups, straws) and food waste. Include everything that gets thrown out that week, even big items such as furniture.

TOP TIP

 Wash any dirty containers before putting them in the bins so they don't smell while you collect them.

 STEP 3

At the end of the week, weigh each of the different containers. Which type of rubbish did you produce the most of? You could even take a family selfie surrounded by the rubbish to share on social media, encouraging others to do the same!

STEP 4

As a family, go through the items you have collected. Seeing all the rubbish in front of them might make them more aware of how much waste they produce. Discuss how you might be able to cut your waste down as a family – there are some ideas for how to do this on the next page!

If you feel inspired by trying this at home, how about trying to get your whole class doing it as a joint project, too?

STAND AGAINST: WASTE

Cutting down the amount of waste we produce depends on two things: buying less stuff in the first place, and being careful about what we do with the stuff we already have.

If you need something, think through it like this. **Start at the bottom of the pyramid, and work up.**

BUY SECOND-HAND

If you do have to buy something, you can probably get it **second-hand**. This saves a lot of money and resources too. Only buy new as a last resort.

SWAP. RENT. BORROW

If you really need something that you don't already have (perhaps you need some special kit for a school trip), could you **borrow** it from someone, or **rent** it instead? Borrowing and renting is much more eco-friendly, and saves your house getting full of unused clutter, too.

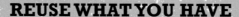

REUSE WHAT YOU HAVE

Do you **REALLY** need a new pair of trainers, or do you just want those new ones because they're cool? Everyone likes to have the newest, trendiest stuff, but the less you care about having the best, shiniest, newest things all the time, the **happier** you'll be, honest!

When you are thinking of getting rid of something, think through it like this. Again, **start at the bottom as the best and most efficient choice**, and work your way up.

DISPOSAL

Throwing stuff away is the absolute **last resort**. Some people manage to produce almost no un-recyclable waste at all. How little can you make?

RECYCLE

Once you can't reuse an item anymore, send it for **recycling**. Recycling still uses energy and resources though, so it's less efficient than reusing things.

REUSE

If you've bought a drink in a plastic bottle, for example, don't throw the bottle out. **Refill** it at home and use it as a drinks bottle. Wherever you can, try to **reuse** the things you **already own**.

REFUSE

Try not to accumulate wasteful things in the first place. If someone offers you a plastic bag or straw you don't need, **refuse it**.

A DIFFERENT SYSTEM

At the moment, it's really difficult to live a zero-waste lifestyle, because unfortunately, the world today just isn't set up for it. But it doesn't have to be this way.

MAKE

CIRCULAR ECONOMY

Remember that linear system we learned about on page 22 – 'take, make and dispose'?

Imagine if instead of chucking away all the old objects and packaging we buy, we sent them back to the companies to be **reused and refurbished**? Or perhaps sent them to an entirely different company who could make use of the old packaging or pieces in a new way?

This idea is called a '**circular economy**', because the resources in it go round and round between maker and consumer (that's you, the buyer), instead of ending up in landfill.

USE

RECOVER

DEPOSIT SYSTEMS

Bottle deposit schemes for drinks bottles and cans exist in some countries, where people pay a little bit extra for the bottle, and get the money back when they return it. In Norway, successful deposit schemes mean that 97 per cent of all drinks bottles and cans are returned and reused or recycled.

THINK AND ACT

Milk deliveries in **returnable** glass bottles are getting more popular again, after a decline in their use. Look online to see if there is one in your area, and if so, **ask your parents if you could sign up to it.**

A BIGGER SCALE

In order for things like deposit schemes to really make a difference to how much waste we produce, they need to be easy and widespread. For example, the scheme in Norway is successful because there are machines and counters for people to return bottles in supermarkets and other accessible locations. Companies who sell drinks in bottles pay less tax when more bottles are returned, so they make it easy for the customers.

Governments and businesses can both help make the necessary changes to reduce our huge waste output — and it's up to us to tell politicians and companies that it's what we want.

WHY IS FOOD WASTED?

>> Did you know that up to a third of all the food produced in the world gets wasted? This is despite the fact that globally, one billion people don't get enough to eat. So why does this happen?

AT THE FARM

In more economically developed countries (MEDCs), food gets wasted before it even reaches the supermarkets. In order to ensure that they can supply however much the supermarkets want, farmers grow lots of food. But the supermarkets' orders are often unpredictable, and the farmers often grow more food than they can sell. They can't make any money from the unwanted food, so it doesn't get picked and sold.

In LEDCs, the facilities for storing and transporting produce isn't always good enough, so sometimes food goes off before it is sold.

IN THE FACTORY

Not all food is sold in the same state it came off the plant. It might be trimmed, chopped, or used in a ready meal or a tin of soup. Wastage happens in the food processing plants and factories, too, as edible trimmings are thrown away, or when the machines processing the food into new dishes don't work properly.

AT THE SHOP

When you go to the supermarket, you don't expect to see empty shelves, or a very limited range of products. But to keep shelves heaving with a large variety of things means it's very likely that some of those items will reach their 'sell-by' date before they get sold. Some supermarkets will donate expired food to charities, but often it just goes into the bin.

AT HOME

A lot of food waste happens at home, too. When people are tempted to 'buy one get one free' at the supermarket, they sometimes end up buying more than they need, and throwing it out because they can't eat it before it goes off.

When we cook more than we can eat, it's often put in the bin, instead of being saved for leftovers, especially in MEDCs where people can afford to waste food. In the USA, for example, 55 million tonnes of food is thrown away each year!

THINK AND ACT

Do you or your parents often put more food on your plate than you can actually eat? **Start with smaller portions:** it's better to go for seconds than to throw food in the bin.

IMPACTS OF FOOD WASTE

The fact that food is unfairly shared around the world means that many go hungry, while others eat too much and suffer from obesity and related illnesses. But food waste is linked to even more problems.

OVERFISHING

Of the fish that we take out of the sea to eat, 35 per cent are wasted. This is very bad news, considering a third of the world's fish stocks are being overfished, meaning they are being taken out of the ocean faster than the population can recover. If we continue fishing and wasting fish catches at the same rate, we will drive all the world's fish stocks to extinction by 2048.

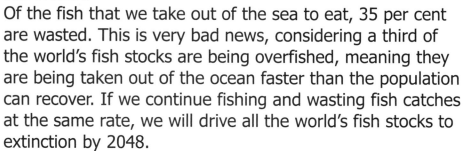

EXTINCTION

One third of the world's land is used for agriculture, and this figure keeps growing. In order to make room to grow more crops, animal habitats are being destroyed. Scientists estimate that around the world, 150–200 wildlife species are going extinct every day, in large part caused by the effects of farming. By producing more food than we need, we are unnecessarily driving more species to extinction.

ERODING SOIL

Soil stores carbon in the form of broken-down plant material, which stops it getting into the atmosphere as a greenhouse gas (read more about this on page 38). Soil is also necessary to grow crops and to absorb rainwater, which prevents flooding. But common farming techniques wear the soil away, releasing carbon dioxide and making it harder to grow food. By overproducing from stressed soils now, we will make it hard to feed everyone in the future.

THINK AND ACT

The world's population is set to rise to nearly **10 BILLION by 2050**. We can feed that many people, but only if we change the way we produce and share food. **Tell people what you have learned about food waste** to encourage them to change their behaviour, too.

WATER WASTE

Agriculture accounts for about 70 per cent of fresh water use around the world. In many places, water from lakes or underground water stores is being used up faster than it is replaced, putting millions of people's water supply at risk. Because food uses so much water to produce, wasted food equals even more wasted water. For example, one kilo of wasted beef also wastes the 50,000 litres of water it took to produce.

STAND AGAINST: FOOD WASTE

It isn't that difficult to reduce food waste at home, it's just a matter of changing habits a little bit. Talk to your family about making some of the following changes.

Some ways to cut your waste

TIP ONE

Plan your meals. Check what food you already have in the cupboard, then **write a shopping list** for the exact things you need to make those meals. Why not get the whole family involved in this, with everyone suggesting a dinner that they can cook? Then, when shopping, only buy the items on the list. Having a plan like this will help stop impulse purchases that don't get used.

TIP TWO

Don't pile your plates really high when serving food. In fact, if you can **use smaller plates** that's even better. This will stop you serving yourself more than you can eat in one go. You can always have seconds if you are still hungry!

TIP THREE

Store leftovers and eat them for lunch or dinner the next day. Extra food that has been made at dinnertime makes a time-saving packed lunch, if stored properly in a sealed box. Just make sure to actually **eat the leftovers**.

Monday   Tuesday

TIP FOUR

Only use sell-by or **expiration dates** as guidelines. They are to do with food quality, not food safety, so just because a piece of food 'went off' a day or two ago, try smelling and tasting it before getting rid of it. If it smells and tastes fine, it should be fine to eat. More caution is advised around meat and dairy than other types of food.

TIP FIVE

If you have an outside space, **try composting** food peelings and other fruit and vegetable scraps. The compost can be used later to grow flowers or more food!

» If you want to help fight food waste at a larger scale, why not look online to see if any food waste charities are active in your area? Some groups run activities such as 'gleaning', where excess fruit and veg that farmers can't sell to supermarkets are picked by volunteers and given to people in need.

POLLUTION, WASTE AND CLIMATE CHANGE

On Earth, all our natural systems are connected, so when we damage one part, it has knock-on effects. Because of this, the dirty truth is that pollution and waste contribute to a really big problem: climate change.

WHAT IS CLIMATE CHANGE?

One of the most serious types of man-made pollution are greenhouse gases that cause climate change. When we burn fossil fuels to power our vehicles or to drive electricity generators, they release carbon dioxide (CO_2) into the air. The Earth's atmosphere naturally has some CO_2 in it, but since the eighteenth century, we have been adding more and more.

CO_2 and other gases in the atmosphere are called 'greenhouse gases'. This is because they act almost like the glass of a greenhouse, letting heat in and trapping it close to the Earth. This is causing the Earth to slowly heat up, causing extreme weather and other devastating consequences around the globe.

THINK ABOUT IT
On average, around 1200 tonnes of CO_2 are released into the air every single second. That's the same weight as roughly 300 elephants.

METHANE, BLACK CARBON AND OZONE

CO_2 isn't the only type of greenhouse gas. Methane is 30 times more powerful than CO_2 as a greenhouse gas, and other gases such as black carbon (in soot) and ground-level ozone act as pollutants, which damage human health, and as heat-trapping gases in the atmosphere that drive storms, flooding and drought. Read more about this on the next page.

DANGEROUS WASTE

Remember how wasting resources and food leads to unnecessary greenhouse gas emissions? Well, waste's contribution to climate change doesn't stop there. When we send rubbish to landfill, it all gets piled up in a big hole in the ground. There isn't any oxygen in landfill, so the waste breaks down 'anaerobically', meaning without oxygen. This produces methane. Along with the burps and farts from livestock, this is one of the biggest sources of methane around the world.

THINK AND ACT

Because so much methane comes from livestock, you can reduce the amount you are responsible for by **eating less meat and dairy**.

IMPACTS OF GREENHOUSE GASES

Greenhouse gases are causing our atmosphere to heat up. Hot air can hold more water vapour than cold air before it reaches the point where it starts to rain. This means weather patterns around the world are changing, with some places experiencing droughts, and other places experiencing serious floods.

CROP FAILURE

The food that we grow depends on having the right kind of weather: a good amount of rain at the right time to water the plants, and the correct amount of sunshine to help them grow. But changing weather patterns mean some plants are not getting enough water, or are getting too much water and are being flooded. Crop failures lead to food shortages, and people going hungry.

THINK ABOUT IT

If humans are struggling to grow food in places where the weather is changing, how do you think the wild plants and animals are being affected?

THINK AND ACT

Go online and search for '**carbon footprint calculator**'. This will ask you questions about your lifestyle to measure the amount of carbon dioxide emissions it generates. Once you have the answer, look on the next page to find ways to reduce it.

OUT OF TIME

Many of the Earth's creatures and ecosystems are very sensitive to temperature. For example, some bird species hatch chicks at a certain time of year when there are the right number of hours of daylight. But the caterpillars that the chicks eat emerge when the temperature is right. Because the Earth is warmer, this is happening earlier in the springtime, and by the time the chicks have hatched, the caterpillars are all gone, leaving them without food. This in turn has an impact on other creatures further up the food chain.

WILD WEATHER

As weather becomes more unpredictable, it also becomes more extreme. Hotter air temperatures make hurricanes stronger, while drier conditions help wildfires to spread. Around the world, extreme weather events are becoming more common, causing more damage and death through droughts, heat waves, flooding and fire.

We all need to make changes in order to combat climate change. Here are some ways that you and your family can reduce your carbon footprint.

Some ways to cut your footprint

TIP ONE

Walk or cycle wherever possible, instead of getting a lift in a car. Public transport such as buses and trains also release fewer greenhouse gases per passenger than private vehicles.

TIP TWO

Get your family to wash the laundry in cool water, and dry it on an airer or line instead of in a tumble dryer. This will cut a lot of electricity usage.

TIP THREE

If your family fly a lot for holidays, ask your parents if you could do an overland trip by train or coach instead. The emissions from aeroplanes are particularly harmful because they are released high up in the sky, where they cause a more powerful warming effect.

TIP FOUR

Grow some of your own food. Gardening is a fun and rewarding hobby, as nothing tastes better than a sweet strawberry or juicy tomato that you have grown yourself! If you don't have anywhere to grow fruit and veggies, ask your parents to buy local, organic foods where possible. This means the food won't have travelled a long distance or been grown with wildlife-harming chemicals.

TIP FIVE

Ask for 'non-stuff' presents at Christmas and birthdays. This could be something like a day at a theme park or a zoo-keeping experience. Most experiences have a smaller carbon footprint than 'stuff' such as toys, clothes and games consoles, and even better, they don't end up as waste once they are broken or you don't want them any more.

≫ One of the most important things you can do is talk to other people about climate change and your efforts to reduce your impact. The more people see others taking action, the more normal it becomes, and the more likely they are to take action themselves.

BE THE CHANGE, SPREAD THE WORD

>> **Campaigning for change and sharing solutions are just as important as taking action yourself. Here are some ways you can amplify your efforts.**

ZERO WASTE WEEK

Launched in 2008, Zero Waste Week is an annual event that happens around the world in September. People, community groups and businesses all try to produce zero waste (or as little waste as possible) over the week. Why not try it yourself? You could get your family to share your attempts online over the course of the week to inspire others to have a go themselves. Search for Zero Waste Week online for tips.

WRITE TO YOUR LOCAL POLITICIANS

Find out who your MP and local councillors are, and write to them. Politicians will only take action on pollution and waste if they think enough people care about it. Explain the problems that pollution and waste cause, and ask them to do something about it.

STREET THEATRE

This can be a really fun way to spread the message to people in your town or local area. Get a group of friends together, and write a short script for a play that explains the problems of pollution and waste. You could have people acting as polluters, as well as people acting as the people and animals that are affected by pollution.

Perform your play somewhere in the town centre. It's a good idea to have some printed materials with the key facts for interested passers-by to read, too. In many places you can do street theatre without asking permission, but it's good to check the rules in your local area first. Always have adults accompanying you.

HOST A SCREENING

Organise a film night at home or at school showing a film about the problems of pollution, waste and climate change. You could show a documentary, such as *Arctic Tale*, or even a fictional film with a relevant message, such as *WALL-E*. After the film, have everyone talk about how the film made them think and feel.

THINK AND ACT
Can you come up with some other creative ways to **spread the word about pollution and waste?**

Glossary

agriculture the practice of preparing the soil and growing crops or raising animals for food

asthma a condition that affects the airways (the tubes carrying air in and out of the lungs)

carbon footprint the amount of greenhouse gas emissions (particularly carbon dioxide) that each person is responsible for through their lifestyle

climate change the changes in weather patterns and temperatures around the world, caused by human activity

composting a process that turns food scraps into rich, new soil

contaminant a substance that pollutes something, making it impure

durability the ability to withstand heavy use without wearing away

emissions something that has been released or put out into the world, such as gases coming out of a car exhaust

eutrophication when extra nutrients get into water and cause too much growth in water plants

extinct when a type of living thing has completely died out

fertiliser a substance used to help plants grow bigger or stronger

fossil fuel a fuel such as oil or coal that was formed over millions of years from the remains of plants and animals

gleaning volunteer harvesting of food that would otherwise be wasted

greenhouse gas gases that, when in the atmosphere, trap the Sun's heat

insecticide a chemical used to kill insects

manufacture to make something

microplastics a tiny bit of plastic

overfishing taking fish out of the water faster than the species can replace itself through reproduction

ozone a gas made of oxygen atoms

ozone layer a layer of ozone gas high in the Earth's atmosphere which helps protect us from the Sun's strong rays

particulates very small bits of solid pollution such as dust or soot

pesticide a chemical used to kill unwanted creatures

plankton tiny plants and animals that live in water

refurbish to repair or upgrade existing objects so they can be used again

respiratory disease a disease that affects the lungs and airways

runoff water or other substances that drain off the land and into streams or groundwater

sewage waste water that is carried away from houses and cities in pipes

versatility the ability to be used in lots of ways

Further Information

BOOKS

This Book is Not Rubbish
Isabel Thomas (Wren & Rook, 2018)
Covering issues like plastics, pollution, global warming and endangered animals, this book is full of top tips for ditching plastic and reducing your rubbish.

EcoGraphics: Pollution
Izzi Howell (Franklin Watts, 2019)
Pollution is fast invading every part of the Earth, from the deepest ocean to the most remote desert to the very air we breathe. Can we reverse the damage before it's too late?

WEBSITES

trjfp.com
A project that started in Leeds, UK, the Real Junk Food Project is now a global network of volunteer-run 'Pay as you feel' cafés and food distribution centres, which take food that would otherwise be wasted and cook and distribute it. The food comes from gleaned fruit and veg, or supermarket stock that isn't sold before expiration. Visitors to the cafés and centres can pay whatever they can afford, thereby providing meals to people in need. Check the website to find a café or project near you.

feedbackglobal.org/campaigns/gleaning-network
Food waste organisation Feedback runs several campaigns, including its nationwide Gleaning Network. This gives volunteers all over the UK the opportunity to rescue fresh produce from farms and get it to good causes. Visit the website to find out about gleaning activities near you.

Note to parents and teachers: every effort has been made by the Publishers to ensure websites are suitable for children, that they are of the highest educational value, and that they contain no inappropriate or offensive material. However, because of the nature of the Internet, it is impossible to guarantee that the contents of these sites will not be altered. We strongly advise that Internet access is supervised by a responsible adult.

Index

TITLES IN THE SERIES

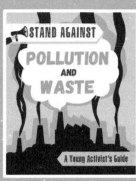

Animal Cruelty

•What is animal cruelty? •Why does animal cruelty exist? •Industrial farming •Vegetarianism and veganism •Unsustainable food •Stand against: Unethical food •Animals in captivity •Entertainment •Sports •Stand against: Cruelty for fun •Cosmetics •Health and medicine •Stand against: Animal testing •Fashion •Wildlife trade •Stand against: Cruel fashion •Pet abuse and neglect •Pet breeding •Stand against: Cruelty to pets •Cruel or not cruel? •Be the change, spread the word

Pollution and Waste

•Know your targets: Pollution and waste •Where does pollution come from? •Impacts of air pollution •Measure air pollution •Stand against: Air pollution •Impacts of water pollution •Investigate water pollution •Ocean plastic pollution •Stand against: Water pollution •Throwaway culture •What do we waste? •Measure your waste •Stand against: Waste •A different system •Why is food wasted? •Impacts of food waste •Stand against: Food waste •Pollution, waste and climate change •Impacts of greenhouse gases •Stand against: Climate change •Be the change, spread the word

Poverty and Hunger

•Poverty and hunger today •Check your consumption •Food availability •Food distribution •Food quality •Stand against: Food inequality •No way to work •In-work poverty •Staying afloat •Modern slavery •Stand against: Child labour •Housing •Welfare systems •Privilege and discrimination •Stand against: Child poverty •Climate change •Intensive farming •Pesticides and herbicides •Growing technologies •Stand against: Future food destruction •Be the change, spread the word

Prejudice

•Know your targets: Prejudice •Measure your prejudices •Where does prejudice come from? •Measure the media •Discrimination •Equal rights •Stand against: Human rights abuses •Privilege •Race •Black history month •Cultural appropriation •Religion •Stand against: Religious misunderstandings •Gender •Stand against: Gender stereotypes •LGBTQ+ •Stand against: Homophobic language •Bodies •Stand against: Negative body image •Age •Be the change, spread the word